Masquerade

Laura Lam was raised near San Francisco, California by two former Haight-Ashbury hippies. Both of them encouraged her to finger-paint to her heart's desire, colour outside the lines, and consider the library a second home. This led to an overabundance of daydreams. She relocated to Scotland in 2009 to be with her husband, whom she met on the internet when he insulted her taste in books. She almost blocked him but is glad she didn't. At times she misses the sunshine.

www.lauralam.co.uk
twitter.com/LR_Lam

By Laura Lam

THE MICAH GREY TRILOGY
Pantomime
Shadowplay
Masquerade

False Hearts

LAURA LAM

Masquerade

PAN BOOKS

First published 2017 by Pan Books
an imprint of Pan Macmillan
20 New Wharf Road, London N1 9RR
Associated companies throughout the world
www.panmacmillan.com

ISBN 978-1-5098-0778-9

1 3 5 7 9 8 6 4 2

A CIP catalogue record for this book is available from the British Library.

Typeset by Palimpsest Book Production Limited, Falkirk, Stirlingshire
Printed and bound by CPI Group (UK) Ltd, Croydon, CR0 4YY

To the readers who kept the magic alive.
Thank you.

PROLOGUE
THE DAMSELFLY

There was no one left alive who remembered the world as I used to know it.

I told the others to call me Anisa. I had gone by many names, experienced many lives in various forms for thousands of years. The land they now called Ellada was a very different place. There were still so many humans, fascinating and frustrating by turns. They lived that one life and then that was it – they either left their mark and they were remembered, elsewise they were forgotten in the fog of time.

Humans were lowest on the hierarchy – though that was not to say they were poorly treated. At the pinnacle were the Alder: tall, ethereal beings, long-limbed and beautiful. Blueish skin, large eyes, those thin necks and willowy waists. They were our guardians, our shepherds, perhaps in some way our gods. They stayed separate, yet they watched us, gave us cryptic instructions, shared their technology with us. Our lives were better with them guiding us, perhaps, but there was also that disturbing sense that those lives were not our own.

In that world there were also the Chimaera, like me. We were somewhere in between the human and the Alder. I was a Theri Chimaera, which meant my primary aspect was humanoid with a slight influence of Alder features, yet large dragonfly wings rose from my back. There had been so many of us. Chimaera with manes like lions or tails like fish. A glimmering of scales on flesh, or nails sharp as thorns. Eyes that glowed blue, purple, or green in the darkness. I had a friend called Matla who flew in warmer skies with me, her wings like a giant owl's. So many lifetimes ago.

Not all of us looked so varied. Many Chimaera were entirely human but for gifts bestowed by the Alder. They were called the Anthi. They lived with us in the gardens strewn throughout the world, when all had been so green and verdant. When one of my lives ended, I'd be reborn into another Dragonfly body. If one was not yet available, I'd spend time in a body of metal and gears until I decided I wanted to live within flesh once again. Sometimes, I hibernated in a small disc called an Aleph. Once, I'd had an entire people that looked like me. Once, I'd had a home.

That world was gone, in fire and flame, in no small part thanks to my own failures. The Alder left us. They could have helped put our world to rights, perhaps, but they did not wish to. The Alder had tasked me and my partner, Relean, with raising Chimaera. Someone murdered my charge, and it haunted me. I never discovered who did it, but I had my suspicions. Years later, when I was tasked with two more charges, I was determined to protect *them with my very life. I loved Ahti and Dev dearly. Ahti was a Theri: scaled, and more powerful than any other Chimaera I'd ever come across. It could overwhelm him, putting everyone nearby at risk. Only Dev, an Anthi, could absorb the powers and bring Ahti back to equilibrium. Dev was a Kedi – both male and female, physically and within.*

Ahti's powers made him a target. A faction of the Alder called the Kashura began to mistrust the Chimaera and their growing powers. They decided they were dangerous and that the world would be better with only the pure, and weaker, humans. I tried to protect Ahti as best I could, knowing the Kashura would want him, for he was the key to their plan.

My protection was worth less than nothing. Relean and I were captured and thrown into a cell with Dev. They took Ahti away, and he was frightened. I could feel his terror, even through the stone walls separating us. Dev could not help him. The world burned, the Chimaera were gone.

The Dragonfly body I wore turned to ash with the others, but Relean had spirited away three Alephs. I survived, but I never found the Alephs of Relean or Dev. My guess is that they perished, all those centuries ago. I had lived many lives with Relean. We had always found each other. Now he had been gone almost as long as we'd been together.

I slept for a long time, deep within the metal, buried in the ground. Eventually, my Aleph was found, sold a few times. Anything the Alder left behind was valuable in this new world that rose from the broken remnants of the old one. Though they did not fully understand how this Vestige worked, they used it, fighting with each other because they were so desperate to collect as much power as they could in their short lives.

My Aleph rested on mantelpieces in fancy houses. Occasionally, I'd awaken from my slumber, listening idly to their conversations, trying to understand how the world had changed. If I reached out to them, no one heard me. I drifted back into hibernation.

Eventually, I ended up in a circus that travelled around Ellada. They used my Aleph in one of their funfair tents, replaying an old recording of my Dragonfly form. Occasionally, the real me would emerge from the Aleph and watch the humans who came to visit. Again, if I spoke to them, no one heard. They saw only the recording, the mist from the card ice in water, the swirling paint on the cloth of the tent. I was called the Phantom Damselfly, and it fit, for I was nothing more than a ghost.

R. H. Ragona's Circus of Magic paused in the city of Sicion last spring. For the first time in so, so many years, I felt a call. Chimaera, powers emerging, reaching out in the darkness. A tarot reader named Cyan, in a circus, reading minds to tell others what they needed to hear. A girl, Iphigenia Laurus, trapped in the gilded cage of nobility, desperate to escape. No, not a girl. A Kedi. Others, dimmer, more distant, but present. Growing.

I was limited in my Aleph form, but I watched them. Eventually, I reached out in subtle ways. It took patience, but I had plenty of it.

One night the Kedi, Iphigenia Laurus, or Gene, over-heard her parents speaking and discovered that not only had a man called Doctor Pozzi left her on their doorstep as a baby, but that her adopted parents planned to operate upon her to make her more 'marriageable'. Gene ran away from home, shedding the dresses and donning trousers, reinventing himself as Micah Grey. He came to the circus, as I knew he would, and joined as an aerialist apprentice. When Micah came to my tent the next night, I spoke to him. He heard me.

I scared him terribly, and he stayed away. Time passed. Micah Grey rose through the ranks of the circus. He grew close to his fellow aerialist, Aenea, though he was too afraid to tell her about his past. Micah also connected with one of the white clowns, Drystan, who was another hidden member of the nobility.

Micah's family searched for him, even hiring a private investigator to try and find him. When the Shadow grew close to his quarry, a shadow of a different sort fell over R. H. Ragona's Circus of Magic. Micah tried to flee, and told Aenea that he was a Kedi, but she was hurt by the lies. Bil Ragona, the ringmaster, figured out who Micah was and captured him, intending to turn him in for the reward to save the failing finances of the circus. When Aenea and Drystan tried to help him, Bil, in a rage, struck Aenea and killed her. Drystan stabbed the ring-master with the hidden blade in his own cane – on purpose or accidentally, it was difficult to say – and they escaped. Several members of the circus gave chase, but it was the night of the Penmoon. When the moon was fullest in the sky, the blue Penglass scattered through the city glowed. Chimaera had an affinity with it, they always did. Micah touched the glass and it brightened, blinding their hunters.

On the run, Drystan took Micah to an old friend who owed him a favour: Jasper Maske, once known as the great magician, the Maske of Magic. Since losing a duel with his embittered rival, Penn Taliesin, fifteen years ago, Jasper had lived in his dusty theatre, tinkering with old Vestige and contraptions for his magic. Drystan collected on his life debt with Jasper and also convinced the magician to teach them the tools of his trade. He did, and those pieces I'd so delicately laid down began to come together.

Cyan, the tarot reader, appeared at the Kymri Theatre after running away from Riley and Batheo's Circus of Curiosities. She helped Maske and the others with the séances, being an understandable boon thanks to her Chimaera abilities. She and Micah began to discover what they were, and bonded together as I knew they must. Drystan and Micah fell in love, slowly, then completely.

When Maske's rival discovered that Maske was teaching magic again, Taliesin challenged Maske to another duel, this time through their apprentices. Desperate for a chance to perform magic again in the limelight, Maske accepted. Micah bowed out of performing, preferring to stay behind the scenes, so Drystan and Cyan were Maske's Marionettes.

Yet the Shadow would not leave Micah alone. With help from his friends, Micah discovered the Shadow was named Elwood, and snuck into his home and found proof that he was falsifying his findings and cheating his clients. With a well-placed package of information left on the Constabulary steps, Elwood soon was no longer a problem, and Micah hoped life as Iphigenia Laurus was well and truly behind him.

The night before the grand duel, one of the machines for their finale broke, and I helped them fix it, showing myself to Maske for the first time. Micah, once more, had to spill his secrets, but at least that time the results were not near as disastrous as they'd been in the circus.

Maske and his Marionettes went up against Taliesin's grandsons, called the Spectre's Shadows, and the duel began. Taliesin never liked to leave things to chance – he tried to sabotage Maske's act. Micah managed to stop it, and Cyan and Drystan finished their performance. They won – the Princess Royal of Ellada herself congratulated them. It was as if everything had finally settled into place for young Micah and his newfound family.

Micah did not realize there was a second Shadow darkening his path. I knew someone followed him, but it took me too long to realize who it was and what it truly meant.

Lily Verre, a woman who worked in a magic shop and had begun courting Maske, was a spy all along. A Shadow working for Pozzi, the Royal Physician himself. Micah had met Pozzi after a séance and he'd warned Micah that he might be ill. Lily followed them from the circus and had Micah touch a disguised Mirror of Moirai, a piece of Vestige that she could use to track his movements.

I had to watch as Micah moved closer to this momentous encounter. Seeing Lily Verre pushing her son in his

*wheelchair down a street in Imachara. Micah finally real-
izing that her son was a Theri Chimaera, skin covered in
a gleam of scales. The very picture of Ahti, and Micah
was so like Dev. They circled closer, caught in each other's
orbit. History was repeating itself, and my heart broke in
both fear and hope.*

*Then Micah fell ill with a fever that I did not see
coming. It worried me, to have such a thing surprise me
so. His fever dream contained many hints about what
happened long ago and what was to come. I wondered
if he would ever be able to forgive me. My little Kedi.
My newest ward. Our last chance.*

1

FEVER DREAM

A fever may burn a man alive. Some of the wise men who called themselves seers would summon a temperature. They said the fever dreams bestowed them knowledge of their fate, and the fate of those who followed them.
— 'Mystics and Seers', *A History of Ellada and its Colonies,* PROFESSOR CAED CEDAR, Royal Snakewood University

Someone carried me.

Disjointed flashes: the pavement, the yellow glow of a street lamp. The sound of a door being opened. Footsteps up the stairs.

Then darkness.

My eyes opened.

Blurred forms surrounded me. I squinted at the brightness. Where was I? At least I remembered who I was. I'd been on the roof with Drystan, following the woman in the red dress, who had turned out to be none other than Lily Verre, someone we'd thought a friend. We had followed her over the rooftops of Imachara. Her child was Chimaera, covered in scales, curled within his wicker wheelchair and well-bundled against the cold and prying eyes. We'd followed her and she'd led us right to the door of someone we had every reason to distrust: Doctor Pozzi, the Royal Physician of the Snakewood Monarchy. The man who had found me and given me to my adopted parents, who had told me that if I ever became ill, it could mean that I was dying.

The last thing I remembered was burning with the fever that still clawed at me and turned the room fuzzy and dim. Drystan had leaned over me: 'I'll take care of you.'

Where had he taken me?

Drystan had told me he loved me. I held onto that love, but even that began to dissolve around the pain of the fever. I dreamed, but only remnants lingered, like a word on the tip of my tongue.

More darkness.

I drifted. When I came back to myself, a face, half-hidden by a doctor's mask, leaned over me. I knew the clipped beard that was underneath and those eyes that imitated warmth but still held coldness at their core.

Behind Pozzi, I glimpsed a shadow of bat wings, but I blinked and they were gone.

A pinch in my arm. A sharp flare of pain. The push of the syringe, and something flowed through the needle and into me. Pozzi leaned closer, peering at me above his doctor's mask.

'You'll be all right, Micah.'

Will I? I asked. And it was only when Pozzi's eyes

widened that I realized I'd spoken to him with my mind and not out loud. No one but Cyan could ever hear my thoughts, but he had. I didn't have the energy to work out what that meant. My mind was heavy, my body burning with sweat and then freezing.

He met my gaze. *It will feel worse before it feels better.*

My eyes closed. I dreamed of fire, pain, and blood. I saw the end of the world.

Part of me knew it was a fever dream. That didn't make it any less frightening.

I was not me. Anisa was flying, or falling, through skies on fire. All was red, orange, black and gold. I reached out my hands and they burned to nothing. There was no pain. I closed my eyes.

I woke up and I was no longer myself. My body was human, my skin the peach and cream of a newborn. No swirling silver markings of my family. No dragonfly wings rose from my back. I was clipped. Earthbound. I skulked through the streets of this strange new city of Imachara, keeping to the shadows. I came to the market square before the palace, with a large stage set up in the middle, but no audience. Storm clouds rumbled overhead.

The phantoms, the parts in this play to come, walked across the stage. The woman in the red dress whose son was eaten from the inside. My new charge knew who she was now, and what she had done. Things might still fall into place the way I thought – hoped – they would. The way the world whispers to me that it might.

The doctor with the clockwork hand appeared onstage,

smiling that self-satisfied grin, though he was as ignorant as all the rest. He did not even know what he wore against the stump of his arm. The ones who sided with him floated around him, waiting in the wings. The young girl with the lie around her neck. The one who was Matla, young Cyan, her powers just beginning to unfurl. The boy Drystan, who despite his lack of power could destroy everything. And my little Kedi, my newest charge, the one called Micah, or Gene, or Sam – my last and greatest hope.

The stage lights extinguished, leaving me in the night. My lungs burned with the memory of smoke and soot. I was alone in the darkness. No one called me forth.

A door in the darkness opened, and the boy Ahti came towards me. But as I reached my arms to him, he fell, his legs unable to support him, his skin grey and green. He wailed, covering his eyes with his hands. He wasn't my Ahti. A flash of bright blue and red light. A dull roar. A young girl, screaming. Micah Grey, the one meant to help, to save everything, crying out. A flash of blinding blue.

They were all dead and gone, and the world dead and gone with them.

Darkness fell.

I knew what I needed to do to stop it, but how could I commit that evil, too?

I would do anything to save the Chimaera.

Anything. Even what was to come.

2

ELIXIR

I have found it. I have found the elixir that will change the world.

— From the unpublished medical notes of the Snakewood Royal Physician, DOCTOR SAMUEL POZZI

When I woke again, echoes of the strange fever dream swirled in my mind.

Drystan held my hand. We were not at home in the Kymri Theatre.

'Where . . . ?' I managed.

'Pozzi's apartments,' Drystan said. His blonde hair stood up around his head in a messy halo. He had dark circles under his blue eyes. 'You've been out for four days.'

I let out a shaky breath, pushing myself onto my elbows. The room was as white and pristine as a hospital room, the floor softened with rugs. The bed's linen was so crisp it crinkled. I wore a plain tunic and felt a surge of panic.

'Where are my clothes?'

'They're here.' Drystan nodded to a chair in the corner.

I lowered my voice. 'Is the Aleph safe?' Anisa's disc. Drystan took the Aleph from my trouser pocket. I held my hand out and he dropped it into my palm. My fingers closed around the metal. Swirling, Alder script was etched into the sides, the Vestige metal shining green, purple and gold in the light. It thrummed in my hand. Anisa was silent.

I'd found her in R. H. Ragona's Circus of Magic; or, rather, she'd found me. I had taken her from the ruins of the circus and she had sent us visions of the past, telling us that all we knew about the Alder, the Chimaera they created, and the Vestige they left behind was a lie. She had said she needed us for a plan to save the world. I never knew how much to believe with her, or how much she kept to herself.

On my arm, where the syringe had pinched me, was an already-fading bruise. I touched the scab of the needle mark and winced at the pain. What had Pozzi given me?

'What happened after . . .' I trailed off. *After I said I loved you and you loved me?* I was almost afraid to say it aloud, just in case it had been a fever dream as well.

'After you fainted, I took you straight to Pozzi. I didn't want to, but I figured he was the only one who could help. He didn't seem surprised to see you.'

'He didn't?'

'No indeed. It was like he'd been expecting us at any moment.'

'I . . . should have told you sooner, that Pozzi said I had a chance of growing ill.'

'Yes. Well.' The words we'd exchanged before my fever had overwhelmed me hung between us, unspoken.

I pinched the bridge of my nose to chase away my lingering headache. I felt stronger, but still not much better than a piece of meat that had been pummelled by a hammer.

'I had the strangest dream . . .' I said.

'What happened?' Drystan drew me closer, resting his forehead against mine.

I pulled back, my eyes darting to the door. 'Not here,' I mouthed. The details of the dream were there – Anisa's end of the world, the threat of a bright light before darkness. An overarching sense of dread and evil.

There was a knock at the door. Without waiting for an answer, Doctor Pozzi entered. He looked cool, collected and impeccably dressed, as usual. He wore no white gloves to cover his Vestige clockwork hand. It caught the light, the brass Vestige within covered with translucent skin, as if trapped in amber.

'Micah,' he said. 'So good to see you awake.' The slightest pause, the smallest look at Drystan. 'There's a fresh pot of tea in the kitchen, Amon.' If he knew Drystan's true name, he did not let on.

I did not want Drystan to go, but he did, pulling the door shut behind him.

'Micah,' the doctor said. 'You gave us all quite a fright.'

'What happened to me?' I asked, scrunching the coverlet so hard I feared tearing the fabric.

'Your body turned against you. It's what has happened in the other Chimaera cases I have studied.'

My mouth tightened. He hadn't used that word in my presence before. Giving up the pretext that I didn't know exactly what I was.

'Your extrasensory abilities grew too quickly,' he went on. 'A spike in your mind, if you will. You're very lucky you were able to see me straight away. Much longer and you might not have made it.'

Gooseflesh pricked my arms. I could have died. I'd never had to worry about my health. Growing up as the daughter of a noble family, I'd been stronger and faster than my friends. I'd never grown ill, not even a cold. When I broke my arm the night Drystan and I fled the circus, it healed weeks faster than it should have. Now my body had betrayed me.

'So you cured me?' I asked.

A small shake of the head. 'I have alleviated it, for now, but you are still reliant on my medication until I discover a permanent cure.' He brought a box from his pocket and opened it, holding the syringe in his clockwork hand. I blanched, gripping Anisa's Aleph even tighter, hoping there was no way for him to glean my thoughts.

Pozzi had never appeared to have anything other than my best interests at heart. He claimed to want only to help me, feeling guilty for how badly things turned out in the end with the Lord and Lady Laurus. Yet I still did not trust him, and was not sure if I ever could. My parents had once decided a doctor could make me more marriageable by performing surgery on me – without my knowledge or agreement. This temporary cure still struck me as a way to 'fix' me, and I was still very, very wary of doctors and their cures.

The syringe was filled with a dark green, viscous substance. It was the drug we had found when we searched the apartments of the corrupt Shadow who'd been working both for my family to find me and, as it turned out, for Doctor Pozzi. I had thought the drug was Lerium, but it was not.

'What is this?' I whispered.

'A drug of my own making. I dosed you four days ago, but I'll give you another dose now. After this, you'll need weekly doses, and you should be safe.'

Weekly. So I was to be completely reliant on Pozzi.

'Any side effects?' I asked.

'Vivid dreams. Possible increased manifestations of some of your emerging abilities.'

Abilities that the Doctor shared. I sent him a tentative thought.

And how did you come by this ability? Are you like me? A Chimaera?

He smiled. *Perhaps.*

So if I decide I don't want to be reliant on your medication, and I run away to Linde or somewhere . . .

Then you'll probably die within a month from a seizure brought on by a fever.

Styx.

'It is not ideal, but it's the best option we have at the moment, Micah,' he said, switching back to normal speech and wiping a drop of sweat from his brow. I guessed it wasn't easy for him to speak mind to mind.

'In the meantime,' he continued, 'you must visit me once a week for your dosage. I'll keep searching for the cure. This medicine is the first step, I'm sure of it. I discovered it when abroad and managed to save several children.'

'What is it made of?' I asked.

'A delicate mixture of many substances,' he said, evasive. 'Nothing unduly dangerous, I assure you.'

'Saying something is *not unduly dangerous* is not wholly comforting,' I said.

Doctor Pozzi managed a rueful smile. 'It's a form of opiate, partly derived from Lerium, but with other additives that suppress the spikes in power your body cannot handle. Some of the additives are from Vestige.'

'Vestige?' I echoed, shocked not just by the answer but by the fact he had given it.

'Yes. Come on, let's get you up and see how you move around.' He held out his hand and I stared at the brass pulleys and the strange, translucent skin. Alder-made, as incomprehensible as all Vestige. I took the hand, cool beneath my touch. My head spun and I clutched the doctor's arm for support. He led me to the lounge, where Drystan sipped tea on one of the chaises.

A flash of light on metal caught my eye. On the mantelpiece was a disc that looked just like Anisa's Aleph. I picked it up, curious, but it didn't hum with power, as Anisa's did. Perhaps it was empty.

'Leave that,' Pozzi said, and I set it down. Pozzi went to his cabinet of curiosities, which looked a lot like the spirit cabinet we used for some of our magician's illusions, except it was topped with a carved and gilded human skull with pointed canines. Doctor Pozzi opened the cabinet door a few inches. A soft green glow emerged from the crack, and then the doctor snapped the door shut. He gave me a bland smile and asked me how I was feeling.

'Still weak,' I admitted.

'Back to bed,' he said. 'Doctor's orders.'

Drystan watched us go, curious. I gave him a nod – an assurance that, later, I'd tell him everything Pozzi told me. No more secrets.

Back in the room, Pozzi held out a small flask for me to take.

I turned it over in my hands. It was made entirely of Vestige metal, glimmering in the light like oil mixed with water. The top was an uncut emerald, polished to smoothness.

'What's in it?'

'We're not entirely sure, but when I fed a few drops mixed with Lerium and a few other ingredients to a child in Byssia, the babe survived the fever instead of succumbing. I call it Elixir.'

'You fed it to a baby?'

'The child was going to die if I didn't do anything. Many cures are discovered in such circumstances.'

I passed the flask back to him, a shiver of foreboding running through me. 'So, you're injecting me with something ancient that could be made of who-knows-what, and it's mixed with an addictive opiate.'

'It's not addictive at only once a week.'

I didn't know whether to believe that. 'And what happens when you run out?'

'There's enough to last me a long while – I have bought as much of this as could be found, no matter the cost, and, as you know, the pockets of the Snakewood family run deep. Finding a cure is one of my highest priorities. I don't want you to die, Micah.'

'That's good. I have no particular wish to die, either. How long of a supply do you have?'

'Several years, at the very least.' He gestured to my clothes. 'You should get dressed and go home with your friend. But I'll see you next week, I trust.'

I picked up my clothes, clutching them to my chest. 'I don't exactly have a choice, do I?'

His gaze was almost sad. *For now, no, you don't, Micah*, he whispered in my mind. With that, he pushed up my sleeve and pushed Elixir into my veins.

3

RECOVERY

In the smaller Northern villages, there are many types of supposed panaceas and poultices for illness. Many studies have been carried out to ascertain their efficacy. Most of them are little more than quackery, but some, especially ones which used Vestige liquids found in the area, proved to be shockingly effective. Yet due to the volatile nature of Alder-age liquids, they are not advised for consumption.

— 'Folk Remedies in Northern Ellada', PROFESSOR SHAWN ARBUTUS, Royal Snakewood University

Before I woke up, Pozzi had told Drystan I'd likely be able to return home that day. Drystan had sent a messenger to the Kymri Theatre from Pozzi's, and so Cyan was waiting at a nearby tea room and we went to meet her after we left the grand apartment block.

She stood to meet us, wearing a Temnian sarong underneath her oversized woollen coat, her long, dark hair braided with ceramic beads. She peered at me in concern.

Are you all right? she asked me.

More or less. For now.

She cocked her head. *That's hardly reassuring.*

I'll explain everything at home. To both of you.

Best explain to Maske as well, at least some of it. He's been beside himself with worry the last few days.

Have there been any shows?

Not since you've been ill.

I winced, hoping I hadn't marred Maske's joy after winning the duel against Pen Taliesin. He couldn't even celebrate with new performances, thanks to my illness.

Is all well with, well, everything? I asked, floundering for words. Only a few days ago, Cyan had told Maske she was his biological daughter. I pushed my feelings and images at her. Sometimes mind-reading could prove useful.

It's still a little strange, but it's good. It'll be better when you're back, safe and sound.

A few minutes later, we were home. The first place where I'd felt truly safe. The Kymri Theatre already looked different, which was jarring. The columns, carved with palm fronds and a sunset, had been freshly painted, the windows scrubbed and the marble front steps swept. It looked like the jewel of architecture it was meant to be, based on the grand monuments of Kymri, the land of hot sands, black oil, and deep blue sea. A hasty sign over the door read, 'Shows cancelled until further notice.'

Drystan unlocked the door and we entered the mosaic-tiled hallway with its newly erected ticket booth – another sudden change – and back to the kitchen.

Maske looked up from the diagram he was sketching and smiled at us.

'Micah,' he said, warmly. 'I'm so glad to see you recovered.'

Overcome with a surge of affection for the man who had taken us all in, I gave him a hug. He always accepted them happily, if a little awkwardly. He patted my back as I pulled away.

'You look well,' I said. 'Victory suits you.' His suit was immaculate, his best silk cravat expertly tied and fastened with an opal pin, and his hair neatly pomaded into place. The largest change was how the worry lines around his eyes had slackened, and he smiled more easily.

Ricket the cat wandered in from wherever he had been napping and miaowed at us. I patted his head, wondering if he'd even missed me.

Maske fixed us some simple sandwiches and some fish for the cat, and I drank a giant mug of coffee, the warmth settling in my stomach. Strangely, I felt better than I had in a long time. My body vibrated with energy as though I'd never need sleep and my concentration was razor-sharp. I was happy, almost floating.

You're high, Cyan told me.

Am I? I guess I am. The drug Pozzi gave me is mixed with Lerium. It was a little like being drunk, but not as . . . loose. I was as focused as a beam of light.

He gave you Lerium? That's one strong opiate.

How long will this last? I asked her, darting a look at Drystan. Did he know I was affected? And if so, how did that make him feel, as a former Lerium addict?

I wolfed down my sandwiches and then stood, my head spinning. 'I think I need a lie down.'

'Quite right,' Maske said. 'Rest up. There's no rush. I don't think we'll start shows again until next week anyway.'

Making my way up to the loft, I still shook with vitality and could not face the thought of crawling under the covers after having just spent four days in a bed. Instead I went up to the roof terrace. Spring had turned to summer, and the air was warm and stifling. I loosened my cravat and stared over the rooftops of the surrounding tenements. A woman hung washing out to dry from her window. Scattered throughout the granite and sandstone buildings were the cobalt blue domes of Penglass, twinkling in the sun and casting their shadows over the stone.

My mind still felt heightened, like I could do anything. I closed my eyes and focused inward, slowing my breath. After several long breaths, the strangeness faded into the background.

My solitude was short-lived. Cyan and Drystan joined me on the roof terrace a few minutes later. Drystan sat close, putting his arm around me. I leaned against him, his presence steadying me further.

'So what happened?' Cyan asked.

I took Anisa out of my pocket, staring at the Aleph in my hands. Within this little Vestige disc was a being older than we could comprehend. Over the past few months, she'd been warning us that Chimaera were returning to the world, and there were those who might wish to do them harm. She was certain that the world was at stake, as it had been all those centuries ago. I wanted to help protect the other Chimaera, wherever they were, but sometimes feared we wouldn't be able to help as much as Anisa was certain we could.

Cyan crossed her arms together, nervously waiting for my response. It was still difficult to believe that she and I were, in a way, like the spirit trapped within Vestige. Cyan and I were Anthi, so we were human but for our extra abilities. Cyan could read minds and communicate telepathically. A few times, she'd sensed events in the future. I had extra strength and Penglass acted strangely around me. Anisa was a Theri, or one of the Chimaera that looked different. The only other one we knew was Lily Verre's child, who Drystan and I had glimpsed just before my fever. He had dark green scaled skin and horns upon his head.

We were all Chimaera.

Growing up, I'd thought Chimaera only creatures of myth. Within the last year, that had not been the case. We already knew of three, four if you counted Anisa, and she said there were others, more and more coming into their powers. I wondered if any others were having difficulties like me, powers turning against them and making them ill.

'Cyan, have you been feeling well? No headaches?' I asked carefully.

'I'm perfectly fine. Why, was your illness related to being Chimaera?' She barely hesitated over the word now.

I shrugged my shoulders.

Pressing the lever on the back of the Aleph, I set it on the ground. Before us, a pillar of smoke rose from the Aleph, faint in the bright light of day. The smoke swirled and formed into the Phantom Damselfly. It always gave me goosebumps when she first appeared, her large eyes staring at us with a blend of melancholy and mystery. Swirling silver tattoos twined about her forehead and along her hairline, snaking down her neck underneath her plain dress. Behind her, gossamer dragonfly wings rose, flapping noise-lessly. Through her transparent body, the darkened outline of the round, stained-glass window of our loft was visible, decorated with a dragonfly of its own.

'Greetings,' she said, her voice echoing. 'I am glad you are feeling better, little Kedi, though I'm worried about what your illness may mean.'

Anisa had nicknames for all of us. I was 'little Kedi', after one of her charges centuries ago. Cyan was 'the one who was Matla', as in one of Anisa's memory-visions, Cyan had seen through the eyes of Anisa's friend, an owl-woman. Drystan she called 'White Clown' for his time in the circus.

'That makes all of us,' Drystan drawled.

I told them everything Pozzi had shared with me, though Anisa had presumably overheard all from within her Aleph. My body had turned against itself. I had to visit him every week until he found a permanent cure – if he ever did.

'And if the same thing happens to me?' Cyan asked.

'Then you'll have to come with me, I suppose, and Pozzi will know you have extra abilities as well.' I turned to Anisa. 'Can you tell us anything about this Elixir?'

She came towards me, resting her ghostly fingers on my face and gazing into my eyes.

'I can feel that it is as he says. Lerium mixed with something Vestige. There are some old elixirs that may do as he claims. But it would surprise me if they'd survived the centuries. Your body is healthy at the moment. Stronger than it's ever been. As it seems to be helping, I advise you to keep taking it. It also enables you to be near the physician once a week and I believe there is much we can learn from him. You recall my visions?'

'Yes,' I said, annoyed at the tone of her question, as if she expected the fever to have altered my memory. 'A man with a blurred face who wishes to kill all Chimaera, just like what happened to you, your partner, and your charges.'

Her face pulled into a grimace. It was low of me to throw the deaths of Relean, Ahti, and Dev at her, even if they had died close to a thousand years ago. Anisa was proof that some grief never fades.

'If Pozzi is the blurred man, he could be the one to kill us by poisoning me for a start,' I muttered.

'That is true,' she admitted with a sigh. 'Although I believe if he'd wished to do so, he could have just let you die already.'

'I don't like the sound of this at all,' Drystan said, pacing around the terrace.

'See if you can steal some of this Elixir,' Anisa replied, looking at me. 'If I have the time to study it, perhaps I can ascertain what's in it. Also, if Cyan does grow ill, it would buy us a little time before we would have to bring her to Pozzi.'

I thought back to Pozzi's rooms. Stealing it from his cabinet of curiosities wouldn't be easy. I remembered what else I'd seen there – the strange little Vestige Aleph on the mantelpiece.

'What was that Aleph I saw at Pozzi's?' I asked her. 'Did you sense anything about that?'

'Sadly, no. It appeared empty to me, or the inhabitant, if they survived, is in deep hibernation. There are so many Alephs scattered about this world. Thousands of crypts that once housed my kind.' She grew quiet, and I knew she thought of Relean. I wanted to offer comfort, but what was there to say?

'What do we do in the meantime?' I asked them all.

'We watch, we wait, we keep our eyes wide open,' Anisa said. 'It is all we can do for now.'

'Not all,' Drystan said. 'Simply sitting around on our arses is a piss-poor plan – sorry, Anisa. I'm going to try and find out more about Pozzi, maybe see if we can find any other evidence of more Chimaera – if we can find others, we can see how common this illness is.'

'I agree,' Cyan said, her right palm rubbing her left forearm. 'I don't like simply waiting to see if I fall ill, too.'

'What you do will hopefully be the right course of action,' Anisa said blandly, her voice echoing with a certain amount of prescience.

I sighed. 'I don't find that comforting.'

Anisa returned to her Aleph, Cyan went back to her room, and Drystan and I climbed down to our loft. My body was still strange and not quite my own, my mind almost detached.

Everything had been wonderful five days ago. We'd won the duel against Taliesin and his grandsons. Maske had learned that Cyan was his daughter. Drystan had said he loved me. Everything had fallen into place. Now my life had fractured again.

Drystan's warm arms wrapped around me. Turning, I rested his forehead against mine.

'We'll get through all of this,' he said. 'We always do.'

So far.

'What did you say?'

'Hmm? I didn't say anything.'

'Strange. I swore I heard you say "so far" but it sounded . . . different.'

My mouth formed a little 'o'. *Drystan*, I thought at him. *Can you hear me?*

He jumped back and swore.

My mouth fell open. 'You heard me!'

'Did you just . . . speak in my mind?' He sounded panicked. 'Can you read my thoughts?'

'I don't know. Do you want me to try?'

'Styx! No!'

I was a little hurt at that.

'I thought only Cyan was psychic,' he said, his eyes still round.

My breath hitched. 'So did I. No one else has ever been able to hear me before Pozzi. Not without Cyan's help.'

Drystan just looked at me. It didn't need a mind-reader to tell he was perturbed at the turn of events.

'It must be the side effects Pozzi was talking about,' I assured him, just as surprised as he was.

Drystan came closer, but we didn't quite touch.

'Are you afraid of me?' I said, my voice cracking. *Am I still a freak?*

'You're not a freak. Never think that.'

I hadn't meant for him to hear the last part. 'Styx, this is just one more strange thing in a series of strange events.'

He hugged me, and those arms were a comfort, a refuge. The warmth, the feel, the smell, the very presence of him centred me. We'd still not been 'together' for very long, and it felt so precious sometimes. So very delicate, like it could shatter at any moment. We curled around this newness, protecting it from anything that could bring harm. Loving him was as natural as opening my eyes after a long sleep.

Putting my hands on either side of his face, pressing my lips to his, I tried to forget everything and only focus on Drystan. 'I love you, Drystan Hornbeam.'

After a long kiss, he pulled back, smiling gently. 'I love *you*, Micah Grey.'

He pulled me to the bed, and I followed.

4

THE FLAME AND THE FIRE

We must rise up against injustice. We must take what is ours. And we will. No longer will we let the Twelve Trees of Nobility soak up all the water, the sunshine, and the nutrients of the world. The rest of us are hungry, and we will be fed.

— Extract from a Forester pamphlet

The next day, the last thing I wanted to do was stay inside.

I'd barely slept; my energy was still so high. Skipping coffee for fear it would make me bounce off the ceiling, I sipped apple juice and munched toast at the breakfast table. Drystan was rubbing his eyes and gulping coffee – he didn't sleep much, after all. I suppressed a wicked grin. Cyan stared at her toast, focusing inward, as if she could sense her body turning against her. Ricket miaowed indignantly in the corner, and Drystan moved to feed him.

Maske came into the kitchen, and one look at his ashen face made my stomach drop. He set the newspaper on the table and the bold headline carved itself into my brain: 'CHIMAERA ARE REAL AND AMONG US.'

That was *The Daily Imacharan*, a respectable newspaper, not some rag printing rumours for the hope of bolstering their circulation numbers. I grabbed it, skimming it.

'That's already out of date, according to the delivery man,' Maske said. 'I'll turn on the radio. Said there'd be an update on the hour.'

Another new purchase that Maske couldn't afford before the duel. It took him a few moments to find the right station, and then the crackly, discordantly upbeat music filled the room.

The two minutes until the clock in the hall struck nine had never seemed so long. The music faded away, replaced with the announcer's smooth tones. It was not a Vestige artefact, though the inventors had spent many hours taking Vestige apart and putting it back together again to find a way to communicate across land and sea.

'Good morning, Imachara. It is nine in the morning, and many of you will be at work, but I hope your employers are feeling generous and letting you listen on one of the days that will go down in history.

'Yesterday evening, a small group of people claiming to be none other than the Chimaera of myth presented themselves at the Royal Snakewood Palace, asking for a meeting with the Princess Royal Nicolette Snakewood and her uncle, the Steward of the Crown. Many, of course, assumed that they were simply pranksters. One of them, however, put on a display that can only be described as magical.

We at Radio Imachara managed to conduct an exclusive interview with one of the guards, who has chosen to remain nameless. He told us there were three people at the gates. One was tall, pale-skinned, dark-eyed, and very handsome, yet looked normal, our guard said, aside from his eyes. They glowed a reddish orange in the growing darkness, like coals. The other was a woman with spots on her skin like a leopard, her teeth pointed canines.'

Drystan and I exchanged a look. Could it be Juliet the Leopard Lady of R. H. Ragona's Circus of Magic? Had another Chimaera been right next to us the whole time?

'The third person was a man with fine auburn hair all over him, slick as a horse's hide. We asked our guard if he thought this could all be done with tricks and cosmetics, but the guard had shaken his head, vigorously. He said the three supposed Chimaera asked very politely if the Royal Family would see them, as they wished to make themselves known to them. They claimed they came in nothing but friendliness and peace, and all three were loyal citizens of Ellada.

'And, Imachara – the Royal Family did indeed let them in.'

He paused for effect. My mouth was so dry I had to steal a sip of Drystan's coffee.

'We do not know what happened once these people entered the palace, but I do know that this morning, at noon, they will address the city. There will be a full security presence, and anyone who wishes to attend is urged to be silent, peaceful, and listen to what they have to say. We will also be broadcasting their words live if you wish to remain in your homes. Whatever they say, I have a feeling Imachara, Ellada, and the Archipelago as a whole will never be quite the same.'

Maske turned off the radio. The silence in the kitchen was deafening.

'Well,' Drystan said. 'I suppose we know what we're doing this lunchtime.'

'You shouldn't go,' Maske said. 'It isn't safe.'

'We can't miss this,' Cyan said. 'It involves us.'

Maske pressed his lips together. 'I can't face it. I'll listen here.' He loved performing in front of large crowds, but he could not stand to be amidst the crush of bodies. After so many years living alone, he was still a hermit at heart.

'We're going,' I said, keeping my voice gentle.

'You need to be careful,' he said. 'Emotions are high. Stay out of the way.'

'We'll watch from the rooftops,' I said.

He nodded and turned back to his coffee cup.

The three of us left our dishes in the sink and almost ran upstairs to finish dressing. My heartbeat hammered in my chest.

Other Chimaera.

Less than an hour later, Cyan and Drystan accompanied me through Imachara towards the Celestial Cathedral. My senses had always been sharp, but now I could detect scents from half a street down, and hear sounds from even farther away. This was not always pleasant – it meant that as well as chimney smoke and unfurling flowers, there was the more noisome pollution of city life; manure, rotting rubbish, stale body odour and that much more. The late spring morning was busy, with shopkeepers setting out their wares, paperboys crying the headlines from the corners, and the engines of cabs and carriages sputtering and growling. Horses drawing carts whinnied. The sun emerged, glinting off the mica in the soot-stained granite of Imachara.

My energy was so high it was hard not to skip down the pavement, despite the dread I should have been feeling. Other Chimaera in Imachara. We would see them, maybe even meet them. We couldn't out ourselves as Chimaera, public scrutiny would fall on us even more than it already had as winners of Maske's duel. Maybe they'd even say we cheated at the magician show by using our Chimaera powers – also not entirely untrue. Still, though. I'd see others like me.

My excitement soon sobered.

The Foresters, the anti-monarchy party, were already here, lining the streets in protest. The Foresters wished for ministries, for democracy, for elections. For the most part, the demonstrations so far had been peaceful, if emotionally charged. A few months ago, a group had splashed paint on the windows of the noble estates in the Emerald Bowl out of town, but the main Forester party was quick to proclaim that they were a fringe group unaffiliated with the main movement. Cyan and Drystan were in varying degrees sympathetic to their cause, even if they didn't agree with their methods. Having grown up in the family I had, and raised to be utterly loyal to the crown, it was difficult to know what to believe.

My stomach dropped – these Foresters were here to
protest about the Chimaera. The Royal Family had let
them into their palace, listened to whatever they had to
say, and given them a platform to address the city. The
Foresters had no say in the matter, and they were unhappy.

This protest was utterly silent. No cries, no fist-fights,
no chanting. Hundreds of people crowded the front of the
Royal Snakewood Courthouse. Many held signs with
slogans: 'FROM THE LOWEST ROOT TO THE HIGHEST
BRANCHES', 'THE TWELVE TREES ARE FULL OF
TERMITES', or the simpler 'FREEDOM FOR ALL'. Other
signs, the paint still wet, proclaimed 'CHIMAERA ARE
FABLES', 'NO MONSTERS IN ELLADA', and 'FAIRY
TALE NONSENSE'. Policiers were clustered around the
protesters, hands resting lightly near their guns, probably
unnerved by the quietness of the crowd.

'The Chimaera aren't here, though, are they?' Drystan
asked, puzzled. 'I thought they were speaking in front of
the Celestial Cathedral.'

'Security probably herded the crowds this way,' Cyan
said. She closed her eyes. 'Yes. They've been here since
just after that announcement.'

There was still an hour and a half until noon and
already the streets were so packed. We threaded our way
through the crowd. Someone pressed a flyer into my hand
and I crumpled it into my fist.

We managed to find a small side street that was less
crowded than the others. Spying scaffolding, we climbed
up to the rooftops.

'Over there,' I said, pointing.

We climbed over the tops of a few tenements, built so close together we only had to step over the narrow gaps between them. Soon, we found another scaffolding-skirted building and climbed down to the second platform from the bottom. We had an excellent view of the Celestial Cathedral. A few children sat on the platform below us, but no one else had been brave enough to climb up higher, so we had space to breathe. The cathedral dominated the square, shining in the sun. The white and black towers representing the Moon and the Sun jutted towards the sky. Its doors were closed, a hasty, temporary stage erected in the middle of the square. Something about it made me shudder – it looked like a gallows.

The last time I had been here was Lady's Long Night, when the service had been interrupted by a very different type of Forester protest. Timur, the leader of the group, had cut the power and threatened to expose a secret that would bring the monarchy down if they did not start acquiescing to the Foresters' demands. As far as I knew, the Snakewoods had not caved to his blackmail. Had Timur ever known a secret at all?

The square below was packed with bodies, but not to the point where people couldn't move. Many more stayed away, frightened by the possibility of actual Chimaera. These people could be frauds, I reminded myself, but so badly wanted to believe that more Chimaera were returning and that we were not alone.

The crumpled flyer was still in my pocket. Drystan and Cyan leaned closer to look over my shoulder. It showed a sketched tree, its branches weighed down with food and gold. Below, people with roots for legs reached up towards the food in vain. There was a short article listing the discrepancy of social wealth and a call to action.

'The other Forester flyers had Timur on them,' I said, remembering his unruly mane of hair and intense eyes. He'd once worked for the palace and the crown, but had turned against the monarchy and now hoped to undo its power. He thought they hoarded their wealth, and so many went hungry who couldn't. He wasn't wrong, but I disagreed with his methods.

'Maybe they realized his face was scaring people off the cause,' Drystan said with a laugh as I put the flyer away.

We quieted, staring down at the crowd. As it grew closer to noon, the square grew even more crowded. The area behind the temporary stage, nearest the cathedral, was blocked off, so the three Chimaera would have an escape route into the church if the crowd grew too rowdy.

Anisa's Aleph was cold as I clutched it within my pocket, next to the Forester flyer. Time passed and the tension grew in the heart of Imachara.

The clock of one of the cathedral towers finally struck noon. The twelve gongs sounded out over the square, and a hush fell over the crowd.

The three Chimaera emerged from the cathedral, hooded and cloaked, surrounded by a security detail. They walked with careful steps up onto the stage. A pulpit with a Vestige amplifier waited to project their voices across the square.

They lined up behind the pulpit and as one, removed their hoods. Gasps and low murmurings rippled through the crowd. Drystan and I exchanged another look. The woman in the middle was definitely the Leopard Lady from R. H. Ragona's Circus of Magic. Vertigo made me woozy, and I gripped the metal scaffolding tight. Juliet had been a friend to both of us, though we didn't know her well. She preferred to keep to herself. Once, I'd asked Drystan if he thought she could be Chimaera, due to her spotted skin and sharp fangs. He'd waved it away, saying she probably had a skin disorder and surgical enhancements. He'd been wrong.

Though the crowd surged forward, no one came closer than six feet from the edge of the stage. Cyan's mouth pursed.

'They've put up a Vestige Shroud,' she said.

My eyes widened. 'I've never seen one of those in effect before.' A Shroud put up a barrier around a set perimeter. Nothing could go in, nothing could go out. The Royal Family or prominent political figures used one whenever they addressed the public, to stave off any assassination attempts. The fact that the family had presumably given the Chimaera one for their own protection would rankle any who felt threatened by these three.

My breath caught in my throat and I leaned closer to the edge of the platform.

Juliet stepped up to the pulpit. The darker rosettes on her skin stood out in stark relief. She'd shaved in the circus, evidently, or her body had changed – she was covered in a soft down of fur, barely visible, but my eyesight was keen enough to spot it. The other two were as the guard had described. One had short hair like a horse's coat on all visible skin. The other man's eyes glowed slightly, even in the bright light of day, the irises a brilliant orange and red, his skin so pale as to almost be translucent. I wasn't afraid of them – how could I be? They were Chimaera, even if they were Theri instead of Anthi like me and Cyan.

Juliet took a shaking breath. She'd performed in front of crowds time and time again, but there she'd simply stood, gazing imperiously at the gawkers who came to the freak-show tent, hissing if they came too close. She'd never spoken to large crowds. I wondered where Tauro was – he'd also been a member of the freak-show tent at the circus. He'd looked part-human and part-bull. He couldn't speak, but understood everyone around him, and I remembered him as sweet and kind. I hoped Juliet was looking after him, somewhere safe, and that he'd escaped a workhouse or worse.

'Good afternoon,' she said, her voice clearly reaching us even on our platform. 'I am called Juliet. My friends here are Henry and Dirk.' Henry was the pale man and Dirk was the russet-haired man. 'I know you have questions. Concerns, fears, hesitations. It's sudden, and change can be frightening. I know how life can shift at a moment's notice.' Her face closed, guilt stabbed me. Drystan stiffened. The circus would have failed anyway, with Ragona's terrible handle on finances, but we'd still killed the circus the night we'd escaped. Aenea's face floated in my mind's eye, the loss and guilt still painful. So much senseless loss that dark night on the beach in Imachara.

'I know our appearance has been widely reported already, but we thought that it would be better for you to hear this from us directly. There's less chance of rumours being construed as facts. The Royal Snakewood family has graciously let us speak.' She paused and licked her lips nervously. Her eyes flashed topaz. My fingers tingled, and I hung onto her every word.

Cyan shook her head vigorously, as if shaking away a fly. 'Stay here,' she said. 'I sense something, but it's faint. I need to be closer.'

'You should stay here,' I said, eyeing the crowd. They were still silent, for the most part, but I didn't like the expressions on some of their faces. 'Or one of us should come with you.'

'No,' she said. 'I can make my way through the crowd quickly, I need only think at them to shift a little out of my way.'

I kept my expression deliberately blank. That was a new skill, or something she'd not told us she could do before.

Juliet began speaking again, catching my interest. When I glanced back, Cyan was already descending the scaffolding.

'. . . we can assure you, we are Chimaera. We've suspected it for a long time. All three of us have always looked different, but over the last two years, we seem to have come into our own. Though we may look strange to you, please know that we are people with feelings, hopes, and dreams. We mean no harm. We only wish to make ourselves known and to reach out to other Chimaera, hidden among us.'

The crowd murmured again, heads swivelling left and right, wondering if the person next to them could be like the three on the stage. Cyan had made her way halfway through the crowd, her shoulders tense. Dread rose up, but I tried to push it down.

'So, if you are like us, please, come see us. We will be staying in the wing of the smaller building behind the palace. This is no trickery. We simply want to find others, to forge a connection, and try to understand why we have returned after so many centuries.'

'Bollocks!' someone cried out in the crowd, and other voices rose with them.

'Please,' Juliet said, her voice shaking. 'We are no threat. That is all we have to say at this time. Thank you for coming and listening. In Lord and Lady's Light, we look forward to brightening Ellada's star.'

'You're cursed by the light!' another called, and others took up a chant of 'cursed, cursed, cursed'.

Cyan still pushed her way through the crowd, almost at the barrier to the front of the stage.

'I don't like her being down there,' Drystan said. 'This crowd is one step from turning nasty.'

Juliet and the others sensed that. They thanked the crowd again and inclined their heads, then began backing away from the stage. The crowd yelled insults. At the perimeter, Policiers and Royal guards called for order. Wordlessly, Drystan and I hefted ourselves over the scaffolding edge and began to climb down towards the square.

Cyan had reached the Shroud barrier and bashed her fists against it. She yelled something, but I couldn't hear. Then Cyan pushed her way *through* the Shroud. A shiver ran down my back. No one was meant to be able to enter if they were on. Juliet turned, her mouth opening in surprise.

In my head, Anisa screamed. Long, loud, terrified, as I'd never heard her before.

Boom.

The sudden sound shook the ground and reverberated in our chests. We almost lost our grip on the metal scaffolding and had just enough time to wonder what it was before we saw the smoke furling from both of the cathedral towers, black and thick. Flames pouring from the windows. People screaming.

Another concussive explosion vibrated through the square. Drystan and I both lost our grip and fell onto the hard, cobbled square. It was only a few feet, but it forced the breath from my lungs.

The towers broke in half, white and dark marble raining on the cathedral roof.

The last explosion reverberated through my body as I lay flat on my back, unable to move. My ears buzzed, my vision swam, slowly steadying to focus on the debris raining from the sky. A piece of brick hit my head, another hit my shoulder, and the world dimmed and quavered. More screams rent the air. Smoke filled the square, swirling motes of embers and ash drifting down like flakes of snow. I coughed, wiping dust from my face, my hand coming away wet with blood.

My head swam with panic and disorientation. 'Drystan!' I called, choking and coughing.

'Here!' Drystan called to my right. About ten people were between us, all moaning with fear and trying to push their way away from the square. My feet had already been stepped on half a dozen times.

Drystan fought his way towards me, his face filthy with soot. Sirens wailed, drawing closer. Everyone who could had already fled the square.

I'd wondered, in the moments before the explosion, if the Shroud had somehow turned off and that was how Cyan had pushed through. Yet even through the explosion, it had held. The square was filled with debris, but all the larger pieces of rock and rubble remained behind the line where the Shroud had been. Where Cyan was, and Juliet, and the two other Chimaera.

Out here there were still injuries. People struggled to their feet. A woman slumped near me, groaned, her eyelids fluttering, blood staining her blouse. She opened her eyes, staring unseeing at the cathedral ruins. Though she was not dead, that glassy stare reminded me of Aenea, killed by the Ringmaster.

I couldn't worry about these strangers. Picking my way through the debris, I tried to reach the cathedral. Cyan.

Drystan stayed close to my side. Blood ran down my temple, warm and wet. Drystan tore off a piece of his dirty shirt and told me to press the cloth to the wound.

'Cyan!' I called, and Drystan echoed my call. Before

us was a wall of boulders that had once been one of the most beautiful buildings in Ellada.

'Cyan!' I screamed again. And then, in my mind: *Cyan! CYAN!*

For what seemed an eternity, there was nothing . . . then a faint: *I'm here.*

My knees almost buckled with relief. *Where are you?* I asked.

I don't know. Somewhere dim and dark.

Are you trapped underneath something, Cyan?

Maybe . . . Her voice drifted away.

Cyan! Stay with me!

She didn't respond, but I caught a few images sent from her: a small patch of sky, a smudge in the corner. It was the ruined stump of one of the cathedral towers. I swallowed against my dry throat, terror pulsing through me. To my left was a pile of rubble which could have matched the images: it must be where Cyan was trapped.

I didn't see the Chimaera.

'Come on,' I said to Drystan.

The ambulances and Policiers were thick in the square. Doctors and nurses worked to treat the wounded. I didn't see any dead, for a mercy. If the Royal Family hadn't put up that shroud as a security precaution . . . it didn't bear thinking about. I focused on the precarious stack of wood, stone, and dirt instead.

'Oh Lord and Lady,' I moaned, swaying on my feet. 'If we move something the wrong way, it could all collapse in on itself.'

Cyan, come on, are you all right? Please, Cyan.

Nothing. Fumbling in my pocket, I drew out Anisa's Aleph, clutching the Vestige disc tightly in my hands. While I couldn't bring her forth, not here, there must be something she could do. She'd been silent since that bloodcurdling scream in my head at the moment of attack. Had she only sensed it in that second before the explosion?

Anisa, you have to help us. The one who was Matla is trapped.

Drystan hovered near me as the chaos swarmed around us. My watering eyes shut tightly. *Please, Anisa. Help me.*

You don't need my help, the Phantom Damselfly whispered in my mind. *You have the power to help her yourself and only need me to point in the right direction. Do not be afraid of your own power. Those other Chimaera – I'd only sensed them last night, and now they're gone. I should have seen this. I should have been able to help stop it. Yet I sensed nothing. Nothing. They were Chimaera. I should have been able to protect them.* Her mental voice was tight with grief.

Cyan did, I said. *She sensed what you couldn't. Now she needs your help. Help her. She is your ward, as sure as I am. Don't let us down.*

A pause, a whisper. *I'm going to take control of you, like I did to fix Maske's automaton. Just long enough to show you how to save her. All right?*

My breath caught in my throat. The last time she had done that, she had not warned me. I had suddenly been a prisoner in my own body as she had walked with my legs, trailed my fingers against the wall, kissed Drystan briefly with my lips. Despite our need for her aid at the time, it had been intrusive and disconcerting to say the least.

But I had no choice; there was no longer a trace of Cyan in my mind at all. *All right. Just find her.*

Anisa flowed into me, a gossamer sheen of blue and purple shimmering over my skin before settling. Drystan watched, his mouth falling open before he checked no one had witnessed the transformation. For those moments, there was no control over my body; I was curled into a corner of my own mind, a silent witness to Anisa's usage of my powers. At least this time I knew what to expect, and was still able to see through my own eyes.

A strange sound thrummed in my ears, and the pile of rocks shimmered. Deep in the rubble, amid the pockets of air, I could see the outline of Cyan's body. My forehead furrowed and then Anisa moved my body forward, setting aside a rock here and there.

'Hey!' someone called behind me. 'The whole thing could crumble and people might be stuck below! Wait for the Policiers and the firefighters!'

Anisa ignored him, moving rocks with my hands. Drystan tried to help but Anisa motioned for him to stop. Before long, she had created a little hole and was reaching into it. A hand clasped mine, and Anisa pulled Cyan out. She was covered in blood and dust, and her eyelids fluttered, but she was still conscious.

'Cyan, are you all right?' Drystan asked her. Her mouth opened but no words emerged.

My stomach dropped. The Shroud hadn't held

throughout the entire explosion. Through Anisa taking over my body, I could sense a few other people trapped in the rubble, their souls shining like burning coals amongst the stone. Seven altogether. *Oh my Lord and Lady.*

They are not Cyan. The medics will help them.

Sometimes I forgot how cold the Damselfly could be.

The medics can't sense the stone like you can. They're people, frightened and hurt. Help them.

A pause.

She did, navigating my body over the rubble, gently moving the rocks aside to find the pockets of survivors, drawing the victims upright through the dust and debris. After her initial hesitation, she didn't stop until we'd helped the other seven people I'd sensed trapped under the ruin out and passed them to the waiting ambulances. At least one of them probably wouldn't make it. His leg was crushed to a mangled mess, and his skin had the deathly pallor of someone not long destined for this world.

Give me my body back, Anisa.

There was another reluctant pause and I tried not to let my fear show.

Anisa.

She took the disc out of my pocket. With a gentle, mental sigh, she flowed out from my mind and body and back into the Aleph gripped in my hand.

Like the last time she had taken my body, I fell to the ground like a puppet with its strings cut. Drystan helped me sit up. My head pounded, probably a result of both Anisa taking my body and the head wound.

Cyan didn't look much better, but at least she was still with us.

'She needs the hospital,' I told Drystan.

He nodded and picked her up, curling her against his chest. Still dizzy, I had to lean on him heavily, but Drystan took us both to the medical queue. We waited our turn, watching the firefighters scurry to put out the last of the flames. I couldn't tell how many had died, but it looked bad.

'Who did this?'

Drystan shook his head. 'I don't know.'

'Foresters,' Cyan whispered. 'A small, violent faction that hate Chimaera. They saw them as a threat to Ellada.'

'Juliet,' I said, my heart hurting.

'You knew her?' Cyan said.

'She'd worked with us at the circus,' Drystan said, his voice just as broken.

Cyan groaned, hiding her face against Drystan's shirt. 'Everything is so loud in my head.'

'This doesn't make sense. Even if the Foresters were against the Chimaera, why attack so quickly? And why have that silent protest and then turn to such violence?' I asked.

Drystan shook his head, mystified. We reached the front of the medic queue. The tired nurse took one look at Cyan and gestured to the next ambulance. We clambered into the back with her where an equally exhausted nurse attended Cyan, making notes of her injuries.

As the engine started and the ambulance rattled down the rubble-strewn streets, I looked out of the small back window at the ruin of what had been the open market square. Just a few months ago, Drystan and I had watched a shadow puppet show there. Now there was no children's laughter, no bright streamers fluttering from market stalls. All was the grey and black of broken stone, and the red of dying flames and drying blood.

5

INFIRMARY

Once there was a sleeping princess, trapped within a castle of fire. A dragon curled around the moat. Each of his exhales kept the stone aflame. The princess was safe from the heat, for she slumbered in an enchanted room. Many a knight and warrior tried to defeat the dragon, to rescue the princess and to keep the hoard of gold and jewels. Every time one approached, the dragon had only to let loose his flames, and the would-be hero perished.

This is one of those stories you may believe does not have a happy ending. No knight ever came to rescue the princess. She slumbers in her enchanted room still, the dragon curled protectively around the castle. She may never be saved. But, depending on her dreams, perhaps she does not need saving.

— 'The Princess and the Castle of Fire', *Hestia's Fables*

The hospital was chaos.

Yelling voices and frantic footsteps echoed down the corridors as harried nurses and doctors rushed to and fro.

The waiting rooms were filled to bursting with crying, anxious family and friends. The smell of blood and smoke was strong beneath the antiseptic cleaner.

The doctors said that, due to space, only one person could come into the ward with Cyan. Though only a small percentage of people within the square had been injured thanks to the Shroud, there were still hundreds who needed medical attention. We'd sent a messenger to Maske as soon as we'd arrived. He came and went through to be with his daughter.

A nurse told us that Cyan was in shock, but that they couldn't believe how unharmed she was considering how much rubble she'd been trapped under. The other people Anisa and I had rescued had not fared so well.

Cyan's presence flickered in my mind.

Are you all right? I asked.

With all the Vestige in the hospital enhancing our abilities, I heard her as clearly as a treble bell.

Sore, but I'll live. Can't say the same for everyone. I felt them die around me, Micah. Especially those three Chimaera. I so wanted to meet them. I'd been so excited by the possibility of meeting others. She sounded woozy from the pain medicine. *It made me realize how very delicately we're tethered to life. Like we're all walking on a barely frozen lake that could crack beneath us at any given moment.*

I didn't know what to say; having learned that very well the night I left the circus. Most of a year later, and the guilt and grief could still take my breath away.

Drystan slumped in his chair, looking as exhausted as

I felt. He leaned close to me. 'What happened back in the square? Was that Anisa in your body again?'

'Yes. But I asked her to help, so this time she had my permission. She did something, channelled my power somehow so I was able to sense Cyan beneath the rubble, even though she was nearly unconscious. And I knew how to move the rocks so the rubble wouldn't collapse.'

'That's . . . something else.'

'Yes. She didn't want to save the others. But I made her.'

'She would have just left them?'

'Aye.'

'Shows her true colours, doesn't it?'

'What do you mean?'

'If a person doesn't have a purpose for her, what use are they?'

'I don't know. She did save them when I asked, so that must count for something, surely?'

Drystan gave me a wry look. 'You're someone she needs.'

There was no answer for that. We waited in silence, the shadows lengthening in the late afternoon sun. My head still hurt and my muscles ached.

Oli, Cyan's beau, came to the hospital. He was as dirty as everyone else, his clothing ripped, his eyes wide and afraid.

He ignored us, going directly to a nurse and asking if he could see Cyan. The nurse went off and returned, shaking her head at him.

'Maske must not want to leave?' I guessed, watching

Oli's crestfallen face. I reached out to Cyan but couldn't sense anything from her. Oli caught our eyes and I raised my hand in greeting, but he hustled past us and out of the hospital without a backwards glance.

'What's that about?' Drystan asked.

'Dunno,' I said, frowning. I surreptitiously linked his pinkie with mine, and we settled down for a long wait.

When the light had almost gone, a familiar figure shuffled out from the hallway that led to the patients' rooms. He crossed the waiting room, heading to the canteen.

'Lord and Lady,' I swore under my breath.

Drystan followed my gaze. 'Pricks in Styx,' he agreed.

'I'll be back,' I muttered, standing. My head swam from rising so fast, and I had to hold onto the chair's arm.

'You all right?' Drystan asked, echoing my earlier question to Cyan.

'I will be when I find out why my brother is here,' I said, and followed Cyril's blonde head to the canteen.

I hovered nearby, but didn't want to call his name – what if he wasn't here as Cyril Laurus, the scion of the Lord Laurus of Sicion? Though pretending to be someone else wasn't exactly my brother's style – that was my role. But why was he here in Imachara, and why hadn't he told me he was coming? Mind, university was starting soon, or perhaps he planned a surprise visit? My mind ran in circles.

He took the mug of coffee from the overworked man behind the counter and turned to meet my curious gaze. He dropped the cup, which shattered onto the floor, while the man behind the counter groaned and dutifully grabbed a mop to wipe up the mess.

'. . . You!' Cyril said, unsure what to call me. I had gone by Lady Iphigenia Laurus, Gene, Micah Grey, and Sam Harper in the time he'd known me. Four names. Three lives.

Then, the unexpected. My brother – my strong, stalwart brother – collapsed into tears and pulled me into an embrace. I put my arms around him, patting him gently on the back. He smelled of home – of his cologne and smoke from the fire and father's cigars, of cloth of good make and my brother.

'Cyril?' I asked, whispering into his ear. 'Why are you here?' The few people in the canteen stared at our unseemly public display. Two grown men didn't often fall into each other's arms in such an open manner.

'It's Mother,' he croaked. 'She came with me to visit after I'd settled into my university apartments. They're . . . just off the square. We were going for something to eat when . . . when the explosions happened.'

Mother.

'Oh, stars. You were by the Shroud barrier?'

He nodded, unable to speak.

'Cyril, is she all right?'

He shook his head against my shoulder. 'They don't know yet. They don't know.'

I pulled away from him, peering into his face. 'How bad is it?'

'She . . . threw herself in front of me. To protect me, and she shouldn't have. I'm bigger than her. She's grown so frail. She was hit by debris. There was a lot of blood, Gene. And now they can't wake her up.'

The shock hit home – my lives, past and present, colliding in a single moment. First Cyan had been hurt, and now my mother.

Admittedly, she and I had never really got along. She had always wanted me to be someone or *something* I wasn't. She was so overly concerned about image, reputation – horrified that someone might find out about my *secret* and ruin my chance for an eligible marriage. So desperate had she become that she'd planned to get me 'fixed', even convincing my father that operating on me to make me a 'natural' female was the best possible chance for future happiness. Without, of course, bothering to ask me whether this was something that would make *me* happy, and I could never forgive her for that. But, almost a year after I'd first run away, I could understand her a little more. She'd tried to do what she considered was best for me, even if that meant she did things that were undeniably, irrefutably, the wrong thing to do.

And now she was lying in a hospital bed.

'Come on,' Cyril said. 'I'll take you to her.'

'But –' Terror rooted me to the spot.

'She's not awake,' he said. 'Don't you want to see her?'

I did. I had seen her from afar a few months ago when she had come to one of Maske's séances. Acting as the stagehand and hiding in the alcove behind the walls, I'd witnessed my mother asking the spirits about me. Cyan had passed along my messages to her. It was the closest thing to contact we'd had.

Cyril took my numb hand and led me through the waiting room. 'My mother,' I mouthed at Drystan, and he met my eyes with surprise and sympathy, nodded in understanding.

My palms grew clammy with sweat as Cyril and I walked down the white corridors before turning into the ward. There she was, tucked into the bed, covered in bandages. She'd always been such an imposing figure – larger than life, looming over me, chastising me for not embroidering enough, or sullying my pinafore, throwing up her hands in despair at my lack of womanly charms. She'd always had a cutting remark, a way to make me feel I'd never be good enough for her.

But since I'd left, she'd diminished. She'd lost weight, sharpening her features. Her hands resting on the coverlet looked so small, so delicate. They weren't covered by their customary white gloves. Rosacea bloomed on her cheeks due to the drink and laudanum. Was this my fault, or was it her own guilt eating at her?

A nurse bustled over. 'Only one visitor per patient, please. We're far too crowded as it is.'

'Please, I'll just be a few moments. She's my mother.' My voice was raspy.

The nurse's face relaxed. 'I understand.' She checked my mother's chart.

'How is she?' I whispered.

'Broken ribs, broken clavicle, but the most worrying is the head trauma. We're hoping she'll wake up soon.'

'And if she doesn't?'

Her eyes filled with pity, and that was answer enough. She left us.

I sat next to my mother, taking her hand in mine as I'd never been able to do before. She had raised me. She wasn't my mother by blood, and Lord and Lady knew we didn't have a deep bond of love and affection. But she was my mother just the same. I'd sometimes imagined returning to the Laurus home, successful and happy as Micah Grey, and fantasised that my parents would apologize for all they'd done and love me unconditionally for who I was, male and female, Gene or Micah. Yet I knew they were nothing but passing fancies, a wish as delicate as a butterfly's wing.

But if my mother never woke up, any chance to salvage a relationship and find any sort of closure or forgiveness would be gone. I squeezed her hand, leaned over and kissed her scraped forehead.

'When you wake up, we'll make everything right. I promise,' I whispered.

There was no response.

Cyan was discharged an hour later, bandaged and woozy. Maske sprung for a hansom cab to take us home, the engine running as the driver unbuttoned his coat in the rising heat. Cyril came with us. He couldn't stand the thought of being surrounded by strangers, and so we offered to let him stay with us for a few days. Sirens still echoed as we navigated through the twining streets.

Arriving home, Maske led Cyan to her room while Drystan and I showed Cyril his temporary accommodation.

It smelled of dust and a hint of mould, as it'd been left unoccupied for so long and we hadn't yet started refurnishing the spare rooms. I took the covers off the furniture and Drystan found some spare linens.

'Sorry it's, ah, not in the best shape,' I said, brushing away a cobweb from the vanity mirror.

'This is wonderful. It's twice as big as the one in the university apartments I'm sharing,' he said, admiringly. 'Maybe I could rent it from you, if Maske wouldn't mind?'

'I'll check with him once everything's settled down. I'd love it, but Mother and Father might wonder where you are.' The thought of having him here filled me with a fierce happiness, cutting through all the fear and exhaustion. To have my brother back, all the time, would be wonderful. I gave him a hug, and he squeezed me until the vertebrae in my back cracked.

As he hugged me, I wondered what Cyan had seen, right before the Celestial Cathedral fell.

We all met on the roof again.

Cyan, pale and wrapped in a thick robe despite the heat, leaning on her crutch. Drystan and me, our hair still damp from our baths. I had stayed in the nearly scalding hot water until my fingertips pruned, scrubbing until all the dirt and dried blood had swirled down the drain.

The sun set, the sky stained red, orange, and yellow. How cruel, for the sun to mirror the death and destruction that had happened just a few hours before.

I brought Anisa forth from the Aleph again.

'The Foresters did this,' Cyan said, with no preamble.

'More specifically, it was Timur. Someone working on his orders.' She paused. Took a deep breath. 'It was Oli.'

'Come again?' Drystan asked. I was similarly flummoxed. Oli was her beau. They met in Riley and Batheo's Circus of Curiosities, and he knew about her power but wasn't afraid of it. Or hadn't been. He was a sailor, and so was often away. He'd helped us with the magician duel, performing as one of our stagehands. We had eaten meals with him, laughed with him. I could not imagine him doing this. It made no sense. Dizziness spun through me, and I hoped it was shock rather than another coming faint.

'I can't . . . I don't want to retell the whole story. Give me your hands. I'll send it to you. Easier that way.'

Drystan and I each took one of her hands. Anisa drifted closer, a gossamer wing resting on Cyan's shoulder.

Cyan's eyes flashed the bright blue of Penglass before she closed them, her head falling forward.

Cyan sat up in the hospital bed. I could feel the pain of her cuts and scratches, the low throbbing of her ankle. She hadn't broken it, but it was a nasty sprain. The pain medicine made her feel sleepy.

Oli had returned and wouldn't leave the waiting room until she saw him. Maske was puzzled – why didn't she want Oli to visit? But she couldn't tell him. Not yet.

'Can you leave for a few minutes for a coffee?' she asked. 'I need to speak to him on my own.'

'Of course, Cyan.' He leaned forward and pecked a kiss on her forehead. The paternal warmth he felt for

her flowed from his thoughts, and she took strength from it.

'Thank you, Maske.' He did not call her by any endearments, and she did not call him Father.

After he left, Oli entered. She stared at him, cold as ice. He stepped back from that glare.

'How much do you know?' he asked.

'Enough. How did you keep it from me?'

He reached beneath his clothes, brought out a small, mechanical Cricket on a golden chain.

'Someone told me if I turned it on, no one could sense anything from me. My mind was my own. They wouldn't even realize I was blocked.' He sounded miserable, but Cyan hardened, refusing to feel pity.

She held out her hand, and he gave her the Cricket, no complaints, no hesitation. Once in her pocket, she could feel the power of it through the cloth, against her thigh.

'Yet you let me sense you in the square. You told me what was happening. You told me to stop it. Why?'

He swallowed. Opened his mouth, closed it again. Cyan was tempted to delve in his mind, uncover all the pieces all at once. Yet the thought of going into that mind she thought she knew so well, seeing how it had twisted away from her, was too raw.

'I should call for the Policiers right now.'

'Why haven't you?' he whispered, hoarse.

'I want to understand why.'

'I thought you suspected. Even though he told me it was Vestige, I thought you'd still snip through it like paper.'

'I've long given you your privacy. Maybe if I'd tried, I could have pushed back, but it never occurred to me. Lord and Lady, I wish it had, for I could have maybe saved lives.'

Oli's eyes darted to the others in the ward, but it was so loud, no one noticed their words.

'I had to, Cyan. I didn't have a choice. And I thought you were sympathetic to the Forester cause. You came to meetings.'

'I went to exactly one meeting and never returned. There's always a choice. And I'm sympathetic to the people having more rights. I'm not remotely sympathetic to killing people on the order of some mad hat evangelical with a personal vendetta against the Snakewoods and Chimaera. You do realize I'm one, right? That if I'd gone up on the pulpit with the other three, I'd be dead, too?'

'You're not like those monsters!' he said.

Cyan recoiled. 'You think I can just read minds because . . . ?'

He shook his head again, refusing to believe. He was closing down, hunching his shoulders, trying to shut her out. *Enough.*

Cyan leaned forward and grabbed Oli's hand. He tried to pull away, but she wouldn't let him. Ruthlessly, she entered his mind.

Oli had been going to Forester meetings faithfully. Timur himself invited him to an exclusive meeting. His most loyal, Timur called them, and all attendees were sworn to secrecy. There'd been a few rituals, a little blurred – perhaps he'd been drinking. Timur ranting how the

Royal Snakewoods were dangerous, were vipers, would protect monsters over their own people. He told them of the Chimaera, claiming all legends were wrong, that they were truly the stuff of nightmares. That, centuries ago, the world had nearly ended entirely because of them, and soon another threat was looming. It was eerily similar to Anisa's warnings to me.

This new group called themselves the Kashura, after the Alder of old who had also worked against the dangers of Chimaera.

He claimed he knew the best way to protect Ellada. Cyan caught flashes of Timur. Persuasive, charming, charismatic. Oli fell under his spell. Cyan never knew, never even suspected. If he was quiet, she assumed he simply missed the sea. When he was away for weeks, claiming to be on short fishing trips to Girit and back, she had believed him. Timur had him do small things for him at first. Trusted him to keep a secret. Oli did, and basked in the praise, and eventually, he came clean about Cyan's ability to read minds.

Cyan jerked back out of his mind. 'You what?'

'Not by name, and I didn't say we were courting.' He swallowed. 'I said I knew you and had to work with you sometimes. So he gave me the Cricket.'

Cyan's rage filled me. It was hot, full, dangerous. Without another word, she took his hand and fell into his memories again.

Only three nights ago, Timur said he knew a way to protect Elladans. He took Oli aside, one on one. Said he had a plan, and there was only one person he could trust.

And so Oli had gone along with the plan to destroy the Celestial Cathedral. It was Oli who had set the bombs in the tower, just before the Chimaera came to speak. He had been lurking, just beyond the Shroud, waiting, watching. Yet just before, he second-guessed himself. Wondered if that Shroud would really hold. He turned his head, and across the square he saw Cyan standing on the scaffolding. He took off the Cricket and let Cyan in, while he stood frozen in fear.

She had come running, but it was too late.

'He lied to me!' he hissed. 'Timur said that he'd do it after the speech was finished and that he'd sound an alarm so the cathedral and the square would be evacuated. Blowing up the empty building was his goal – a symbol of the wealth the monarchy squandered. Later, when I thought perhaps he would target the Chimaera, I still thought that Shroud would hold. I believed no one would be harmed. He'd promised me that.'

'Yes, and you were stupid to believe a word he said.' She turned from him. Her heartbreak hurt me. She loved him, but love cannot erase evil, intentional or not.

'If I were you, I'd turn myself in,' she whispered. 'I should turn you in, but I . . . I can't.' Her voice broke. 'I don't want them thinking I'm involved with your fringe Kashura. You tell the Policiers what you know, and you can stop any of this happening again. Go, Oli,' Cyan said. 'I never want to see you again.'

His jaw worked. His opened his mouth, but then simply thought: I'm sorry.

It's not me you should be apologizing to, *she sent back.*

It's all the innocent victims here in the hospital and all those in the morgue.

He closed his eyes. She stood.

'Send in the Policier in the lobby,' he whispered. 'I'll tell him everything.'

'You'll tell him everything except about me and the others.'

She held his eyes and used just a little of her power to force the suggestion on him more firmly. If only she could have trusted him to do the right thing on his own.

He squared his jaw, nodded once.

Cyan left. She would never see her sailor again.

Cyan let go of our hands.

Her eyes were dry, but pain radiated from her. 'If I'd known, I could have stopped it. I tried, but couldn't get there in time.'

I didn't want to say that if she'd been any closer at all, she would have died.

'We can't know everything, one who was Matla,' Anisa said. 'I did not sense it either.'

Drystan pulled a face. He thought she never sensed anything of use, and at times, it was hard to disagree.

Anisa caught the look. 'I can sense almost nothing of the future any more. There are too many possibilities. I feel blinded. It is most disconcerting.'

'Welcome to how most of humanity feels,' I said, echoing words I'd once said to Cyan when she couldn't read Doctor Pozzi's mind.

'To call themselves the Kashura, the group that nearly

ended the world all those years ago, is . . . brash. They do not even know what they invoke with that name.' Anisa looked sick. I felt the same.

'Did Oli come clean, then?' Drystan asked.

'I lingered in the hallway, listening. He told them everything, except about us. He's at the Constabulary headquarters now.'

'I'm sorry, Cyan,' I said, taking her hand.

She squeezed. 'I am, too.'

Anisa looked out over the growing darkness. 'The sun has set on a terrible day. Let us hope that more like it do not follow.'

6

SYRINGE

I lost another one today. My third loss. I need to do something soon. I have to save them, or there will be none left. What will my patron say?

— From the personal diary of the Snakewood Royal
Physician, DOCTOR SAMUEL POZZI,
while abroad in Byssia

A week passed. Our cuts and bruises healed. My mother still did not wake up.

Cyril went to visit her every day at the hospital, but I hadn't been able to go back and face the sight of my fierce mother reduced so small.

Our small troupe had stayed indoors for the most part, venturing outside only for food and newspapers. The temporary sign proclaiming 'No Shows Until Further Notice' remained on the door.

We heard sirens call more often. More Forester protests occurred almost every day. I never heard the word Kashura. Riots broke out in the Penny Rookeries, the poorest part of town. Some demonstrations even took place within the noble sectors of the Gilt and Glass Quarters, at least until the Policiers arrived to break them up. Rumours circulated of the nobility fleeing to the Emerald Bowl, far away from the riff-raff. I remembered that some Foresters had still gone to the forest of the Emerald Bowl, throwing bricks at one of the estates. They were now building higher walls and hiring security.

Within the city, Banshees and other Vestige security tripled in price on the black market overnight. Food was already creeping up in price, as traders from the other islands of the Archipelago hesitated to bring their wares to Ellada's ports. The streets were nearly empty, some of the windows boarded. Imachara was a ghost town, holding its breath and wondering if the Celestial Cathedral attack was the first domino to fall.

If Ellada looked weak, the other islands would use that to their advantage. Ellada had, after all, subjugated them on and off for centuries as the former head of an empire. Yet it had only ruled through the perceived threat of superior Vestige that made any war against them useless. Vestige was breaking down. All knew this. The other islands were well aware that this threat was now rather empty. Byssia, Linde, Northern and southern Temne, and Kymri all watched and waited.

I hoped this was only a brief period of unrest as people came to terms with what had happened in the Celestial Cathedral. Imachara, the sprawling metropolis and head of Ellada, had always been wild and a little dangerous. It had never felt so unsafe to me that I needed to take a weapon with me whenever I left the house, but now I kept a little dirk inside my boot, just in case.

Though a dirk would do little if there was another explosion.

The Foresters were quick to say that they had nothing to do with the explosion. Timur gave no public speeches, almost as if he were no longer a part of the party. A woman named Lorna Elderberry spoke for them now, claiming that their primary aims were still to reform government, and that they had no political stance on these so-called Chimaera. There was still no mention of the Kashura in the papers. They kept that name to the shadows.

The Palace had offered no proof that the three who spoke to the square were actually Chimaera. All mention of them so far focused only on their physical differences. Surely the Royal Family must know of their other powers. Or perhaps some Theri didn't have powers. Did Lily's son? I'd thought of that little boy often. He was the only other Chimaera I knew of, now that Juliet and the others were gone. Anger and grief for those three haunted me. I'd wanted to connect with them as I had with Cyan.

Cyan had told Maske what Oli had done. It was strange, knowing he would never again enter the Kymri Theatre. He had been taciturn and rarely said more than two words unless he truly had something to say, but I'd liked him. He'd seemed steadfast, so the fact that he had been so easily swayed by Timur rattled me. If he could turn Oli, Timur could probably convince a great many others to do his bidding. Now, Oli was in prison, and likely would be for a long time.

Cyril went back to his apartments to meet his university friends occasionally, but for all intents and purposes, he had moved into the Kymri Theatre, at least until Mother woke up. Maske didn't mind, nor did Cyan or Drystan. I was ecstatic. Poor Drystan might have been a little put out – I spent every spare moment that wasn't magic and séance practices with my brother, catching up on the last few months. We filled each other in on the details of our lives; I told him about how I'd met Drystan, and he told me about a girl in one of his lectures he fancied. It made me realize just how much I'd missed him. My protector. My brother. My friend.

Cyan kept to herself, processing the loss of Oli, wrangling with her guilt. She wished she'd seen the signs, done more. She thought she could trust him. Her thoughts drifted to mine more often, almost as if her mind quested for reassurance that I was still a friend. Each time, I let her in. She'd leave a glow in my mind and retreat, and that was all the comfort she needed. Cyan would recover, but she would be even slower to trust.

All too soon, the week had passed. My energy, so briefly returned to normal, took a sharp downturn again. A low fever returned; my bones were heavy.

Despite my apprehension, it was time to go back to Doctor Pozzi.

Doctor Pozzi tapped the syringe, popping any lingering bubbles. The dark green fluid in the glass looked ominous.

Even since that morning, I'd grown weaker, to the point that I'd had to lean on Drystan as we walked across town.

Forcing myself to watch as Pozzi pressed the needle into me and pushed the plunger, I felt better almost immediately. I wondered whether it was really working, or if my mind played tricks on me.

As soon as he took out the needle and applied a bandage, I pushed my sleeve down. Drystan was in the front room again, drinking tea. He might even have had a chance to pick the lock on the spirit cabinet and pinch some Elixir, like Anisa had asked us to.

Pozzi asked me questions about how I had been feeling, the normal clinical observations between patient and doctor. And then he surprised me.

'I heard about your mother.'

Of course you have.

'Have there been any improvements?' he asked.

'Not really. My brother has gone to see her frequently.'

'But not you.'

'Not me.'

'I know one of the coma specialists at the Royal Snakewood University. I'll write him a letter and he will examine her if he hasn't already.'

'You'd do that?'

A wave of the clockwork hand. 'Of course. If – when she wakes up, you should speak to her. I remember what she looked like when she held you in her arms for the first time. There was love there.'

I looked away. 'She didn't look at me like that later on. But thank you for writing to the specialist. I know my brother will appreciate it.' This was not a conversation I wanted to have with him. Any favour came with strings attached.

I changed the subject. 'What do you think about the Celestial Cathedral attack?'

'I think it made quite a statement.'

'Surely you have more opinion than that? Three Chimaera were killed. Did you know them?'

A shake of the head. 'No, I'd not seen them before. I wish I'd been able to meet them, see if they would permit me to make an examination.'

'Do you think they had extra abilities or were ill?'

'That's what I would have determined. I mourn the loss of such a valuable dataset.'

Yet he didn't seem to mourn the loss of the lives themselves. Was a life only research to him? I shivered. Tentatively, I tried to reach out to him with my mind. For a brief moment, I sensed something, just beyond reach. It was gone. I wanted him to open up to me, to prove I could trust him, that he wished me no harm. Yet his mind was as inscrutable as his blandly polite expression and smooth voice.

Pozzi didn't seem to have noticed anything. 'This attack has toppled the delicate balance of Ellada, no question about it,' he continued. 'The Royal Family, all the Twelve Trees of nobility, anticipate this is just the beginning.' The Twelve Trees were the most powerful and noble families in Ellada. My own adopted family, the Laruses, were members, but their influence had waned over the last few generations. With the money Pozzi gave my parents when they adopted me, the Laurus family had risen again.

'They really think there'll be more attacks?' I asked.

'They've put the Princess in hiding in the palace. She's not to see anyone she doesn't know. She can't venture out, not that she did often before. All her food is taste-tested. She must be kept safe. There have been threats against her life.'

'Against the Princess Royal? She's only seven!'

'She's the heir to the throne. Her age does not matter.'

'Why are you telling me this?' Surely it was all confidential.

'I assumed you would find it interesting. Do you not?'

'I do. You must be one of the few that can see her, being her physician.'

'This is correct. I've tended her since she was a babe, except for the time I was on sabbatical. She's already lonely. She only sees me and the Steward, and one or two closest friends, though I'm hoping the Steward will allow her more freedom soon.'

I'd had only a taste of that cloistered life as Iphigenia Laurus, and it'd nearly suffocated me. I wondered how many friends the Princess had, and if she could trust them. Many said the Steward wanted nothing more than to hold on to the throne as long as he could.

'Do you think it was the Foresters?'

'It seems that way, though they're careful not to claim credit. The attack was partially shielded, but several still died. Those who fear the threat of Chimaera still seem to be flocking to them, all the same.'

'Why hate something that they aren't even sure is real?'

'Because they don't understand it. The idea that

something could exist so far beyond their ken means most will fear them.'

'Even if they said they meant no harm?'

'Even so.' Pozzi looked me over again. 'Have your magic shows begun again?' This time it was his turn to change the subject.

'Not yet. We'll be performing tomorrow night.'

He hesitated.

'Why?' I asked, frowning at him.

'You know, your manners haven't improved much since I first met you.'

'That they haven't. What's that look mean?'

'I don't know if such a rude person deserves what I'd offer.'

It took me a moment. He was *teasing* me. How very bizarre. Fine. Two could play this game.

'Please, my most prestigious of royal physicians in all of Ellada and the Archipelago, what, pray tell, does that considering look mean that you are planning?' I asked, deadpan.

He broke into a laugh and I found myself almost smiling in turn; then hardened myself against him as I remembered how cold his eyes had looked upon waking from my fever dream. It would be dangerous to grow to like him, when he'd hired Shadows to find me and kept so many secrets.

'I was thinking of asking the Steward if he'd allow entertainment for the Princess Royal. If I vouched for the performers.'

And that time I understood.

'You would ask us to perform for the Princess Royal again?'

'And whatever members of the court are let into her coterie of trust.'

'All of us?'

'I don't see why not.'

'Why?'

'You really are a suspicious one, Micah Grey.'

'Yes, well, I've had need to be.'

He sobered. 'That you have. I remember how Princess Nicolette loved watching you perform at the duel. Keeping her happy keeps the Steward happy, and that keeps me content.'

Curiosity got the better of me. I'd only spoken to the Princess Royal once, after the duel. And she'd been a sweet girl, delighted by the performance. I'd like to see her again.

'It's not my decision, but Maske's. But if he's amenable, then of course we'd be delighted to perform for the Princess.'

He nodded. 'You ask Maske, and send me a missive with his answer. Then I'll speak to the Steward and let you know, perhaps at next week's appointment.'

Pozzi was genuinely pleased. His thoughtfulness for the young Princess was touching, but I still didn't trust him. This was the man who had hired Lily Verre to spy on us for months, for who knows what purpose.

Lily hadn't come to the Kymri Theatre since my illness, for which I'd been grateful. But I knew she wouldn't stay away for long. We needed to know where she had been, and why she was bringing her son to Pozzi for treatment. He must be ill, like me. My thoughts strayed to Cyan. She said she was fine, but it was difficult not to worry.

Doctor Pozzi's hand – the human one – rested on my forehead, startling me. 'Are you feeling all right, Micah? You've gone cross-eyed.'

I tried to slow my racing thoughts and find the words. The Elixir was hitting me, hard.

'I'm fine. There's just been . . . a lot on my mind lately.'

I'm sure there has.

'Is there any other treatment?' I asked, determinedly speaking aloud.

'No, you're all done for today, Micah,' Pozzi said. 'Are you feeling normal?'

'Normal as possible, I suppose.'

'Right. Keep track of any unusual side effects.'

'Like what?' I said, my stomach tightening.

'Strange dreams, new abilities you haven't experienced before, any physical changes. They should be minor, but I might be able to adjust the dose to lessen any you experience.'

Great, so I could sprout horns by next midweek.

'Horns are unlikely, Micah.'

Styx.

'I'll see you next week, Micah.'

I pulled on my coat. 'Yeah. Next week.'

I walked through the dark streets of Imachara. My strides were long and soundless, my cap pulled low over my forehead, my coat tight against my shoulders. Should anyone see me, I was nothing but another shadow, flitting through the city.

I reached the cemetery, the wrought iron gates imposing.

The guard was on the other side, in the shelter of the gatehouse. He smoked a pipe, the blue-grey smoke curling around his head, his lantern the sole speck of yellow in a world of black and grey. Carefully, so carefully, I picked the lock, looping the chains back. Pouring a little bit of oil into the lock, I eased open the gate and slipped through. Keeping to the darkest shadow under the ivy-covered wall, I crept closer to the guard.

Sleep, *I* thought *at him.* Sleep deep. Dream of what you want the most. Dream you are far away from this place of death.

His eyelids grew heavy, his head falling to his shoulder. The pipe fell to the ground, extinguishing in the grave dirt.

I smiled.

I hadn't brought a shovel. There was one here – there always was. I took the key from the sleeping guard's pocket and opened the guardhouse, taking the shovel and making my way to the freshest grave.

For a long time, there was no sound but the soft fall of dirt onto a rising mound to my right. I sank deeper into the ground, closer to my prize. I had no love of the work, no anticipation of the grisly task aside from what it could give me. The end result. The shovel hit the coffin with a thunk.

'One.'

I awoke in the dark, curled around Drystan with goose-flesh prickling my skin. As I burrowed closer to him, he made a sleepy sound of contentment. I stared towards the dark stained-glass porthole at the end of the loft, thinking over my dream. I knew it was no night-time vision, but more like I had tapped into someone's psyche, perhaps as a result of the recent dose of Elixir.

I tried to fall back asleep, but every time my eyes closed, I saw the grave being dug into, the body being lifted out. I shuddered. Why was someone out there stealing corpses? And how was I seeing them do it?

7

FLAMES AND RAIN

You want to know what I think of the growing Forester situation? I think they've the right idea about these Chimaera. I know they said they didn't do it, but we all know the truth. There were those three monsters, and the Lord and Lady showed them what they thought of their kind, right in front of their own church. I think the monarchy is a lump of phosphorous, and the Foresters are the rain.

— Anonymous unprinted letter to *The Daily Imacharan*

I slept late the next day.

I might have slept badly, but still almost skipped with energy. I took the stairs two at a time. We'd be starting our magic show again tonight, and I was annoyed that they'd let me sleep through the morning practice.

I skidded to a stop in the kitchen. At the table sat Lily Verre, talking to Maske about the Foresters, spreading butter onto a slice of bread. I tried to school my features into faint surprise, but I could feel the blood draining from my face.

Lily Verre.

Drystan and Cyan sat at the table, putting on their best performances of acting a little bored. Cyril was there as well, but I hadn't told him anything about Lily. We also hadn't confronted her. We weren't sure of the best way to do it. And so we hesitated, frustrated but frozen.

Maske had fallen in love with Lily Verre, or the Lily she pretended to be around him. It made her betrayal of spying on us for Pozzi hurt all the more. We didn't know what they wanted from us, and that also made our next move difficult to calculate.

'I say, Sam, are you feeling quite all right?' Lily asked, the knife hovering above the bread. 'You look so terribly pale.' She called me by my false name of Sam Harper, though she must have known my other names.

I sat down, pouring a cup of coffee from the carafe on the table. It was only lukewarm. 'I'm fine. Just a little under the weather, I suppose,' I said, hoping my voice was even. Shielding myself as much as I was able, I reached out to Cyan. She'd recovered from the worst of her injuries, though she still limped a little and she'd shown us the rather nasty cut on her ribs. *Can you get anything from her now that you know?*

Not a thing. She's still shielding herself with a bunch of mindless chatter that's impossible to break through. It must be so difficult for her to keep up.

Her whole charade must be. It also means she might suspect what you can do. Which is . . . not good.

She nodded, almost imperceptibly, as she took another bite of her sandwich.

I had no idea what to do. Should we confront Lily? But then, that would be playing our hand just as much as if I'd confronted Pozzi at his home the other day.

Drystan looked between us, clearly guessing we were speaking to each other. I reached out to him and Cyan, unsure if he'd be able to hear me: *We'll do nothing for now. But soon, I want to find out what she's really up to.*

One side of his mouth quirked in agreement.

Lily Verre spoke with Maske, laying her hand on his arm and looking up into his face, hopefully unaware that we knew she was a viper in our nest.

That afternoon, we scrubbed the theatre to prepare for the first magic show since my illness.

'We really need to convince Maske to hire cleaners,' I puffed as we mopped the stage floor.

'Agreed,' Cyan said, her face pink.

When we were finished, the place shone like the jewel it was. I changed into my performance suit for the first time in weeks, and it felt comfortable and right. I couldn't wait to be back out on that stage, seeing the audience hanging on to our every move. The stage was my home, just as much as the actual building of the Kymri Theatre. It was somewhere I could be myself, in a strange way, despite the magician persona I adopted.

That night, Maske and his Marionettes returned to the stage.

Cyril agreed to man the ticket booth for us and do some of the easier stagehand tricks, as now we did not have Oli to help us. I checked on my brother a few times, and he smiled and laughed as he passed out the tickets and took in the coins. I knew it was a charade. Underneath he was worried about Mother, and about me. Helping out like this was good for him, and helped distract him from his worries.

I was performing tonight alongside Maske and Cyan, who would be Maske's assistant. We would be swapping roles often now that we regularly performed – sometimes it would be Drystan and Maske, or Cyan and Maske, or all three or four of us. But Maske always performed. He was the big name, and he hadn't been allowed to perform for fifteen years, and so the Maske of Magic was in each show no matter what.

Behind the stage, Drystan set the gramophone playing. This moment still filled me with a thrill – the violin, the piano, the deep thump of the drums, and the expectant silence of the audience. The pause, the breath before the show began. The magic appeared.

We told a story through our illusions. It helped string the acts together and created a thread for the audience to follow. Some ended up being more autobiographical than we realized, sitting around the battered kitchen table, nursing warm drinks as we plotted and planned. The finale we had beaten Taliesin in had been the story of Maske, letting his hubris overwhelm him and having to pay for it before ultimately finding redemption again.

Before going onto the stage, I turned on the Glamour I wore around my neck. With the flick of a tiny switch it altered my appearance, changing the colour of my hair and eyes. We'd been pretending to be Elladans raised abroad in Southern Temne. I'd still not grown used to wearing a different Elladan face and clothing from a culture that was not my own, and I never would. It was not for me to use a costume. Cyan taught us more of Temnian ways to ensure we did not make fools of ourselves, and I enjoyed learning. I could hold a basic conversation in Temri now. Both Drystan and I had to wear Glamours as we were considered fugitives, still hiding from the Policiers. If only we could appear on the stage as ourselves.

Standing in the centre of the stage, I took deep breaths as Maske launched into his introductory patter. He claimed a Seer had given him power when he gifted him this very theatre. Maske now shared the magic with me, one of his trusted students.

Maske held out his hands, and blue light emanated from them. I looked away. Even though it was only an illusion – a simple flare of chemicals – the light still reminded me of the night I had run away from the circus and used Penglass as a weapon when the glass glowed under the full Penmoon. I'd blinded those circus folk pursuing us, and while none of them had been friends, they hadn't been enemies, not even the ones who had played cruel pranks on me when I had been the circus's newest performer.

On the stage, I recovered from my flinch and held out my own hands so that they glowed green. The audience gasped with delight as the chime of bells and strings rose from the gramophone.

Maske and I moved to either side of the stage, gesturing to the centre at a screen painted with cranes and clouds. Maske said that, though the Seer claimed to be the most powerful magician in the land, we had recently been challenged by a Temnian princess, who agreed to show her powers here tonight. We would see which magic was the stronger.

The story alluded to our recent magic duel, and tied a little into the current problems with the Kashura Foresters. After we won against Taliesin and his grandsons, we had decided to work our acrobatic skills into the illusions. That had meant long hours of physical work, oiling away the rust that had gathered in our joints and muscles since Drystan and I left R. H. Ragona's Circus of Magic and Cyan had left the rival circus, Riley and Batheo's Circus of Curiosities.

Cyan stood in the middle of the stage, wearing a Temnian sarong and introducing herself as Madame Damselfly. Her face was decorated with glittering silver paint, swirling at the corner of her eyes and across one cheek. She raised her arms above her head and rose from the floor, aided by hidden cables, until she hovered six inches above the stage. Like us, her hands sparked with false magic, and her colour was red. She lowered back to the floor, throwing us a challenging look.

Maske took his place at the head of the stage, bowing out of the performance to preside over our small duel, a pale echo of the one that had changed our fate so completely.

Cyan and I squared off from each other.

One, two . . . three! she counted in my head.

The unseen wires raised us above the audience. Behind stage, Drystan and Cyril helped us fly.

The crowd below us craned their necks, some of them open-mouthed. We'd used the best-quality wires, so even those squinting their hardest shouldn't be able to see the thin supports in the dim lights. We swung towards each other and away. At one point, our faces nearly touched, and our hands sparked with ersatz magic. Behind stage, Drystan handed Cyan's wire controls to Cyril before climbing to the gridiron above, dropping down two silken sashes that reached the stage's wooden planks. Slyly, Cyan and I unlatched our wires, which slid back up to the gridiron, before reaching out to grab the sashes, wrapping them around the arches of our feet and ankles as make-shift footholds. We reached out, letting our fingers alight again, red and green meeting in the middle in another shower of sparks. We flipped upside down, our bodies forming mirrored crescent moons, and confetti and glitter fell from our hands.

The audience applauded, and I couldn't keep the smile from my face. Our circus lives and our new illusionists' lives melded into something new. Each swing reminded me sharply of Aenea. She had taught me the trapeze; taught me how to fly. High above the stage, it was as if the performance honoured her.

But Cyan was across from me, not Aenea, and the show painted us as rivals, not partners. The music from the gramophone rose. Untwining ourselves from the silken sashes, we continued our magic duel. Cyan put a small pile of white feathers on a table, shrouded it for a moment with a silken scarf, then pulled the silk away to reveal a white dove. The bird cooed as she set it on her shoulder and bowed. Paix, the dove, then flew up to the gridiron, where Drystan had a treat ready and his cage.

I responded to Cyan's challenge by flipping through the air and showering her with paper blossoms that appeared from mid-air. She brushed them out of her hair impatiently and took out a bow and arrow. Cyan jumped into a handstand, her skirts bunching up to reveal the loose pantaloons favoured by Kymri women. Using her feet, she aimed the bow and arrow at me, suspended above her. The audience held their breath as she took final aim and then let the arrow fly.

The audience gasped. The arrow *thunked* into the target a few inches from my head. Scattered applause broke out, and I bowed to the crowd. Up above, Drystan unhooked the support and I fell to the floor in a flurry of sparks. I struggled to my feet and a large, red piece of silk emerged from my sleeve. After draping her in the silk and pulling it away, Cyan was gone. The audience gasped again, and before them, I stood tall, the proud victor.

Cyan reattached her wire and dropped down from the gridiron to land on my shoulders. We held our arms out and bowed as one.

But during the pause just before the applause, we heard a loud *boom*.

It was close enough that the entire theatre shook, dust falling from the ceiling.

Silence.

There were a few scattered claps before they trailed away, realizing it wasn't part of the act.

Then the wail of sirens.

Boom.

The theatre shook again. Cracks appeared in the walls of the auditorium. Smoke trickled in through the windows. Just in case there was a fire, I ran to the side of the stage and pressed the emergency lever. The sprinklers in the ceiling began to rain, and within moments, everyone was drenched.

People panicked. Screams tore through the theatre, reminding me of the day in the square. They scurried over the velvet seats, desperate to leave.

'Everyone go outside, away from walls! Stay close to each other. We don't know quite where this blast has come from.' Maske's voice boomed in the stadium. Next to him, Cyan sent her awareness over the crowd, subtly urging them to leave but remain calm – no trampling, no pushing each other out of the way. Drystan used the hidden passageway underneath the stage to appear on the other end of the theatre and help guide people out.

Parents clutched their children close. Strangers lent others a hand if they stumbled. Within a few minutes, the theatre was empty.

Cyan and Maske picked their way over the puddles to join the others in the street.

'I'm going to go upstairs and grab Anisa's Aleph and try to find Ricket,' I said. 'I'll meet you outside in a minute.'

'This building isn't sound, it's dangerous,' Maske

protested. 'We don't know where this came from exactly. What if the Kymri Theatre was a target?'

'It wasn't,' Cyan replied. 'It happened a few blocks over, judging by the noise.' Maske still didn't know that his daughter could read minds.

'I'll be all right,' I said, trying not to think of collapsing ceilings. 'Go help the others, see if you can find out what happened.'

Reluctantly, they let me go. Climbing the stairs to the loft was not easy. The building seemed sound enough, but the cracks were worse on the upper levels, the hallways riddled with debris. In the loft, I stifled a sob.

Half of the roof had collapsed. All of our belongings were covered with broken shingles and dust. Stumbling and coughing from the smoke, I made it to the bedside cabinet and took Anisa's Aleph, stuffing it into my pocket. I took one lingering look around our room, then heard a frightened little mewl.

'Ricket,' I said in relief, crouching down. The cat ran towards me and I scooped him up in my arms. He purred in fear, huddling against me.

Out on the street, most of the audience of the Kymri Theatre had stayed together, clustered close in the drizzling late spring rain, despite the fact that most of them were strangers. The next street over, the sky was red with the glow of flames, the sky above it black and purple with smoke. The theatre had sustained less damage than some of the other buildings on the street. A few near the end of the block were little more than precarious rubble. My neighbourhood. Our home.

Was the fire spreading? On my tiptoes, I craned my neck as if that would help me see through the buildings.

Then I realized what was burning: the Museum of Mechanical Antiquities.

'How bad is it?' I whispered.

Cyan closed her eyes and her awareness brushed across me. I jerked in shock. I'd never felt her reach out to others like that. I could almost see it – a delicate net of purple, blue, and green. The web of her power spread through the streets before coming back into her. She opened her eyes. *It's the museum and half the buildings on that street.* She spoke in her mind only to Drystan and me.

'No,' I whispered out loud, horrified. Within the Museum of Mechanical Antiquities were priceless Vestige artefacts. Many of them were on loan from Doctor Pozzi's private collection. Did he know this was happening?

'What is it?' Cyril asked.

'Nothing,' I said, too quickly. Though we lived so near to it, I hadn't gone back to visit as the museum brought up too many memories of an afternoon spent with Aenea there. Now I could never return.

So much Vestige lost in the flames. It had to be the Kashura. The Museum contained relics from the Chimaera and the Alder. Did they distrust Vestige, too?

Closing my eyes, I tried to push away the image of the clockwork woman's head burning. Anisa had worn a body like that, when she didn't wish to inhabit flesh. A beautiful woman, gears and clockwork showing beneath synthetic skin. I hoped, somehow, that Vestige could not burn.

The fire isn't spreading, Cyan thought, relief colouring

her thoughts. *The wind is in our favour and the firefighters are there.* She sent me flashes of images from the minds of people watching the aftermath of the attack: firefighters wielding hoses, the flames hissing as the water hit. People, weak with smoke inhalation, wrapped in blankets. Ambulances at the ready to take away the injured and the dead.

We all looked at my pocket.

Anisa, I ventured. *Will you help?*

A pause. *There is nothing I can do. But the firefighters will soon have the flames under control.* She did not sound regretful. They were, after all, simply humans who live a short life and spark out.

Did anyone die? I asked Cyan.

She nodded imperceptibly. I wondered who, and how many. I clutched Ricket closer, feeling his warm fur against my cheek.

Was it the Kashura?

Hard to say – no one on that street saw who set the explosion. My guess is yes. Her face tightened. *Yet again, I didn't sense it. I couldn't help.*

You can't help everyone, Cyan. Timur knows there's someone out there who can read minds. He'll have had the attacker wear one of those Cricket necklaces. He couldn't hate all Vestige, if his followers used it, though perhaps he viewed it as a necessary evil. This Timur was an enigma; I wanted to know more about him, why he was so intent on harming Chimaera, what he hoped to gain. This government he wished to create would not flourish under his care. Not if he considered violence a meaningful form of protest. My hope was that these acts would drive many away from their cause, yet fear could also be excellent at clouding a person's better judgement.

There was a lot of Vestige weaponry in the museum, wasn't there? Cyan asked.

Yes, I said. *An entire room of Vestige weaponry. It was defunct, though.*

Are you sure about that? I'm betting they won't find a lot of it in the wreckage.

My mouth fell open. Timur and his followers might have just stolen a large cache of Vestige weaponry, and set the explosion as a way to cover their tracks. And if they could somehow find a way to make the weapons work again . . . ? I shuddered.

The evening was cold. The audience dispersed, their shoulders hunched. As soon as the last of them was gone, Maske started to cry. Cyan put her arms around him, sending him comfort. Where were we meant to go? The Kymri Theatre was damaged enough that we couldn't stay there.

The rain had soaked us all completely. None of us were wearing heavy coats.

'We can't go to the insurance office until tomorrow,' Maske said, wiping his eyes. He took a deep breath and squared his shoulders. 'The Kymri Theatre is safe enough to go in and get some things. We'll spend the night at Taliesin's old place.'

As part of the terms of winning the duel against his old rival, we'd inherited his theatre. It had just sold, but Maske still had the keys. So we went into our ruined home and packed some clothes, our coins, whatever possessions we could fit into a carpet bag each.

Drystan let out a low whistle when he saw the ruin of our loft. The stained glass of the dragonfly was smashed into pieces on the floor.

Drystan gave me a hug. 'Don't worry. It can all be fixed and be just as it was.'

'I hope so.'

We shook the dust out of our rain-sodden clothes and packed the rest of our things. Maske locked the door and we looked up at the Kymri Theatre, with most of its roof collapsed. The brand new paint on the column was smoke-stained. We would not be living here again for quite some time.

We walked the twenty minutes to Taliesin's old theatre. Many people still roamed the streets, curious about the flames. The Policiers would soon be swarming the neighbourhoods, urging people back to their homes. There were no shouts for justice and no crowds looting. Everyone appeared sad and confused.

If the Foresters did admit responsibility, would that peaceful acceptance last, or would there be demands for retribution? Once the shock wore off, I feared there would only be more riots.

Taliesin's old theatre, the former seat of the Spectre Shows, was dark and cold. Initially, Maske had considered keeping the theatre, opening another branch of Maske's Marionettes and finding other magicians to fill the stage, but then dismissed the idea.

'You are my Marionettes. My family. I need no other,'

he had said. And he wanted no more reminders of Taliesin and their long-lasting feud. Last I heard of the old magician, he had sunk further into his Lerium addiction, his health continuing to fail. He was still a rich man, but no longer a magician allowed to perform on stage. Did he miss it, as Maske had missed it all those years when he had been prevented from performing?

We found rooms to sleep in and started fires in the hearths. Ricket trotted off to sleep in Maske's room. Drystan and I chose a small chamber with two sofas. We spread our sodden possessions in front of the fire to dry, and pushed the sofas together for a makeshift bed.

'Maybe Maske can stall the sale, and we can use this theatre until the Kymri is fixed?' I asked. After having our first performance in weeks, I didn't want to stop.

'I don't know. I think it'll take at least a few months to fix the Kymri. The buyers might not want to hold off that long. I think they plan to turn it back into a private residence.'

I sighed. 'This is awful.'

'I know. It will work out, though. It has to.'

The sofa was lumpy and uncomfortable, and I couldn't settle.

'Stop being so restless,' Drystan complained after an hour of this.

'Sorry. Can't sleep.' I feared falling asleep in case I dreamed of the grave robber, or of the clockwork woman in the Museum of Mechanical Antiquities, the flames spreading, shattering the glass display, claiming her.

Drystan sat up, rolling his head side to side until the vertebrae snapped. 'Me neither.'

We stayed up for a few hours, simply talking to each other. Not about the Kashura Foresters and the Chimaera, or what happened at the Kymri Theatre. We made up silly stories, each of us trying to make our next section all the more outlandish – our way of trying to distract ourselves. By the end of it, we were curled up with laughter until our stomachs hurt.

It was what we needed. To try and forget everything and enjoy each other's company. Who cared what was outside the small room, with its warm fireplace? It didn't matter. Not that night.

Under the cover of night, I limped my way to the university hospital. I'd covered myself in false wounds and grime and hunched my back to hint at a life of poor nutrition. I looked just the part of the Penny Rookery ragamuffin.

The university hospital was overcrowded as usual, but quiet at this time of night. A nursing student who had drawn the short straw and had to do a night shift led me to a bed. She checked my wounds and with a subtle, mental push, she thought she tended real wounds rather than dye and cornstarch.

She was the only one in the wards as the other patients slept. Doctors were in the next room, but I sensed they were playing dice to pass the time. I cast my awareness over the patients until I found a suitable candidate.

The nurse settled on the sofa in the corner, pinching the skin of her arms to stay awake.

Sleep, *I thought at her.* Sleep.

Her head fell to her chest, her body sliding sideways.

Sleep, *I thought at the rest of the ward, though my energy ebbed drastically at sending so many into dreamland.*

I approached my target. A young man, handsome. Strong jawline. Good teeth. The bed next to his was empty. I picked up the pillow.

I hesitated. I shouldn't care about what I was about to do. He was unimportant in the grand scheme of things. But then, aren't we all?

Inching closer, I pressed the pillow over his face. He was so deep in his dreams, he barely struggled at all.

Quick. Painless. And I'd sensed the illness in that body I needed. The boy wouldn't have made it anyway.

As everyone slumbered on, I stole the spare doctor's clothing from the supply closet and wheeled the boy out of the hospital as everyone slumbered on. The boy's head bounced awfully as I wheeled him to where I needed to go.

'Two,' *I whispered.*

I awoke with a gasp, cold again despite the blazing fireplace.

Drystan heard me and wrapped his arms around my shoulders. 'Lord and Lady, you're like ice.' He rubbed my fingertips. 'It's all right. Just a bad dream.'

'Yes,' I whispered, still shivering. 'Just a nightmare.' A little thread deep within me wondered if it was something more. I told him about both dreams.

'Well, that's creepy. Stealing a corpse.' Drystan sighed and leaned back. 'Then killing to create another. A psychiatrist would have fun psychoanalyzing that, I'm sure.'

It had been so real – pressing the pillow over the boy's face. The smell of the antiseptic of the hospital, undercut with the scent of sickness. The way the boy struggled and then went horribly limp.

'What do you think it means?'

'Dunno,' I said. 'I don't want to talk about it any more.' I moved closer against him, still shaking. I couldn't bear to think about cold, or corpses, or grave robbers. Thoughts were too dangerous, too tangled.

We didn't say a word, but neither of us slept any more that night.

8

THE OPERATING THEATRE

Neonatal death. Low temperature. Jaundice. Atypical anatomy: tail, caul, ichthyosis. Cause of death: unknown.
— Unsigned medical notes, Royal Snakewood University

The next few days were not filled with good news.

We went to the insurance office first thing in the morning, taking all of our belongings with us and locking up the Spectre Shows Theatre. First, Maske hired a surveyor to assess the extent of the damage to the Kymri Theatre. It was as we feared; the building was sound enough, but it wouldn't be safe to live in during renovations. Maske tried to find out if the sale of the Spectre Theatre could be delayed for a few months, so we could use it for our shows while the Kymri Theatre was fixed. No such luck; the owners wished to move in immediately.

The biggest problem was an issue with the insurance. While nearly destitute, Maske had had the smallest premium, and in the scant weeks since the duel he had not yet amended it. This meant that the insurance would not pay out. The sale of the Spectre Theatre would cover the damages, but in the meantime . . . we were broke. Again.

Maske found cheap rooms in a tenement in the Penny Rookeries. The walls smelled of mould and the bed frames were more rust than metal. The fireplace in the lounge didn't draw out the smoke properly until Maske went in to fix it, emerging covered head to toe in soot. We had a decent view of the street and the docks in the distance from the grimy window.

I hadn't spent much time in the Penny Rookeries, but I knew that this was the area of the city with the most support for the Forester protests. Here, people were so ground down by poverty that they'd support anyone trying to better their lives. I worried for Cyril, who, no longer having a place to stay, went back to the flat by Celestial Square, but came to visit us often. As he walked through the streets completely oblivious, he stood out a mile with his rich clothes. Heads turned and eyes glowered at him as he passed. I'd have to get him to dress down for his visits to us, otherwise he'd soon find himself in trouble. The rich were not welcome in this area.

After the latest attack by the Kashura Foresters, Imachara enforced a sunset curfew.

Personally, I didn't see how this would dissuade more attacks, and in fact, it might make people more vulnerable. One of the attacks had happened in broad daylight. Those who worked late shifts applied for special dispensation papers, which they had to carry with them after dark.

Some liked the fact that the capital took action, and

they complied. Those in the Rookeries who took work when and where they could find it said it was taking away what little freedom they had. Protests grew more frequent. I could hear the chanting from our new room in the afternoons, as they started in the Rookeries and then marched through different neighbourhoods in the city.

We had pamphlets and leaflets shoved through our letter box every day. Blocky letters urged us to protect Ellada. More Chimaera were hiding, and they must leave the island. Many were also wary of immigration from the other islands, claiming it was because there could also be Chimaera there, but mainly because they were xenophobic, afraid that immigrants would steal jobs from Elladans.

'This is such rubbish,' Drystan said, crushing a few pamphlets and throwing the ball towards the wastepaper basket in the corner. He missed.

'Dangerous rubbish, though. It's nonsense, based on fairy tales and rumours, yet they're turning people against each other.' We'd heard of people accusing their neighbours of being Chimaera, based on anything from a sudden stroke of good luck to a patch of dry skin that they insisted was scales. People mistrusted each other, wondered who else was hiding among them. Someone like Tauro would be at high risk, whether they were Chimaera or not. Fear and hatred breeds nothing but more hatred and fear.

'This isn't going to stop,' Drystan said, looking out of the window down to the empty street below. Curfew had just fallen. I wrapped my arms around him and rested my cheek against the side of his neck.

After we'd settled into our small, sad rooms, Maske told us in no uncertain terms that we were not to let our skills go to waste. When we'd first learned magic, we'd done several street shows, and that would be our trade again. Whatever coin people threw into our hats would be our day-to-day spending money. We began practising in the cramped lounge, adapting our stories for the streets. It was a completely different challenge. We couldn't use wires, and people could crowd around us at all angles. At times, I worried I'd tear my hair out, trying to find ways to make it work.

A few more days passed.

All too soon, it was time to visit the doctor again.

I made the trip alone, brave enough to go to Doctor Pozzi's without needing Drystan to accompany me. My energy had plummeted again; I could barely keep my eyes open after practice ended. I slept later and later in the mornings, until Drystan would pull the covers away and I'd protest at the sudden cold.

Drystan and Cyan were perfecting their street routine this morning, which they would air for the first time in the afternoon. Cyril was at university, registering for classes and attending his first lecture before visiting Mother in the hospital.

Striding through the cramped streets of Imachara, dodging the fetid puddles and feeling guilty at ignoring the beggars pleading for spare coins, I thought of my brother. I'd not been able to speak much to Cyril in the past few days. He was spending any spare time at the hospital, sitting by Mother's bedside, hoping she'd wake up. He kept inviting me to go and I kept declining, part of me fearing to see her so small and weak. The other part feared sitting there and her actually waking up, seeing who her daughter had become. I didn't want to see the revulsion on her face.

The doorman at Pozzi's building let me in. He knew me by sight now. Heading to Pozzi's apartments, I knocked on the door, and the Doctor opened it himself. He kept few servants.

'Good morning, Micah,' he said, welcoming me inside. My eyes lingered on the cabinet of curiosities as we passed it. How would I be able to distract Pozzi long enough to try and steal some Elixir?

In his consulting room, Pozzi already had the syringe prepared on the table. 'I'm afraid our visit today will have to be short. I've been asked, as a favour, to cover a University class. One of their professors, a colleague I've worked with a number of times in the past, has fallen ill and is unable to make it.

'I'll be going to the palace after and asking whether the Princess requires any additional entertainment in her confinement to the grounds. They've tightened security since the latest attack.' He paused, as if something had just occurred to him. But I knew that everything he said was calculated. Nothing caught him by surprise. 'Normally I'd take my assistant, but he's in a lecture of his own. Do you wish to accompany me to the University? I think you might find it rather intriguing.'

'You have an assistant?' I asked, curious.

'Of course, but he does not often come to my private home. He assists in experiments at my laboratory. Bright young chap, destined for great things.'

'So today you're going to a lecture?'

'It's an anatomy lesson.'

I suppressed a flinch. My stomach crawled. The thought of seeing a dead body filled me with horror but also a small, sick fascination.

'I'll go,' I said, surprising myself.

'Wonderful. I know you have your hesitations about doctors, what with how you were treated growing up. Yet medicine is not something that needs to be feared. It is its own sort of magic, I find. You may be more interested than you once supposed.'

I made a noncommittal noise.

Doctor Pozzi picked up the syringe. 'Hold out your arm and roll up your sleeve, if you please.'

Ice flowed through my veins again.

Doctor Pozzi defied the current fashion of hiring a chauffeur by driving the carriage himself.

'I went abroad on sabbatical a number of years ago,' he said, as if I'd asked him a question. 'Much of my early research into Chimaera was conducted in Byssia and Linde. I've grown used to doing things my own way. After I was trapped in the jungle with a missing hand and a stump about to grow septic, once I recovered, I began to chafe at having servants dress me, feed me, and drive me everywhere like a child.' He'd told me how he lost his hand: a Cyrinx, a large, dark violet cat, had attacked him when he was deep in the Byssian jungle. I had seen one of the cats in the circus. She'd definitely looked at me like I'd make a tasty meal.

In this way, though, I was similar to Pozzi. Even as Iphigenia Laurus I'd been uncomfortable with being treated like a porcelain doll, far preferring to escape and climb scaffolding or trees with my brother.

My thoughts drifted. In the front of the carriage, I watched Pozzi's clockwork hand move the brass controls of the carriage with ease. The smoke from the exhaust stung my nose.

'I was grieved to hear about the damage to the Kymri Theatre. I hear you're staying in the Penny Rookeries until it's repaired.' The Doctor clicked his tongue. 'Not the best part of town – especially with all the civil unrest at the moment. I've a spare apartment in the Gilt Quarter, if you'd like to stay there.'

I knew I should be grateful, and flattered. Pozzi had been nothing but polite and kind to me. Yet everything about him reminded me of what my parents had done, and the doctor was wrapped in secrets. He spied on me, and I already felt far too reliant on him. 'Thank you for the offer, but it's only temporary, and the Penny Rookeries has an undeserved reputation. Yes, it is a poor area, but hardly dangerous.'

'At the moment . . . At least until the Foresters grow more proactive. There's been far too much violence already.'

I wondered if he knew they called themselves the

Kashura. 'Did you lose much in the fire?' I asked, steering the conversation slightly. He owned many of the collections in the Museum of Mechanical Antiquities. I'd seen his name on placards, months before I'd met him.

He gave me a sidelong glance. 'I did, but not as much as I would have even a few scant months ago. That museum had been dying a slow death. I had taken out many of my most prized possessions already.'

'Did you take away the clockwork woman?' I asked, unsure why my heart lifted in hope. She'd terrified me, when I'd seen her that afternoon with Aenea. Those gears beneath her skin, the way her features would shift into perfect emotions when a little boy put a coin in a slot and pulled levers with different moods. A disembodied head forced to pantomime for the world to see.

He gave a little smile. 'I did. When did you see her?'

'Last summer.'

'I removed her at the end of the summer. Their security wasn't strong enough any more. She is safe. But a lot of my smaller treasures were lost. Alder clothes, jewellery, some defunct weaponry. A shame.' His hands tightened on the controls, his only hint of anger.

'I heard rumours that much of the Vestige weaponry went missing,' I chanced.

Another sharp glance out of the corner of his eye. 'Difficult to tell in the wreckage.'

'But most Vestige doesn't burn. And if the Foresters have them . . .'

'Then they won't know how to use them. The ones in the Museum ran out of power centuries ago. Even if they had power packs, they wouldn't work. If they did steal them, it was for nothing.'

I was about to ask him more, but we pulled up to the University of Medicine, part of the Royal Snakewood University. I climbed down the steps of the carriage, straightening my suit. Pozzi put his gloves back on, hiding his false hand.

The guard at the gate let us into the courtyard, filled with lush trees and walkways. A few patients lounged in the sun, some in wheelchairs and others bandaged. The patients were usually middle-class: bankers or successful businessmen who couldn't quite afford the private doctors' surgeries. They'd be seen by the professors of the medical university, or the senior students about to finish their degree.

But many of the poor were also treated here, in a separate wing, by students in their first few years of study. Most of the time this was fine, but sometimes inexperienced students made mistakes. The poor understood the risk. It could be as dangerous as going to a charlatan in the back alleys of my new neighbourhood.

I licked my lips. The university itself would be crawling with nobility, who were the bulk of the students. I feared coming across someone who knew me from my previous life. I wasn't wearing my Glamour, as I wasn't performing. Rationally, I knew that it was unlikely. My brother had once run into me by chance at a park in Sicion, and he hadn't known me until I'd changed my voice closer to my old timbre.

I followed Doctor Pozzi through the labyrinth of

corridors, taking his briefcase so as to look more like an assistant. It was heavy, and I wondered what was in it.

We entered the operating theatre. The class was primarily full of young men, though I spied a few women amongst their ranks. They all had notebooks open in front of them, pens and ink at the ready, and though they muttered amongst themselves, their eyes frequently strayed to the metal tank in the middle of the room. It was covered with a cloth. We all knew what was inside.

Doctor Pozzi motioned for me to sit in an empty chair and I did, passing him his briefcase. I had no notebook, no prop to help me pass as studious. The other students looked at me curiously – their stares prickled the back of my neck.

'Good morning, students. I am the Royal Physician of Imachara, here to cover for the esteemed Doctor Mulberry.' Low murmurs erupted in the ranks as they realized they were staring at the most powerful doctor in Imachara. He must have been close to this Doctor Mulberry to agree to cover for him. Why else would he have deigned to come here and perform a dissection for student doctors?

He finished introducing himself and then talked passionately about the necessity of studying the intricacies of the human body, how it was a combination of nature and machine. To fix it, he said, we must understand its systems, how everything is connected. He took off his glove to demonstrate, wriggling his Vestige fingers under the bright surgical lights. He had every student under his spell, and even I was impressed by his enthusiastic speech. He was like a magician, almost, pulling back a veil to reveal the mysteries of the human body.

Pozzi lectured for about twenty minutes, and then the time came for the dissection. With a showman's flick of his wrist, he took away the cloth covering the Vestige tank. The body floated within a light green substance. Through the murky liquid, I could tell it was a man with grey hair, but nothing more.

'This is a piece of Vestige known as an Ampulla,' Pozzi explained, pointing to the container. 'Corpses stored within it do not decay. This is useful with such a shortage of cadavers.'

The top of the Ampulla opened, and the cadaver rose from within. The man had been in his sixties when he died. His body had been shaved, and his eyes were closed. He had a hawk nose, and he looked almost as if he were sleeping. But the texture of his skin was wrong: too dry and stiff. It was very clear that no one inhabited that shell any longer. The smell of formaldehyde and embalming fluid, chemical and yet somehow earthy, permeated the room.

Down the man's chest, a huge Y-shaped incision had been made. I couldn't stop staring at the bloodless gash from the bottom of the neck to just above the groin.

'This is one of the first lectures of the semester, so you have not seen this cadaver before, have you?' Doctor Pozzi asked the class. They shook their heads.

'I suppose I have the privilege of introducing you, then. He will be your cadaver for the semester, and slowly, you will dissect or watch every part of him being dissected.

These anatomy classes change your perception of the human body forever. So far, you have seen diagrams in books, the muscles perfectly butterflied, bloodless, pristine. Or you've seen wax models, intricate in their detail. But you have not sliced through actual flesh, peeled it back, recognized what it is within us. What makes us human. This is what you shall discover.'

He paused, meeting most of the students' eyes in turn. I shivered when his eyes brushed mine. 'We have no way of knowing what this man was like in life. Judging by those bruises around his neck, he was a criminal hung for his crimes, his body then donated to science. But that's only one facet of the story. That tells us almost nothing about him. What were his crimes? Why did he commit them? Who did he love, who loved him, who did he leave behind? You'll never find out. But you will always be aware that he was once a man. His chest once rose and fell with breath, the heart that you are about to cut out of him and hold in your hand like a mango once beat blood through every vein in his body, powering that organic machine. And you have the gift of his body to see how every part of him fit together, and it's how you will learn, one day, how to fix others when a part has broken down, to stop them from turning into a corpse.

'You will probably give him a name at some point. When I taught, I encouraged this. He is your teacher, just as much as I am today, and all your professors will be.'

At the end of his speech, we were all silent. Faces were grave as his words sunk in. I'd never thought much about how doctors were trained. Nobility filled many of the roles, as doctors, especially ones starting out, were pitifully paid. Later, they could amass a generous wage, especially if they achieved a rank like Pozzi's. It was considered a vocation, a calling to heal. To me, they'd always been my bogeymen – featureless people hidden behind masks as they studied me, quantifying me, writing about me like a specimen. I'd always imagined that was how they saw me, and every patient – as a problem to be fixed, not a person with a past and a life and a future.

I remembered Doctor Ambrose's face, tapping the tablet with his stylus, hidden behind his moustache as he decided without telling me that I should be cut into his notion of a woman. Pozzi had taken me here deliberately to show me that there were doctors of different types; that not all of them were like the ones who'd treated me as a child.

I could see that these doctors were a far cry from the emotionless automatons I'd encountered in my past. Some of the students weren't much older than me, and looked nauseated at the sight of the wrinkled, preserved flesh of the unknown man. They were swallowing and clutching their pens too hard as they made shaky notes. Others were unperturbed.

Doctor Pozzi called a few students down from the top benches to watch more closely, and they clustered in a rough semi-circle behind the body on the slab. Pozzi gave me a meaningful look, inviting me to come closer, but I shook my head minutely. The operating room grew quiet, reverent, almost as if it were a church, the body on an altar and Pozzi the priest.

When he pulled back the skin on the chest, I wanted to throw up.

The skin rolled back, stiff. Beneath was what could only be described as old meat, and the remains of old fat, like scrambled egg. A few students looked a little green around the gills. I gripped the desk in front of me hard, determined not to retch in front of a room full of strangers.

Pozzi chose one of the students clustered nearby to dissect the heart. The sternum had already been cut through, but they still had to remove the cage of the sternum and ribs to access the heart underneath.

The boy couldn't have been older than twenty. He rolled his neck before reaching into the chest and taking out the sternum. I gaped at it held in his hands, resisting the urge to rest my fingers against my own ribcage. He gazed into the cavity of the dead man's chest, the other students peering over his shoulder. Pozzi invited all the students to walk by and look at it while the heart was still within the chest.

'In reality, we should ideally have one cadaver for every five or six of you, and we'd be in the laboratory, but there's a drastic shortage,' he said as they filed past.

A student raised his hand, tentative. When Pozzi nodded at him, he asked, 'I never understood that. Don't plenty of people die?'

'Unfortunately, yes, plenty of people die each day in Imachara, especially in the recent fires.' *Fires*, I thought wryly. I suppose that's one euphemism for Kashura Forester attacks. 'But you have to specify that your body can be used for science. Most elect against it, and so we have access to criminals and a few people who die in the hospital on campus, and that's it. It's not enough, but we make the most of what we have.'

My mouth went dry. I remembered the dreams of the person winding through the streets, and through the cemetery. The sound of the shovel, and the *thump* as it hit the wood of the coffin.

Rising with the last of the students, I was determined to push away my squeamishness and see what lay within the human body. The man's face was red with rosacea. He had a notch missing from his ear, which in some gangs of Imachara meant he had killed someone. His heart nestled behind his rib cage, which had now been spread like wings. I could hear my own heartbeat thundering in my ears. This was what was within all of us, slippery organs in shades of purple and yellow and red, save for the bright green of the gallbladder.

Pozzi selected another volunteer to make the cuts. He chose a girl with spectacles and hair in a long braid down her back. She picked up the scalpel with her gloved hands, which were steady as a surgeon's. Deftly, she reached into the dead man's chest before bringing out the heart like a prize. It rested in her hand, bloodless and dead. Pozzi clapped, congratulating her, and motioned for her to pass it to another student, who weighed it on a nearby set of scales. Each student came up and held it for a second of silence. Then the doctor asked her to put it back into the cavity.

He chose yet another student to fold back the sternum and put everything back as it was, resting the flaps of skin together. Once it was done, the man still looked very dead, the gash of the Y incision dark and ugly. Pozzi lowered him back into the coffin-like Ampulla tank. I was glad when he was out of sight. My skin still crawled.

Pozzi looked at all the students, future doctors of Ellada.

'Your professor will be back next week, and you will continue to explore this man's body. Remember that even though we all have the same organs within us, there will be slight differences as well. If you cut the exact same spot on every person, without first deducing exactly where each organ is, you could do more harm than good. Remember that. Do not grow too proud and believe you know everything about the human body. There is always more to discover. Hidden depths you cannot fathom. Never forget that in many ways you will always be a novice. But that does not mean you should not strive to learn all that you can, to push the limits of what we can yet understand.'

The students broke into solemn applause. I couldn't stop looking at their hands, all of which had just held a dead human heart.

I lingered after the students left. If I'd been raised without doctors constantly poking and prying into my privacy, perhaps I'd be less mistrustful of medicine. Maybe I'd even be interested enough to go into it, to discover others who were like me. As it stood, I was still wary of doctors. It was my main fear about Pozzi – that I was nothing more than another experiment, an unwilling subject.

The door to the surgery room opened and a young man came in, slightly out of breath.

'Doctor, I came as soon as my lecture ended. I thought I could help you finish.'

'Ah, hello Kai. Kai, this is Micah. Micah, this is Kai, my assistant.'

Kai gave me a little bow. He was little older than me, and a few inches shorter. He was chubby, with an open face and the hint of a goatee. He wore a heavy coat despite the warmth within the operating theatre. His hair was brownish and curly. His smile was hesitant, shy, but genuine.

I held out my hand and shook his. Kai had a surprisingly strong grip. 'Nice to meet you,' I said.

'You came in good time. These Ampullas are annoyingly heavy to move. We'll need all three of us. I can't be bothered sending for the morgue orderly.'

Kai needed no further encouragement. As we wheeled the Ampulla out of the lecture hall and down the corridor towards the morgue I thought of the room full of silent, dead bodies floating in tanks, chill and unmoving, and shuddered.

At the morgue we were greeted by a young Byssian doctor. His dark hair was shaved close to his head and he was very tall, his skin black, his eyes brown.

He shook Doctor Pozzi's hand. 'We are so pleased you were able to come and cover for us at such short notice, Royal Physician.'

'Not a problem, Doctor Maral. It's always thrilling to see the young minds that will grow to be the great medical minds of the next age. We must always pass the torch.'

'That we must.' Doctor Maral lapsed into silence.

'Is everything all right, Doctor?' Pozzi asked, all smooth concern.

We'd reached the morgue. Doctor Maral took out the key and opened the door, wheeling the body inside. I couldn't help but peek over his shoulder. More tanks, filled with unseen bodies. The blast of cold air from the room hit my cheeks. Doctor Maral closed the door and locked it again, putting the key back in his pocket and patting it.

'We've finished the autopsy you were interested in. I thought . . . I thought you might wish to see the body before we begin preservation. Any additional observations you have would be invaluable.'

Doctor Pozzi tried to hide it, but his eyes gleamed. 'I'm happy to take a look, if you believe you'd find it helpful. I take it my assistants may join me?'

'Of course, though I ask you do not mention what you see to others. I trust in your discretion.' Doctor Maral led us to another door at the back of the morgue. He took out another key, unlocked it, and paused, waiting for our answers.

'You have my word,' Kai said, serious.

'Mine, too,' I added, though I hid a frown, wondering if this was the real reason he had brought me to the university today. What was beyond that door?

Doctor Maral nodded once, and pushed open the door. The air was cold, and I shivered beneath my coat. The body on this slab was also stored in an Ampulla tank, the hair on the skin glistening.

It was Dirk. The one who had been with Juliet and the other one, pale and red-eyed, whose name I'd already forgotten. His eyes were closed and he had a Y incision across his chest like the anatomy subject. Countless cuts scored the short, slick fur that covered his body. On his face, arms, and hands it was russet, though darker than I remembered as it was wet. His stomach was dappled lighter with white and grey.

'He was at the Celestial Cathedral,' I said. 'One of the three Chimaera who called for peace.'

Kai sucked in a breath, snuck me a look from beneath his lashes.

'Very tragic,' Doctor Maral agreed. 'One of the bodies was never found. The third was too damaged to perform an autopsy.'

My hand clenched into a fist. 'Which body was not found?'

'The leopard woman.'

My heart lifted. Maybe Juliet hadn't died but had managed to escape. If she was smart, she'd leave Ellada on the first boat and stay well away from those who wished to harm her. If only I could have spoken with her, just for a few minutes. She might have had answers.

'How different is this man's biology?' Doctor Pozzi asked, clearly fascinated. Kai also held on to every word. I wondered how much he knew of Chimaera, how involved he was with Pozzi's work.

'Not significantly. Entirely the same internally. Just the addition of this hair, here. Brain structure is slightly different, certain areas more developed. We're still consulting with a brain surgeon to return with his full report. The implications could be astounding.'

Like the ability for telepathy, or telekinesis.

'It's a shame we can't use him for students,' Doctor Maral went on. 'We're so short of corpses. Yet there's so much uncertainty with that attack, and we've more work to do with him. Can't risk students damaging the specimen.' He sighed. 'It's a shame how far the current corpses have to spread around the students.'

Doctor Pozzi turned serious. 'Don't turn to resurrection men.'

Doctor Maral looked affronted, but also guilty. 'We never would.'

Resurrection men. They crept into graveyards to dig up fresh bodies, selling them to universities or anatomy schools. Doctor Pozzi asking Doctor Maral not to use them was pointless, even I knew that: pretty much all universities employed resurrection men on the sly. Not enough criminals were hung to meet the demand. Perhaps I was dreaming about someone finding bodies for quick funds. Yet maybe they weren't searching for simple corpses for anatomy and they wanted corpses that were different from the norm. Like Dirk.

My eyes couldn't leave the smooth curve of his skull, fitted back together after doctors had come to saw it open, take out the brain that had housed all his thoughts and memories. What had this man been like? How had he felt about being Chimaera, and what other abilities had he possessed? He was a man murdered solely for looking different, killed while explicitly asking for peace and understanding. Now they'd taken his body and pulled it apart, peering within, trying to discover what made him tick.

They'd do the same thing to me if I died and they knew I was Chimaera. My breath came fast and shallow, and I swayed on my feet. Without a word, I turned and fled the cool room, nearly running through the main morgue and out into the blessedly warm hallway. A few passing students looked at me curiously as I sat on the cool tile of the floor, head between my knees, trying to gain my breath back.

Pozzi came out a moment later.

'I should have realized how upsetting that would be for you. I'm sorry.'

'I'm fine,' I said, not fooling either of us.

He passed me a few coins. 'I must stay here and discuss the subject with Doctor Maral and Kai, but you take a cab home. I hope you found it enlightening, if a bit unnerving.'

'It was interesting,' I said, and that wasn't a lie.

'It's not easy to see people after the light of life has left them, I know.' I did not respond, and we stood in silence for a moment before he continued. 'Have you spoken to Maske yet about my offer to perform for the Princess?'

'Not yet. I'll check with him tonight and send you a missive in the morning, but I'm sure he'll be most agreeable. Thank you.'

'Wonderful. I'm sure the Princess would enjoy it immensely. Well, I'll let you go on your way. Travel home safely, and my apologies again for upsetting you. I forget how non-doctors aren't quite as hardened to the sight of death.'

'I hope I never am,' I said. He gave me something resembling a smile and turned away.

9

THE PRINCESS AND THE LILY

All have heard the tale of Olivia Hyacinth. While her story may have had a basis in fact, it has grown to a myth in the retelling. Her child was stolen by a Chimaera while she was hanging out washing on her farm in Girit.

She'd only turned from her babe for a moment, and when she turned back, a Siren had him in its slick, four-fingered front paws. The creature had no hair, and skin like a salamander's, orange as a sunset and speckled with black spots. Her child was wrapped in a blanket, and the creature wasn't touching the baby's bare skin, which was lucky, as many Sirens have a touch of poison.

'Please, give me back my child,' Olivia implored.

The creature only stuck out its sticky tongue in response, as if testing the air.

Desperate, Olivia grabbed for the child, but the Siren darted out of the way, and within a blink was gone.

Olivia screamed in rage and soon took to the swamps where the Sirens were said to nest, searching until, finally, she saw the speckled orange Chimaera. It had been six *months by this point, and her heart hurt to see her baby so much bigger. But he was still alive, a smiling boy with wispy dark curls. A few drops of skin oil in the baby's milk a day had made the baby immune to the Siren's deadly touch.*

Olivia took out her weapon and snuck closer. She knew that nothing would keep her from her child. Not even one hundred Sirens, or the Lord of the Sun or Lady of the Moon themselves. She moved silently through the swampy marshlands. The Siren had curled up to sleep protectively around her child. Olivia didn't hesitate, and struck off its head. Her child cried, but soon quieted when she picked him up. She went back to her farm, keeping an even closer watch on her child from thereafter.

— Myths and Legends of Ellada and Girit, PROFESSOR CAED CEDAR, Royal Snakewood University

When I returned from Pozzi's, the first thing I did was ask Maske if he wanted to perform for the Princess.

Whatever the Royal Family would pay us to perform would be a lot more than any coppers earned on the street. Maske's eyes lit up with glee when I told him.

'Oh, I do wish this, indeed I wish,' he said. Performing for the Princess would mean we were favoured by the Royal Family, which would result in more séance and magic show bookings from the nobility throughout Imachara and the Emerald Bowl. By the time we were back in the Kymri Theatre, coin would flow through his coffers again.

I wrote the missive then and there, paying a boy to run the message to Pozzi's apartments.

Maske ran into his room, which was stuffed to the gills with the contents of his workshop, to begin planning the show. As he slammed the door, dust fell from the ceiling.

The tenements where we stayed had no roof garden, so Drystan, Cyan and I crammed into mine and Drystan's room so I could tell them why I had returned so late from Pozzi's appointment.

Anisa emerged from her Aleph, as ethereal as ever. I told them everything, and filled Cyan and Anisa in on my two strange dreams.

'I'm not sure who's behind it, or why I'm eavesdropping on the crimes, but it's worrying.'

'Could Pozzi be behind it?' Drystan asked.

'Hard to say. Maybe, but why would he need bodies?'

'Were the bodies human or Chimaera?' Cyan asked.

'That body I saw in the morgue was Chimaera, yes. The ones in the dreams didn't look obviously Chimaera, but we know that doesn't mean much if they were Anthi. Can you sense anything, Anisa?'

'I'm almost completely blind now. I *hate* it. I feel powerless.' Her transparent hands clenched into fists. 'No body, and now not even glimmers of what's to come. Only darkness.'

We lapsed into a temporary silence, mulling it over. The view from Drystan's and my room was not inspiring. We looked directly onto the broken windows of an abandoned building. In the early afternoon, shouts from below and the rumble of engines floated through our thin windows. Our temporary home was so different to the Kymri Theatre. After dark, that area of town was quiet, but here, everything was always alive, curfew or no. Though the quarters were cramped and none too nice, I liked the brief change of scene. It was the polar opposite of my childhood in the richest parts of town. If Pozzi had decided to give me to a poorer family rather than one in the Third Ring of nobility, I might very well have grown up somewhere like this.

I sighed. 'So why would our mystery grave robber need corpses?'

'Experimentation seems the most likely reason. I can't imagine Pozzi sneaking around graveyards at night or creeping into a hospital to suffocate someone.'

'He has that assistant, Kai. Though to be honest, I can't imagine him doing it either. He was very diffident.'

'Could be an act, like Lily.'

'Maybe. What if the university is doing it? To see if they can somehow learn more about the Chimaera? One of the corpses in my dream went missing from the university hospital, I think. That Doctor Maral was very keen on learning everything he could about the one body he had.' The horrible Y incision on Dirk's chest haunted me. The university had taken apart one Chimaera already. What was to stop them from procuring more to further their research? A prestigious paper in the right journals could make doctors rather wealthy from resulting lecture tours. Some of the doctors who saw me as a child had used me to make their fortunes. Chimaera were different. Exotic. The masses would be fascinated and fearful. Call us monsters. Exhibit us around the world, just like the circus freak show, but wrapped in a false veneer of respectability and the pursuit of knowledge.

'It is curious, but I'm not sure if this corpse-stealer is our most pressing concern. Hopefully if you have any future dreams, you will be able to deduce a little more about whoever this is. In the meantime, isn't it time you confronted this Lily Verre about the fact she has been spying on you and reporting to the Royal Physician?' Anisa looked pensive.

There was an awkward silence. As usual, she was right and cut to the heart of the matter. We'd all been putting it off. Something had to be done, but none of us knew what.

'Isn't it better she doesn't know the game is up?' Cyan asked. 'Then we can control what information reaches Pozzi and what doesn't.'

'To a point, perhaps. Personally, I am quite curious to know what Pozzi has on her that ensures she will do his bidding. I have a feeling it is not something she truly wishes to do, but rather something she is being forced into doing.' Anisa raised an eyebrow.

A loud bang from the direction of Maske's new workshop caused us all – save Anisa – to flinch.

'I feel bad, keeping Maske in the dark about all of this,' I said. We had not told him about Lily. Again, she had not been around much as we moved – letting us settle in, she claimed. But I wondered if she sensed that we knew about her. Was she avoiding us? Yet it was cruel to know that Lily was false and not tell our benefactor. Poor Maske was oblivious. But if we told him, his attitude to her would change, and she'd realize we knew she wasn't who she claimed to be.

And then there was everything else. Maske thought Pozzi was simply the prestigious Royal Physician, and was delighted that he was a patron of our art. He did not know that the Doctor was the man who had found me on his doorstep when I was a babe – or so he claimed – and though we told Maske I needed to see Pozzi weekly, we kept the reasons why vague. Maske was curious, of course he was; but I doubted he thought about it over-much, especially with all the recent troubles.

'If we tell him about Lily, he's going to be heartbroken,' Cyan said. 'I feel just as you do about hiding all this from him, but though he seems to be keeping it together, he's not coping well. The Kymri Theatre has been his home for decades.'

'If we figure out what this Lily Verre is up to, then we can ascertain what her motivations are for seeing Maske,' Anisa said. 'Is he but a pawn to her, or is he something more?'

'I think she's using Maske. If we know her game, then we could have power over her,' Drystan said. 'I think we should do what we did to Shadow Elwood. Search her apartments when she and her son are visiting Pozzi, and see what we can find. If we find a secret we can hold over her, then we can skew the information that reaches Pozzi.'

'So we follow her, and when she takes her son to Pozzi, then we strike?' Cyan asked. She too had some misgivings, but she was curious. So was I. Either Lily Verre was a

Shadow who had no qualms following anyone and pretending to be in love with someone, or Pozzi had power over her. And it didn't take much to guess what it might be.

'Pozzi is probably dosing her son with the same Elixir he's giving me,' I said. 'Threatening to take it away would probably drive her to do anything. What if that's all he has on her? That'd be enough, wouldn't it?'

'She's hiding more, I'd bet on it.' Drystan paused, and gave a little smile. 'If I was still the betting sort, of course.'

I didn't like him even joking about that. He and Maske had met at the poker tables in the underbelly of Imachara. He'd still never told me the details of what happened to them there, but I knew it involved card-counting and cheating drug lords.

'Fine. Who'll take first watch?'

'I will,' Cyan said.

'We shouldn't have to wait long. Her son will probably need to be dosed once a week.'

'By this time next week we should have our answers, then,' Anisa said. 'Take me with you when you go and I'll help however I can.'

'All right,' I said. 'I'm not going to tell Cyril about this, so keep him out of it. He doesn't need to be dragged into my trouble.'

I only saw my brother once every few days now. His schedule was gruelling, with hours of lectures and labs, and many more in the library. Then, he usually went to sit with Mother in the hospital. He no longer asked me to come with him.

'Turn me off,' Anisa said. 'I still have a decent amount of power, but there's no point wasting it.'

I'd never considered that before. 'What happens if you run out of power?'

'When it gets low, we'll have to find another Aleph and transfer me to it. Otherwise, I'll die.'

'How long do you have?'

'Don't worry, little Kedi,' Anisa said. 'Though I am touched by your concern, I have plenty of time left yet.'

'Goodbye for now, Anisa,' I said. She inclined her head at me, and I switched her off, putting the little disc in my pocket.

'Well,' Drystan said. 'We better start practising if we're going to perform for the Princess, shouldn't we?'

10

STREET MAGIC

A blink is all you need. A second of distraction, and you trick them with that precious moment. Magic is both the easiest and the hardest thing you will ever do.

— From the soon-to-be published memoirs
of the *Maske of Magic*

The next day, we did street magic.

Maske wanted nothing to do with street performances when there was the strong possibility of performing for the Princess. 'When I've sorted out this new device, I'll do it,' he said at breakfast, oil smudged across one cheek, before he returned to his room. I doubted he had slept a wink.

Street magic wasn't the same as performing in the Kymri Theatre, but it had its own challenges and its own rewards.

We decided to perform in the merchant part of town. Rich enough that people would have spare coins to throw our way, but not rich enough that Policiers would chase us off. We set up our makeshift stage – a threadbare Arrasian rug – and set out the hat for coins. We wore our full magician regalia, me and Drystan in our suits, Cyan in her Temnian sarong. The street was busy, and many did not give us a second glance.

The air was loud with calls, the clop of horses' hooves, and the ceaseless footsteps of hurrying pedestrians. Nearby a blacksmith rang an anvil in a steady beat. Dust choked the air, and the sun beat down on the windows of shops and the tops of the heads of people rushing past. From two streets over, we could smell the butcher's row: old blood, offal, and the smell of meat about to turn. Two young women were walking down the street. They had no big bags, no children, and did not seem to be in a rush.

'Excuse me,' I called to them with a smile. 'Would you care to see some magic?'

A pause. A shy smile in return from one, a sceptical raise of the eyebrow from the other. 'All right,' said the disbeliever, with a tilt of her chin as if to say: *impress me*.

'May I see your ring, just for a moment?' I asked the shy one. She wore a simple wooden band around her thumb. 'I promise, it'll just be for a second, and then it'll return to you safe and sound.'

She hesitated.

'Here, you may hold my ring as insurance.' I passed her a silver band. She took it and then slipped her ring off her finger and handed it to me. A few more people gathered, wondering what we were doing. Cyan might have been pushing minds, just the slightest bit, to draw attention to our corner of the street.

I took the wooden ring from the girl. A quick close

and open of my fingers, and it was gone. The sceptic puffed up. 'If you steal it—' she began.

'Never fear, miss. As I said, it'll be back in a moment. Now,' I said, holding my hands wide. 'Would you be impressed if the ring showed up in my pocket?'

'Yes,' the shy one said, hesitantly.

'Well.' I reached into my pocket. I brought a small wallet, opened it, unbuttoned a smaller pocket within, and revealed the wooden ring, chained to the wallet itself. I unclipped the ring and passed it back to her.

The shy girl gave a delighted laugh, and even the sceptical lady was grudgingly impressed.

'Now, please pass me back my silver ring.'

She patted the pocket where she had stored it and then reached in. Her fingers came up empty. She gazed at me with wide eyes.

Another quick flourish of the fingers, and the silver was back on my finger. Both of the girls clapped.

We performed more sleight of hand with a pack of cards as the crowd gathered. We chose the correct cards, made them disappear and appear in pockets, on the bottom of shoes, underneath hats. Drystan did a trick he'd performed at the Elmbark's on the Night of the Long Lady, telling a story of love and jealousy, having the right characters – the jack, the king, the queen – appear at just the right time.

For some of the performance, we used our acrobatic skills – handstands, cartwheels, and flips. These impressed the audience just as much as the magic, and I spied one small child trying a cartwheel of his own before his mother stopped him from smashing his head on the cobblestones. By the end of the performance, our hat held plenty of coin. It'd help us buy food, as almost all of our money was now tied up in the sale of Taliesin's theatre and the repairs on our own home.

We thanked everyone, took our coins, and packed up our things.

'One of us should go back to Lily's,' I said. We'd been taking turns watching her apartment building the last few days, trying to have one of us there at least a few hours at a time.

We couldn't go back to Maske's to drop off the props, for we wanted him to think we were still out performing. We went to a tea house, setting the props under the table. The waiters disapproved but did not object. Cyan would watch our things as we tailed Lily.

'I prefer doing this bit of the job,' Cyan grinned, leaning back in her chair as her tea steeped.

'It'll be your turn again before you know it,' I said making a face at her.

She sighed. 'True enough. When do we make our move?'

'Soon,' I said. 'I just want to see what we can discover from afar, first.'

So far, all our attempts to tail Lily had failed. We'd wait for hours outside her apartments, yet she never emerged. We were not hopeful as we made our way to her blocky tenement building yet again.

Dutifully, Drystan and I went to another tea house, one which gave us a direct view of the entrance to Lily's apartments. It was here – a few weeks ago, at the very table where I now sat – that I had realized Lily Verre was the woman in the red dress I'd seen in visions. Our tea arrived. A Penglass dome to the right of the tea house cast the veranda in blue shadow. My eyes kept snagging on it. Penglass always called to me, especially on the night of the full moon, but this was stronger. It was as if the Penglass emitted heat, and I wanted to unfurl in front of it.

Turning my back on the glass, I focused on my cup. 'This is nice,' I said, raising my tea and clinking my glass to Drystan's. 'Like a date.'

'A romantic date of spying on a Shadow with a Chimaera son who may or may not wish us harm.'

'Yes, well, we don't have the time or the money for any other dates, so I'll take what I can get.'

Drystan laughed, and we settled down to drink our tea.

After half an hour of waiting, Drystan nudged me with his elbow. 'There she is.'

Lily came out, without the wicker chair or her son. She wore a hat festooned with flowers against the early summer sun. We followed her at a distance. Using my Elixir-enhanced powers, I reached out to her mind. But like Cyan, all I heard was an incessant chatter of noise. She kept it up whether or not she thought we were near, then. Where had she learned to shield herself, and what was she hiding?

Then, suddenly, Lily was nowhere to be seen. It was a busy market, with thick crowds and stalls packed as closely as possible. Perhaps she knew we were following her before we'd even begun. After a few minutes' fruitless search, we headed back to the Penny Rookeries.

On the way home, I kept turning my head to the left. It was like the Penglass at the tea house, like heat emanated towards me, and I was as transfixed as a moth to a flame.

When I slowed down for the third time, Drystan asked me what the matter was.

Telling him about the Penglass, I craned my head. 'This is different. It's like I'm drawn to a person . . .' Our eyes met, and at the same time we whispered: 'Chimaera.'

As soon as we said it, I knew it was true. Somehow, I was sensing another Chimaera. Not Cyan. It was someone new, someone different, yet somehow familiar.

I followed the feeling, Drystan trailing behind. A street later, the feeling faded, leaving behind only a vague, warm blush.

'That was bizarre,' I said.

'Potentially very useful, though. If this Elixir has strengthened your powers and you can sense others, you could find more. Maybe even find some answers from one of them.'

'Or draw myself right into danger.'

'That too. Let me know if you feel it again, but don't go running off after anyone on your own, all right?'

I nodded. A headache bloomed at my temples, growing stronger with each step. By the time we reached our rooms, my vision was blurring and it was as though ice picks skewered me through the temples. Drystan settled me into bed and then went back out to help Cyan carry the magic props back from the other tea house.

I reached out with my mind, trying to sense any other Chimaera. There was nothing until Cyan rounded the corner and came back. She burned like a flame in my mind.

When she came up, it was almost too strong. Somehow, I pulled back until she was only a glow. Drystan told her what had happened. Cyan rested her hand on my forehead and pressed gently into my mind, reliving the memory. She jerked her hand away. 'That's incredible.'

'And frightening,' I said.

'Yes.'

They left me, and I napped. I did not dream of the grave robber, but instead of Timur, the leader of the Kashura.

He stared right at me with those intense eyes, that shock of curly hair. Fury radiated off him in waves. He was in a sumptuous room, surrounded by his followers, none of whom I recognized.

'Have you found any others?' he asked. 'What about the girl young Oli mentioned? The one who could read minds, even influence them?'

One of his followers shook his head. 'Nothing yet, sir. Yet the hunt continues. It shouldn't take long until we find either the woman who escaped the cathedral, or another one.'

'Concentrate your efforts. Find one strong enough and we can find the rest,' he said.

The sound of voices woke me. Groggy, I sat up, but at least the worst of the headache had fled. The dream had left me unsettled.

Running my hands through my hair to try and tame it, I opened the door to my bedroom and froze.

Within our cramped lounge, Maske, Lily – her

ridiculous hat set beside her on the sofa – and Doctor Pozzi were having tea with Drystan and Cyan. Ricket was asleep on Lily's lap. Traitor.

I felt awkward in my rumpled clothes, my eyes still gummy with sleep. I'd taken off the Lindean corset I wore beneath my clothes to bind my breasts. Sleeping in it was nothing resembling comfortable. Granted, in the heat of summer, it also itched terribly, but if I wanted to dress as a boy, it stayed on. Hunching my shoulders to hide my small breasts, I bit my lip with nerves.

Maske couldn't contain his excitement. 'The good Doctor has just confirmed we will be performing for the Princess in a few days' time!'

We smiled back at him, but all of us were hesitant. Me and Drystan because there were likely people in the palace we'd know, and Cyan as she was still uncomfortable around the nobility. She'd been sympathetic to the Foresters and their mission to bring more democracy to Ellada, but now, thanks to the violent actions of the Kashura, she'd turned against the party. Performing for a monarchy she was not loyal to was not her preference, but she would do it, both for the money and for Maske.

'Well,' said Doctor Pozzi, putting on his white gloves to cover his clockwork hand, 'I should probably return to the palace and give them your acceptance. Thank you for the tea, and it was nice to meet you, Miss Verre.'

I only barely managed not to scoff. Lily met my eyes, then glanced back at Doctor. 'The pleasure's mine. Good day, Royal Physician.'

I walked the doctor to the door. On our crumbled front steps, he put on his top hat.

'Why are you doing this for us?' I asked, tired of dancing around everything. Perhaps I'd forgotten more of the etiquette my mother had taught me than I thought.

'It's not for you,' he said.

I blinked in surprise.

He paused. 'That came out harsher than I meant it to. But I'm doing this mostly for the Princess Royal. She's lonely. For several weeks after the magic duel, your performance was all she would speak about, she enjoyed it so much. When she found out I knew you all, she begged me to speak to the Steward about letting you come and perform for her. So I am merely following her wishes.'

'What's she like?' I'd only met her briefly, after the magicians' duel. She'd been as excited as any other little girl, though her smile had dimmed a little in the shadow of the Steward looming above her. The Princess's parents had died in a gyrocopter crash near Byssia when she was a toddler. Her uncle, the Steward, was to rule in her stead until she came of age at sixteen, but it was clear to all that the Steward relished the throne and might not give it up easily. The Princess, not even seven, was torn between power plays. Her life would not be easy.

'She's a jewel, our Princess. I just hope that she won't crack. Pressure makes diamonds, after all.'

And with that, he left.

11

THE SHIMMERING GIRL
AT THE PALACE

*Once there was a girl with dragonfly wings, who soared
above the world. She looked down and saw happiness,
and sadness, and wide expanses with no one at all save
the animals and trees and rocks and streams. She flew all
the way around the world, writing down whatever she
saw. When she came back, she did not show anyone her
little journal. It was her version of the world, and she
wanted to keep it for her alone.*
— 'The Dragonfly Girl', *Hestia's Fables*

We went to the palace two days later, following the instructions sent by courier on sumptuous regal stationery.

The Steward sent a gilded carriage for us. Maske, Cyan,
Drystan and I squeezed into it and enjoyed the rare luxury.
My brother wanted to come, but his name was not on
the invitation and I did not want anyone to see us together,
lest they make the connection between him and his missing
sister.

The carriage jostled, the engine purring and smooth.

Drystan, Maske and I wore smart dark suits with cravats that matched Cyan's green sash. Drystan and I also had our customary Glamour disguises. I often wondered what we'd do when the power for the Vestige tools ran out. Glamours were beyond our price range just now, and the prices would only go up.

Cyan kept looking out of the window. She wore an Elladan dress of dark blue damask, a sash of Temnian green silk at her waist. She hadn't painted her face with the swirling Alder designs as she often did when she played Madame Damselfly, but she'd lined the lids of her eyes in silver, which sparkled as the light hit it.

Cyan couldn't help but be curious about the interior of the palace. She turned to me, knowing my mind reached towards hers. *Think of all that tax money sitting in marble columns and silver cutlery. Wrapped up in mansions in the Emerald Bowl and lavish apartments in the city. The Snakewoods and the Twelve Trees take so much while their subjects live like they do in the Penny Rookeries.*

I could not disagree with her. Living in the Penny Rookeries, in the neighbourhood where the Foresters had begun, had made me think differently about the monarchy. Every day I saw thin beggars holding out hands for coins. We gave them what coppers we could spare, but we knew it was not enough. Hungry children played in alleyways unsupervised, and others, not much older, worked in factories twelve hours a day. Poverty was everywhere, with no hope of reprieve. Yet here, in one room of the palace, was enough gold to feed everyone in that neighbourhood for over a year. Why did the nobility need so much, when so many others had a greater need? The bulk of the Forester cause made sense.

As the carriage waited by the imposing metal gates of the palace, I looked out over the square where the Celestial Cathedral had once stood proud. They'd cleared away the rubble, but the broken foundations were like a scar on the city's face. Flowers lined the square, tributes to those who had been killed. There were nubs of extinguished candles, and notes written by the victims' family members and other sympathizers were tied to posts, fluttering in the wind. There was talk of Imachara erecting a memorial statue and rebuilding the cathedral – which all sounded well and good, until people remembered it would be taxes from Ellada's already overstretched coffers that funded it.

The guard looked at our official invitation and then spoke through a Vestige communicator to the palace. After a long pause he nodded and opened the metal gate, letting the carriage through.

It was not a case of simply walking into the palace. We were led to an alcove and asked to empty our pockets. Anything that could be used as a weapon was taken away. They patted me down and I had to lie, awkwardly, that the binding corset beneath my shirt was for a problem with my back.

After we had all been searched, we were led into another room and asked to wait while our gear was unloaded from the carriage and likewise searched. Anisa's Aleph was hidden in one of our equipment cases, and with a little mental push from Cyan, they did not search that one too closely. It was more a show of control than anything else. Most of our magic props could have been used as weapons – the séance table, the wires and hooks, even the wands. If they really meant to take away potential weapons, we'd be forced onto the stage with nearly nothing.

We were kept there, watched by the guards, for nearly three quarters of an hour. None of us said much, all too aware that the guards would report our conversation word for word back to the rest of security.

Despite it all, though, I was looking forward to seeing Princess Nicolette. She was old enough to start noticing when people kept secrets from her, or perhaps lied to her for her own good. Seven was when I started resenting the doctors my parents kept taking me to, when I started mistrusting them telling me it was for my health. What sort of person would the Princess grow up to be? The Steward himself kept out of the public eye, for the most part. He was uncharismatic in his few speeches on holidays. People mistrusted him, hence the rumours flying thick and fast that he wanted to keep the throne. I had only met him the one time I'd met the Princess, and I couldn't read him either. I hoped he treated her well, taught her what she'd need to know to rule in these uncertain times. Though the violent Kashura arm of the Foresters did not have much support, the people still wanted change. They were growing impatient, and afraid. That could breed more violence, and more sympathy towards it.

She was still a child, and I remembered how her face had lit up as she watched the magic show. On stage, she'd given Maske, Drystan, and Cyan medals to thank them for the performance, stiff and regal; but afterwards, she'd asked me questions as any normal child might. I hoped we could bring her a little magic again.

Finally, we were led to one of the salons to set up. The ostentatious display did not impress me as it once might have. Now, it was entirely too much. Soft glass globes tinged pale pink and orange lent the room a dreamy glow. The entire place was made out of marble threaded through with gold. The columns around the dance floor were purest white, but the floor was a pale rose-tinted marble, with smaller tiles of a deep amber stone marking out the design of the Twelve Trees of Nobility. A large, twining Snakewood tree was ringed with a circle, surrounded with different leaf shapes like the hours of a clock: Snakewood at the twelve o'clock spot, surrounded by Ash, Balsa, Cedar, Cyprus, Ebony, Elm, Hornbeam, Oak, Poplar, Redwood, and Walnut.

They were the original families of nobility, in power since Ellada became the largest empire of the Archipelago. Centuries' worth of wealth was shared between them, political alliances made through marriages. Sometimes their fortunes could fall, briefly; previous generations of my own adopted family, the Lauruses, had lost wealth in risky business ventures. It was one of the reasons they'd taken the child Pozzi gave them, and the hefty sum of money that came with me. It meant they could rejoin the higher rings of nobility and take advantage of the societal perks associated with that.

Before us was the stage, a smaller but more ornate version of ours at the Kymri Theatre. Seeing it gave us all a pang, reminding us of the cracked plaster and broken stage of our home. More glass globes were suspended over the polished stage like clusters of pale grapes. Servants were setting out chairs, and we oversaw the seating placement to ensure that no one would be sitting at an angle that might let them see too much and spoil the illusions.

We set up and went through a few practice rounds. The servants lingered and watched, becoming our rehearsal audience. They applauded for us at the end. Hopefully this meant word of Maske and his Marionettes would spread throughout the palace, and perhaps some of the other servants would come to our Kymri Theatre when shows started again.

Near the end, after we were packing up, I caught sight of Princess Nicolette peeking around the door. She was with her nurse. When the Princess met my eyes she smiled, recognizing me. I gave her a wink and she blushed.

As she turned, I saw a flicker. It was as if feathers of light emerged from her skin, then re-settled and disappeared. It reminded me of the shimmer when Anisa took over my body, or the occasional glitch that could happen when a Glamour ran low on power. Her nurse saw, her eyes widening. With a frightened look at me, she took her royal charge away. No one else had seen.

I hadn't imagined it.

We finished our rehearsal and went back to the Penny Rookeries. Our apartments looked all the tawdrier after the grand ballroom.

'The Princess couldn't be controlled by an Aleph, could

she?' I asked, as we clustered in the lounge. Maske was, as usual, back in his new workshop-bedroom. Cyan and Drystan shrugged and then looked to Anisa, who I'd asked to join us.

'It could be an Aleph. Any being containing a consciousness like me could flicker like that. However, I'd wager it's more likely a Glamour low on power, as you thought. Or sometimes, if there's feedback from other articles of Vestige, it can interfere with a Glamour.'

'Curious, curious,' Drystan said. 'Why would the Princess be wearing a Glamour? Don't we have enough to worry about already?'

'It seems there is one more worry to add,' Anisa said.

'You, ancient damselfly, have no sense of humour,' Drystan told her wryly.

She narrowed her eyes at him, which made me nervous. I never knew quite what Anisa thought of Drystan.

'Any other dreams?' Anisa asked me.

'Just the Timur one.' I'd already told them about that, along with the feeling of sensing other Chimaera. 'And I've not sensed anyone other than Cyan, either.'

'You've not been able to procure any Elixir?' Anisa asked me.

'There hasn't been a chance. I'm trying to think of a distraction for next week.' My tone was defensive.

'Take Drystan with you,' she said. Drystan frowned at her. 'He can do it. The sooner the better.' I noticed she didn't volunteer a way to help.

'We're on it. And we'll see what happens on Saturday,' I said. 'And we're still looking out for Lily going to Pozzi's.

We missed her last week, but hopefully we can follow her this week.' I rubbed my temples. It was, as Drystan said, too much to worry about, and there was only so much space in my mind. All we could do was push forward and hope luck gave us a break.

We each went to bed.

But there was no escape for me there.

The two corpses lay in a row in the dim laboratory. They were still fresh, and the serum I used kept them in that suspended state, free of further decay, but it wouldn't last forever. I needed Ampulla tanks, and sooner rather than later. My experiment needed to work within the next few weeks or I'd have to start all over again with new cadavers.

I drifted closer, hefting the syringe in my hospital-gloved hands. The one nearest to me was the woman who had committed suicide. Wires poked from her veins, connected to machines pilfered from the hospital. Her long, dark auburn hair curled over her shoulders. She must have been lovely, this girl who decided that life was a battle too difficult to fight. I wondered what finally drove her over the edge.

I unwrapped the bandages, wincing at the sight of the ugly wounds. I touched her hair, then pushed back her grave-dirt-stained sleeve and pushed the syringe into the crook of her elbow.

The gashes on her wrists still did not heal.

'This will work,' I told myself. 'This has to work.'

I tried once more. And slowly, so slowly, the dead flesh began to knit back together.

I smiled, and then turned to the man I'd killed at the University Hospital.

'Your turn.'

I woke up, shivering. The whole bed was cold, as if I had no body heat to warm it. Drystan lay curled into a ball away from me. I shook him. He didn't wake easily. I had to try several times before he finally stirred.

'What's the matter?' he asked, his voice blurred with sleep.

'I had another one of the dreams,' I whispered.

He put his arms around me. 'What happened?'

I told him all I'd seen.

'Experimenting on corpses.' He sighed. 'It has to be Pozzi, surely. Him or Timur. You dreamed of him, too.'

'Maybe him. He did want Chimaera. Perhaps he'd settle for dead ones, too. I can't tell whose eyes I'm looking through, whether man, woman, or Kedi. It could be Lily or Kai, working at Pozzi's request. It could be Timur, or one of his followers. It could be someone working for the Royal Family. The Steward was interested enough in the three Chimaera to let them speak to the city. It could be someone entirely unrelated. We simply don't know.'

The person in the dream never looked down at their clothing. I had an impression of long, dark sleeves and those hospital gloves, but that was all. I sighed. 'I'm so tired of this. Every time I turn around there's something new to contend with.'

'I know. It'd be nice to go at least a couple of weeks without some sort of catastrophe, wouldn't it?'

'That it would.'

He pulled me closer. 'You're cold as ice.'

'I guess riding the minds of people committing crimes with cadavers steals all my warmth,' I said, pressing closer to him. He was so leanly muscled that he didn't seem to keep any of his heat, and it radiated from him like a furnace.

He stroked my hair from my face, his other hand making lazy circles on my back. I shivered in a different way. My lips pressed to the square of his jaw, the small hairs at the base of his neck tickling my cheek. I always turned to him after nightmares, but he was always there to comfort me. As if after dreaming of death I had to remember that I was alive. He pulled me closer, and our shirts rucked up, our bellies pressing against each other.

I sat up, drawing him up with me and pulling off his shirt, running my fingertips along the tips and grooves of his muscles. He pulled off my shirt. My breasts were small, but just fit into the palm of his hand. We shimmied out of the rest of our clothes, leaving them in a heap on the floor, exploring and losing ourselves in the other.

I was still so cold, and I let him melt me.

12

THE BOY WITH HORNS

Hush, my child,
and fall into sleep,
to have your dreams of wild
worlds and oceans deep.
Let your troubles slip and fade,
You'll dream forever, or so the doctor said.
— A banned Elladan lullaby

Lily Verre left to visit Pozzi with her son the day before we were to perform for the Princess of Ellada.

As soon as Cyan spied Lily leaving her building, pushing her son in his wicker wheelchair, she'd run back to the Penny Rookeries to fetch us, as we were too far away for her to reach us with her mind. Luckily we had a free afternoon that day while Maske tinkered in his workshop, tweaking the props we'd be using at the palace. We gathered supplies, wearing dark civilian clothes. Unlike when we snuck into Shadow Elwood's apartments, we wouldn't have the cover of night, and we'd have to take a different approach.

I hid in the alleyway near the entrance to Lily's apartments. Cyan paused in front of the door, rummaging in
her bag for something. The doorman stood stiffly at attention in his buttoned coat and cap. Drystan wore scruffy
clothes, his fair hair hidden by a cap and his face smudged
with dirt. He darted down the street and grabbed Cyan's
bag.

'Help!' Cyan screeched, wringing her hands and acting
the part of the helpless maiden. 'Thief!'

The doorman hesitated and then took off after the
fleeing thief, perhaps hoping to impress the damsel in
distress. Cyan, quick as a snake, opened the door and
slipped inside, and I followed. Moments later, Drystan
came in as well, wiping his face clean of grime. We knew
Lily's number thanks to her letters for Maske, and so up
the stairs we went.

Halfway up the stairs, a wave of exhaustion overwhelmed me and I stumbled. Before Drystan or Cyan
could notice, I forced my feet forward. I'd been tired all
day, but now, wiping my burning eyes, it was as if I hadn't
slept at all. Time for another dose of Elixir.

Drystan took out his lock picks and set to work. I
turned on the Eclipse, a Vestige artefact that would disable
any other Vestige within a small radius. We'd borrowed
it from Maske before, and if he ever noticed it go missing
temporarily, he never commented on it. We didn't anticipate Lily Verre was solvent enough to own Vestige alarms,
but it was better safe than sorry.

With a satisfied sigh, Drystan finished picking the lock.
It opened with a little *snick* and the door swung inwards.

We crept inside, closing the door softly behind us. Through the haze of exhaustion I wondered what, if anything, we'd find in the home of Lily Verre.

It was dim inside, the apartment being one of the cheaper ones at the back of the building where the sun was blocked by other tenements. Cyan flicked on the light, and we all froze.

Lily Verre sat in the middle of the room.

'Hello, you three,' she said calmly, in her true voice rather than the one she affected as the widow dating our mentor. 'How nice of you to come calling.'

One eyebrow arched, her chin lifted. She rose in a smooth motion. 'Sit down,' she ordered.

Unsure what else to do, we obeyed, perching across from her on the sofa. One thing was for certain – she was a far better Shadow than Elwood had ever been. She must have waited until Cyan began her ploy with the guard and then hurried back to her apartments to wait for us. I had to appreciate her skill. My body tingled and my mind filled with Chimaera warmth. Her son was in the next room, strong as a furnace.

I wondered what she had planned for us.

The apartment was unassuming, with no personal knick-knacks or belongings. It could have been a hotel room. My damp palms slipped on the dark red leather of the sofa. Paintings of generic landscapes of rolling hills dotted with cows and sheep lined the wall. There was an empty desk of dark wood with locked drawers. A book-shelf lined another wall, heavy with leather-bound tomes, but I couldn't read the peeling gilt titles from where I sat.

'When did you know that we knew?' I asked, my mouth dry.

'I knew you'd figure it out at some point. You took longer than I expected. You followed me from the cafe to Pozzi's a few weeks ago. I wondered if you'd accuse me then, give up the game, but you didn't. Which I found curious. Didn't take much to deduce that you'd try to sneak in. Would have been useless, even if I wasn't here. There's nothing to find.'

'What have you been telling Pozzi about us?'

Her eyes darted away, but not before I saw the regret there. 'More than you'd like.'

'Where's your son?' I asked, as if I couldn't feel him burning the edges of my mind.

'Frey's in the bedroom.' Her voice softened when she spoke his name.

'How old is he?' Cyan asked.

'Seven, and he's all I have in this world. Or all I did have, before I met Maske.'

'Don't pretend you care for Maske,' I said, my voice sharp. 'You used him to get closer to us.'

She shook her head. 'Initially. But he's a sweet man, and cares for me. And I for him.'

'He cares for the person you pretend to be around him,' Drystan said.

Lily Verre flinched. She changed the subject. 'My son nearly died two years ago when his scales and horns appeared.' I remembered the one glimpse of his face I'd had, when we'd followed Lily. The light had caught on dark green scales.

His too-small, too-flat nose, the nostrils long and thin. The small horns poking from the scarf wrapped around him. The long, thin fingers, the nails dark and sharp like claws.

'He's Chimaera,' I said.

She nodded. 'Yes, though I do not know how. The person who sired him was not.'

Cyan and I exchanged a look. We didn't have to send our thoughts to know what the other was thinking: his father could have had unseen abilities. Or his mother. Was Lily like us?

'So I went to the Royal Physician. It was before he went away on sabbatical. I had heard rumours that he was studying birth anomalies. Frey was in a coma, and I thought he would die. Pozzi was able to save him. I was in his debt. I still am.'

So it was as we suspected – if she was telling the truth.

'You've not recently turned Shadow,' Drystan said, lifting his eyebrow at her. 'You're better than Elwood, whom I'm sure you know was hired to find us last year.'

At his name, her lip curled ever so slightly. 'I was a Shadow long before I met Pozzi, yes. And Elwood, well, I can't say I'm particularly sorry to see the end of him. He stole plenty of cases from me over the years, and charged outrageously for shoddy work.'

'I've never heard of a female Shadow,' Cyan said. Neither had I. And judging by Lily Verre's true accent, if this was it, she had been born to nobility or rich merchants. There was a story here, that was for sure. How had she become a Shadow?

'You wouldn't have heard of me as a female Shadow,' she said. 'I dressed as a man. Alban Verani.'

We gaped. I didn't know much about him – he was active when I was a small child, but Cyril had found him interesting and told me stories. Alban Verani had been one of the best Shadows in Ellada, and one of the youngest. He'd also been quite the mystery – no one knew where he had come from. He solved almost every case he took on, but people never learned anything about him. He'd supposedly died two years ago, though there were conspiracy theories about what had really happened to him: that he'd been murdered by the Eel of Imachara, the Lerium Lord. That he'd decided he'd made enough riches and retired from his life as a Shadow. That he'd been driven out of Ellada by other Shadows. No one would have guessed that he had been this small blonde woman before us now.

The look on Cyril's face when I told him would be priceless.

'Yet that's not the complete truth of the matter. Life has a way of being more complicated.' She hesitated, then squared her shoulders. 'I was assigned male at birth, yet when I was a little younger than you, I realized that was not correct. I am female, though it took me many years to let that side of me flourish. I continued dressing as a man, and working as a Shadow was easier in trousers.' Her face closed. 'Yet it was constrictive. I married, and I kept the truth from my Andrea for years. She guessed, though, and when I told her, she accepted it. Even celebrated it.' Grief was in every line of her face.

My mouth opened, then closed again. I'd heard of

people who transitioned to another gender, but I had never met anyone who had done it before. I peered at her more closely, but she still looked exactly like Lily to me. 'So there is the truth of it. What now, my doves? You know what I am. I know that you know. There's much knowing of things now. Where do we go from here?' She smiled as if this was all terribly amusing, but underneath I sensed she was nervous.

'Stop reporting to him,' I said.

'Not that simple. I have to give him at least a little something every time I bring Frey for his medication.'

'He needs regular treatments?' I asked, my voice growing dry.

'Once a week, just like you. The Elixir slows the changes, keeps him far healthier than he would be otherwise.'

'What about when the Physician was away on sabbatical?'

'He gave me Elixir, and I administered it. But once he returned, he disliked giving me caches of it, so I have to visit him again.'

'What do you know about it?' I asked, rubbing the spot in the inner crook of my elbow where Pozzi stuck in the long needle.

'Not much. Just that it's part Vestige, and it seems to work.' But she paused.

'You know more than that,' Cyan said with certainty. 'If you want us to have a shot at trusting you, you need to tell us. Cease that incessant chatter in your head and let me in. I can already filter through some of it.' She smiled, and Lily blanched. I was surprised that Cyan was so forthright, but she must have been able to realize that Lily already knew some of what she could do.

'Have you told Pozzi about Cyan?' I asked.

Lily's mouth twisted. 'I told him I had suspicions that she could do more than she let on, but not the exact nature. Fine. I shall lower my defences, and Cyan shall project it to you. But do not delve deeper than what I offer to you freely. It is my mind, my privacy. Do I have your word on this?' She stared at Cyan, unblinking.

Cyan stiffened. 'You do.'

'Very well.' She paused. 'What you see will completely change your opinion of the Royal Physician.'

'We've never trusted him,' I said, my mouth dry.

'And that is wise of you. But even so, I don't think any of you have fully suspected what sort of man he truly is. Remember, Cyan, no peeking in corners you shouldn't. I'll know if you do. And you need my help.'

Cyan's face was pinched. 'I gave you my word,' she said.

Lily Verre closed her eyes. Cyan kept hers open, but her eyes rolled up into her skull until only the whites showed. For a moment, they glowed the bright blue of Penglass, and then her head slumped forward.

I took Drystan's hand in mine, warm and comforting. And then we closed our eyes and let the images project into the darkness of our minds' eyes.

It was like when I was thrown into the past memories of Anisa when she wanted me to understand more of the Chimaera she had raised, an age, an eon ago.

The images jumped: Lily rested her hands on a woman's pregnant belly, spreading her fingers on soft skin, feeling the movement within. The baby kicked, and the woman laughed.

'Lily,' she said. 'Did you feel that?' The baby kicked again.

I-as-Lily thought of Andrea, and my throat closed with tears. The scene cut to the birth. I held Andrea's hand, and she was surrounded by doctors as they scrutinized her.

Andrea began to bleed. At first the doctors were not concerned, but then their eyes grew worried above the gauze masks. They tried to usher me from the room, but I would not leave. My Andrea looked at me as she died, her hand growing slack in mine. The grief threatened to unhinge me completely, so I did my best to close off all feeling. I sat by my wife, completely numb, as she grew cold.

The doctors surrounded us in their frantic ballet, trying to save the child. Eventually they pushed me away, and I sat hunched in a corner. I wanted to die.

A few minutes later, a thin, high cry cut through the barrier I'd erected around myself. My head lifted, and I saw a tiny, moving fist.

'The child has a caul,' one of the doctors said, shamed.

'Cut it off,' the other doctor, a woman, instructed. 'I'll not hold with superstition here.'

The caul was cut, delicately enough that it did not scar his face later in life.

The female doctor wiped my son free of blood and looked down at him, frowning.

'*What is it?*' *I asked, terrified. 'Is my son all right?*'

Her brow smoothed. 'I just thought for a moment I saw something odd. He's small for his age, and he's not kicking his feet.'

They set him in my arms. He was small, but his cry was fierce. If he had died, I would not have lasted the night. I would have joined my wife and my child. Yet he survived, and so I brought my baby home. Around where the umbilical cord was cut, there was a cluster of small scales. Later, they fell off, but I always remembered them, delicate. I kept one in a box.

I worked as Alban Verani to support us, but the rest of the time, I was Lily Verre. I saw my son, aged five, at the playground, so much smaller than the other children. Never able to walk. So many broken bones. Yet, strangely, they healed much faster than they should have.

Two years ago Frey suffered from seizures, and all I could do was turn him to one side, press down his tongue with a spoon, and hold him as he jerked and I sobbed.

He fell into a coma for four days. I took on no new cases. I stroked his skin, singing his favourite songs, my throat stiff with tears.

Frey's eyes opened, but he did not see me.

I rubbed cream onto his dry skin. When the skin flaked off, there were the scales, almost invisible. He burned as if with a fever. And then there were the strange bumps on his forehead. I wondered if they were growths of cancer. It would have explained the seizures, but not the scales. I held cloths to his forehead, wondering if there would be another coma and if he would wake up from it.

The doctor who had birthed Frey stood in front of me, arms held out. She did not know what was wrong. But she was the one to tell me of the Royal Physician. She told me not to tell him she had given me his address, or she'd lose her licence – or worse. I kept her secret.

The vision shifted. Rather than flecks of memory, Lily told us the tale directly, peppered with flashes of reminiscence.

Sometimes I wished she had never sent me to the Royal Physician. And then I hated myself for daring to think such a thing, because then my child would be dead. And that would be worse, far worse, than dying myself.

I went to Pozzi. Alone, because my son could not be moved from his hospice bed at home. I wouldn't let them take him to the hospital, for fear they'd see the scales. My friend since childhood, Erin, had become a nurse. She cared for him, and I knew she said nothing to anyone else of Frey's anomalies. Then she grew ill, a cancer eating her from within, and she could care for him no more.

At first the Royal Physician pretended he had no time for me, that he could not help. But once I insisted and told him a little more than I wanted to, his curiosity was piqued enough that he came back with me. As soon as he saw Frey, he dosed him with something from a syringe. Immediately the seizures ceased, and several days later, Frey woke up.

I was so grateful, and saw Pozzi weekly for Frey's treatments after that. I staged Alban Verani's disappearance, letting that last remnant of him fall away. I don't know how, as I was always very careful, but the Royal Physician discovered that I was Alban, though he never asked me to investigate for him. Not for a long time, in any case.

When he finally did, I was hesitant. Spying on youths, little more than children? Pozzi said they were runaways, but he made no promises to return them to their parents. I took the case because I was curious as much as because I owed him for Frey's life.

Once, though, when I was waiting in the front rooms of Pozzi's apartment while Frey was being dosed, I went snooping. Sneaking into his spare office, I rifled through the locked drawers of his filing cabinet, careful not to disturb anything.

And it was there that I discovered old medical records dating back years. And on one of them was my wife's name.

He was the Royal Physician then, but he still owned a practice in Imachara that specialized in prenatal and neonatal care. The same practice Andrea had gone to.

I'd never seen him. He'd never treated her personally, as far as I knew, but he'd overseen her medication. I remembered going to the practice, watching Andrea pulling back her sleeve as the nurse administered a needle, right in the crook of her elbow, with something Pozzi had told them to give her.

It took a long time, and a lot more digging, but eventually I found out the truth: Pozzi had done something to Frey in the womb. I don't know what. Frey probably would still have been weak and had seizures. His leg muscles might still have atrophied enough that he couldn't walk. I have an uncle with the same condition. I don't fully know what Pozzi did to my son. But I do know that, had Pozzi left my wife alone, Frey would not have scales. Or horns.

The memories that had illustrated the story faded, and the backs of my eyes were dark once again. I opened my eyes and looked at Lily Verre in horror.

'Yes,' she said. 'I'm certain he made Frey a Chimaera. And, in all likelihood, he did something to you as well. Kindled latent powers, or created them to begin with. The Royal Physician is experimenting on you, my son, and probably others. I don't know why, or to what purpose.'

I couldn't speak. Neither could Cyan. Even Drystan was struck silent. Why would Pozzi do this? He was clearly not afraid of Chimaera, like Timur and his ilk. But to create and bring them back? Cyan was nearing twenty. He'd been doing this for a long time.

'This is why you can trust me,' Lily said, her voice shaking with emotion. 'He changed my son without my consent. He then had the gall to pretend he was helping me, when truly he was manipulating me as neatly as a marionette. He doesn't know that I've found this out, or I sure as Styx hope not. I'll help you take him down, and I'll delight in it.'

If she was lying, she was a master actor. I thought of her son again. His hairless head, the dark green skin, the shimmer of scales. If Pozzi had done this without her consent to her child, that would make her despise him to her very core.

And if the rest were true? Pozzi told me he'd found me as a baby, left on his doorstep. If that was truly what had happened, had my birth mother, whoever she was, left me there because she knew Pozzi had done something to me during her pregnancy? What about Cyan? Riley and Batheo was often based in Imachara, never travelling as much as R. H. Ragona's Circus of Magic. Had Pozzi, or a doctor in his employ, treated Cyan's mother during her pregnancy? So many questions that we'd probably never know the answers to.

I reached out tentatively to Cyan and Drystan, shielding my thoughts as best I could.

What do you think?

Cyan's lips thinned. *I honestly have no idea. I want to believe her, but what if she deliberately crafted a tale that would win our sympathy? And if he wants to destroy Chimaera, why is he also creating them? Creating . . . us.* Cyan shivered.

Drystan's thoughts were hesitant, still uncomfortable with the fact that we could hear him at all. *It's a pretty tale, and I think much of it is true, but not all of it. She still has secrets she's keeping from us. Too much to hope that you did pry deeper into her mind, Cyan?*

She narrowed his eyes at him. *I told her I wouldn't, so I didn't.*

We both heard Drystan's mental sigh. *Moral codes are so inconvenient at times.*

I shot him a look. *I think we need her help, but, like pretty much everyone else in our lives, we won't trust her.*

Joy, Cyan thought. *More balancing acts.* She sent an image of her juggling eggs, and then them all breaking on the ground with a wet splat.

Cute. Drystan's thought was wry with amusement.

Lily watched our silent conversation, her face impassive.

'All right,' I said, speaking for the group. 'We're in. Where do we start?'

Lily smiled and leaned forward. 'Oh, my sweet dears,' she said in the affected voice Lily Verre had used when we first met her, before returning to her normal voice. 'I thought you'd never ask. Next time you're at Pozzi's, you need to steal some Elixir.'

Drystan laughed.

We turned to him.

'Just doesn't seem that easy, is all,' he said, though a smile still played around his mouth.

What is it? Was he amused because Anisa had instructed us to do the same?

Later, he replied, with the slightest glance at Lily.

'It won't be,' she said. 'I'm always in the room with Frey now when I visit. I wish now, so much, that I'd kept spare Elixir, but Pozzi made sure I'd run out. I don't like to leave him alone with my son. I don't have the chance. But you could do it. You wait with Micah sometimes, don't you, Drystan Hornbeam? I'm sure you could spirit some away.'

He stiffened at the use of his full name. 'Don't call me that,' he said, his voice tight.

She smiled sweetly. 'Of course, you were stricken from the family tree. Must have slipped my mind.'

I didn't like the power play between them. Drystan's face was blandly polite, but underneath he was furious. She had so carelessly played another card in her hand, showing that she knew, and probably had known for quite some time, exactly who Drystan was. His family still had a case open for finding him, though he was the estranged son they were ashamed to speak about. I wanted to comfort him. Scaring him like that was not a smart move on her part. He'd never warm to her now.

And I worried what else Lily knew that she hadn't yet shared. How much she knew about me. 'Why do you want us to steal it?' I asked. Anisa wanted much the same thing, though in all my visits, I hadn't seen a way to open Pozzi's cabinet of curiosities without him knowing.

'I have someone who might be able to tell me what's in it. If we can find a way to recreate it, then we can break our dependence on Pozzi.'

'Or you can discover if it's making things worse,' Cyan said.

Lily met her eyes. 'Yes. Frey has powers, like both of you. They are very strong, and sometimes they can overwhelm him.'

'What can he do?' Cyan asked.

'Telepathy,' she said, with a nod at Cyan. 'Telekenesis. The ability to affect the weather, sometimes, or at least so I suspect.' Her features were pinched tight.

'My powers are stronger after I've been dosed,' I said, slowly. 'You think he's making that happen deliberately?'

'It could be. You're an experiment as well. He wants to know what is possible. No matter who he has to hurt to find out.' Lily's lip curled. 'And he won't get away with it.'

There was a call from the other room. 'Mum!' The feeling of warmth from that room strengthened in my mind.

We all froze.

'You may as well come and meet him.' Lily went to the bedroom, opened the door. We followed her. Unlike the unremarkable and sombre lounge, the bedroom was cheery, full of bright colours. There was a bookshelf, plenty of toys and framed artwork, presumably by Frey.

Frey was in his wicker chair, his scaled fingers holding a crayon as he coloured. No, he wasn't colouring – he was practising his alphabet and writing simple sentences.

His eyes turned to us. They were a luminous green in the dim light of the lounge. I felt his power come off him in waves.

'Hello, sweet,' Lily said, her voice softening.

'Hello, Mum,' Frey said. His voice was soft, but sounded different to a normal voice. Almost as if it had a built-in echo.

Like Anisa.

'I've finished,' he said, proudly holding out his paper. Lily read the sentences copied from *Hestia's Fables*, and praised the illustrations he'd done in the corners. The handwriting and drawings were both much better than I could have achieved at his age.

'It's lovely, Frey,' she said, taking it from him as though it were precious.

Frey looked at us, wary but not fearful. 'Who are you?' he asked, his voice barely audible.

'Frey, this is Micah, Cyan, and Drystan. Remember, I told you that you might see them today? They're here to help me, and help you. You might see them around now and again. You needn't be frightened.'

'I'm not,' he said, but one hand went to his cheek, and he turned from us as though ashamed. How many strangers had he ever come across without being heavily veiled?

'Can I have more paper?' he asked.

Lily passed him a few more sheets. He began to write and draw again, as though we weren't there. Lily rested her hand on his shoulder and kissed the top of his head. He did not respond, but as we left the lounge, he looked up at us. I gave him a smile. One corner of his mouth quirked before he went back to his paper. It was something.

'He's shy,' Lily said when we were back in the lounge. 'You're the first new people he's met in quite some time, so he wasn't sure what to make of you. I have to keep him hidden. Especially after what happened at the Celestial Cathedral.'

'I understand.' I felt sorry for poor Frey. Locked away in that bedroom, no matter how bright and cheery it was. Never meeting anyone. Just like the Princess. And it was all possibly because of Pozzi.

It made me pity Lily, too, much as I didn't want to. But how difficult it must be, to raise a child who required a lot of caring on her own – or almost on her own.

'Who helps you with Frey?' I asked.

'I used to have a girl come to help me, but she married a merchant and they moved to Northern Temne. I'm here for him most of the time, but if I need to go out, I ring for Pozzi and he sends an assistant to help out.'

'Who is he?' I asked, though I suspected I knew the answer.

'His name is Kai. He's a student at the university and helps him from time to time. I don't trust him a whit, but he is good with Frey.'

Interesting. It was another way to keep tabs on Lily and her son between sessions, and a way to observe an experiment subject regularly.

'How can you stand to look at Pozzi?' I asked. 'How can you look at him and be civil, knowing what he might have done?'

'I honestly don't know how I manage,' she said. 'Sometimes I fear I'll snap and attack him. But I feel keeping him close is the wisest course. Find out what he's up to. Find out his weaknesses. And then take the bastard down.' She looked at us, grave. 'I am truly sorry for lying to you. For pretending to be someone I'm not. I didn't have much of a choice. I know it will take a lot for you to forgive that, if you ever can. But you have an ally in me.' Another pause. 'I ask that you not tell Maske that I am a Shadow just yet. I feel it should come from me.'

'Does he know . . . everything?' I asked, unsure how to phrase the question.

One of her eyebrows twitched. 'He knows everything except that I am a Shadow and that I have Frey. I have not lied to him about my past, and he has embraced it just as Andrea did. I am lucky to have him in my life, and I am aware that he does not deserve my lies. Sometimes life makes liars of us all. I can only hope he will forgive me.'

'We won't say anything,' Cyan said. 'But you should tell him sooner rather than later.'

'I will try. This I promise.' She led us to the door.

I wished Cyan, Drystan, and I could trust her. But we only trusted each other.

Back in the Penny Rookeries, everyone went to our bedroom. I took Anisa's Aleph and brought her forth. The early afternoon light filtered through her transparent body.

'Why did you laugh when Lily said we needed to steal Elixir?' I asked Drystan.

'I stole some already,' he said, a little sheepish.

'What?' I asked.

'Well, I stole it twice, to be precise,' he clarified.

That didn't help. 'When?' I asked.

He gazed between us. 'The looks on all your faces are absolutely priceless.' He spoke to me. 'Remember when we searched Elwood's, and we found that box of what you thought was Lerium?'

'Yes . . .'

'Hold on.' He went to his trunk, rummaged around, and then held out a vial. 'I liberated him of one.'

I licked my lips. 'Because you thought it was Lerium?'

He gave me a stern look. 'Look, I obviously haven't smoked it or injected it, so I didn't steal it for that reason.

It didn't look . . . right, and I thought it might be important.'

Cyan frowned at us, not quite understanding.

Can I tell her? I asked Drystan.

A tiny shrug of one shoulder, which meant I could, but he wouldn't relish more of his secrets being spilled.

Drystan used to be a Lerium addict, I told her, and she gave a nod.

I didn't know much about that period of his life, and he didn't like to speak of it. But the fact he'd stolen what could have been a drug without telling me made me nervous. What if he had taken it? Would one hit be enough to send him into full relapse?

'You said you stole it twice?'

'When I took you to Pozzi because of your fever. He asked me to leave so he could talk to you. I grew curious. My fingers accidentally slipped and opened his spirit cabinet.' He shrugged. 'Oops.'

He took out another vial, this time filled with little rocks of raw Elixir. 'I just took a bit from a nearly full vial. I figured he wouldn't miss it, unless he weighed it religiously.'

'Why didn't you tell us when Anisa asked us about it last time?' I asked.

'I don't trust you, Anisa,' he said, bluntly.

Silence fell.

Anisa's face was impassive.

It was more than that, I thought. He didn't want to admit to the stealing. He wanted to keep the secret to himself for a time, to see if he could solve it.

'I was trying to figure out how we could find out what it is first,' he said, confirming my suspicions. 'Have it tested on my own, then show it to everyone. But I haven't had much luck. There's plenty I could ask, but none that I would trust.'

'Are you going to let me see it now?' Anisa asked.

Drystan shrugged. 'Might as well, I guess.'

He set it down on a small table and Anisa went to it. She held her palms over it, closing her eyes and concentrating.

'It's Vestige, naturally, but it has . . . a lot of components,' she said. 'Too many memories and impressions for me to make sense of.'

'What a surprise,' Drystan said, taking it back. Anisa's gaze turned steely.

I couldn't help but agree with him. Oftentimes, it was when Anisa's powers would have been the most useful that they didn't work; or so she said.

'So are we going to give it to Lily? See if she can find anything?' Cyan asked, trying to break the tension.

Drystan shrugged. 'I don't think we should just yet. Get to know her a bit better. Observe Pozzi this weekend at the palace, see if there's anything else we can discover. I still want to try to find out more about Lily Verre, and her alternate past as Alban Verani.'

Drystan slipped the vials back into his pocket. I didn't like him keeping them. I was high after my injections, and at the end of each week, I craved the next dose. The Elixir Drystan stole could have the same effect, or be even stronger on him. And he wasn't Chimaera – what if it was extra dangerous for him? Yet if I took them away from him, he'd think I didn't trust his ability to remain clean. And it'd been years. I had no way to know if he would fall hard and fast again. It felt traitorous to doubt him.

Elixir. The Princess. The Kashura Foresters, and a growing fear of Chimaera. The Royal Physician perhaps creating Chimaera. A grave robber stealing corpses, perhaps of other Chimaera. Lily Verre and her son. Anisa's prophecy. My mother. The pressure sometimes threatened to crush me. It was too much.

The sun set, the golden glow resting on the cracked plaster of the walls. I leaned against the windowsill. The sky was aflame in orange and yellow, the clouds tinged dark purple and red. The flecks of mica in the granite buildings sparkled in the low sun and tinged the grey with dusky pink.

I turned from the bright sun just as the door opened.

My brother, Cyril, entered. 'Maske said you were in here . . .' he began, and then his voice trailed away. He wasn't looking at me, but beyond, at the transparent figure of Anisa, the damselfly ghost.

I tried in vain to come up with an explanation that didn't sound completely ludicrous, but my mind was blank.

'Hello, Cyril Laurus,' Anisa said, shattering any hope of me pretending she was a projection from the circus, unable to speak or reason.

His mouth dropped open comically.

'I'll explain,' Anisa said, clearly relishing his shock. 'I

am called Anisa. You recognize me from the circus, where I played a monster in that ridiculous pantomime play. Your brother-sister knew what I truly was, or at least a little, and he took me from the circus when he fled. I am a Chimaera, and have lived more lives than you can possibly imagine.' She smiled, but it was the furthest thing from reassuring.

'Gene?' my brother asked me, slipping back to the name he'd grown up calling me. 'What in the world?'

'Cyril,' I said, weakly. 'There are certain things I must tell you.'

13

THE HOSPITAL

When a child under twelve is injured, it's common prac-
tice for any child present to "call upon the fairies" to help
heal them. The other child or children will circle the
injured child thrice, chanting "sprites, take flight, we need
your might to spite the blight!" Sometimes the child will
kiss the other on the forehead; a target for the fairy to
know where to sprinkle their magic dust.

— A History of Ellada and its Colonies, PROFESSOR
CAED CEDAR, Royal Snakewood University

I turned off Anisa, and Cyril's eyes bulged as the Phantom
Damselfly turned to smoke and disappeared back into her
disc. Drystan and Cyan wisely went to the lounge to leave
me to speak with my brother alone.

Cyril looked at me, hurt I'd kept this from him.

'I'm different,' I began.

Cyril frowned. 'Yes, I know.'

'I don't just mean my . . .' I gestured to the area between

my legs. 'You know I was never sick growing up. Rarely hurt myself, and if I did, it healed quicker.'

Cyril nodded, slowly. 'I remember.'

'It's even more than that. I've started having . . . abilities. And the first time I realized was when I saw the Phantom Damselfly in the circus.'

Cyril opened his mouth, but I held up my hand. 'Please. This is hard. Let me get it out all at once, and then I'll answer any questions.'

'All right.'

I took a deep breath. 'When I saw her, she was in a haunted tent, and they ended up closing it down because she frightened people so much. But she didn't terrify anyone as much as me. When I saw her, she spoke, calling me a Kedi. No one else could hear her. I thought I'd gone insane. When she was in the circus pantomime she stared at me every night, as if waiting for me to ask her all the questions I had. When I left the circus, I had to take her with me. It was almost as if I didn't have a choice.

'I learned more about Anisa. She's Chimaera, Cyril. From the Alder age. She's ancient. She knows so much, though she keeps a lot of it to herself. She frightens me, but I think I do trust her. She has her own agenda, but she cares for me, Cyan, and even Drystan and Maske, in her own way.'

I paused, sending a thought downstairs: *Can I tell my brother about you?*

A few heartbeats of silence. *If you think he'll keep it secret.*

He will.

'Then Cyan came. And she's different, too. Cyan and I . . . we can read minds. Her much more so than me. I can only glean a little, here and there. We're Chimaera too.'

Cyril didn't blink. But as promised, he didn't interrupt. I knew he wanted to, the questions building, but he pressed his lips together so they wouldn't escape.

I told him the rest – how Anisa had sent me visions from the past, how she feared the Chimaera that re-emerged could be targeted and hurt. Someone was trying to destroy us, and she feared that, like last time, the world itself could burn. That we had to stop this blurred man she'd seen in her visions, though we did not know how. I told him about my growing illness, how the doctor who gave me to our parents turned out to be none other than the Royal Physician and now I had to see him every week. As I told the tale, Cyril's eyes grew rounder until they were nearly bulging. When I finished, I was strangely deflated. I pressed my own lips together.

'This . . . this is a lot to take in,' Cyril said.

I nodded.

'It's hard to know where to start.'

'Take your time.'

And he did. We sat in silence in the growing darkness. Cyril's head was bent, and I stared at his crown of curly blonde hair. He worried his big hands in his lap.

'I don't know how you've dealt with all of this,' he said.

My eyes filled with tears. I'd just told him impossible things, and in all likelihood he should have thought me cracked. But instead, his first thought was how difficult it was for me.

'Lord and Lady, you're the best brother,' I managed, sniffling.

He gave a strangled laugh and held out his arms. I went to them. Cyril gave such wonderful hugs – firm and warm and safe.

'You can really read minds?'

'Well, like I said, Cyan is a lot better than me. I've only received a couple of impressions.' *But I can speak to people like this.*

He jerked. 'Holy Styx.'

'I know.'

Cyril shook his head. 'What does it mean, though? There were the Chimaera at the Celestial Cathedral. How many of you are there?'

'We don't know. They're definitely returning, and we're not sure if it's by chance, deliberate creation, or both. Whatever it means, the world will change. The three Chimaera called for acceptance, and at least two of them died for the crime of asking for understanding. More out there might not be afraid, but it'll be hard to convince any others to go public with the Kashura's violent discrimination. Everything is hanging over us like a thundercloud. Any moment, the lightning will strike and the floods will come.'

'That's melodramatic, Micah.'

I half-laughed, half-choked. 'A little. But doesn't feel like that much of an exaggeration.'

He broke away from my embrace and grew still, eyes widening.

'What is it?' I asked.

'You can read minds.'

'Ye . . . es. I thought we'd established that.'

'You need to come with me to the hospital.'

I swallowed. 'Why?'

'To see if you can reach Mother and wake her up.'

My mouth opened. Closed. The thought had not even occurred to me. The day of the explosion, seeing her had been enough of a shock, and I'd avoided thinking of her as much as possible, to dampen the tangled feelings I had. Could I reach her and bring her back?

Cyril looked at the clock. 'We still have time before visiting hours are over.' He grabbed my hand. 'We're going.'

I didn't want to go. I didn't want to see her. That one glimpse of her in her sickbed had been more than enough. But Cyril was right.

I had to try.

But before we left, I knocked on Cyan's bedroom door. She grabbed her coat. My fledgling abilities might not wake up my mother, but if Cyan couldn't succeed, perhaps no one could.

The nurse showed us to Mother's ward right away, and then hurried off to her next patient. The ward was still full of people recovering from the attacks, but our corner was quiet. I reached up and pulled the privacy curtain around the bed.

My mother looked exactly as she had the last time I saw her. Shrunken. Subdued. I didn't sense anything from her. How could either Cyan or I hope to reach her?

We clustered around the bed. Cyril pushed an errant strand of hair back from her face. He'd never dare to do something like that if she was awake. At the moment she might be a weak, sleeping lamb, but I remembered her as a fire-breathing dragon.

'Has Father been up to visit?'

Cyril's head bowed. 'Just once, right after it happened. He keeps saying he'll come up more often but . . . well, you know how Father is.'

Yes. Father was never there. Not even for his wife.

My fingers fidgeted, and then I steeled myself and took her hand. Her skin was papery and cool to the touch. The rosacea on her cheeks from her frequent drinking had calmed.

Cyril had hope painted starkly on his face. But I didn't know if we'd be able to do anything for her.

I tried first, questing with my newfound abilities. Her coma was like the deepest sleep, as though her mind was encased in Penglass and I could only slip off the sides. Letting go of her hand, I shook my head.

I was relieved. I didn't want to touch her mind. What if I reached her? I'd be hit with the anger, the disappointment, and the guilt she surely felt about me.

Cyan took her hand next. She closed her eyes, becoming still as stone. I sensed her reaching and as her mind quested, I thought I saw the echo of that web of light I'd seen on the night of the fire at the Museum of Mechanical

Antiquities. A tiny line appeared between her eyes. The minutes ticked past. Cyril and I did not speak, for fear of breaking her concentration. Sweat appeared on Cyan's brow.

Eventually she broke away, her eyes opening, gasping as if coming up for air.

'I thought I was close at one point, but she's in too deep. I couldn't reach her.' She collapsed against the chair. 'I'm sorry,' she said. She looked exhausted, and after this she'd go home and sleep for ten hours straight to recover. Gratitude welled up within me, that she'd do this for us.

'Try again, Micah,' Cyril urged. 'Once more. Just in case.'

I closed my eyes. I came across that barrier again, smooth and hard. I pushed against it. I pushed harder, as though I smashed against impenetrable glass. I stopped. My energy ebbed, and a headache pounded at my body's temples.

And then I stopped trying so hard.

I eased against the barrier. And then I melted into and through it. It was as though I floated in a void, darkness cut through with threads of blue, like Penglass. Up ahead was a shadowy figure. My mother, wearing her most fashionable dress, with her corset tight, her best bustle, those white gloves and her favourite parasol. She meandered through the darkness as though strolling through the park on a summer's day.

Mother! I called out.

She paused, then kept walking.

Mother! I called again.

She turned towards me, her face blurred by the swirling blue light. She raised a hand, but hesitantly.

The blue light swirled, brighter and stranger. I blinked and my mother was gone. I was back on the outside of whatever barrier lay around her mind.

Cyril shook me. He was above me, strands of blonde hair falling into his eyes.

'I'm on the ground,' I said, dazed.

'You fell off your chair,' Cyan said, her worried face appearing next to my brother's.

My shoulder hurt. Cyril helped me back to my seat. 'Anything?'

'Sort of.' I told them both what had happened, keeping my voice low.

Cyan tried one last time, but after a few minutes, she came back. 'I couldn't even get past the barrier.'

'Have you ever come across anything like that before?' I asked her.

'Never.'

Cyril slumped in defeat. 'I knew it was a small chance,' he said. 'But I couldn't help but hope . . .'

Cyan gave us a sympathetic look.

If she's in that deep . . . she began.

I know. I know.

Then she might never wake up.

Cyril was silent on the way back to the Penny Rookeries.

'Thank you both for trying,' he said in the entryway. The carriage waited below to take him back to his shared flat by the Celestial Cathedral.

'I only wish we could be of more help,' Cyan said.

'Maybe . . . if we keep trying, we'll be able to break through.'

We all thought it unlikely, but Cyril thanked her just the same with his impeccable manners.

After Cyan went to her room, my brother lingered, squeezing my shoulder. 'I came here to tell you something earlier, before . . . well, before I saw a ghost and learned you and Cyan are magical.'

Put like that, it sounded rather silly. 'What was it?'

'I received an invitation to your magic show tomorrow at the palace, for the Princess.'

'How'd you manage that?' I'd told him about it as soon as we found out, but because it was only the very inner circle of royalty and nobility attending, it didn't seem possible he'd be able to go.

'Remember Tara Cypress?'

I resisted the urge to make a face. We'd never been close, and I'd never particularly got along with her.

'She's a lady's maid at court to someone invited, and she managed to find me an invitation as well. I'll have to get there early and have every inch of me searched by the palace guards, but I can be there.'

'That's wonderful!' Talking about this was far easier than discussing what had just happened – or, rather, failed to happen – at the hospital. So I told him about what I had noticed at the rehearsal, the way the Princess had shimmered. 'You'll be closer to her than we will – can you watch out, see if you notice anything as well?'

'Lord and Lady, Gene, you think the Princess is a . . . Chimaera?'

'Maybe.'

'I'll see what I notice, and try and eavesdrop on the other people there.'

I didn't like getting him involved, but we needed all the help we could get. 'Thank you, Cyril.'

'Anytime, little sister.' He frowned. 'Or brother. Sibling?'

'Call me what you like. They all fit.'

I gave him a last hug and ran up the stairs before he could mention Mother again.

14

THE FETE AT THE PALACE

I couldn't believe I was able to go to the Snakewood Palace for one of their summer fetes, Winnie. I wish you could have been there to see it. It was the most magnificent display I'd ever seen in my life, and I don't know how any celebration could ever top it. But it must be possible, for this was just a "small party", as they kept calling it, not a birthday or other grand event. But the food, and the glass globes, the music, the gowns! It made our debutante ball at Sicion's Ballroom look like little more than a country hall with some garlands thrown about. I still can't believe my luck. When no one offered for me after the debutante ball, I thought my life was over. But now I'm lady's maid to my cousin, and perhaps here at court I'll find myself a husband after all!
— Letter from Lady Tara Cypress to
Lady Winifred Poplar

From outside, you'd never have guessed a royal party would be underway that night.

I'd passed the palace before when celebrations were on. Lights glowing from every window, music drifting down onto the streets, more lights speckled through the trees of the grand promenade. But now, under the threat of Kashura Forester attacks, all was quiet. Wise, too, for such ostentatious displays and blatant waste of taxpayer's money would not be well regarded.

We entered through a side gate and endured the customary searches by stoical-faced guards. As before, we slipped Anisa's Aleph through security.

Doctor Pozzi came to greet us and take us to the stage. He was perfectly groomed, as usual. It was the first time I'd seen him since Lily Verre told us what he had done to her. I shored the walls within my mind, not wanting him to catch even the smallest stray thought. I wished tearing down his walls and unwinding every secret curled in the coils of his mind was possible.

'I'm looking forward to the performance,' he said. 'I'm sure it'll be as fantastic as all the rest.'

Smiling at him, hoping it didn't look as tight and strained as it felt, I told him we needed to finish setting up.

'Of course, of course.' He left us, to my great relief, and we hurried to finish preparing for the show. From behind the curtains we peeked out as several members of Ellada's social elite entered the ballroom, sipping wine, nibbling food plucked from silver trays held by palace servants, and murmuring softly amongst themselves. I recognized a few of them. Lord Wesley Cinnabari, who had been at a séance we'd performed for the Lord and Lady Elmbark on the Night of the Dead near midwinter. That had been one of our first large bookings with the nobility, and that séance and the others that followed had helped us finance the duel with Penn Taliesin. There was Tara Cypress – we'd been presented at our debutante ball together an age ago, along with Lady Winifred Poplar. There was my brother Cyril, trying to blend in, keeping close to Tara. There were a few young girls I didn't recognize, around the Princess's age. In the middle of them was the Princess Royal herself, wearing a pink gown sparkling with crystals, her security guards never far away. She seemed subdued, quiet, barely speaking to the other girls. Her uncle, the Steward, was laughing and moving around the room greeting guests.

The enGlamoured Drystan, cheek to cheek with me as we looked through the gap in the curtains, suddenly stiffened.

'I didn't think he'd be here,' Drystan whispered.

I followed the direction of his gaze: his father. Lord Nigel Hornbeam. The resemblance was obvious, his features were echoed in Drystan – pale hair and eyes, strong jawline.

'Are you all right?' I asked, resting my hand on his shoulder. 'Do you want to sit this one out?' Even as I asked, my mind tried to plan an alternate show. We'd lost Oli as a stagehand and we couldn't use Cyril. We could do it without Drystan, but it would be trickier.

'No,' Drystan said, touching the Glamour around his neck as if for reassurance. 'I'm not all right, but he won't recognize me with this. He'd never expect me here.'

With Pozzi's Elixir enhancing my gifts I was even more sensitive to his emotions than usual, feeling Drystan's pain almost as acutely as he did. My throat closed; panic thrummed through me. It reignited my own feelings of displacement and guilt: the part of me that still regretted cutting my family out of my life, too.

Maske came onto the small but grand gilt-and-marble stage to introduce the show. He would be performing the bulk of the tricks tonight, while we had supporting roles. It was understandable that he'd want the majority of the limelight: performing for royalty in the palace for a private party was a career highlight. Even his adversary Taliesin had never managed that.

'When I was a young lad,' Maske began the act, 'I thought there were no magicians in my family. My father was a woodworker, and his father before him, and his father before him . . . or so I thought.' He paced the stage slowly, as if lost in memories.

I manoeuvred the lantern, slotting in the small silhouettes Drystan had carved from flat pieces of wood and moving them slowly left to right, so that there was a constant stream of shadows accompanying Maske's tale.

'I was working late into the night. Most of the time, my father created furniture to sell, but he always taught me that we should master true art from the wood. So I was carving a cat, looking at my little pet sleeping in front of the fire.'

With easy sleight of hand, a little carved cat appeared in his palms. He made it disappear and then asked a member of the audience to stand and pat their pocket. The volunteer – the Treasurer of Ellada – took out the carved figurine, incredulous, to scattered applause.

Maske sat down in a chair on the stage, pantomiming nodding off to sleep. 'I was so tired that night, and fell asleep in the middle of carving. I was lucky I did not cut myself.

'At first, I thought I dreamed, for there in front of me was a great mage.'

Behind the scenes I crashed the cymbals, and Maske threw a powder that flashed bright green. When the smoke cleared, Drystan, nearly hidden by a huge cloak, appeared before him. Even beneath the Glamour's illusion, it was clear that his features were pinched with tension. Yet he performed perfectly.

'I am your great-great-grandfather, Jasper Maske,' Drystan declared.

'You look a little young,' Maske said, and the audience chuckled. 'You lie, or I am dreaming. My family has been naught but humble woodcarvers for generations.'

'Are you so sure? The magic calls to you, doesn't it?' Drystan asked. 'It sings to you, deep in your blood. It's always been there, and it always will be. I am here to unlock it.'

Drystan twirled, his cloak flaring out behind him, showing his magician's suit. He levitated in the air and pressed his hands to either side of Maske's head, looking deep into his eyes. With another flash of smoke he ascended to the gridiron above stage, leaving Maske alone.

The rest of the story was Maske learning his 'magic' and delighting the audience with his tricks. As it was a smaller stage, he couldn't perform as many grand-scale illusions as at the Kymri Theatre, but his arsenal of prestidigitation was impressive nonetheless. A shower of coins fell from his bare palms, even with his sleeves rolled up. He made a rose bush grow from a seed he planted, and water pour from a vase that appeared to be empty.

He disappeared into the spirit cabinet, and reappeared at the back of the audience. I smiled. It was one of the earliest tricks we had learned, and though I had not liked being tied within the cabinet, the fact that Drystan had been crouched in the dark with me, close enough to kiss, had made it easier to bear.

Peppered throughout the performance were card tricks of all sorts. Maske flitted through the small audience, asking them to choose a card and always having it appear in an interesting way. He'd ask the participant to throw the entire deck in the air and stab the chosen card with a small knife. Another card appeared within a block of ice, and still another in a woman's handbag on the other side of the room. Even I, who knew the truth behind every trick, could not help but be impressed by the ease with which he performed them. There was no hesitation, no awkwardness. Everyone knew it was sleight of hand, yet no one could catch him.

Behind the scenes Cyan and I pulled levers, provided sound effects, and did all we could to bring the show to life.

After all the tricks were done, Drystan returned, dressed as Maske's supposed long-dead relative. 'You see,' he said, with a sweep of his cloak. 'Destiny cannot be denied. A magician I was, and a magician you are.'

Maske bowed to his 'great-great-grandfather', and Drystan bowed back. The curtains fell.

Everyone broke into applause, but my eyes didn't leave the Princess. The dark ringlets of her hair bounced as she clapped. Her smile was wide. That was what I'd wanted. To make her as happy as she'd been the day of the magicians' duel, rather than the sombre girl who had walked in here.

After we'd bowed and left the stage, we packed up our gear.

'I miss our theatre,' Maske said glumly.

'I know,' I said. We all did. 'How much longer until the repairs are finished on the Kymri?'

'Another month at least,' he said. 'And it'll cost every copper we made on the sale of the Spectre Theatre. I'll never short-change my insurance again.'

'Good call.'

When we finished packing, we mingled in the ballroom. The nobility came to congratulate us on the performance. Maske glowed in the approval of such illustrious company.

We ate a few of the leftover treats, but before long most of the guests left to attend the main feast. Maske had been invited to join them, but not us.

The Steward was about to leave for the feast, but paused with the Princess, accompanied as always by her guards, and Pozzi to speak to us.

'That was an excellent—' the Steward began, and then stopped short, staring at the Princess in dismay. She'd gone rigid, hands against her sides, mouth open as if in a silent scream.

'I'm sorry, Uncle,' she gasped. 'I've been trying to contain it all night, but—'

The Steward ran to her, but he was too late. The Princess fell to her knees, and her skin shimmered as it had on the day of our rehearsal.

Drystan, Cyan, and I all froze. Around my neck, my Glamour grew hot, and then there was a snap of pressure. Drystan's disguise was gone, as mine must be. Guards surged forward, grabbing our upper arms in case we were a threat to the Princess.

Her disguise was gone as well.

She sprawled on the ground, panting. The Glamour hidden under her own dress had fallen out, swinging from a gold chain around her neck.

No longer was she the girl with pink cheeks and dark ringlets. Instead her skin was tinged cobalt blue, smooth and poreless. Her hair was short, dark blue stubble against her scalp. Her features were sharper – the blades of her cheekbones, her brow, her pointed chin. Her eyes were all pupil, with no whites or irises. She grimaced and her teeth were sharp, the canines pointed. Though the same height as her Glamour image, her neck and fingers were thinner, her limbs more slender.

The Steward looked unchanged. Either his Glamour had held, or he didn't require one.

'Lord and Lady,' Drystan breathed. Pozzi knelt beside the Princess, prepping a syringe. He was not surprised. Cyan, Drystan, and I exchanged a look. It was Elixir.

I decided to chance reaching out to Pozzi with my mind – the first time I had ever willingly chosen to do so. *Is she the same as me? Is she Chimaera?* Yet I had sensed no warmth from her, as I did with Chimaera.

No. He pushed me out of his mind completely, as if slamming a door in my face.

The Steward watched the doctor avidly as he tapped the air bubbles from the syringe and pressed the needle into the crook of the Princess's arm. Her head lolled back, and she panted loudly. Even her tongue was tinged blue.

If she wasn't Chimaera, what was she?

I couldn't help but be glad that Maske wasn't here for this. The three of us were used to bizarre sights, but we'd protected him from the strangeness of the world as much as we could.

The medicine began to take hold over the Princess. The lines on her forehead smoothed. She rested her head against Pozzi's shoulder for a moment, gathering strength.

Then she looked up at us and met our gazes. I kept my face blank. She wasn't repulsive. On the contrary, she had an ethereal sort of beauty, as if she were a strange, fey creature of old. . . and the fey were based on the . . .

Alder, Cyan whispered in our minds.

I should have seen it. The Alder had created the Chimaera, possibly the humans, and the Vestige we now depended upon. They'd vanished without a trace centuries ago. Some said they died with the Chimaera, but I knew from Anisa's visions that they'd disappeared into the stars. The Princess looked a little like the Alder I'd seen in those visions. Two Alder had come to give Anisa the charge of a small Kedi, Dev, untold centuries ago. Yet the Princess looked far more human than those two tall creatures had.

The guards stared straight ahead, as if they saw this sort of thing every day. Perhaps they did.

I chanced another look at the Steward. He still looked the same, and I spied no chain around his neck. No – there was a change. The barest darkening of his eyes, a blue tinge to his fingers, his fingernails a deep purple, almost black.

Our monarchy was not human, and they were not Chimaera. What were they?

'You cannot say a word about this to anyone,' the Steward of Ellada said, looking at us. 'Not a word.'

He's wondering if he should kill us to keep the secret, Cyan said.

You maybe didn't need to share that with us right this very moment. I wanted to throw up.

'They're trustworthy,' Pozzi assured him, and the Steward gave us another considering look.

The Princess held the Glamour pendant in her blueish fingers, turning it over. 'It's broken,' she whispered.

'We have others,' her uncle said, kneeling down beside her. His voice was gruff, cold. It chilled me. The Princess's brow furrowed, and she looked as if she would cry.

She looked up at me with her midnight-dark gaze. *I can't cry*, she thought at me clearly, gesturing to her strange eyes.

No one else heard her but me. I couldn't even feel surprised. She'd just been dosed with Elixir and could speak mind-to-mind, like Chimaera. Did the Elixir strengthen any abilities she had, like it did mine?

'It'll be easier to keep them quiet, considering who and what they are,' Pozzi said.

The Steward gave him a sharp look.

Don't, I sent to Pozzi, but it bounced uselessly off his walls.

'There's a few reasons I'd trust them,' he continued, smiling serenely. 'One: they are Chimaera, the Anthi kind, and are hiding their nature after the attacks on the three creatures near the Celestial Cathedral. Two: these ones –' he gestured at Drystan and me – 'are the escaped clowns from the circus at the end of last summer.'

'The ones who set off the Penglass?' The Steward bristled, taking a step back. The guards gripped us tighter, until I winced. 'And you knew both these facts and still brought them here to perform in front of Princess Nicolette?'

The Princess looked at us in fear, her eyes wide.

'Micah is a patient, and thus I protected him under doctor-patient confidentiality. The Penglass behaved strangely, but there have been no other occurrences,' Pozzi said smoothly. 'If they say anything, we can expose who and what they are, and no one would believe the word of felons. They have no proof, and you know how the public currently feel about Chimaera.'

The Steward's jaw worked. 'Well I do. I should never have let them speak to the people. A moment of weakness. Or a hope that if they'd accept those three, they'd perhaps accept us, if they discovered what we truly were.' His gaze sharpened. 'We cannot afford even rumours.'

'We'll do more for you than keep our silence,' Drystan said. 'We'll do everything within our power to help you, however the crown needs.' As ever, Drystan was quick to find a way to turn the situation to our advantage. Or, at least, for us not to be killed or thrown into prison.

The Steward didn't dismiss the offer out of hand, which I found interesting. He could have scoffed and called us children, but he didn't. He instead considered us honestly: the students of Jasper Maske, the greatest magician in Ellada. Able to gain entry to the most prestigious houses, as well as the parlours of lower merchants. Good enough to entertain royalty.

I hated that Pozzi had thrown down the chips of our past on whatever he was betting.

'This one is strong, even stronger than the others,' Pozzi said, gesturing at me.

What others? I knew of Frey, but his powers were far stronger than mine. Was Pozzi protecting Frey? Cyan was also stronger than me, and hopefully adept enough at hiding her powers that Pozzi didn't know all she could do.

The Steward nodded. 'The Princess's life is in your hands, then. For if word of this reached the Kashura, they would find a way to expose her. Us. And the Ellada you know would crumble to dust in a heartbeat.'

He knew the true name of the Foresters' violent arm. 'But what is going on?' I asked, finding my voice.

The Steward hesitated.

'You can trust them, Uncle,' the Princess said, her voice ringing with the prescient certainty I had heard sometimes from Anisa. The Chimaera was in her Aleph, hidden within one of the cases below stage. I was sure she was listening, waiting, watching, as ever.

The Steward gave the slightest nod. The guards released

me, Drystan, and Cyan. My upper arms tingled unpleasantly.

'I'm part Alder,' she said. 'All of the Snakewood family is.' She was only seven, but she sounded older, as if in shedding her disguise she had also shed the persona of a young child. 'Centuries passed and we started looking human again, just like you. But then, a few generations ago, it started changing. I look more different than my parents, or so my Uncle says.' Her parents had died before she could even hope to remember them.

Part Alder. I remembered what I'd read in one of Professor Cedar's books in the Kymri Theatre library:

> *They say magic left the world with the Chimaera and the Alder. Whether they perished or abandoned us for the stars, the magic has leeched from the earth and left us only its scattered remnants. Its Vestige. They say perhaps, if the Chimaera and the Alder ever return, magic will as well.*

I supposed magic was as good an explanation as any for what we could do.

'I've always had to wear these. Even when I was a baby,' the Princess continued, holding the broken Glamour in her hands.

She'd always had to hide. Always had to hide the truth. Like Lily Verre's son, Frey. Like I had to, in a way.

If someone had found out about me, the worst that would have likely befallen me was that I wouldn't have been able to marry. She could lose a crown, maybe even her life. It was all too easy to imagine her and Frey hated and hurt because they looked physically different, like Juliet and her two friends.

The Elixir in her veins had taken full effect on the Princess. Power emanated from her. She was just as strong as Frey, if not more so.

'Are the other Alder really gone, then?' Cyan asked.

'As far as we know, we're the last. I suspect there may be more in hiding, their abilities latent,' the Princess said.

Just like the Chimaera are hiding, I thought.

'Do you feel better, my Princess?' Pozzi asked. 'Any ill effects?'

'I'm quite all right, thank you, Royal Physician,' she said, primly. 'I am very hungry, though.'

The Steward laughed, but it was hollow and didn't reach his eyes. He nodded to one of the guards, who turned smartly on his heel and left. The Steward took the Princess's hand.

'Come, then. Let's take you to your rooms, and your maid will bring you up a tray.' The Princess's hand was lax in his, as if she'd pull away if she could.

He looked at us again. 'I'm sure I'll be seeing you again soon. I may have need of you.'

He's thinking that we could perform for people and then report back all we see and hear, Cyan reported. She could read the Steward's mind more easily than that of his Royal Physician. Cyan was being delicate. The Steward wanted us to spy for the crown. Life was never dull for us, that was certain.

'Goodbye,' the Princess said. 'I did enjoy your magic

show very much.' She paused. 'And thank you for not screaming. Once, a maid saw me and she shrieked so loudly I thought my ears would burst.'

The Steward's jaw tightened. I wondered what had happened to the maid.

A guard returned with a small bag, which he passed to the Steward with a deep bow. The Steward opened it and put the new Glamour around the Princess's neck. She closed her eyes and concentrated. The blue tinge faded from her skin. Dark hair grew from her scalp in a bristle and then lengthened into ringlets that fell to the shoulders. She appeared to gain enough flesh that she no longer looked as frail. Her eyes transformed from all black to bright green, eyebrows appearing above them as if drawn on.

'That's . . . not how Glamours usually work,' I managed. They usually had to be pre-programmed, and it took ages to get them right. When they were turned on, the new illusion settled over your skin in an instant, rather than almost . . . growing on, as it had with the Princess.

'I can control it myself, even a little without the Glamour, sometimes,' the Princess said. 'It helps me concentrate, though. Good evening, and thank you again.'

We bowed low, grateful it helped hide our incredulous faces. They took their leave of us, a few guards remaining. The future monarch and her Steward were human and Alder. If the world were to find out, Ellada could well descend into chaos. Some would worship them as gods or saints. Others would seek to destroy them. I had no idea what the Kashura would do. Chimaera, they hated, but they'd named themselves after an Alder group. What of the royal families in the other islands – were they the same? Alder, Chimaera, Kashura. As if the past were repeating itself again.

The guards stood, still as if made from stone. I was uncomfortable that they had witnessed the whole scene. Pozzi noticed my nervous gaze.

They won't remember any of this, he sent me.

I flinched at him in my mind, but I was curious enough to answer: *what?*

Palace guards agree to look at a Lethe after any shift where they overhear any secrets. That'll happen on this day for certain.

I shuddered. A Lethe was a pendant, often with a stylized snake on its face, and it could erase memories. Whoever held the Lethe controlled which memories were affected. If the person didn't know how it worked or was overly reckless, they could take too much, leaving the victim hollowed out. The thought that the palace guards would willingly give up their memories and trust whoever held the Lethe . . .

'I think it's time for you three to head home,' Pozzi said. 'It's certainly been an interesting evening.'

'That it has,' Drystan said. He and Cyan went to gather our cases and ask the guards to send for a carriage.

'You told him our secrets,' I said to Pozzi, anger returning.

'I had to. And I'd do well to remind you that, as a citizen of Ellada, your allegiance is to the crown as well, is it not?'

I didn't answer.

'If he didn't know you were useful to him, then you'd

be staring into the red eyes of a Lethe right now. I trust you know not to breathe a word of this to anyone.'

'Of course we do,' Drystan drawled, coming back into the room. 'We're not about to tell a country on the brink of civil unrest that their royalty isn't even human.'

'They are human. Just a touch Alder as well. I hope you'll forgive me telling him, but he is, after all, my employer and regent of the land. He's irritated at me for having kept secrets from him before. I assure you, what I did will work out best for all concerned.'

Or best for yourself? I thought, but tried to keep the thought from him.

'Good evening. I'll see you in a few days, Micah.' He took his leave.

Drystan and I lingered in the room a moment. I reached out to him, and we pressed our foreheads together. His Glamour hung from his neck. Neither of us had bothered turning them back on. What was the point? We'd been wearing false faces for too long, anyway. When we performed magic again, we'd find a way to shed them, and I'd be glad of it.

Yet Drystan reached over and switched my pendant on.

'For tonight, at least, we should keep this. If we leave the palace with different faces than we had on entering, people may notice.' With a sigh, he turned his on as well. Our features shifted, ever so slightly.

'Not as elegant as the Princess,' I said.

'No.'

The door opened and we broke apart, expecting to see

Maske or Cyan. Instead, a very different face appeared: Lord Nigel Hornbeam.

He seemed surprised to see us. Drystan was tense beside me.

'Shouldn't you have gone by now?' he asked, haughty and superior. 'Where have the Princess and the Steward gone?'

'They just left, my lord,' Drystan said, his voice strained, giving a little bow.

Nigel Hornbeam's brow furrowed.

'You should probably be on your way, then. It was a nice performance. I'm not usually one for magic, but it was clever.'

'Thank you, my lord,' Drystan managed. How many years since he'd last spoken to his father? Five or more.

Nigel Hornbeam turned his back on his son and left him, all without knowing who he was actually talking to.

'Drystan . . .' I began.

'Let's get back to the others,' he said, curtly.

I followed him, wanting to offer comfort, but unsure how.

We finished packing up our magic supplies and left the Royal Snakewood Palace behind.

That night, I woke up to the sound of Drystan sobbing.

I'd not been asleep long. Drystan lay propped up against the pillows. He'd brought up a bottle of port from the kitchen, and he'd made good work of it, judging by how little liquid remained.

He'd been crying for some time. His nose and eyes were red, his cheeks damp.

I didn't say anything, just opened my arms. He drained the last of the port and set the empty glass on the bedside table with a clatter.

He moved into my arms, hiding his face against my neck as if ashamed. He absolutely reeked of the sweet alcohol. It worried me. He'd drunk in the circus at the bonfire, and he'd have the odd glass of drink in the evenings here at the theatre. Once he'd bought a bottle of horrible, cheap gin, and we'd sat on the pier overlooking the circus on the beach and drunk it as we entrusted each other with secrets.

But I wasn't used to seeing him drunk. And I knew he didn't like to be inebriated, not after he'd lost over a year of his life stoned and drunk and running away from reality however he could.

His tears dampened my neck. I stroked his hair. He didn't want to speak about the pain of his father being right there and not recognizing him. And even if he had realized, Drystan was the estranged son, the rotten branch pruned from the family tree.

Eventually, his breathing slowed. He'd cried himself to sleep. I pressed my eyes shut against my own tears, and tried to follow.

This laboratory below the university was ancient, but it would serve my needs well enough. The two bodies were in Vestige Ampulla tanks I'd stolen earlier that night from the university. It hadn't been easy to bring them down here, but I'd managed eventually, inch by painful inch. I was covered in grease and dirt and my scalp itched with sweat.

My new laboratory was underground; the only light was the flickering lights of stubs of candles and the green glow from the tanks. The tables and benches were covered with beakers, some simmering over gas burners. The air smelled of damp and chemicals and freshly-turned earth.

Two bodies floated within the tank. They looked perfect. The man was from the university hospital, the woman from the grave.

Ampulla tanks would help keep the bodies fresh, but they would still slowly decay, even with regular injections of the serum. I pressed my palms against the glass.

'Soon,' I whispered. 'Soon this will all fall into place. My task will be complete.'

It was time for the first experiment. I turned on the tank closest to me, fingers running over the controls, slowly figuring out how they worked.

The girl's body rose, her hair floating about her face. I'd taken great care with her, brushing her hair until it gleamed. The auburn strands undulated gently in the waters of the tank. Her skin was bone-pale, but would be the colour of the palest pink rose once blood pumped through her veins again. I imagined her alive, radiant. I smiled.

The body fell to the floor of the tank, the hair falling over her face. The control panel sparked, and the precious vessel within jerked with the force of electricity. I frantically banged on the controls, but I couldn't open the tank.

Within moments, the body was boiled, and even a new tank and more serum wouldn't be able to save it. I bashed at the controls again, and the liquid fled the tank.

I wanted to scream at the top of my lungs, but then someone might hear me. My breath came raggedly through my nose.

I dried out the corpse and set her aflame in an old bathtub with the help of a Vestige Brimstone solution, until nothing was left but ash.

Still so far away from what I needed. Now I needed to find and steal another tank.

And another human girl, freshly dead.

I awoke just past dawn, every part of my body aching.

'What the Styx is going on?' I asked. Drystan turned over in the bed, but no one else answered me.

Yet I knew someone who must be able to give me *some* answers.

I grabbed the Aleph, and went into the lounge before pressing the switch. Anisa appeared. She was fainter in the early light.

'What do the dreams mean?' I asked. 'Are you sending them?'

'The grave-robbing dreams?' She shook her head, as if mystified. 'It's still happening?'

'Yes. Whoever is stealing the bodies is trying to bring them back to life.'

She closed her eyes and her awareness spread through me, picking at the memories of my dreams. 'I can't sense who they are,' she said sadly. 'It's as though it's blocked.'

'What do I do?' We still didn't know who it was. The body didn't feel like Pozzi, and this time I'd caught a glimpse of bare hands. No clockwork. Timur, or one of his Kashura?

'I am afraid I have no answers for you, little Kedi. You could try to search, but I have a feeling this resurrectionist is very clever. We can only hope that he will slip.' She looked worried. 'It bodes ill, and it speaks of desperation.'

Before I could answer, she turned away from me and disappeared back into the Aleph. And even when I flicked the switch again, she did not reappear.

15

The Nickel Daily

If the monarchy continues to bury its head in the sand and ignore the discontent of its people, there will be trouble. We cannot deny it any longer.
— Editorial, *The Nickel Daily*

When I woke up, my body was too heavy to move. My throat itched, and my eyelids refused to stay open. I tried to sit up, and fell back against the pillows.

'I feel ill,' I told Drystan, 'almost like I did when I collapsed.'

'Your appointment with Pozzi is tomorrow. The Elixir must be wearing off.'

I shivered, hating being this dependent on it.

'Are you all right?' I asked him.

'I have a bugger of a hangover,' he admitted. 'Feel like Saitha stepped on my head.'

Saitha was the elephant of R. H. Ragona's Circus of Magic. I'd helped look after her right after I joined.

'Aside from your head, how are you?' I pressed.

Drystan shrugged. 'Been better, but I'll live. Let's go to breakfast. I need to drink my weight in water and coffee, and eat some grease.'

'Grease on its own? Delicious.'

'A whole vat of it.'

We bantered on the way down to the kitchen, and the jokes lifted Drystan's spirits.

When we entered the kitchen, our smiles faded. Cyril had come to visit, and he, Maske, and Cyan were huddled together over the newspaper, worry emanating from them.

'What's happened?' I asked.

Maske pushed the paper towards us. It was an entire issue devoted to the current political situation in Ellada. It wasn't the *Daily Imacharan* or one of the other big newspapers, but a smaller rag, the *Nickel Daily*.

'The Steward didn't want people to see it and ordered it all pulped or burned,' Cyan said in a hushed voice. 'But I heard about it, and found one this morning.'

Drystan and I read side by side. The newspaper claimed that we were on the brink of a civil war. Forester support was growing and finally, whispers of the Kashura were going mainstream. Some thought violence was a necessary evil for the greater good. People still stared at their neighbours out of the corners of their eyes, anonymously sending letters to the Constabulary, convinced the old lady upstairs or the baker down the street was secretly Chimaera. Accusations of hidden scales, witchcraft, the evil eye all abounded.

Three months ago, I wouldn't have said that Elladans were particularly superstitious. I'd since changed my mind.

Mistrust of the Royal Family had been growing steadily, judging by the newspaper article. Focused on our own troubles, we'd been a little cut off from that sentiment. Maske read the newspaper every morning, but those against the royalty knew better than to print such sentiments, at least until today. Some evidently thought the Snakewood family was behind the Celestial Cathedral attack, using the Chimaera as their agents to harm the public. Never mind that the casualty number that day was low thanks to the security measures of the Royal Family. Others thought the attack had been a plot from one or more of the other islands to weaken Ellada's powers. The Colonies successfully sued for independence, but some of the older generations thought we should still be an empire. The article capitalized on that fear, stating that the colonies were planning on levying trade barriers to watch us flounder on our own once war broke out.

It didn't take a Shadow to understand why the Steward would want this banned. It attacked the monarchy's decisions directly and showcased Ellada's weaknesses. No matter how much they tried to hide this, copies would still circulate, or rumours pass in whispers behind hands. Throwing whoever wrote this into prison and shutting down the newspaper would make little difference at this point. Word had spread, and we lived in a country where to speak out against royalty was rarely done.

I had grown up never questioning, never seeing how the nobility behaved, how differently the branches of the Twelve Families lived compared to those in the lowest roots of society. Even when I'd run away and lived on the streets and eked out a simple life in the circus, I'd never stopped to think and wonder why the world was like that for so many. Did it have to be?

'I wouldn't be surprised if a Kashura sympathizer wrote this,' Cyril said. My brother folded his hands together, thinking.

'It's likely, yes,' Maske agreed. 'This would be an effective way to undermine the monarchy. Incite others to do their dirty work for them. Styx.'

I set the paper down. 'Civil war still seems a stretch. People are upset, angry, afraid – but afraid enough for war? A full class revolt?' Naively, I'd hoped this mess between the Kashura, the calmer branch of the Foresters, and the monarchy would sort itself out with no more bloodshed. Too much to hope for.

'It might be enough to ignite the flame,' Cyril said.

His words made me flinch, for they reminded me of something Anisa had once said to me: 'One leader to spark the zeitgeist, and the world changes.'

I made myself a cup of coffee, stirring in milk and sugar. Outside, the Penny Rookeries awoke. How many people out there had read the newspaper already? How would they react? I was still exhausted and worn down, and the beginnings of a headache pulsed at my temples.

We were silent as Maske brought out bread, butter, and preserves. We spoke of other things, trying to drive the thought of war and uprisings from our minds.

'You did well last night,' Cyril said, biting into a slice of toast.

'Thank you,' I answered. 'What did the guests say? Anything interesting?'

'They all watched what they were saying. Lots of small talk. I did overhear something between Lord Hornbeam and Lord Cinnabari, though.'

I suppressed another wince and didn't look at Drystan. 'What did you hear?' Cyan asked.

'Lord Hornbeam was annoyed to see the Royal Physician there and kept glaring at him out of the corner of his eye. He muttered to Lord Cinnabari that he hoped the Physician would go on another sabbatical. Cinnabari mentioned he'd enjoyed the Physician's last book and the recent article in the Royal Snakewood medical journal. But I think it was more that Lord Hornbeam hoped the Physician would go away and not be so close to the Royal Family. When the Physician leaned down to ask Princess Nicolette something, Hornbeam looked like he'd pop a blood vessel.'

'Interesting,' I said. 'Maybe Lord Hornbeam hasn't been around the family as much, especially when Pozzi's treating the Princess. Maybe he doesn't know about her.'

'Know what about her?' Cyril asked. Maske frowned at me.

Styx. I was so tired I was letting things slip. 'Sorry, I'm not allowed to say. The Steward made us promise, and he's not someone I want to break promises to.'

'Not even a hint?' Cyril said, flashing me his cheekiest grin.

'Nice try, but sorry. I don't think breaking a promise to our monarch is a good idea. He could Augur us to see if we told anyone.'

'That's a good point,' Maske said. But neither of them was happy to be left out of the secret.

Cyril looked at Drystan. 'Sorry, but . . . do you know Lord Hornbeam?'

Drystan waved his fingers. 'Everyone else knows, so I guess you may as well. I was once Lord Hornbeam's son.'

Cyril's mouth formed an 'o' as he put it together that the young man sitting across the table from him was the estranged son of the Hornbeam family. 'We . . . played hide and seek together a few times!' he sputtered.

Drystan burst out laughing. 'That we did. You were good at it, as I recall.'

'I can't believe I didn't see it before.'

'The mind sees what it wants to see, not what is there.'

Cyril's gaze flicked to me as he realized I was seeing the boy who sparked all those rumours years ago. It would've been almost comical if I wasn't so nervous. Drystan was always one to keep his secrets to himself. He'd been annoyed at me when I'd told Cyan about my past, thinking I was foolhardy to trust her so quickly. I couldn't even remember if we ever told Cyan Drystan's true name, if she'd figured it out, or plucked it from our minds.

'I see,' Cyril said.

'Did you hear anything else?' I asked, desperate to change the subject.

'Nothing of note.' He finished his coffee. 'I have to head to my lecture, then I'm going to the hospital to visit Mother.'

'I've lots of practice this afternoon,' I said guiltily, in

response to his unasked question. I'd told him I'd perhaps try to reach her again, or that Cyan would, but neither of us had returned to the hospital.

Maske raised his eyebrows and took a bite of bread, but said nothing.

Cyril sighed. 'All right.' He finished his coffee and washed his plate and cup.

Drystan threw away most of his breakfast and grabbed his coat before Cyril even left the table. He didn't wish us farewell or say where he was going.

Poor Drystan, Cyan sent to me.

Leave him his thoughts.

I have, but there's no shielding myself from those emotions. He's hurting.

I know. He didn't want to be around any of us just now.

The next morning, before my appointment with Doctor Pozzi, Drystan said he wanted to take a walk through the Penny Rookeries. Cyril had come over again first thing, books in hand, saying he studied better here.

We all had a quick breakfast, and then Maske returned to his makeshift workshop, but Cyan and Cyril lingered over another cup of coffee, talking. I heard the laughter as I put on my coat. I was so tired, my movements were jerky and hesitant. I didn't really want to leave the flat. I'd rather have gone back to my bed until it was time to visit Pozzi. After that visit, I'd be more than willing to go for a walk, perform street magic, jump backflips.

'They seem to be getting along well,' Drystan said, with

a meaningful raise of his eyebrows in the direction of the kitchen and Cyril and Cyan.

'You don't think . . . ?' I'd been so caught up in my own troubles, I hadn't noticed anything between them. 'I thought Cyan thought he was a rich twat.' I remembered her snapping at him on the Long Night of the Lady.

Reaching towards Cyan revealed nothing. She was closed to me. So was Cyril. My powers were weaker when I needed my next dose. When I tried again, I could just sense that Cyril was very interested in what Cyan was saying, his eyes lingering on the curve of her lips. I jumped back from his mind.

'Oh, Lord and Lady, he likes her. A lot. I feel like a peeping Tom.' The effort had also winded me. I tried to hide it. Drystan was acting almost normal again, and I didn't want to risk him sinking back into his doldrums.

'Well, you were peeping. Leave them be. None of our business.'

Chastened, I followed him out to the street, throwing a quick goodbye to Cyan and Cyril, hoping my blush wasn't too obvious.

Outside, summer was truly arriving. The air was hot and sticky, and my clothing immediately itched and clung to my skin. We passed a grocer's, and the apples smelled so good that I bought two and we ate them as we walked down the narrow, crowded streets.

Evidence of poverty was everywhere. None of the streets were properly cobbled, and I had to pick my way carefully so I didn't trip in the divots or step in horse droppings. The homeless people on the streets made my heart ache.

I kept my purse full of coppers and gave them what I could, but it still felt like it was not near enough. The faces I passed had the scars of smallpox, rotten teeth, and were too thin from hunger. More Forester posters were in the windows than I remembered. Sentiment against royalty was turning, as they kept promising a better life and never delivering. Councils had given the Steward petition after petition, new budgets, yet hardly anything was actively done. Drystan thought that Ellada's coffers were distressingly empty, but that they couldn't let the country know how poor we'd become for fear it'd only bring on conflict all the faster.

We drifted closer to the docks. The air smelled of fish, both fresh and not so fresh, and the acrid smell of fish guts. Stallholders hawked their wares and tried to entice us to purchase some shellfish or herring. I'd never been keen on fish to begin with and shook my head, continuing on. Drystan bought a small bag of smoked kippers and I pulled a face.

'You're not kissing me after eating those,' I said.

'You won't be able to resist my charms,' he said.

'I will if you smell like a fish. Sorry.'

We laughed, and it was so good to simply walk through the streets, not thinking about performing or politics or worrying about being pursued and trapped. At another stall, we bought some iced lemonade and found an abandoned dock, sitting with our legs over the sides.

'It's like that night in the circus,' I said, sipping my tart drink. It helped wake me up.

'Except that was night time, the air didn't smell so

much like rotten fish, and we were drinking really bad gin instead of me nursing a particularly violent hangover.' He squinted into the sunlight. His hair shone bright gold, freckles speckled across his cheeks like cinnamon. I wanted to kiss him, but hesitated, feeling like I couldn't be physically affectionate while we were both dressed as men and hating that pause. Though he did still smell of kippers. I settled for putting my hand over his and squeezing.

Drystan leaned back on his forearms, closing his eyes. 'I never want to drink port again.'

I chuckled, but it faded away. 'What do you think of the *Nickel Daily* article?' I asked. It was still on my mind. Drystan was good at knowing all the different angles of a political problem.

'I think it overstated how close we are to the possibility of civil war. The Foresters and the Kashura are at odds more than they are together. The Foresters, now that Timur's out, are actually well organized and have a solid plan to try and get more rights for the people. If it was just them on their own, I think they might be able to effect a lot, peacefully. But the Kashura are giving them a bad name. They have to expend so much energy separating themselves from that faction that it takes energy away from all they need to do. And then I think there's internal strife, too.'

'How so? And how do you know about it?'

'I don't. I see it in the streets. I read all those posters. A lot of Foresters joined the party under Timur. They liked him. His vision, his energy. They know that going through bureaucracy is difficult, arduous, and it might not result in anything. The article was right when it said some might think violence is the way to go, in the short term.'

'That's a trap, though, isn't it?' I mused. 'If you join a violent group to topple one system, and that actually works, you still have leaders who are used to violence. Will they simply stop and become peaceful again?'

'That's the question.' Drystan rubbed at his eyes, wincing. 'I have no idea what'll happen.'

'Do any of us?'

'Don't think so.'

We stayed there, finishing our lemonade, until the bright sun threatened to burn us. Reluctantly, we stood and walked back through the twining streets of Imachara. It was time to visit Doctor Pozzi again.

16

SWEET ELIXIR

The thing about addiction is that I know it's what will kill me. It won't be a carriage in the road, or a common flu, or even the slow creep of cancer. It's almost certain that Lerium will be what ends me. And there's a strange, awful sort of comfort in that.

— From the anonymous memoir of a Lerium addict, discovered and published post-mortem

Pozzi took what felt like forever to prep the syringe.

I almost hissed at him, mentally willing him to push the needle in quicker.

Then he injected me, and it was all I could sense. That sweet, cold ice flowing through my veins. It was as though, before, my body was threaded with darkness, and then when I was injected, the drug was bright light that washed it all away. It purified me and I felt born anew.

I was addicted. There was no point denying it any longer. Even as I craved it, I hated it. I was high but also heightened. My senses sharpened, and the power within me grew stronger. I was alive again.

After a few moments, I came back to myself.

'Better?' Pozzi asked.

'I suppose,' I said guardedly, even as my insides sang. Being dependent on the drug made me feel weak, and I despised that I now looked forward to visiting Pozzi, if only for my fix. If it wasn't for him I might not have needed the drug in the first place. He could have lied completely about my past, and never found me on his doorstep at all. More likely, my mother died in childbirth and he'd simply kept me until he found another home. One where he could keep an eye on me, to see how his experiment fared.

He put his things away. This was the part I hated the most. I'd gained what I wanted. I had no desire to sit and visit and have tea with the man I didn't trust, but it always happened anyway.

We went into the lounge, where Drystan waited. I wondered if he'd stolen anything else from the cabinet of curiosities.

No matter how much time I spent with the Royal Physician, I would never truly know him. Did anyone? Yet I could still try to learn certain things.

'Did you always know of the Princess's condition?' I asked as Pozzi brought out his Vestige tea set. I wouldn't have minded owning one myself – it kept liquid hot as long as it was in the teapot, whether it'd been boiled an hour ago or last month.

'As soon as she was born, yes. I was the one to deliver her.'

I had more of an idea of what childbirth was like now, thanks to Lily's visions. And Pozzi had dosed Lily's wife when she was pregnant. I glanced at him out of the corner of my eye with new suspicion. Had he somehow worked this change in the Princess, to continue his scheme? No, the Princess had said the Alder traits went back centuries. But if they'd recently been growing stronger rather than weaker, maybe Pozzi had something to do with it.

I found it incredible that the Snakewoods' secret had been kept all these years, despite the Glamours and Lethes. They had covered their tracks very carefully, trusting no one but the Royal Physician.

Had they misplaced their trust? Would he really go that far – treating royalty as his own laboratory rats?

'You could barely tell, at first,' Pozzi went on. 'A tinge of blue here and there. As she grew older, it grew stronger. And, sometimes, I wonder if her childlike innocence is an act. She's wickedly intelligent, and sees more than she might. Good for a monarch, but perhaps unfortunate for a lonely little girl.'

I thought of the magic show and how most of the guests had been adults, and those few that were her own age she'd largely ignored.

'Does she have any friends?'

He shook his head. 'No true friends that I'm aware of. Every now and again she'll have play dates with other children. She plays the part well, but it's more like she endures them. She'd rather be on her own in a room with no windows, where she can turn off the Glamour. She loves to read and learn. The Steward encourages her to stay separate. It's safer.'

I pressed my lips together at that. Safe, but isolating. I peered more closely at Pozzi and almost gasped. 'You're afraid of her.'

Drystan stayed quiet, watching our exchange, his blue eyes calculating.

'No. Fear is not the right word. I am . . . wary. I have studied people with different abilities, but no one who is part Alder. I'd not have believed it but for the proof in front of my own eyes. But I've known her for her entire life, and she is sweet, if different. I like to flatter myself that I am one of the few people she has genuine affection for.'

His words rang hollow. Pozzi found her fascinating, as he did me and Frey. I did not doubt that hidden somewhere he had pages and pages of observation notes, and rued that he could never publish his findings.

I didn't answer, but sipped my tea. It was mint, and the taste of it reminded me of the night I'd snuck down to the kitchens at my old house in Sicion for a midnight meal. On the way back, I had heard my parents discussing me. Mint tea would always be reminiscent of the night my life changed irrevocably. When I left Iphigenia Laurus behind and became Micah Grey.

'We must be getting back,' I said. 'We're performing this afternoon.'

'Ah, yes, the street performances?'

'Yes.'

'I'm glad to see you are not letting the political situation deter you. And how very gallant, to perform for the everyday people after the Princess.'

I stifled a scoff.

'Hardly gallant,' Drystan said. 'Everyone deserves entertainment, and we must keep our skills sharp for when the theatre is reopened.'

'Naturally. Well, I'm afraid I must be off. I've been asked to cover another lecture at the university. Do you fancy coming again, Micah? They'll be dissecting the liver.'

I suppressed a shudder. 'No, thank you.' But that reminded me of the resurrectionist dreams. 'Have any more bodies gone missing?' I asked, hoping I sounded nonchalant.

'Yes, another one early yesterday morning; a young woman. From the hospital for the poor again. Strange, isn't it? They've set up guards, but those stationed by where the body was taken were found sleeping like the dead, and would not wake for hours. It's a puzzle, right enough.'

I hadn't dreamed of the woman being stolen, and why not, when I'd eavesdropped on so many of the others? It was a puzzle. And I was staring at the man who might be behind it, or knew who was.

I had a front-row seat to it all, even if I did not know who starred in the show.

Drystan and I made our farewells. On the way to the door, I passed the mantelpiece, and noticed the disc that had looked like an Aleph was no longer there.

* * *

'You didn't take the Aleph thing that used to be on his mantelpiece, did you?' I asked as we made our way back to the Penny Rookeries.

'No. Too obvious. I wanted to take a look at it, but it wasn't there. He's changed the lock on the cabinet of curiosities, too. I couldn't hope to crack it.'

'So he knows we stole from him?' My stomach clenched.

'Probably. For whatever reason, he's not accusing us of anything. Today . . . has not been a good day.'

Physically, I felt magnificent. Mentally was another matter. I was dependent on a drug whose supply I could not control. So many events swirled around me and it felt like I was caught in the vortex. Drystan looked as close to crying as I felt.

We went to the park and sat on a bench, watching children play in the sunshine. We were going to miss that afternoon's street show. Either Cyan would do something alone, or there'd be no magic on our corner that day. I couldn't find it within myself to care.

'Do you want to talk about it?' I asked.

'No. Not now.'

Taking his hand, I squeezed. We stayed in the sunshine, under the green canopy of the trees. Behind me, three or four streets away, I sensed a low, warm glow. Another Chimaera perhaps, one I didn't know. The right thing to do would be to follow, try and meet whoever it was. Instead I stayed with Drystan, letting the yellow, buttery light fall on us. In that moment, he needed me more.

17

AHTI'S SCION

When I was little, I used to walk through the gardens at my parents' house in the Emerald Bowl, looking down at the flowers. They were the perfect size to be teacups for fairies, I always thought. I went through the dark green leaves, my feet sinking into the grass. I wasn't looking where I was going, and the ground fell off sharply, down to a ravine. I slipped, but managed to grab a root. I hung there, my feet dangling. I was only six or seven. I remember thinking how quickly all can change. One minute, you seem to be in a fairy's realm, and the next, your life is in danger. It took a long time to crawl back up, and my nightdress was stained. Mother berated me for it the next day.

— From Micah Grey's infrequently updated diary

Each day we performed street magic. Maske and Cyan held seances, with Drystan and I helping behind the scenes. A week went by, and then another, and I almost fancied we had fallen into a routine. Work, perform, practise. Drag through the last two days of the week. See Pozzi, have Elixir flow through my veins, and feel marvellous for the next five. The Steward didn't call on us. Drystan seemed to recover from the shock of seeing his father. Yet I could not shake the feeling that it was but a brief respite before the storm.

I was right.

Lily Verre came to visit Maske. She'd been 'on holiday' for the last three weeks, though Drystan, Cyan, and I knew that she was still at her apartments. Maske was utterly delighted to see Lily, pulling her into a passionate embrace. I made a face behind their backs. Cyan, not missing a beat, 'sent' me and Drystan an image of her retching. Drystan disguised his laugh as a cough.

Lily stayed for dinner. I wished Cyril was here to lessen the tension. Cyril was as diplomatic as our father, able to steer a conversation into safer waters. Instead, we pretended we knew nothing about Lily Verre except what she had told us in her guise – a widow dating Maske who had worked for a time in the magic shop, Twisting the Aces. She'd quit that job months ago, of course.

Near the end of the meal, Maske went to fetch dessert.

Trouble is coming, Anisa said out of the blue. Her Aleph was in my pocket, as usual.

What? I asked her.

Answer the door. It's about Frey.

There was a knock at the door. No one ever called this late.

I sent my awareness past the door, and Cyan did the same. We sensed a young man, nervous. *It's Kai, Pozzi's assistant*, I sent Drystan and Cyan.

I opened the door, and sure enough, there was Kai. He

still wore his bulky coat despite the warm night. He asked for Lily. She came, and we retreated, Cyan and I mentally eavesdropping. The blood drained from my face. Kai squeezed Lily's shoulder and left, almost running back to the carriage to wait for her.

Lily emanated terror, and locked eyes with us just as Maske returned with the cake. Lily slipped her own mask back in place.

'Who was that at the door at this hour?' he asked.

'Someone trying to pass us a Forester pamphlet,' Drystan said.

'I'm sorry, my dove,' Lily said regretfully, patting her stomach. 'I'm afraid I cannot eat another bite. I've been battling a bit of a headache all day, and it seems to have come back in full force.' She touched her temple.

'I'm sorry to hear that,' Maske said. 'Would you like to lie down in my room? You can have your cake later.'

'I don't wish to trouble you. I think I'll head back home. And if I have sugar this late, I might never get to sleep!'

Maske looked crestfallen, and she gave him a kiss on the cheek. 'I'll see you soon for the opera. I'm ever so looking forward to it, my love.'

I felt guilty. Lily claimed she loved Maske and it was no act, but how could I believe her when she'd lied about so much else? Maske loved the Lily that he thought he knew, but he didn't know she was the most famous Shadow in Imachara. It wasn't fair, but I was too cowardly to tell him and break his heart.

Lily left, but we nodded to her. We would follow to her apartments as soon as possible.

Something was very wrong with Frey.

We ate Maske's dessert as quickly as we could, a cake he'd made himself flavoured with cherries and almonds. I barely even tasted it.

We helped Maske clean up, and then, though we knew he wanted us to linger in the kitchen and chat, we made our excuses, pleading exhaustion. He went to his makeshift workshop and bedroom, and before long we heard the distant sounds of a little hammer on brass. In our rooms, we put on light summer coats, and I grabbed Anisa's Aleph. Then it was out the fire escape and down a drainpipe.

'This could be a trap,' Drystan said as we started towards Lily's apartments.

'Maybe,' I agreed.

'She was terrified,' Cyan said. 'And I'm curious about Kai, aren't you?'

'Of course,' I said. I'd met him briefly at the hospital, and since learning he was Frey's caretaker, my suspicion had only grown.

We slunk through the streets as quickly as we could, darting into alleyways at times to avoid the notice of the night watchmen. There were far more of those on the streets than even a few months ago. It must have stretched Ellada's coffers to deploy them, but they had to ensure that people kept to their curfew. For all the good it probably did. If the Kashura wanted to attack the city, they would attack, curfew or no curfew.

What happens if we're caught out after dark? I asked Cyan.

Fined and arrested, she said. *Maybe even a beating for*

our trouble. I swallowed and kept an even sharper eye out for the night watch.

At Lily's apartments, the doorman had evidently been bribed, for he let us in without hesitation and told us to make our way to number 209 as quickly as possible. He held his hand out for a tip, and we gave him what scattered coins we had in our pockets. Luckily, this doorman was not the same one we'd duped the last time we were here.

The door opened almost immediately after we knocked. 'Thank the stars,' Lily said, practically dragging us inside.

Kai was still wearing his coat, wringing his hands. 'I didn't know what to do. He was fine and then he went into a fit and collapsed. I was . . . was going to go to Pozzi first, but then I heard a woman whisper in my mind to go to your address. She said . . . she was the dragonfly woman, and you would know what that meant.'

My gaze flickered to my pocket.

We went to Frey's bedroom. The bright colours and drawings warred with the worry emanating from Lily. Frey was unconscious. The low light glinted on his green-black scales and the curves of his horns. The *power* that emanated from him was almost unbearable. Cyan and I took involuntary steps back.

'What's wrong?' Lily asked.

'He's rupturing power everywhere. The air is thick with it. It can't be good.' I staggered again, my temples throbbing. If before he'd been a furnace, now he was a forest fire.

Drystan and Lily looked uncomfortable. They couldn't

feel a thing. Cyan was a bit green around the edges. And Kai . . .

'You feel it, don't you?' I asked him.

He nodded, uncomfortable. I wanted to know more about him, but I couldn't spare the time.

Memories of Anisa and her old charges came to me. Frey was similar to Ahti, and that Chimaera had nearly destroyed the world.

Bring me out, Anisa said. *They should know who I am.*

I took the Aleph from my pocket and set it on the ground.

'This is the dragonfly woman, Anisa,' I said, looking into Kai's eyes as I flicked the switch.

It did give me a small sense of satisfaction to watch Lily and Kai's shock as the smoke swirled into view and Anisa appeared. The Phantom Damselfly went straight to Frey's side. Normally, it was difficult to tell what the Chimaera ghost was thinking, but now she was clearly concerned.

'Dev, come here,' Anisa commanded, and, with a start, I realized she meant me, even though she'd called me by the name of one of her ancient charges.

'I don't know—'

'No time for doubts. We must contain this or you will all be at risk.'

Her words sent a shiver down my spine. I didn't doubt her – the power held a threat, and the air smelled alive and stormy, as if lightning could strike at any moment.

'Reach out and take his hand,' Anisa instructed. 'We don't have long.'

Outside, the skies opened in a torrent of rain, the wind lashing against the windows. The clouds completely hid the moon, as if nothing but a water-laced abyss existed outside of the small window.

I took Frey's small hand in mine. It was hard and scaly, and far too warm. His fingers tightened around mine like a vice. I gasped. He leeched power from me, my energy flowing into him. Within moments, I was as poorly as I had been the morning before I'd last been dosed with Pozzi's Elixir.

The stuffed animals by the window rose into the air, spinning slowly. The books tumbled from the bookshelves, falling to the floor and then rising again, their covers flapping like birds' wings. Everyone in the room screamed.

'He's hurting me,' I gasped.

'You must take control,' Anisa said.

'I . . . can't . . .'

Drystan darted forward. 'Stop it!'

I half-fell to the bed. A scream tore from my throat.

Drystan grabbed my hand, trying to pry me from Frey, but as soon as he touched my skin, the power leeching from me spiked, caused him to fly across the room. He crashed into the wall before falling to the floor.

'You can take control, little Kedi,' Anisa said, her voice echoing through the room. 'You have to, or all is lost. There is not much time. One who was Matla, lend him your strength.'

Cyan clasped my other hand. Immediately, I felt more grounded within myself. But all too soon she fell against me with weakness. I could barely see and had no idea

what Drystan or Lily were doing. Perhaps they still tried
to free us, but my mind was full of swirling blue light.

I had to do something. If I didn't, then Frey, Cyan, and
I would die – and perhaps everyone within a set radius,
too, if Frey's powers grew too strong. It would be like
the Forester attack in front of the Celestial Cathedral, or
worse.

I reached towards Frey with my mind, but it was as
though I reached for a whirlpool. I swirled through it,
hunting for the frightened little boy who must be hiding
in there somewhere.

There. Off in the distance of my mind. A small spark.
The smallest star.

'Frey,' I called to him. 'Frey Verre.'

'Who are you?' His voice was high and wailing. 'What
do you want from me?'

'We met before, at your mother's. I'm Micah, do you
remember? You're frightened and your power has gotten
away from you.'

'I don't want to go back. I like it. The world is bigger
here.'

The whirring colours were strangely hypnotic. Everything
was various shades of blue, like that one memory I had
from Anisa. When she'd found her charge dead, they'd
lived inside a Penglass dome, and everything was soft and
cool but for the red blood.

It was the same swirling colours as the vortex of my
mother's mind.

'Your mother needs you,' I urged. 'She's so worried for
you. You don't wish to upset her, do you?'

A pause. 'No.'

'Come on, then. Let's go back.' It was as if I held out my hand, though where we were we had no bodies and were only light.

I reached to him, but it was like reaching for my mother at the hospital. He was too far away, or he was like smoke that slipped through my fingers.

'Come on, Frey,' I said. 'Reach towards me. You have to help me.' I didn't want him to disappear. If he was lost, would he be in the same kind of coma as my mother?

Then, so faintly, he connected with me. His grip strengthened. The swirling light around us slowed. The bright, eye-watering blue grew dimmer, that same bright-dark azure just after the sun has set but the stars have not come out. Everything darkened to black.

I returned to my body, which hurt as though I'd been stepped on by a horse. Several times. And then kicked for good measure.

Groaning, I raised my head. Frey looked at me, black eyes alert, as fresh as if he'd just awoken from a nap. Unfair.

Cyan, her eyelids drooping, looked as awful as I felt. The bedroom was a mess, torn books and toys everywhere, the pictures fallen from the walls, the glass shattered. I could hear the frightened thoughts of the neighbours, wondering if there'd just been an earthquake.

Drystan dragged me to my feet and crushed me tight in his arms. I fell against him, hardly able to stand. I was numbed to all emotions, shocked into silence. It was like after Anisa's memory dreams, or after I woke up after the bodysnatching nightmares. I still wasn't entirely sure who I was. Though I hadn't been experiencing someone else's life, I'd been away from my own body. I wanted to sleep for days, but only after I'd eaten my body weight in food.

'Are you all right?' Drystan whispered into my ear.

'I think so,' I said.

'I gave you some energy back,' Frey said, propping himself up with his elbows. The covers had fallen back, exposing his skinny legs. 'I didn't want you to be too tired.'

If this was how I was after him giving me some energy, I didn't want to think how I'd feel otherwise.

Anisa smiled at us. 'Perhaps there's hope yet.'

The vision of the world ending she'd sent me, remembered from hundreds of years ago, could give anyone nightmares. I didn't want history to repeat and restart.

Lily clung tight to her child, resting her cheek against the top of his head. The love she possessed for him flooded through me. It was too strong. With difficulty, I erected the barriers, blocked out her relief. Kai watched everything in wide-eyed wonder, pressed against the wall, almost willing himself not to be noticed.

I clung to Drystan, hiding my face. The light hurt. Everything hurt.

'Thank you,' Lily said. 'I don't know what you did or how you did it, but thank you.'

'How do we stop it from happening again?' I asked the Phantom Damselfly, my voice hoarse.

'Frey must learn to control his powers,' Anisa said. 'Others like you can perhaps contain it, for a time, but in the end, it comes down to him.' Her eyes went distant, and I knew who she was remembering.

'You didn't teach Ahti, all those years ago?' I asked.

She looked away. 'I tried. I thought I had. But when they hurt him, all my teaching was not enough. And Dev was not there to help him. And so they were lost, and the world nearly lost with it.'

'How do I learn?' Frey asked. 'I don't want to hurt anyone.'

Anisa smiled at him, almost sadly. 'We'll start now. For all we have is time and now is as good a time as any.'

'Wait. We still don't know much about Kai, here,' Drystan said, nodding to Kai. Startled at being addressed, the young man hunched his shoulders. 'You work for Pozzi. We don't know if we can trust you. What's to say you won't report everything back to the doctor?'

'I – I won't,' Kai said. 'I hate him.'

I blinked, surprised. At the hospital, he'd hung on the doctor's every word.

'He's playing the same game I am,' Lily replied.

The problem, I wanted to say, *is that we aren't totally certain of your game, either.*

'What do you do for him?' Drystan asked.

'I help him in his private laboratory, or when we conduct lectures or autopsies. I'm never with him when he goes to the palace.'

'Before you ask,' Lily added, 'no, he doesn't help experiment on pregnant women or babies or whatever the Styx Pozzi is really doing. Kai is a medical student, and helps with Pozzi's most banal projects.'

'I see you for what you are,' Anisa said. She flapped her wings, slowly. 'Show them what you hide, and they will understand.'

He stooped his shoulders again, but took off his coat. Underneath, he wore a bulky jumper. Awkwardly, he took this off and then stood.

Wings like a bat's spread from his back. They jutted out through holes cut in his shirt. They were a different shade to his skin, greyer, and small enough that when folded across his back, they did not create a noticeable bump.

'Can you fly?' I asked.

'No. They're too small.' His voice was sharp. The few people he'd shown these wings had probably all asked the same question.

'Does Pozzi know about them?'

'Of course he does. I'm fairly sure he created them in me. He saw my mother when she was pregnant.'

'How did you start to work with him?'

'My mother told me her suspicions. I went to him, claiming I wanted to learn, and he took me in. He funded my schooling, made sure I met the right people. It's only in the last few months he's trusted me enough to help with certain experiments. But I don't trust him. I never have, I never will. I'm using him to get what I need, and waiting until I can find proof of what he's truly doing.'

Cyan stepped closer to him. 'Can I check that you're telling the truth?' she asked, holding out a hand.

He stared at her hand, nervously licking his lips. Then he straightened his shoulders, stretching out his small wings again. 'Yes. I have nothing to hide.' He took her hand and held it tight.

She didn't need to touch him, but it was a gentle lie, that he thought she did. Her eyelids fluttered closed. She softly stepped into his mind to examine him. She only stayed long enough to discover what she needed before stepping back and opening her eyes.

'He's telling the truth.'

He took his hand back, rubbing the skin. 'I hope that clears the matter.'

We wanted to ask him more, but Lily spoke up. 'Now, I'd like to ask more about you, Anisa, and your history,' she said, almost hesitantly. 'I am truly grateful for all your help but I have no idea who you are. A transparent ghost just saved my son with the help of a boy and a girl with powers that should not exist. And no, I didn't know you were Chimaera, not definitively. I want answers.'

'Very well, Shadow,' Anisa said, calmly, the veneer of detachment back in place. Lily had her own nickname.

She told Lily, Frey, and Kai small amounts about herself – that she had lived many lives in many bodies. Some of flesh, some of machine, but usually not for long in an Aleph like the one she lived in now. How she was tasked by the Alder to raise Chimaera with extra abilities and teach them, whether they were Anthi or Theri. Anisa skimmed over the period of her life she'd shown me, of Ahti being tortured by the original Kashura, who had wanted to take his powers – the rare dual ability to both move objects and affect weather. Instead, they triggered a catastrophe that almost resulted in the end of the world.

'I'm trying to ensure that this doesn't happen again. I will always protect Chimaera.'

Lily looked mistrustful, and I couldn't blame her. But then, I didn't trust Lily either. I trusted that she loved her son and would do whatever it took to keep him safe: including betraying us all, if she felt she had to. Kai was inscrutable.

'Frey,' Anisa said. 'Look at me.'

He did. 'I remember you,' he said in wonder.

'You do?' Anisa asked, for once taken aback. 'From where?'

'I don't know,' he said, shrugging. 'It was a long time ago.'

We all stared at him, unsure what to say.

'My chair?' he asked.

Kai went to get his wicker chair and lifted Frey from the bed, settling him into the seat and tucking blankets around him. I couldn't stop staring at the wings as they moved along his back. I wanted to reach out and touch them. Would they feel warm? Would they be rough like Saitha the elephant's skin, or smooth like leather? I felt guilty for my curiosity.

'I'll teach him the basics of control for now, but the little Kedi can probably help as well. They seem to have an affinity for one another.'

Kai sent me a startled look, but said nothing. Lily was unsurprised – she knew that secret, then.

Don't talk about me like I'm not here, I sent Anisa. She ignored me.

'What does affinity mean again?' Frey asked.

'It means you two get along,' Lily said, with a nervous glance towards me.

'Oh. That's true. I only met you one other time, but you seem very nice.' He nodded. 'So do the rest of you,' he added, as if he realized it might be rude to leave the others out.

It was unnerving, how unafraid Frey was after his fit. But then, perhaps he didn't know how close he'd come to being lost. His words worked to break the tension, and we managed weak chuckles. I liked Frey. He still reminded me of the Princess. They both had to hide their differences. They were both lonely. Lily wanted to protect him, but she also cut him off from the world. He had no friends his own age, and couldn't leave the house without being heavily disguised.

What childhoods. By Frey's age, I knew that I had a secret, but mine could be hidden. I could play with other children. I doubted Frey or the Princess had ever laughed with abandon at something their friend said until they gained a stitch in their side. Never had a mud fight. Never been free to be children.

'All right, Frey. Close your eyes,' Anisa said.

He did as he was bid. The scaling on the backs of his eyelids was very delicate. Anisa walked him through simple meditation, asking him to clear his mind. He had trouble settling down, but when he did, the power that still sizzled around him calmed, as if it drew deeper into his body.

'Yes,' Anisa said. 'Yes. Whenever you are frightened or feel the energy escaping, come to this place. Block everything out. Right here, right now, you are safe.'

She taught him more meditation techniques, until the room felt almost normal again. Cyan sat on Lily's bed, her feet drawn up under the skirt of her dress, her arms around her knees. She was fascinated by the lessons, and I found myself planning to try some meditation myself, to see if it'd calm my mind.

When the sky was lightening, Anisa said that was enough. Kai had fallen asleep on the sofa, his coat covering his wings. In the way of some children, Frey was calm and unconcerned by the magnitude of the days' events. I envied him, that he didn't constantly fear what the morrow would bring.

He yawned, and the light glinted off his scales again. I thought of how bundled he was whenever they left the apartments.

'Have you ever tried using a Glamour?' I asked Lily.

She blinked. 'I had wondered, but I can't afford one and have never been able to try. Is that how you change your appearance for your magic shows? I thought it might be cunning cosmetics.'

Taking the Glamour from around my neck, I fiddled with the controls. It took a long time to program the Glamour perfectly, but at least I could see if it would work at all. Though I still ached with exhaustion, I was so curious.

I slipped the Glamour around Frey's neck. He picked it up in his hands and turned it over. I turned it on and the illusion settled over his features. It was crude, and his horns were still visible, but his skin turned the same shade as his mother's, and his bright eyes turned a more normal shade of green. Lily held her hands over her mouth.

'What is it?' Frey asked. 'What did it do?'

I hesitated, wondering if I should show him. What if it made him feel embarrassed about how he looked normally? Lily saw my trepidation.

'Remember how I said that people don't understand things, sometimes? Like your scales, and how they're beautiful, but some people have tiny minds and might not think so?'

'Yes,' he said, his hand going to his cheek. Though it was now the colour of peaches and looked just as soft, it would still feel scaly to him.

'And so we have to cover you up when you go out, so that these sad people don't stare at you, or make mean comments, and make you feel at all like it's bad to be different. This is another way to do that. But I want you to know that I wish we didn't have to hide it at all. You know that, don't you?' Her eyes shone with tears again.

He shrugged. 'Yes. Can I see now?'

She passed him a little hand mirror. It was cracked from falling off the vanity.

He frowned as he looked at the mirror. Gently, he touched the horns, poking from his forehead. I hadn't given him hair, either. 'I look strange.'

Lily laughed, though the sound came out harsh, and switched off the Glamour. The scales returned. Frey watched the transformation and passed the mirror back. He yawned and said he was tired, and then closed his eyes. Within moments, he was fast asleep. Lily ran her hand over his scaled scalp.

Kai had awoken. 'Can . . . can I try?'

We passed it to him. He caught the trick of it sooner than Frey had, and he only had his wings to erase. He looked at his smooth back in a full-length mirror in Frey's room.

'How much are they?' he asked when he reluctantly passed it over.

'They're not cheap.'

'I'll find a way. I'd give anything not to have to wear coats like this in summer.' When his wings reappeared, though, he wrapped them around himself, touching one lightly. He didn't hate them any more than Frey hated his horns. He hated that he had to hide them.

'Thank you,' Lily said. 'I really thought I was going to lose him tonight.'

'More than just he would have been lost,' Anisa said. 'I am glad we drew him back from the brink.'

'You must all be tired,' Lily said. 'I won't forget what you've done. I've not told Pozzi much about you, though, to be fair, recently he hasn't asked. I suppose since he sees you once a week, Micah, that satisfies most of his curiosity. But if you wish for me to feed him false information, then I will. No questions asked.'

'Thank you,' I said. As a Shadow, the offer of falsifying information to her paying client was not given lightly. Shadows usually prided themselves on their honesty, though of course there were always exceptions.

We bid our farewells. Anisa transformed back into smoke and returned to her Aleph, and I pocketed it. It had been interesting to see her training Frey. She'd been a teacher, so long ago. She'd taught Chimaera to control their powers, but for what larger purpose?

And what skills did she know that she could also teach me?

At the door, out of sight of Kai and Frey, Drystan turned to Lily. He reached into his jacket pocket and brought out the vial containing the tiny fleck of Elixir.

She cradled it in her hand, as though it were precious. 'Thank you,' she whispered. 'I'll send it to my friend tomorrow morning. Maybe then we can finally discover what it contains.'

Drystan said nothing, but was the first out the door. He held his back straight and stiff.

We were silent as we returned to the Penny Rookeries. Curfew was still in full force, and we kept to the shadows. The streets were empty, and we saw only one night watchman, easily avoided. As soon as we'd climbed the fire escape and climbed into the bedroom, Cyan went to her room.

Drystan sat on the bed, staring blankly at the rug.

'I'm all right, Drystan. We're all right. I know it was—' I began.

'I couldn't do anything,' Drystan interrupted.

I stayed silent.

'When Frey was hurting you. I couldn't do anything. There was no way for me to help. I was completely useless.'

'That's not true—'

'It is. I couldn't even touch you without being thrown across the room. You and Cyan have the powers, the abilities. I can pick a lock, but otherwise I can't help much at all.'

'That's not true,' I insisted. 'After I came back I needed

you and you were there. You held me and helped me come back.'

I received a wan smile at that. 'When I couldn't reach you it was . . . terrifying.'

'I know.' I sat next to him on the bed and put my hand over his.

'I feel useless,' he went on. 'And then I feel guilty for thinking like that. Like I'm some child left out of a game I can't play. You're part of something. Anisa's worried for the Chimaera. You're the one she said could help. Not me.'

'There's more ways to stop them than just powers,' I said, picking my words with care. 'Say, for instance, what happened to me today happens again. I can't defend myself when I'm like that. I couldn't even see. I'd need you to help keep me safe. It's a different battle, but that doesn't mean one is better than the other.'

He sighed, running his fingers through his hair. 'I know. I suppose I'm a bit jealous, which seems ridiculous when I see how much grief it causes you and Cyan. She has to hear the stupid, cruel thoughts humans think. You're reliant on Elixir, though it seems to have expanded your powers. It's still amazing, what you two can do. Even that boy Kai had those wings, and probably other powers besides. Sometimes I imagine what kind I'd have.'

'And what are they?' I asked, curious.

He leaned back on the bed, crossing his arms behind his head. 'There's a few. I wouldn't mind being able to convince people to do things. I'm already pretty good at that, mind, but a bit of a stronger push. Or maybe the ability to be invisible.'

'You could then become quite the jewel thief,' I said.

He laughed. 'Wouldn't hurt. I'd steal you an emerald as big as your head.'

'We'd have to sell it. I don't think I could wear a ring the size of my head on my finger. But that's a romantic gesture. Until we're caught and thrown in prison.'

'Then, with my power of invisibility, I'll break us both out and we'll pick up right where we left off.'

'Hmm, I suppose that would be rather handy.'

That won me a smile. 'I'm being stupid.'

'No, you're not.' I leaned back on the bed next to him. 'I'd be jealous too. And you shouldn't feel stupid for saying how you feel.'

He sighed and held out his arms, and I crawled into them. 'You're right. I feel better after having my little strop about it.'

'Good.'

We were silent. I listened to his heartbeat. His fingertips stroked my scalp through my hair. Eventually, our eyes closed and we drifted to sleep.

18

RETURN TO SNAKEWOOD PALACE

Attention: security throughout the Royal Snakewood Palace is to be doubled. Shifts are lengthening from nine to ten hours. Anyone willing to work extra shifts, please report to Head of Security immediately, and new vacancies will be posted imminently. Current guards are encouraged to recommend names of friends and family they can personally attest to being strong, capable, and trustworthy.
  In the Royal Snakewood's name,
  Palace Security.
      — Personnel Memo, Royal Snakewood Palace

A few days later, we received a letter during breakfast. As soon as Drystan came back to the kitchen carrying the heavy, creamy envelope, I knew what it would be.

We'd received another invitation from the palace.

Maske was excited. The last fee we'd received had paid for most of the repair of the roof of the Kymri Theatre. With another fee of the same amount, Maske said, we could afford a better apartment.

'I sort of like this place,' I said. 'It has charm.'

'The hot water's stopped working and every time we turn on the stove we worry it's going to explode,' Cyan said. 'And there's mould in my room.'

'Charm?' I said. She mimed throwing something at me and I pantomimed ducking.

It would be good if we could have larger accommodation. We were cramped in this four-bedroom apartment after the sprawling rooms of the Kymri Theatre. Magic props took up a lot of space.

Drystan, Cyan, and I didn't share the same enthusiasm for returning to the palace. We knew all too well that it would be more than just a magic show for the Princess. The Steward had left that almost-threat hanging in the air: he might have use for us. We had volunteered our services. I would put gold coin down that the Steward would be appraising us again, and if he found us worthy, would collect on that promise.

Maske was jolly the rest of the day, occasionally punctuating the tuneless humming to wonder what in the theatre we would fix next. 'The kitchen? The gridiron? Recreating the mosaic in the hallway?'

We didn't have the heart to tell him that the price for these things would be far steeper than he knew.

That afternoon, the Penny Rookeries threw a street party. We were invited to perform magic. Most people knew us in the neighbourhood by now. Every now and again, we'd perform street magic in the Rookeries, refusing to take anyone's coins, knowing full well they had none to give.

Sometimes people would stop us on the pavement when we weren't doing magic, to greet us and tell us how much they enjoyed our shows. I'd spied a few people playing with packs of cards, trying their hand at their own tricks, and it'd made me smile.

The street party was a way to unwind. Even those loyal to the Forester cause were exhausted by the tension throughout the city. There had been no more Kashura attacks, yet people still feared their neighbours, others calling for a freeze on immigration to Ellada. Rumours of more attacks were thick in the air.

We went down to set up in one of the squares, dressed in our magician's costumes, and Drystan and I wore our Glamours. Most of the cobbles were loose, and many were missing. We spread out our rugs and props as people set up food and casks of ale. A local tavern keeper gave us some mugs of his best as a thank you for our performances.

The party started early, as it'd have to finish before nightfall. Soon, the square was packed with people. A band on the other side of the square played jaunty tunes. A crowd gathered around us, and we began our show.

We hadn't crafted our usual act, lacking the space to fully implement any of our magical plays, and as people came and went, they'd likely lose the thread of the narrative. And so we drew on our now-wide array of tricks – cards, coins, flowers, and more. Cyan even took out her old tarot deck and set up a table nearby, reading fortunes. She told me earlier she hadn't read fortunes since she left the circus, but that she wasn't as resentful or afraid of it any more. But she wouldn't be looking in people's minds to tell their fates, only reading the cards that were there.

After a few hours, we tired of the street magic and stopped. Lily came to visit and she and Maske went off together, arm in arm. We knew we should tell Maske who Lily truly was, but at the same time, it seemed as if she should be the one to tell him. I wondered how Kai and Frey were faring, back at Lily's apartment, and whether or not they wished they could be here.

We wandered through the square, purchasing snacks. We had sausages in rolls with onions and peppers, more mugs of ale, and later, gooey, just-baked chocolate biscuits. My stomach was happily full. I liked being surrounded by the crowd of loud, cheerful people. A temporary dance floor of cheap wood had been erected in front of the band. Cyan danced a jig with me and then Drystan. We twirled about to the sound of fiddles.

Afterwards, breathless, I had more ale, the world growing warm. It reminded me of the bonfires and dancing after the circus. For a few brief hours, I was able to push all the troubles from my mind.

On the day we were to go to the Snakewood Palace, Maske lost his voice and came down with a fever.

He struck the pillow with his fist when we told him he'd have to stay behind. He couldn't very well narrate the show without his voice, and the guards wouldn't let him near the Princess looking as sick as he did. He lay back in his bed, defeated. I made him a cup of tea while Cyan and Drystan finished packing up the kit.

Maske thanked me and fell into a deep sleep. I doubted he'd wake up before his tea was stone cold. I couldn't help but be thankful he'd be staying behind. We hadn't told him about the Princess's secret, for we were true to our word.

The carriage from the palace arrived, the footmen making short work of the heavy boxes of our kit. We set off and the palace soon came into view, the turrets stark against the overcast sky.

After the seemingly endless search through our possessions, we were led into the same room where we had performed last time. We unpacked, painting our faces and changing into our costumes, and then waited for the Princess.

She came in with her two friends who had been at the other party, whose names I didn't recall, and another girl. She walked in front of them, stiff and proper, and settled at the front of the stage, rearranging her skirts. Cyan fed us the names of the girls we didn't know: Miss Laya Oakbeam and Miss Katharine Huckleberry. The last face I most definitely did recognize: Darla Hornbeam, Drystan's youngest sister. Drystan stared at her avidly.

I gave Drystan's shoulder a squeeze and then we entered the stage. Drystan would be narrating in Maske's absence, with me and Cyan performing. The show had been designed so as to only briefly require a stagehand.

We'd run the programme by the Steward and his council beforehand, and luckily they'd approved it. They didn't want anything too political, they said; but perhaps they hadn't noticed that the tale was more so than they realized.

It was one of my favourite of the magic plays we'd developed. I hoped the Princess enjoyed it.

'A long time ago,' Drystan began, 'there was a princess who lived in a faraway land. She had many friends, but sometimes she liked to be alone to watch the sun set and the moon rise.

'One day, she went to a tower that faced the west, as it had the best view. She hadn't gone to that tower in a long time, for she'd found the gargoyle statues frightening. Yet one of them did not seem so fierce, so she stood beside it as the last of the sun faded.'

With his foot, Drystan tripped a hidden lever, which caused a long swathe of silk to fall over the stage for just a moment. He tore it away, revealing Cyan and me in costume, freshly emerged from the trapdoor under the stage.

Cyan was dressed as the Princess, wearing a Temnian robe, her hair freshly braided with beads. She wore a tin crown studded with glass jewels, but under the light of the glass globes it looked as fine as any coronet.

I was not so pretty. My skin was painted entirely grey, my hair dusted white with chalk. I wore old, ripped clothing, likewise dyed grey and chalked. I stared straight ahead. A gargoyle statue.

Drystan, behind stage, moved the glass globes to mimic sunset, and another silken cloth fell against the backdrop. This one was dark blue and dotted with stars, embroidered by Cyan and Drystan, as I was still hopeless with a needle and thread.

As the last 'ray' of light left the stage, I shook myself

awake, a small cloud of chalk rising from me. Cyan jumped back in shock.

'Good evening, Your Majesty,' I said.

The girls in the audience tittered, but not Princess Nicolette. She watched us closely, her falsely green eyes locked on us.

Our story began. I introduced myself as the gargoyle, giving my name as Petros. Cyan crept forward again, curious. I told her that I was under a dark spell, and that I'd been placed on this windy tower as punishment.

Drystan added a timely sound of wind blowing and thunder, thanks to a whistle and a rattling sheet of metal.

I stood on the low wall of the tower and stretched. My constructed wings rose behind me, fully articulated bat-like wings made of metal, wood, and leather. They were crude echoes of Kai's. Again, murmurings came from the other three girls in the audience, but not the Princess. I stood on my tiptoes, ensuring they had a full view of my wings. I glanced down at Cyan and saw a flash of an emotion I could not place, and then it was gone. Though I frowned at her, I did not break character. Hopping down from the wall, I held up my hands to stop Cyan from fleeing the 'tower.'

'Wait,' I called. 'If you stay, I'll show you magic, and tell you tales of such wonder that you have never heard. The world is wider and wilder than they have told you. Do you not yearn to see the spark?'

Hesitantly, she returned, perching on the wall.

The magic show began in earnest. With prestidigitation, I made more of the carved wooden puppets I'd used in the lantern appear, the movements blending seamlessly with the tales I told the princess of lands far away, filled with other Chimaera that I had flown to see. Behind stage, Drystan helped with sound and lighting effects.

Then I, as the gargoyle, grew despondent.

'You can no longer fly,' Cyan said, sadly.

'No, I am enchanted. By day, I am hard as stone. By night, I live, but I cannot leave the top of this tower. I cannot fly.' I shrugged my shoulders and the constructed wings flapped.

'Why were you cursed this way?'

'They're afraid of me,' I said. 'They think I mean them harm, though I'd do no such thing.' Not subtle. 'A wizard decided to trap me and was hailed as a hero for saving the kingdom from danger. No one realized until it was too late that he was the monster, not me.'

Cyan stood. 'I know magic as well,' she declared. 'Perhaps I can free you, and you may fly again.'

My eyes went wide with hope. 'You would do that?'

Cyan closed her eyes, sifting through the audience's minds to find out which display would impress them best. She clapped her hands together and the hidden chemicals she palmed sparked. Drystan manoeuvred behind the scenes, and Cyan lifted into the air, held aloft on a strong, nearly invisible black wire.

She began to mutter in Temri, peppered with the odd bit of Alder. She clapped her hands again and, thanks to Cyril, the glass globes bloomed, as if lightning was in the room. Drystan created another clap of thunder. Cyan lowered herself to the ground, panting.

I sighed. 'It was a lovely display, but it didn't work.'

Cyan looked crestfallen. 'Are you sure?'

'I am, my Princess. For look, the sun returns.'

On cue, Drystan and Cyril moved the glass globes so that the stage filled with the soft oranges and pinks of sunrise. I returned to my perch and settled myself back into my statue pose.

As the 'sun' rose, I froze. Cyan touched my shoulder and jumped back.

'So cold! As if made of stone!' she exclaimed. She stared at me in amazement, and then gathered her skirts to flee.

Another drop of the curtain, and then Drystan appeared back on the stage, taking up his role as narrator. Below stage, Cyan and I readied ourselves for the second half of the show.

Drystan stared at the audience, chin held high. 'The years passed, but the princess continued to visit the gargoyle at the top of the tower. As she grew from princess to queen, she searched for a way to break the gargoyle's spell. For over these many years, they became close friends, and the gargoyle, with his many years of experience, often gave her sound advice for her kingdom.

'But sometimes, the princess despaired – could Petros ever truly be set free? Could she undo the punishment he was wrongly given?'

Drystan disappeared with a flourish of his cape, leaving us to take the stage.

Cyan had changed into another costume, a dress with long, flowing sleeves. Her new crown rose high from her brow. She stood on stage, stiff-backed, as regal as the queen she was meant to be.

'I've searched far and wide,' she said. To her left were several books which levitated, thanks to more hidden wires, twirling slowly. They were more sedate versions of the flying books we had seen in Frey's room. 'I've emptied libraries and asked the greatest scholars and folklorists throughout the Archipelago about the myths of gargoyles. But no one knows anything that could free you. I'm so sorry, Petros.' Her voice broke. 'I don't know how to save you.'

I turned my head and jumped down from the tower perch. 'I do not think there is a way to free me, fair Queen. I have long since resigned myself to this fact. I am content to stay here, looking out on the horizon to protect you from evil, as long as you continue to visit me.'

Cyan shook her head. 'That is not enough. I want you to be free, to fly as I promised you.'

I smiled at her sadly. 'Seeing the world through your eyes is freeing enough, my Queen. Thanks to you, I know all that happens in our lovely land. Your stories are my sustenance. For even if I was free, where could I fly? The world has changed so much since I was young. People would fear me, and perhaps even hunt me. No, my Queen, please. Do not spend a moment mourning my situation. I am where I need to be. With you. I am home.'

At my words, the glass globes shifted to dark blues and purples. But the light that shone on me was all reds, oranges, and yellow. With another lift from unseen wires, I spread my wings out wide.

'I'm freed,' I said, delighted. I gave a short flight around the stage, moving my mechanical wings. The audience clapped as Cyan clasped her hands over her mouth in delight.

'But how? Why only now?'

'I do not know. Perhaps the Lord and the Lady decided I had suffered enough.'

Drystan finished the story:

'But even though the gargoyle was freed, he stayed by the side of his queen, through all her long years. He flew throughout the kingdom, protecting the borders. He became her adviser in earnest, though others still feared him and called him a monster.

'With the curse broken, the gargoyle aged. And when the Queen died of old age, her gargoyle soon followed.'

The glass globes brightened again, with Cyan, Drystan, and me on stage. We bowed to applause. The Princess's companions smiled and clapped, even Drystan's sister Darla, who in my memory was sombre. The Princess smiled like the rest of them, but there was a small line between her eyes, as though she still contemplated the storyline. The allegory was fairly evident – Chimaera, like the gargoyle, meant no harm.

Darla looked at me, frowning. I straightened my shirt, nervous. I was wearing the Glamour and male clothing – there was no way she could recognize me as the girl who had sat across the table from her at afternoon tea parties in the Emerald Bowl. Yet I was relieved when her attention wandered elsewhere.

The Princess came to us, clasping our hands and thanking

us for the performance. It seemed as if she'd enjoyed it, but knowing she wore so many different personas for different people made it difficult to tell for certain. At our duel with Taliesin, she'd smiled and clapped, bright with excitement. Had that been real? I hoped so.

How are you feeling, Your Highness? I chanced asking her with my mind.

She started, but recovered her composure. *A lot better than last time, thank you*, she replied.

I'm glad, I said.

I've been wanting to speak to you. Can anyone hear us?

I strengthened the shield around our minds, so even Cyan would not hear. *It's safe. What did you wish to discuss, Your Highness?*

I'm growing ill a lot. Collapsing like I did last time. The doctor told me you are having treatments too. And others.

Others. Me and Frey; were there more? Was Kai treated? Why hadn't I thought to ask that?

Yes. I take Elixir injections once a week, just like you do. But I'm not sure how I can help. We are . . . different.

I'm scared all the time, and no one understands. I can't tell anyone. Her eyes darted towards her friends, speaking amongst themselves and nibbling on scones and cakes laid out by the servants. Well, not Darla. She still had no sweet tooth.

Yes. I do know what that's like, I thought.

The Doctor will fix us, she said, determined. I looked into her hopeful face and I wanted to weep.

Perhaps he will, is all I said.

We'd been silent and staring at each other too long. I turned away from her and busied myself with my magic props.

Maybe neither of us needs to be cured, I sent her.

Her eyes widened and she smiled at me genuinely, eyes as bright as the night of the magic duel. *I do like you, Sam Harper.*

Please, call me Micah. It's my real name. And I like you too, my Princess.

Call me Nico.

Nico. I flashed her a little smile, marvelling at the fact I'd just called the future monarch by a nickname.

The Steward entered with a few bodyguards and servants, to lead the Princess and her companions to their lessons.

But the Steward lingered. Drystan, Cyan, and I all bowed low to him as etiquette dictated with a murmured, 'Your Highness.'

'Good afternoon,' he greeted us. His lone bodyguard stared straight ahead, a statue made of flesh and bone. Soon, he could forget every word we were about to utter.

And, if the Steward decided we knew too much, he'd do the same to us. I shivered.

'Another enjoyable show, I hear. My apologies that I could not attend, but I was needed elsewhere.'

'You are a busy man and we completely understand, Your Highness,' Drystan said.

'I've learned more about you since our last visit,' the Steward said with that same, inscrutable calmness. Cyan stared at him hard, and a frown line appeared between her eyebrows.

He's wearing a Cricket, she whispered. *Can't sense a thing. He either knows or suspects, and neither is good. He also has an Augur, so ensure you do not lie outright, but you can withhold aspects of the truth without triggering it.*

'Yes, Your Highness?' I chanced, when no one else made a move.

'Of course, with the little our Royal Physician told me, I had to delve deeper to ensure you are safe enough to have around my niece. What I found was most interesting.'

My mouth was dry. He did not seem to expect an answer this time. That little smile still played around his mouth. Here was the man in charge of a kingdom, of a former head of an empire. Here was a man who knew every piece in play, and delighted cornering us into a checkmate.

'You,' he said, nodding to Cyan, 'are Cyan Zhu. You grew up in Riley and Batheo's Circus of Curiosities, the daughter of Temnian immigrants. After suspicious circumstances involving a lion tamer, you left the circus.'

Cyan swallowed. 'The way you phrased that, Your Highness, makes it seem as if I was involved. I was not.'

'No, no, I am well aware the tragedy was an accident. Yet there is a strange spate of rumours about the exact reasons for your disappearance.'

One of his hands went to the hollow of his neck, where he wore the Cricket disguised beneath his clothes. Cyan's back stiffened.

'In any case, should I have need, I believe your certain skills will prove most advantageous. Can I rely on you?'

Cyan did not hesitate. 'I am a loyal citizen of Ellada. What you need, I will give.' *Unless you ask me to do something undeniably wrong and against the spirit of Ellada.* She shot me a look out of the corner of her eye, and I gave her the most imperceptible of nods.

'And Ellada thanks you for it,' the Steward said. 'And you,' he said, next turning to me. 'Maske insists on referring to you as Sam Harper, but we both know that is not your name. It's not even Micah Grey, the young fugitive. It's Iphigenia Laurus, the runaway. Your parents are very worried about you.'

I forced myself not to react, but it was all I could do not to faint. The Steward had done his homework on us. 'They are,' I managed.

'You're a little harder to deduce. You seem strong; by all accounts you were a very healthy child. No evidence of wrongdoing prior to that night at R. H. Ragona's Circus of Magic, and none since.'

I nodded, not trusting myself to speak.

'Tell me what you can do, Iphigenia Laurus.'

The name made me wince. 'Micah Grey is the name I now use, Your Highness.'

His eyes narrowed. 'Micah.' His voice was flat with a warning.

Taking a deep breath, I told the truth. 'I rarely grew ill, until I needed Pozzi's treatments. If I am injured, I heal faster. I can sometimes glean the thoughts and emotions of others. That's all.'

He paused, waiting to see if his Augur would chirp. He nodded. 'Thank you for telling me the truth. I know this is not easy.'

I breathed a little easier. The Steward turned to Drystan, and my shoulders tensed again.

'You were an interesting surprise as well,' the Steward said. 'Amon Fletcher is yet another pseudonym. But I did not expect the son of my most trusted adviser to be one of the escaped clowns from R. H. Ragona's Circus of Magic.'

'I don't have any abilities,' Drystan bit out.

'Oh, I know. But you are still very useful to me. Card-counting, petty theft, drug dealing, and picking locks. This could come in handy. I also figure that, since I can't dangle the threat of exposure, I have to use a slightly firmer hand.' Another pause, a studied glance at his fingernails. 'You have a young sister. Darla, is it? She was just here. A lovely young girl – her debutante ball is this year.' The Steward smiled. 'It would damage her prospects if word were to spread about what her brother has been up to. Might harm your father's standing, although you're probably not bothered by that. Am I wrong?'

Drystan didn't collapse, but it was a very near thing. My ears rang and Cyan's mental walls had fractured, her fear and confusion spiralling into the room. I had only met Darla a handful of times, and though I didn't like her, the thought that the Steward would so cavalierly speak of ruining her future chances left me cold. I'd faced a life without prospects. It was hard for a young woman of means to remain on the shelf, especially if it was due to a scandal in no way her fault. In that moment, I hated the ruler of our country.

The Steward could ask us to do almost anything, and we would have to do his bidding. The Steward of Ellada, one of the most powerful men in the country, knew all of our secrets and dangled them over us. He was shrewd and knew he could not rely on our loyalty to the crown alone. He let us know that he could destroy us with a wave of his pinkie, sending us to prison for the rest of our lives if we refused him.

It was a pretty trap. And how easily we had stepped into it.

'Are . . . you asking us to do anything?' I managed to ask, voice shaking.

The Steward smiled, and he shed that polite facade. His smile should have had pointed teeth. 'Not now. Not yet.'

'Why not hire proper spies? Even knowing our secrets, we're hardly professionals, Your Highness.'

'No, that you aren't. Yet the Princess's secret is spreading far too quickly for comfort and I don't know who to trust. The Kashura have agents everywhere. I don't trust you, but I trust that you wish to remain free. Blackmail and bribery are not my usual way of business, but in this case, they are a necessity.' He spread his hands widely, but made no further apology.

'We will do as you bid, Your Majesty,' I said, bowing and hoping it was to the right depth. Growing up, I'd focused on memorizing the proper curtsies. Drystan followed, stiffly, and Cyan sank into a shaking curtsy.

The Steward of Ellada let us go. For now.

19

THE NEEDLE

Lerium is one of the most powerful drugs known to man. It was not consumed by the public until the last century. Before that, it was a sacred substance used only by priests in the remote mountains of Byssia. A foolhardy Elladan trekked through the mountains on his own, and became trapped in a snowstorm. He would have died, had not a passing priest seen him shivering beneath a pine tree and taken him to their monastery. The priest may have later regretted his decision.

The priests had one of their ceremonies, and the Elladan, breaking their hospitality, stole some Lerium and tried it himself. The high was the best the man had ever experienced, and this was a man to try as many substances as possible. He brought some back with him to Ellada.

The secret was out. Within a matter of years, Lerium was no longer the exclusive providence of Byssian priests. But Byssians were very canny about it. They kept the recipe and the source of the drug secret, so Ellada could not copy it. Though the drug has ravaged many in Byssia,

Ellada, and all the former colonies, at the same time, it has made Byssia incredibly wealthy.

Yet if that man had perished in the snowstorm, would Lerium still be the well-kept secret of the priests? Would all the people who have since perished from the drug still be alive? Very possibly.

— 'Lerium', paper and lecture by PROFESSOR IONA DOUGLAS, a student of PROFESSOR CAED CEDAR, Royal Snakewood University

Drystan only barely managed to hold it together until we were home. He sat in the carriage, still as could be. None of us could bring ourselves to speak and Cyan had her mental walls locked tight. I was as surprised as anyone at the ruthlessness of the Steward, but at the same time it was somehow inevitable.

Drystan had tried to leave his family and Elladan politics behind, and now he was drawn back into their orbit. The Steward had toyed with all of us, but him most of all, showing that he could still shatter the life Drystan thought he'd left behind. The Steward hadn't threatened my brother. Perhaps he felt he didn't need to, or through his network already knew of Cyril's staunch loyalty to the crown and didn't wish to taint it.

It was all because Pozzi had told the Steward enough secrets to pique his interest. He'd arranged this as neatly as everything else. In some ways, the Royal Physician and the Steward were two sides of the same Elladan coin.

I'd hoped that despite everything, the doctor had our best interests at heart. Now, I dreaded my next visit, even as the thought of more Elixir sent a thrill of anticipation through me.

When we entered our flat, Maske rang the bell from his bedroom impatiently, urging us to report. I couldn't help but be glad that he hadn't been there for this.

'Don't tell him,' I whispered. 'He doesn't need to be drawn into our troubles any more than he already is.' They agreed.

Maske had also received a letter from the insurance company the day before, saying that the renovations of the Kymri Theatre would be delayed due to Forester protests around the area and limited shifts due to curfew.

I still did most of the talking, telling Maske the Princess had enjoyed the show and asking how he felt. He said he was feeling better and would soon be able to dance a jig.

'But maybe not just now,' he added, ruefully. He asked for more details, and so I kept speaking until the sound of my voice lulled him to sleep. He slumped against the pillow, his hair rumpled and his mouth hanging open in a most un-Maske-like fashion. Cyan put her palm on his forehead.

'His fever's broken,' she said. 'He just needs sleep.'

We left him, dimming the lamps, before returning to our bedroom. The room was stifling, so I opened the window. Outside, the air was crisp and chilly, but the night was clear.

'Are you all right?' Cyan asked Drystan.

'No,' he said, shortly.

'Me neither.' Cyan wrapped her arms around herself

and stared up at the stars. 'We can only hope he never calls on his favour.'

'It's only a matter of time.' We should never have accepted Pozzi's invitation to perform for the Princess. The strings attached had tied us too tightly.

We lapsed into a silence filled with worry. My hand clasped Drystan's, giving him what wordless comfort I could. The moonlight shone its faint silver light on the three of us.

I awoke in the middle of the night, alone in the bed. The space next to me was cold. I waited a few minutes, wondering if Drystan had gone to the toilet, but he didn't return. I left the bed, my bare feet cold on the floor.

He wasn't in the bathroom. I reached out with my mind and sensed him in the tiny spare bedroom, the one we used for storage of our magic kit. Bizarre. If he couldn't sleep, he'd surely go to the kitchen or the small lounge, with the banked fires to take away the evening chill. Foreboding surged through me as I made my way to the room.

I could not sense his thoughts through the door – for all my recent surge in abilities, I wasn't anywhere near as talented as Cyan.

Frozen with indecision, I wanted to knock but at the same time feared to discover what he was doing in there. Did that mean I didn't trust him? It was his own business, and I'd kept my own fair share of secrets from him in the past.

I strained to read him again, but only sensed . . . elation?

I'm probably going to regret this, I thought before pushing open the door.

For a moment, the room seemed empty aside from the covered magical props, and I squinted. There, in the corner, Drystan lay curled up around himself.

'Oh, Styx,' I said in dread. In front of him lay a spent syringe, and I knew it was Elixir. If I hadn't spent so long tied up in my own fear, I might have been able to stop him.

'Drystan.' I rolled him onto his side. I'd read somewhere that you should do that, in case they choked on their own vomit. He was shivering, his eyes rolled up into his head.

'Oh, you *stupid* fool,' I said, my hands fluttering over him, unsure what to do. I had no experience with this, and no idea how Elixir would affect him. What if it was poisonous to someone not Chimaera?

Drystan's eyes opened and focused on me, sharp as knives.

'I sense the threads of the world,' he said, clutching the front of my shirt. 'They're made of light. The blue of Penglass, the orange of sunset, the red of blood. I sense them all.'

'I'm sure you do,' I said, speaking to him calmly, though my heartbeat pounded in my ears.

'No, you don't understand. It's like Anisa said. Everything is written in the world, if only you have the ability to read it. And she's right. Someone wishes to hurt the Chimaera. But it's so cloudy. I see the man behind it, but his face is . . . blurry?' He rested his face in his hands. 'It's beautiful and terrible to read the world. Oh Gods, what have I done? I . . . just wanted to be better than myself again. For a little while.'

'Oh, Drystan,' I said, stroking the hair back from his face. 'You don't have to be better than yourself. You're wonderful as you are.'

'No,' he said forcefully, pushing away. 'I can't help you. The day the cathedral fell, I couldn't help you. The other day, with Frey and you and Cyan, I was thrown across the room by power like I was a feather. But now I can – with Elixir, anyone can be at least a little Chimaera. Maybe that's why they're so afraid of you.' He struggled to sit up. 'It means I could help you if I keep taking it!' The words tumbled from his mouth, faster and faster. 'Maybe I'd gain a power, like moving objects with my mind, or turn invisible, or fly! It's not for the high. You have to believe me. I didn't do this just for the high. I'm not an addict . . .'

He shook even worse. I swallowed, my mouth dry with fear. 'You shouldn't have done this without telling me. Elixir is risky, and you didn't know how it'd affect you. We don't even know what's in it yet.'

It could be dangerous because you're not like Cyan and me, I wanted to add, but bit my tongue. I knew he felt left out because he did not have extra abilities. Yet I never thought he'd do something so foolhardy as to risk addiction with a drug we didn't understand.

'I wasn't going to . . . I was just going to look at it.'

He fell against me, resting his head against my thigh. I pushed the sweaty hair back from his forehead. I wanted to be angry with him, but how could I? He was hurting.

Seeing his father must have brought back memories of the time just after he left. He'd stolen Elixir months ago and hadn't taken any, but it was too much at once.

'How much of this did you take that night from Elwood's place?' I asked him. 'Answer me honestly.'

'A few vials.'

Earlier, he'd said he'd only taken one.

'How many exactly?'

A soft breath. 'Six. Five, now.' His voice grew fuzzy, his eyelids drooping.

I shook him. 'Stay awake.'

'I'm awake. I'm awakened. More than I've ever been.' His eyes widened. 'Did you know there's no one like you in the entire world, Micah Grey?'

'Yes, I did. There's no one like you, either. We're all unique.'

'Yes. *Yes.* There's so many lives. Each with their own story. Their own joys. Their own sorrows. How could I go so long when I was young, never giving them a second thought? How could I have been so selfish?'

'You learned from it. You moved on. You're not the same person you were when you ran away, Drystan.'

'You always see through me, Micah. Always see to the heart of it. Even when I hid from you, behind the veneer of the White Clown. And you're still here. You're not afraid.'

'Why would I ever be afraid?'

'I was a terrible person,' he said, and he was crying. 'Maybe I still am. I might destroy my sister's prospects. My father's standing would be compromised. Look, I can't even resist sticking a needle into my veins. I swore I would never do this again. I promised Maske, years ago, and then I fail under his own roof. I've disappointed him. I've disappointed you. I disappoint everyone.'

'Stop with that nonsense, right now, Drystan. I won't stand for it.' At my sharp tone, he looked up at me, blearily.

'You have never disappointed me. You were one of my first friends in the circus, even if you scared me half-senseless when you did that weird thing with your eyes.'

That startled a laugh from him and he made his eyes vibrate in his sockets, just like he had the night I met him.

'Ew! Don't do that.' He managed to make me laugh too, but it faded. 'I mean it. When I told you who I had been before, you kept my secret. You've saved my life. You accepted me, you loved me, and you weren't afraid that I was different. Do you realize how much that means to me? Ever since I can remember, my mother always told me that no one could love me as I was. That I had to hide and change what I was to be accepted. You never have. Not once. I'm so grateful to have you, to love you and have you love me.'

My outpouring of words sputtered to a halt.

Drystan broke down, weeping openly. I gathered him even closer, tears falling from our eyes.

He babbled to me of what the world was telling him, how he wished he could fly. When the cold of the claustrophobic room made us both shiver, I drew him up and led him to the kitchen, setting him at the table and making him drink some tea and eat some toast. This proved to be a mistake, as he couldn't keep the toast down. I cleaned him up.

'Come on,' I said. 'Come upstairs.'

He leaned heavily on me. He smelled of the mint tea I'd given him. He kept mumbling, but I couldn't make out what he was saying. Halfway back to the bedroom he stopped and looked up at the ceiling.

'Above us is so much open space, yet we hide from it under roofs and towers. Maybe if there are a Lord and Lady up there, we're afraid for them to see what we're really up to behind closed doors and under the roof slates.'

'Or we build roofs because it's cold and rain is wet.' I urged him on again. Far off, I sensed Cyan awakening from slumber, alarmed. *Leave it*, I told her. *This is between us.* She drifted away, but left the smallest tendril of concern behind.

I managed to half-drag Drystan to bed. I took off his sweat-stained shirt, then left him long enough to fetch a large glass of water and a damp cloth. I forced him to drink all the water, hoping it would help. I used the cloth to wipe away the sweat from his skin. He lay in bed and shivered, eyes staring upright, pupils large and dark. Sometimes he'd mumble, but often he was silent, lost in the throes of the drug.

The drug affected him far more than me. I ended up feeling alert, powerful, a little high but still able to function. Drystan was on a whole different trip. I understood Drystan's desire for an escape. He stopped responding to me when I spoke to him, his breath coming in great gasps.

His pulse was fast. I sat next to him, holding his hand. Using my new awareness, I could tell he wasn't in enough danger to need to go to the hospital or the doctor. Was this how he had felt, that day Frey's power had grown so strong? So powerless?

Hours later, the drug finally began to loosen its hold. I held him close as his shaking slowed. His eyes opened, the beautiful blue bloodshot.

'You're still here,' he whispered.

'Where else would I be? I'm always by your side.'

His breath caught in his throat. 'Oh, Micah. I don't think I've ever loved anyone as much as I love you.'

I kissed him. He kissed me back and clung to me. I held him until he fell asleep.

Then I left the bed, tucking the covers around him. And, methodically, went through our room, into every nook and cranny. Nothing.

I crept back to the bed and whispered in his ear: 'Where's the Elixir, Drystan?'

Drystan mumbled, but I couldn't catch it. I asked him again.

'Mmmh. You'll just take it.'

'Where is it, Drystan?'

A brief, sleepy whine. A sigh. 'Bookshelf in the lounge. Behind the history of Lerium.' He laughed softly and then settled back into sleep.

Typical. I waited until his breathing was steady, and crept to the lounge. He wouldn't remember telling me that he'd hidden it in plain sight. I found the vials Drystan had lifted from Shadow Elwood's apartments. My fingers shook as I held them, and despite everything, I was tempted to take an extra dose of my own, to feel that rush of magic. Somehow, I resisted.

Unsure where to hide them. I ended up sneaking into Maske's bedroom and workshop. He slept soundly in the bed. I found a cupboard filled with old, spare brass springs and cogs, hiding the vials at the very back. I locked the cupboard and I hid the key in another drawer. It'd mean awkward questions if Maske needed to access that cupboard, but judging by the state of the coils, he'd brought them 'just in case' and would probably never actually use them.

Then I went back upstairs and crawled back into bed with the boy I loved, my tears falling into his hair.

20

SIDE EFFECTS

When stories speak of Chimaera granting wishes, the people in them always waste them. You don't need three – you only need one. Wish for unlimited power, which you can control and understand completely. You could use that for anything. Why wish for land or money? Power can create that. Some things are beyond power's control, you'd say. What of love or human emotion? Power could change that too. Power can do anything.

— Anonymous

We did not speak of it the next morning.

Lily sent word, and Cyan and I went to her apartments. Drystan stayed behind, weak and suffering from the after-effects of the Elixir.

Anisa had urged us to see Frey as much as we were able, to work on focusing and controlling his power. I was exhausted from the night before, and wanted nothing more than to lie in bed until the sun was high in the sky, but that was not to be. Cyan and I told Maske that

Drystan was unwell, and we just wanted some fresh air, for the day was beautiful. Maske nodded, saying he'd be in the workshop as usual. He still took things easy as he recovered from his own illness. And so easily, we told him another lie.

What happened last night? Cyan asked as we walked through the streets.

I swallowed. She already knew, but we went through the motions. *Drystan used some of the Elixir he stole from Shadow Elwood.*

Is he all right?

I think so. I hope so.

She reached out and took my hand, pressing it tightly. *It's hard for him. I've sensed it. But I think he will be fine. This was his sign that he needs to truly look at how he's feeling. Reconcile his old life and his new.*

As usual, she'd found a way to express it perfectly. Drystan needed to mend the broken pieces of his life, the various people he had been. The spoiled nobleman. The drug dealer and the card sharp. The clown in the circus, and now the magician who had turned his life around. He couldn't shed the guilt of who he used to be.

We'd reached Lily's apartment building, and I was glad; I didn't wish to discuss it any more. The doorman let us in as usual, and Lily welcomed us into the lounge. Kai wasn't there. She offered us tea, and as a gesture of good faith, we accepted. As soon as the tea was poured, she told us:

'I gave that sample of Elixir to my friend, as I promised.'

'Who's the friend?'

'Someone who works at the University.'

I stiffened. 'Pozzi has many friends at the University.'

'She is not one, I assure you.' Lily fidgeted. 'She has results, and they confirm what Pozzi has told us, for the most part. Part Lerium, and part some sort of Vestige substance. She's running further tests, trying to find out anything more. But there's so much about Vestige we don't know.'

I tried to think of what it could be. Some sort of liquid? But most of the Vestige items I'd come across were gadgets and machines, nothing that could potentially be ingested. Yet the Vestige we knew about was only a faint echo of what must actually exist. In one of Anisa's dream memories, she and Matla, the owl-woman, had gone to Linde to rescue Ahti. The Kashura, those Alder who hated Chimaera, wanted to implant something into him – perhaps one of those? But that had been half a world and centuries ago.

'Who is this woman who tested it?' I asked.

'She's one of the chemistry professors. Her name is Professor Teak, and she helped me now and again when I was a Shadow. She's one of the few to know of my double identity, and she's never told anyone. She specializes in looking at the chemical components of Vestige, though she often focuses on machines, such as automatons. She can keep looking, see if she can recreate it.'

I didn't like the thought of more people knowing our secrets, yet I could see that Lily yearned to tell Professor Teak and find the answers as much as I did. What the

Styx was Pozzi injecting into us? My fingers rested on the crook of my elbow.

What do you think? I asked Cyan.

Honestly, I don't know. It's to do with Elixir, so it's your call.

'If you think she's trustworthy, then tell her. Though, obviously, leave our names out of it.'

'Of course.' Lily sighed. 'I feel like we're coming closer. Like it's all just beyond our reach.'

'I don't know,' I said. 'I feel like it's further away than ever.'

We drank our tea. Lily took the cups into the small kitchen and we made our way to Frey's bedroom. It was difficult to concentrate on the lessons, my mind whirring with possibilities.

'Focus,' Anisa admonished. I sighed and turned back. Frey was likewise restless, growing bored within five minutes. We persevered. Meditating, building mental walls, drawing the power in closer to his chest. Once instructed, Frey was quite quick to pick up on things.

Cyan shook her head in amazement. 'With his walls that tight, I can't sense anything from him at all.' There was no trace of that fierce, terrible power.

Once Frey had accomplished building mental walls, Anisa instructed him – and, by proxy, Cyan and me – on directing power. She showed us how to keep ourselves shielded but for one small beam to focus. The first time he tried, Frey was able to levitate one of his teddy bears.

It didn't work for Cyan, whose abilities were telepathic rather than telekinetic. Tentatively, I tried myself. I took a deep breath and cleared my mind, imagining the bear lifting and hovering.

Nothing.

I cleared my mind again, thinking of the cool, blue light of Penglass. Focusing was like trying to move my ears and moving my eyelids instead. I tried once more. The teddy bear gave a sad wobble. I let out a breath, and it stopped. I tried again, and again, until a migraine threatened to overwhelm me. It didn't move again, no matter how hard I tried, and it never rose.

I wasn't sure whether to be relieved or disappointed. Still, I had made it move, with nothing more than the power of my mind.

Next, Anisa had Frey focus on creating the illusion over his features again. I lent him my Glamour, and Anisa walked him through programming the small controls on the back. It took much longer, for Frey kept wanting to give himself purple eyes or bright green hair, which made me smile. Eventually, though, he could use the Glamour to focus the illusion.

Frey stared back at us from his new face. His skin had lightened to peach and his eyes were a less luminescent shade of green. His fingernails were pink as seashells instead of dark claws. Brown curly hair on his head, with no sign of horns. He looked a little sad when he looked in the mirror, and I didn't know what to say to him. If only the world was not so afraid of scaled skin and horns.

Soon, even Frey and his boundless energy flagged. He yawned, stretching his arms over his head. As if connected to him, Lily entered to bring some snacks for us and to move him in his chair. The former Shadow kept looking at Anisa out of the corner of her eye, and I couldn't blame her. Anisa took a bit of time to grow used to. We nibbled at the treats – crackers and cheese, apples and celery.

When the afternoon lengthened, we took our leave. Anisa disappeared back into her Aleph and I tucked her into my pocket. After eating, Lily had put Frey to bed, and he slept deeply, the illusion of normalcy gone.

'Until next time,' Lily said. 'I'll let you know as soon as I have more answers.'

I nodded. 'More answers to raise more questions.'

My stomach fluttered as I climbed the stairs to our loft. Drystan had said little when I'd dragged myself out of bed that morning. When I returned, he greeted me kindly, even if he was subdued. I wondered if he'd gone to the library to discover his cache of Elixir was gone. If so, he didn't mention it.

He'd washed, and his golden hair curled about his ears and forehead. I perched next to him on the bed, unsure what to say.

'I noticed something this morning,' he said.

'What?' I asked, with some trepidation.

He pulled up the sleeve of his shirt. There, in the crook of his arm, was a dark little mark. Right where the needle had gone. I squinted, moving close enough to touch his skin. The skin was dry, and I brushed away the flakes of dry skin. There was a dark spot. Dark green.

'What the . . .'

'I know,' he said, his voice shaking. 'It's the same shade as Frey's skin.'

'How do you feel?' I asked, trying to dampen my growing alarm. 'Is it spreading?'

'I feel fine. It hasn't changed. No extra abilities. Tired, but that passed.'

I rolled up my sleeve and peered at the crook of my elbow. How had I missed it? The marks weren't near as pronounced as Drystan's, but where the needle went into the vein were tiny dots, like dark green freckles.

'So he is causing changes in us, too.' Of course it made sense. I must have known. It was so clear, so obvious.

'If you went off Elixir, I doubt anything would happen,' Drystan said, rubbing at the mark again, as if he could erase it. My guess was that he'd always have it.

'But what about the fit? Or the fact I feel so tired before treatments?'

Drystan thought back, his brow crinkling. He looked much better than he had this morning. I could tell that focusing on this problem was easier for him than having to face what happened last night. 'The night we won the duel against Taliesin. Pozzi was there, at the party afterwards, wasn't he?'

'Yes.' I remembered the sight of the theatre, filled to bursting with revellers, Maske grinning from ear to ear. Cyan reuniting with her parents after she'd fled the circus, and then finally telling Maske that she was actually his biological daughter. 'I spoke to him.'

'Did he give you anything?'

My stomach turned. 'He gave me a glass of wine. I had one sip.'

Drystan nodded. 'There you go. He pulled a magic trick of his own on you. Basic misdirection. Caused the fit, let you believe it was due to your health, and then started dosing you once a week. That explains why Cyan has had no symptoms, despite her powers being undeniably stronger than yours.'

My skin itched. 'That manipulative bastard. But what if I stop and he was right?'

Drystan stared ahead. 'Well, we have enough Elixir for a few more treatments, if we need to.' His jaw worked. 'You hid them well, I hope?'

My mouth opened, then closed. I could only nod.

'Well . . . then that will help for a while. Otherwise, I suppose we hope this friend of Lily's can figure out what's in it, and if need be, we somehow recreate the formula.'

I swallowed. I hated this. Not knowing if I could trust my own body not to turn on itself.

'I'm meant to see Pozzi in two days. What do I do?'

Drystan looked at me. His eyes were dark and haunted. 'I don't know. Last night I thought I had all the answers of the world at my fingertips. Today I feel as blind as a newborn mole rat.'

'Should we ask Anisa?' I asked.

'She'll give us no straight answers. I don't know if I trust her any more than Pozzi, to be honest.'

My eyes darted to the bed stand. Anisa's Aleph was in the top drawer. I never knew how aware she was when she was in there. Sometimes she spoke to us, but often it was as though she were hibernating, or asleep, to save power.

'Pozzi being the one to destroy the Chimaera doesn't make sense, as he's been creating them,' I said.

'Timur seems the more logical choice. He has already killed Chimaera, and was looking for Cyan.'

I shivered. 'Gods, what if he hasn't stopped looking for her? The Steward knows about her now, and we don't know how he found out. What if Timur somehow accesses the same information?'

Drystan sighed. 'We worry about that if it happens. Oli never gave her up, as far as we know, so that's something. We can only do what we can and adapt to whatever life throws at us next.'

I leaned back on the bed, feeling so tired. After I closed my eyes, Drystan settled down beside me. He put his arms around my shoulders, and I turned my face to his neck. Neither of us could bear to speak any longer. And so we both drifted off into sleep.

There was no rest for me there. It was not as clear a dream of the resurrectionist as before, but flashes of carrying a body into the laboratory, brushing grave dirt from blonde hair, and watching the corpse sink into the Ampulla tank. Of fingers pressing against dead flesh, sticking syringes into inert veins. Electric bulbs buzzing in their sockets, somewhere deep underground.

And throughout it all, a feeling of panic, of desperation.

Of time running out.

21
THE SPARK

*You cannot raze us down. We will rise up, our own
branches to the sky.*

— Extract from a Forester pamphlet

We stayed in bed late the next morning, neither of us
willing to face the day. Maske was still weak, so he did
not knock on our flimsy bedroom door demanding we
begin practice or hit the streets to earn our coins.

Our bodies curled around each other, we drifted in and
out of sleep. When Drystan finally awakened properly, I
kissed him, my lips gentle. We tasted of morning breath,
but neither of us cared. We didn't speak, but we told each
other how sorry we were with our movements, with our
bodies. Everything else fell away and we lost ourselves
and found ourselves all over again.

Afterwards, we dressed and I proposed we went out,
just the two of us. There were enough coins in the box
by the bedside table for us to have lunch in a not-so-nice
restaurant and tea at a cafe.

Maske was a little annoyed we were bunking off work, but he waved us away. Cyan stayed in her room, sensing we needed to be left alone.

We went to the second-largest square after the Celestial Cathedral, near the smaller Lady of the Moon church. It was made of dark blue marble threaded with white, painted with silver stars. A full silver moon was suspended from the two towers on thin wires, the light catching the corners. Most churches represented both the Lord and the Lady, but smaller ones chose one deity. The Lady of the Moon churches were frequented more often by women who prayed to the feminine side of the Couple. As someone in between genders, I was more comfortable in the churches devoted to both. It had been a long time since I'd prayed with anything approaching sincerity.

We had a lunch of chips and cheap cuts of beef and pickled vegetables. The price of food had already risen so much since the beginning of the summer. Our meal was silent, almost stilted. For the first time in a long time, I was tongue-tied around Drystan, and he was the same. Secrets had threaded their way through our relationship. We couldn't let them fester.

I pushed away my meal before it was finished, my appetite gone.

After our sad excuse for a date, we wandered into the Lady of the Moon church. Inside, everything was dim and quiet, a few lit candles mirroring the stars. We sat in the pews, our heads bowed, but I did not know if either of us truly prayed.

When we left the church, Drystan reached out, linking

his pinkie with mine for a few moments before letting go.

On the way to a tea house, my head swivelled to the right. That sense of warmth in my mind returned.

'There are at least two Chimaera that way,' I said, indicating with a jerk of my chin.

It was only after we turned down the cobbled street that we heard the angry shouts of a protest. Forester, Kashura, or monarchists? I moved closer to Drystan, the fear in my stomach growing stronger.

The protesters had stopped the traffic on one of the long promenades that led to Snakewood Palace in the Glass Quarter. Signs waved in the air, and people stood shoulder to shoulder. Even the scaffolding was packed, so we could not perch on it as easily as we had that day at the Celestial Cathedral.

'We should leave,' Drystan said. 'There is no Shroud if there's another attack, at least not that I can see.'

There had not been any large-scale attacks since the day the Kymri Theatre had been damaged, but small-scale fights and riots still happened on a regular basis. Shop windows were smashed, goods stolen. Graffiti accusing people of being monarchists or Chimaera was scrawled across doors. There had been far more peaceful protests and vigils, yet today the mood of the crowd was angry. The distant call of sirens echoed through the spaces between buildings. The protest had just begun, despite the crush of people.

On the scuffed, exposed brick wall of one of the sides of the building, Timur's face appeared. It was a Vestige projection. Wherever he was, it was somewhere he could not be arrested. The same could not be said of his followers, who stood on a small stage in the middle of the promenade, wearing long, dark robes and blank masks on their faces – half golden, half silver. The sun and the moon, the light and the darkness within us all. The imagery took me aback – there had been no rumours of the Kashura being religious zealots, but I suppose the imagery was evocative and served their purpose, no matter what their beliefs. They did not seem like people, but sentinels meting out justice.

Two people stood with their faces covered by bags, their arms held tightly behind them by the men in the robes. They were the Chimaera whose warmth I sensed.

'We can't leave them,' I whispered.

'Oh, Styx,' Drystan muttered, but resolutely he started pushing his way through the crowd.

'Thank you for coming, each and every one of you.' Timur's voice floated down the promenade, deep and commanding. 'All of you seek change, all of you wish to protect this island we call home. You know that we are under threat in so many ways. Our monarchy lets us starve while they live in gilded rooms, eating food we could never dream of tasting off the finest china with the finest silverware. And strange, unnatural creatures are returning to our lands, many from the other islands of the Archipelago. We do not know what powers they hold. There are such rumours. Some can supposedly read our innermost thoughts, influence our actions. Not even our minds are safe.'

Fearful murmurings moved through the crowds, others calling out in anger. Timur's projection nodded, solemn.

'I know, I know this is not easy. It is a trying time for Ellada. Uncertainty is a difficult beast to tame. Yet we are strong, and we are fearless!'

The crowd's yelling grew to a dull roar. It reminded me far too much of that day in the Celestial square. Pushing our way through people was agonizingly slow. Several pushed back, and someone trod painfully on my foot. Still, we persisted, darting through the small spaces like minnows swimming upstream. The fear within me grew. I wished Cyan were here, able to tell us who the people beneath the sacks were, or the people behind the masks.

'I am but your humble servant,' Timur continued. 'Helping enact the will of the people. I tried to work within the system, to help change Ellada for the better from the inside. Yet the termites have eaten the very hearts of the trees of the nobility. We must rebuild the core of Ellada, and keep our island safe from harm.'

As if on cue, the sentinels tore the sacks off the heads of the two Chimaera. Drystan and I let out cries of dismay. On the left was Juliet the Leopard Lady, her head lifted in defiance but her eyes sparking with fear. Next to her was Tauro, the bull-man from R. H. Ragona's Circus of Magic. He lowed, shaking his head, the ring through his nose catching the sunlight.

We were still so far from the stage. It was growing harder to move forward. The shoves grew stronger, some people yelling at us to stay back. Ignoring them, we pushed closer. There was no plan. No way to stop them. Yet we could not simply turn away.

'These are the Chimaera infiltrating our land,' Timur said, voice rising. 'The leopard woman claimed to mean no harm, but we know what terrors the Chimaera are capable of. Untold centuries ago, they nearly destroyed the world, and I am certain that, should they and their foul magic be allowed to return, the same will happen once again. We must send them out, far away from us. The Chimaera and their sympathizers in the monarchy will otherwise destroy our nation. Out there are Chimaera who could destroy the world, but do not fear. I search for them, and I will protect you.'

'Fell them!' someone yelled in the crowd. It turned to a chant: 'Fell them, fell them, fell them.' As if using a timber metaphor softened the cry for murder.

The Policiers arrived, unfurling from their carriages, surrounding the edges of the crowd. Their Vestige-amplified voices called for all to disperse peacefully. The mob shouted back, pushing against each other. Timur's projection watched what was happening avidly, his eyes glittering, almost as if he were waiting.

The crowd kept their eyes on the Policiers, and Drystan and I used their wavering attention to move closer to the stage. Juliet's head turned towards me and she met my eyes. The hope on her face pained me. Tauro saw us too and began making noises. One of the sentinels elbowed him hard in the ribs and he whimpered. Rage burned through me.

Someone pushed to my right. I turned, and Cyan looked

up at me. There was no point asking how she knew to find us, but I was so glad of her presence.

'There must be something we can do,' I said. 'Can we help influence the crowd to leave?'

Cyan shook her head. 'Too many of them, and they're too riled up. I think we can help Juliet and Tauro, though.'

She took my hand in hers. Before we could even attempt to link minds, however, the crowd behind us began to scream.

My first thought was that there had been another explosion, but there was no deep, reverberating boom.

'A Policier struck someone,' Cyan said. 'He's fallen, and he's bleeding badly from his temple.' She paused, blanched. 'He's dead.'

Chaos erupted. People began attacking Policiers, and they fought back. More sirens echoed through the city to mix with the hoarse yells of the crowd. It devolved into a riot within five minutes. Cyan, Drystan and I pushed our way through to the stage. The sentinels were tense, their hands straying to weapons hidden beneath their robes. Cyan took my hand again and her mind touched mine. A side effect of helping Frey control his powers was that we had better control of our own. The two of us were stronger. Cyan sent out a thin tendril towards the sentinels. Though we walked right up to them, their heads did not turn, and no one in the crowd noticed us. Juliet and Tauro shrugged free of the sentinels' hands and we ushered them off the stage. It was not easy to push our way out past the crowd, especially as the violence increased. Warning shots crackled in the air, and we all winced – at least, I hoped they were warning shots. Tauro kept making low, frightened noises in the back of his throat. I took his hand, squeezing. Policiers fought with civilians here, too, and Cyan was shaking with the effort of keeping people from noticing us. Eventually we slipped past the edge of the mob and into the relatively quieter streets off the main promenade.

We didn't speak until we found a deserted alleyway. Cyan leaned against the wall, breathing hard. I was almost as exhausted. Juliet put her arms around Tauro, leaning her head on his hairy shoulder. Drystan was a little green around the edges, his withdrawal still taking most of his energy.

'You saved our lives,' Juliet said.

'Surely they wouldn't have harmed you,' I said, but Juliet shook her head.

'I'm not sure. They might have. Either in front of that whole crowd, or behind closed doors. Timur despises us.'

'Are you actually Chimaera?' I asked, trying to keep the hope from my eyes.

She pressed her lips together, nodded. 'Are you, too? None of the guards even blinked when you took us from them.'

'Yes,' I whispered, and Cyan nodded too.

'I'm not,' Drystan added, and his voice was bitter.

'All this time, we were in the circus and we never knew another was right there,' Juliet said in wonder.

'I mean, we wondered,' Drystan said. 'The lovely teeth had us curious. Not surgical implants then?'

Juliet flashed her long eye-teeth. 'Nay. They came in

after I lost my milk teeth. Gave my mother quite the shock.'

Tauro was smiling at us. I'd missed him. He couldn't speak, but he understood what we said. He was a gentle giant, and I'd worried about him after we left the circus, afraid he'd have to join a workhouse. Juliet had protected him, or tried to.

'Do you know many others?' I asked.

She shook her head. 'Just . . . the other two.' Her eyes filled with tears, and she bowed her head.

'I'm so sorry for what happened at the Celestial Cathedral.' My apology felt useless.

'Aren't we all?' she sighed.

'Do either of you have any extra abilities?' I asked.

She shook her head. 'None that we've noticed. We're simply physically different. Dirk might have had some, but if so didn't choose to share that with me. He was very guarded.' I tried not to think of him spread on the operating table, the gash down his chest.

'I'm sure you could stay with us if you need shelter.' It would be beyond cramped, but I could not turn them away.

Juliet gave me a smile. 'I thank you, but there's no need. We have friends we can rely on. I want to take Tauro away, somewhere safe. It's time for us to return to Byssia, leave this island that hates us.' She looked away from us. 'You may think that cowardly, but I find my desire to fight, to reach out and work for peace, it's all fled.'

I reached out and put my hand on her shoulder. 'It's all right. I understand.'

Drystan, Cyan, and I emptied our pockets, giving them

what coins we could. Juliet wrapped a scarf around her head, leaving her face in shadow, and Tauro put up the hood of his coat so only his stubbly chin showed.

'Will you be all right?' I asked.

Juliet shrugged. 'Who knows? I hope so. And I hope you are safe as well. You should consider leaving, too.'

I took a shaky breath. 'It's still my home. I have to believe that most people here are better than Timur and his ilk.'

'I fear you will be disappointed.'

'We're magicians these days,' I told her. 'We usually stay at the Kymri Theatre, but it's being repaired, so we're at the Penny Rookeries now.' I gave her the address.

Her eyes widened. 'You're Maske's Marionettes?'

'Guilty as charged.'

She gave us something approaching a true smile. 'I'm glad you two have found success. What happened at the circus . . . well, it was terrible. Bil destroyed it all. Yet us circus folk are a strong sort. We always land on our feet.'

'We do.' I gave them both a hug, and Drystan did the same. Cyan shook their hands.

With a last wave, they were gone.

Even this far from the promenade, I could still hear the sirens. The alarm calling the curfew sounded, even though it was hours before the sun would set.

As we hurried back to the Penny Rookeries through streets filled with people hunched with fear, I asked aloud, 'What does this all mean?'

Drystan's face was hard. 'I think Ellada is now at civil war.'

22

THE RESURRECTIONIST

'I am devastated by the desecration of the grave of my daughter, Rosalind. Of course I am. She'd been put to rest, and that rest has been disturbed. I know that my daughter is gone, hopefully already leaving the river Styx for her next life. But I feel it's important for her shell to remain interred, if only for the peace of mind of me and my family.'
— 'Snatched from the Grave', an interview
with ROBERT ARCHER, *The Daily Imacharan*

When we arrived home, Cyan disappeared into her room. I was covered with the sweat of the crowd, and Drystan felt the same. He ran a fresh bath, the ancient pipes creaking and shaking. The tiny bathroom smelled of mould, the grouting permanently stained no matter how hard we scrubbed it. I shed my clothes, helping Drystan out of his. We lowered ourselves into the bath, the water almost too warm.

It was not romantic. Both of us were too upset to turn to each other for comfort. We lay in the bath, barely fitting, our legs touching, each lost in our own thoughts. Juliet and Tauro were Chimaera. They were safe, thanks to us. Had Timur wanted the fight with the Policiers to break out? His sentinels must have discarded their robes and masks, disappeared anonymously into the crowd.

This was only the beginning.

The monarchy would impose even stricter rules after the attack by the Policiers. The Kashura would respond with more violence. The public would be caught in the middle. It was a mess, and I did not know how they could contain this before it grew into even more of a problem.

When we came out of the bathroom in clean clothes and towel-dried hair, Maske motioned us to come into the kitchen.

'Time for a meeting,' he said. He still wasn't fully recovered, and coughed wetly. Cyan was already sitting next to him.

He's tired of secrets, she said, spoiling Maske's surprise.

'It's time I knew what you three were actually up to,' he began. 'I know what's going on out there, and life is about to become more difficult and more dangerous. What are you involved in? It's nothing to do with the Foresters, is it?'

I almost bit back a laugh. 'I promise you, it's definitely nothing to do with them.'

'Come on,' he said, almost gently. 'It's time to take me out of the dark. Tell me everything.'

'We can't tell you quite everything,' Cyan said, hesitant. 'It would be treason to talk about some of it.'

That gave him pause. 'Well. Tell me everything that wouldn't involve treason.'

We almost came clean. We still didn't tell him about Lily, and therefore Frey, as we were cowards. So now Maske knew that there was a secret involving the monarchy, and that we'd known one of the Chimaera at the Celestial Cathedral square, and that we'd saved her again tonight. He knew that we ourselves were Chimaera, and about Anisa and her visions. I told him of my grave-robber dreams, and the Kashura, and Timur's anger against the Chimaera. I told him of the Elixir and what it did to me, that it enhanced the powers I did have. Of course, I didn't tell him more Elixir was hidden in his very bedroom, for fear Drystan would sneak in and pick another lock.

After it all, I was breathless.

'Lord and Lady,' Maske said.

'It's a lot,' Drystan said.

'I thought you were going to tell me you were sneaking off to Forester protests or something.' Maske blinked, his eyes blank. 'This may take me some time.'

'We understand.' Cyan laid a hand on her father's forearm. 'We should have told you much sooner. Yet it's not exactly an easy subject to bring up.'

'Also, not much of it makes sense. There are so many gaps in what we know,' Drystan added.

'That seems true. It's hard not to be hurt that you kept it all from me, though. Did you not think I would wish to help?'

'We didn't want to burden you,' Cyan said. 'You were

so upset by the damage to the Kymri Theatre. You had your own troubles.'

'Of course I did. And I do. But first and foremost, I am your friend, your mentor. I would far rather know your troubles, and do all I can to help you, than hide away in ignorance.'

We were all sheepish. I opened my mouth, wanting to tell him about Lily, about Frey, about another piece of the puzzle with missing pieces. But my throat closed, my mouth snapped shut. It would come out eventually. The longer we hid it, the worse it would be. Hadn't I already learned that, lying to Aenea for fear she would be hurt by my secrets? And it had cost me so much.

'Thank you for telling me, truly. But I think I'm going to go to bed now.'

He stood, and took the whisky bottle with him into the bedroom. We lapsed into guilty silence, then broke off to our own rooms.

The next day, I saw Pozzi once again. Took my medicine, let it fill me with light. Drystan did not ask to come, and it was easier than me having to turn him down. Sitting alone in the lounge while I was dosed was too great a temptation with a spirit cabinet full of Elixir right in front of him.

Later that night, curled up in bed next to Drystan, it took me ages to fall asleep. The instant before I drifted into slumber, I knew that I would not dream. Instead, I would see.

The man and the woman floated in their separate tanks, their watery coffins. They were both naked. The resurrectionist had replaced the woman destroyed in the last experiment. The new one was still young, still beautiful, but this time with hair so blonde it looked almost white, her skin tanned from the sun. Her hair floated about her head like seaweed. There were no wounds on her. I wondered how she had died.

The resurrectionist moved towards the tanks, breathing shallowly. In the dream, their heart pattered within their chest. The fingers danced along the controls.

As ever, I wondered: was this happening now? Had it already happened, or was it all still to come?

The electrical bulb dangling above buzzed and then popped, leaving the damp laboratory in darkness but for the soft blue tinge of the tanks. Impatiently, the grave robber took a candle from their bag, lighting it and setting it between the metal tanks. The plain white candle was very similar to the ones we used for séances, but they were also used in churches. It made the laboratory seem like some sort of altar, a sacred space, the bodies depictions of dark gods.

The tanks whirred. The bodies arched as the full power of the Vestige tank took effect. The tops opened, the slab at the bottom of the tank rising until the corpses emerged from the water, glistening.

Except they no longer looked like corpses.

They both had flushes to their cheeks, and their chests rose and fell. Their hearts beat, marked by spikes on the small monitors by the tanks. Yet there was a stillness to them. Though their bodies had somehow come back to life, whoever had once possessed these shells was still long gone.

The body I trespassed within rummaged in the bag again, bringing out two Alephs. If I could have, I would have frowned. What was happening?

The resurrectionist connected the Alephs to wires attached to each corpse's temples. Whatever they were doing, it would not be good, but there was no way to stop this. No matter how I tried, I could not move even the pinkie of the body I rode within.

The person fiddled with the consoles. Then they stopped, gazing at the suspended bodies. 'Let it work,' the resurrectionist whispered.

They hugged their arms to their body, then moved forward, pressing a button on the tank containing the woman's body. The Aleph shimmered, lights of blue, green, and purple twining from the device and along the wire before settling on the corpse like a second skin. The body started, and the resurrectionist stepped back from the flailing limbs, watching avidly. The body arched and convulsed, the mouth opening and closing like a fish. The last of the shimmering colours faded into the skin, before the body slackened.

She struggled to sit up. It took a few tries, for the muscles were weak, but she managed. Water dripped from the wet ropes of her hair, which lay over her shoulders like molten gold.

'Anisa?' the resurrectionist asked.

'It worked?' the woman asked, a hand moving to the

hollow of her throat, eyes widening in shock. 'I didn't expect to see you.'

Who was she looking at, and was this truly Anisa in a human body?

'Just a moment, and I'll explain everything.'

She peered at him. 'Poor little bat-winged boy. Drawn into the game like all the rest.'

It fell into place.

Kai was the grave robber, working on Pozzi's orders. All those protestations that he hated the Royal Physician just as much as us. All lies.

'Not exactly,' the voice said. I could tell it was Kai's, now, even feel the wings pressed underneath the too-tight jacket. Yet the inflections of his voice were all far too smooth.

'Ah.' Anisa's eyes flashed. 'You're not the bat-winged boy at all. Not truly.'

One of Kai's hands started the other tank, connecting another metal Aleph to the corpse.

Using all the strength I had, I pulled myself out of the vision and away from Kai's body.

Awakening with a gasp, I jumped out of bed.

'What's going on?' Drystan asked.

'Put on your shoes and coat. We need to go to the university. Kai is the grave robber, and yesterday Pozzi must have stolen Anisa.'

'What?'

'No time.' I shoved my feet into my boots, not even bothering with socks, and shrugged on my coat. Cyan opened the door, awakened by my panic, putting on her own coat. It was deep in the middle of the night. We opened the stiff front door as silently as we could and ran to the university, keeping to the shadows. Mercifully, the streets were silent, and we didn't see any Policiers. Perhaps Cyan gently gave them a push, urging them to turn down a different corner, away from us.

We were all panting by the time we arrived at the university. What if they'd left? In the last dream vision, I'd seen the stamp on the side of the Ampulla tanks. University property, and my guess was that they were in an underground laboratory, long abandoned.

Drystan picked the lock and Cyan strode in first, leading the way.

'Are they there?'

'They're waiting for us,' Cyan said, and I could only shiver.

I had no idea what to think. Anisa had a body. Had this been her plan all along?

The door to the lab was already open.

We walked in, gazing at the three people before us. Kai was hunched over, hands on his mouth, as if he were about to be sick. Anisa wore a robe wrapped around her new form. The candlelight flickered over her skin, still damp from the liquid in the Ampulla tank. That body was breathing, living –when only an hour before, it had been dead. Now Anisa lived in a corpse. The other body, the man, still floated in the Ampulla tank, dim and dark. In the corner, Pozzi waited, standing apart from the others, his face as inscrutable as ever.

'Anisa?' I asked, my voice catching on a sob.

She came closer to me, but I pulled away. 'I'm so sorry, little Kedi. I did not know this would happen.' Though her voice was still tinged with a long-forgotten accent, it no longer echoed.

'What the hell are you playing at?' I asked Pozzi. 'And you.' I turned to Kai. 'I thought we could trust you.'

Kai didn't move, only kept his hands over his face. Pozzi moved closer. 'Don't blame him. He did not know what he was doing.'

'What in the Styx is going on?' Drystan asked.

'An experiment,' Pozzi said. 'One I could tell no one about. On the Steward's orders.'

'You're breaking your word.'

Pozzi nodded. 'Indeed. I feel I've interfered in your lives enough, that you deserve to know what is happening. I owe all of you apologies that you have every right not to accept.'

My head spun. 'Explain. For the love of the Lord and Lady, stop your riddles.'

'No more riddles. No more games.' He was the solemnest I'd ever seen him. 'The Snakewoods asked me to bring Chimaera back to the world, as much as I was able. I was only too happy to agree to try. The Steward funded all of my research. I rose through the ranks of doctors and became the Royal Physician because he wished me close. For years I was lost in my work, convinced that what we were doing was worth it.'

'Like dosing pregnant mothers so their children would be Anthi or Theri?' I asked.

Kai lowered his hands from his face.

'Like dosing me with Elixir each week only to enhance my powers, but pretending it was because you were saving me? A cheap magic trick, and I fell for the misdirection.' My voice had gone high, shaking with anger.

'Like so.'

Cyan bristled next to me.

'I never questioned it. I thought what we were doing was good. Worthwhile. Once I helped birth Princess Nicolette and saw her blue-tinged skin, I thought she was Chimaera too, even wondered if the Steward had somehow dosed her himself. Then he told me himself that the family was Alder. He wanted the Chimaera to return, to protect him and his family as the Chimaera had protected and helped the Alder centuries ago. I liked knowing that I was helping bring magic back to the world, even if I knew it had a rational, scientific base. It felt magical, anyway. Like I was chosen.

'The Steward slowly had me do more experiments, deeper and more challenging. He gave me a selection of Alephs, like this woman Anisa's, but they were all empty. I thought, perhaps, the one I tried –' he gestured at the man floating in the tank – 'might work, but obviously that was not to be. The Steward wanted me to bring back ancient Chimaera, so they could teach us more of the old ways and help us on our quest. I tried for years and thought it must be doomed to failure, until I realized you had a working Aleph all along.'

'So you made Kai steal bodies?'

Kai finally met my eyes. 'I did not want to.' His voice shook with anger. 'I did not have a choice.'

'No, indeed he did not. I couldn't do it myself. Fear of being recognized, and this hand isn't as strong as you might expect.' Pozzi waved his clockwork hand.

'I remember none of it,' Kai said.

'I hadn't quite cracked how to awaken Alephs, but I did discover that if I gave myself a large dose of Elixir, I could take over a Chimaera body, though only for a few hours. I did that with Kai, then Lethed him afterwards. I did ask you if I could borrow your body, and you said yes, though I erased that.'

'If I did, I regret that,' Kai said, his voice thick with tears.

My face drained with horror. He'd stolen Kai's body, like Anisa did once to me. What if Pozzi had taken my body for some nefarious purpose, then erased all memory of it?

'I helped bring back Chimaera,' Pozzi continued, 'though I cannot claim full responsibility. Others have come into this world on their own. I have proven we can bring back Alephs into bodies, to help bolster the numbers of Chimaera, should we need. You did consent, Kai, even if you can't remember. I know that is scant comfort.'

Kai turned his face away. 'I definitely did not consent to killing a man to obtain a body you couldn't even use.' He gestured to the Ampulla tank. 'I can't even remember doing it properly. Just . . . flashes. Now I'll have to live with that for the rest of my life.'

Pozzi hung his head. 'That was me, not you. I killed

them. I could say I didn't have a choice, but that's a lie. There is always a choice. The Steward wanted the freshest bodies possible. He thought someone important might have been in that empty Aleph. The man in the university hospital would have died anyway, though that does not excuse what I did.'

With that, Kai stood and left. I could not blame him. Though I wanted nothing more than to follow him, we needed more answers.

'The Steward thinks he needs Chimaera to protect him, but then he experiments on women, creates us without our consent, and threatens us. Why would he expect us to be loyal?' I asked.

Pozzi stared into the distance. 'He thinks war can't help but break out, and when that happens, Chimaera will turn to the crown. And you weren't ever meant to find out about the experiments. Why would you suspect?'

'And why the sudden treason?'

Pozzi was still staring, his clockwork fingers moving restlessly. The underground lab was damp and smelled of stone and moss. The lightbulbs flickered, casting his face half in shadow. 'It was far from sudden. It was slow, considered, measured. Yes, I willingly agreed to perform these experiments, but after creating you, of course I felt protective. The Steward wanted this for his own gain. He cares not if you're destroyed. He only sees Chimaera as potential soldiers, as powers he can harness and control. If there's one thing I've learned working for the Steward of Ellada these past decades, it's that once he sees power, he never lets it go.'

'And that doesn't bode well for the Princess when she comes of age,' I hazarded.

'No, indeed. It was not any one thing, but so many. The final straw was killing for him.' He met my eyes. 'What would I do if he thought a Chimaera wasn't loyal enough? Would he ask me to destroy what I had created? I was protective of you and Kai and Frey especially, as I saw you grow up. I became personally invested in my own experiments. A rookie mistake, perhaps, but not one I regret.' He smiled, but as always, it never reached his eyes. 'I started worrying for the Princess's future, decided I was far more loyal to her and the crown than the current Steward in guardianship. Even as the thought of bringing back past Chimaera from Alephs excited me, I wondered if that was still the right course of action. They'd already fought their war. Would they want another?' He shook his head. 'I cannot undo what I've done, yet I also can't say I regret my life's work. The world is better with Chimaera and Alder returning to it, that I know, deep in my heart. It's not magic, perhaps, but it's still a wonder.'

None of us had any response to that. 'Were you in on this?' I asked Anisa instead.

'No, little Kedi,' she said, softly.

'You weren't surprised when you awoke in a body.'

'When he stole me from you, he asked me what I wanted. He wouldn't have done this if I'd said no, but would have kept searching for another Aleph.' She moved over to the tank with the inert, dead man and picked up the Aleph. 'I wonder who had been in this one, before it ran out of power.' She held up the disc. 'This could have been my grave. I was lower on power than I let you know, for fear of worrying you. Pozzi came at just the right time, so of course I said yes. I cannot help you if I'm dead.'

I swallowed. Drystan and Cyan clustered closer to me, their arms touching mine. They were the only ones I could trust. The only ones who didn't have their own reasons for using me. For the crown, for some vague prophecy.

Anisa came closer and took her hand in mine. This was the first time she'd ever been able to touch me. Her hand was warm. Solid. Alive. She ran a finger down my cheek, and then she touched Cyan's and Drystan's faces, just as gently. She kissed each of our foreheads, feather-light. It reminded me, incongruously, of the night of my debut, when the women of the Twelve Trees had kissed each young woman on the forehead, welcoming us into adulthood. With Anisa, it was more of an apology.

'Your experiment is done, Pozzi,' I said. 'We are not your subjects any longer.'

Pozzi's face closed to us. 'I know, Micah. Cyan. Anisa. I know. It's worth little, but I am sorry. So very sorry.'

We left him with his corpse and his laboratory.

23

PROPHECY OF LIES

You feel as if you know what the world is. What it wants of you, what it demands of you. But then, in a moment, all shifts, and you realize you never knew anything at all.
— From the soon-to-be published memoirs of the Maske of Magic

Kai sat across the street from the university, his head in his hands. I wasn't sure if he'd waited for us, or if he'd been too overwhelmed to go home right away.

Cyan went over and took his hand and he rose, following us. It properly hit me about halfway home from the university. The sun was just rising over the granite buildings, the sky peach and pink. Curfew had not broken, but we were too exhausted to keep to the shadows. We could only hope no watchmen found us.

Kai came back with us, for he'd been staying in one of Pozzi's apartments. He kept looking at his hands as if he did not recognize them. His body had gone places, done things, all without him knowing.

In eavesdropping on Kai's grave robbing, I did not think my body properly rested. Pozzi's drugs hadn't caused all of the fatigue. Though I didn't want to, it was hard to trust Anisa, walking beside us in the body of a dead girl. She could have taken over bodies while in her Aleph. What if she'd worked with Pozzi, taken over Kai to do his bidding? Pozzi had never specified which Aleph he'd used to make Kai more susceptible to his will.

I remembered what Anisa had said to me in my dream the first night after I'd seen her in the Pavilion of Phantoms at R. H. Ragona's Circus of Magic. She'd touched my face with a transparent finger, as she'd done tonight: 'I know your secret, little Kedi,' she had said. 'And I know what your future will bring. You poor thing.'

Did I want to know the truth?

Dawn continued to lighten the sky. Curfew broke as we approached our neighbourhood and people began passing us on their way to work, looking askance as we shuffled through the streets, wild-eyed and desperate.

We arrived at the Penny Rookeries apartment. I'd never been so glad to see its cracked stones, the one broken pane in the window in the lounge temporarily mended with oilskin paper.

Kai, Anisa, and Cyan sat at the table, while Drystan and I collapsed on the sofa.

The door to Maske's bedroom opened. He peered at us, blinking sleepily.

'This is rather early to be having visitors,' he said, glancing curiously at Kai and Anisa.

'We've had a Styx of a night,' I said.

'Wait until I've had my brew,' Maske said. 'Then tell me everything. Anyone else for a cup?'

We all said yes. Anisa couldn't disguise her excitement. She hadn't tasted anything in a few millennia, I supposed.

Maske brought through the cracked mugs, milk, sugar, and a carafe of coffee. We procrastinated, taking our time preparing our cups. The coffee did little to wake me, but unsettled my stomach, making my limbs even more jumpy. Anisa drank three large mugs with relish.

'All right,' he said. 'Tell me what's happened now.'

'Well. This is Anisa,' I waved to the blonde woman with knowing, ancient eyes. 'You two have met.'

'Hello, magician,' she said.

Maske startled. 'How?'

I opened my mouth to try and explain, but the exhaustion settled over me so heavily that no words would come. Anisa took over, her voice smooth, never faltering. Meticulously, she laid out everything. How Pozzi had been experimenting on women to create Chimaera, including Cyan's mother. How the Royal Family was distantly descended from the Alder, yet the features came through most strongly in young Nicolette. At least it was Anisa performing treason. We had not technically broken our promise to the Steward.

Next, she introduced Kai, Pozzi's former assistant, and explained that he was also Chimaera. She skimmed over the fact that he had done the actual grave-robbing, and I was grateful for her tact. Kai was one small step from a breakdown. His shoulders were so hunched the outlines of his wings showed through his bulky coat. Cyan still held his hand. She didn't use her powers on him, but she was a calming presence for him all the same.

'So what do we do now?' Maske asked, and my heart warmed. We did not deserve him.

Seeing me sway in my seat was answer enough for him.

'First, you sleep. We'll figure out the rest later. Kai and Anisa, you can take the sofa and the chair. I'm afraid there are no other beds. We had much more room at the Kymri Theatre.'

'You'll be back into it soon,' Anisa said, but I could no longer tell if that was prescience or wishful thinking.

Maske only smiled sadly and retreated to his room, to reappear with blankets and a pillow. Cyan lent Anisa a blue dress, as they were close enough in size. Both the sofa and the chair were old and sagging. They would not be comfortable.

'You sleep, Kai,' Anisa said, settling into the chair and pulling a ratty blanket around her. 'I've slept for centuries.'

I found a small bag of jellied fruits in a cupboard and gave them to Anisa. She ate them happily. At least someone was finding some pleasure in this strange morning.

Kai laid down but his eyes were open, meeting mine beseechingly. 'I'm afraid of what I'll dream.'

'I know. Me, too.'

I did not sleep easily that morning. I lay close to Drystan, listening to the sound of his breathing. We didn't speak, but he stroked my hair until he drifted off.

I stared out the window, over the chimneys of the next tenement.

Every time I closed my eyes, I thought of the floating man in the Ampulla tank. We should have destroyed the tanks before we left. Pozzi said he was finished with his experiments, but what if that was just another lie? Yet, despite everything, the idea of breaking something Vestige felt sacrilegious. Plus, in one of the visions, the corpse had healed. Perhaps that could be used to help the living. There was so much about Vestige we did not know.

After a sleepless morning, I stayed in bed until the early afternoon.

Drystan got up and returned with a cup of coffee. I took a few sips and then dozed fitfully. A little later, Cyril came to visit before his lecture. He sat with me. I tried to fill him in on what had happened, but I was still so tired I couldn't remember what he did or didn't know. He sat with me, holding my hand.

'Any change with mother?' I asked.

'No. No change. Will you visit her again soon? We should try again. You almost reached her last time.'

'I will,' I said. If I decided to miss my next dose of Elixir, my powers might grow weaker. They might return to their former, erratic state. The chance to help my mother might have already passed me by, and I'd let it, due to my own fear. Cyril left when I drifted off again.

Cyan woke me. *Come to the lounge. Right now.*

Fear flooded through me, and I flung myself from the bed.

It was almost evening. Lily was in the lounge, her face streaked with tears, her hair falling from its plait.

'Frey is gone,' Cyan told me. Lily only sobbed harder.

'What—?' I started, but then the front door opened. Lily looked up in fear.

Maske came into the lounge, holding a bag of groceries, and saw the whole messy scene. Lily in tears; Kai, Cyan, Drystan, and I surrounding her. He stopped short, setting the food on the table next to the door.

'Lily? What's wrong?'

'I'm so sorry, Jasper,' she said, and she did not use the voice of Lily Verre, the merchant's widow, but the Shadow Lily Verre. Gone were her flighty mannerisms, her high titter of laughter. She pulled off her mask. I couldn't bear to watch this unfold, when I was so raw from the events of the night before. We had put off telling him, to try and avoid hurting him. Now he would only hurt all the more.

'More secrets, I see,' was all Maske said, but he was wary, every line of his body radiating the hurt he felt.

'My name is Lily Verre, but I have had to keep things from you,' she said. It was the first time I'd seen her hesitant. 'I had to put on a fake voice, and initially I had to grow closer to you for a job. I'm a Shadow. Oh, Jasper, I swear I'll explain everything to you as you deserve, but right now my son has been taken, and I have to find him.'

'Your son . . . ?' Maske echoed, faintly.

'When did you notice him missing?' Drystan said, forcing her to look at him. He was brusque, and she responded to it, falling back into her Shadow training.

'Half an hour ago. I went out to fetch some food for dinner and when I returned, he was gone. No sign of breaking in. But he couldn't leave on his own. I asked the doorman who had left recently, and he'd seen no one. It's as if he vanished into thin air.'

I opened my mouth. Closed it. 'Where have you gone? Have you seen Pozzi?' Kai was here, and the only other person who knew about Frey, as far as I knew, was the Doctor. My stomach sank with dread.

'I would never have taken him anywhere without telling you,' Kai said.

'I know. I know. But I'd hoped he'd convinced you to come here for a visit – he has grown fond of all of you – rather than the alternative.'

'Don't you have a Mirror of Moirai? You used it to track our movements.'

Her lips tightened. 'I never let Frey near it. Didn't want people to be able to find him so easily. I regret it now.'

Maske missed nothing. 'A Mirror of Moirai? You watch Lily's son, Kai? You all knew of this?' He couldn't even look at us.

'I'm so sorry,' I said.

'We were afraid of hurting you. And it didn't seem our secret to tell.' Cyan gave Lily a hard look.

'I want to fix this, Jasper, I truly do, but my son is missing. We'll go to Pozzi first. I can only hope he's there.' Her eyes were dry, but her hands shook.

'We'll find him, Lily, I promise.' I closed my eyes, trying to stretch my awareness, but it couldn't go far. The only Chimaera flames I sensed were Cyan's and Kai's.

Maske backed away from us. He turned his shoulders from Lily. The repairs on the Kymri Theatre would be finished soon. Within a week or two, he'd be back on the stage, performing as the Maske of Magic. He thought his life was about to go back to the triumphant victory he'd only been able to enjoy for a few weeks after the duel. Everyone in this room had misdirected him with our lies.

'Jasper,' Lily said, and the word was filled with love, with sadness, with fear. 'We have to go,' she said.

'I'll grab my coat,' he said, sighing.

'You don't have to,' I said. 'You can stay while we look for him.'

'If I can help, I will. I can't shake the feeling that this is much bigger than my own hurt feelings. Everything is coming together.'

The first time I'd met Maske, he'd thrown a séance for us, to decide from our reactions if we were worth taking in. Anisa had used him to warn of her visions, but before that, he had mentioned images he saw in the crystal ball while in a trance that tied back into Lily and Frey. I had always assumed that was Anisa as well. Either that, or Maske had a touch of prescience himself.

'Thank you, Maske.' Drystan said.

Maske pulled his hat low down over his eyes, so we could not see his face.

Before we left, I went to Maske's workshop for one of the hidden vials of Elixir. Cyan came with me. Drystan knew what we were doing, but stayed away.

I prepped the syringes, tapping out the air bubbles as I'd seen Pozzi do. I didn't want to take any more of the drug, even as I still craved it, but we needed all the help we could get. I pressed the needle into my skin and pressed down. Another faint green mark to add to the others.

Then Cyan took her first dose. Her face was pinched with nerves. I couldn't help but fear it would somehow affect her differently. Would it make her as high as Drystan? But no. Though her head fell back and her eyes closed tight as the drug did its work, when she opened them again, her mind was clear.

'My gods,' she whispered. 'I can sense everything. Everyone. So clearly.' She let out a breath, pressing her hands to her temples. I sensed her building her walls, blocking out enough of the noise that she could hear herself again.

'That's something,' she said when done, looking down at the Elixir bottles.

'Yeah. The comedown might be difficult. I was always exhausted, but that might have been because of my eavesdropping on Kai.'

She squeezed my hand. 'I'm sorry I didn't sense it.'

'No one did. Not even Anisa, apparently.'

Kai tentatively poked his head in and saw what we were doing.

'You're welcome to one, if you think it will help,' I said.

Kai shook his head. 'That enabled Pozzi to . . .' he couldn't finish the sentence. 'I'll never go near that.'

I winced. 'I'm sorry.'

'Are you ready?'

'We are,' Cyan said, rising in a smooth motion. We followed her back to the lounge.

'This is big, whatever is happening,' Drystan said. 'I

feel the same as Maske. It's all coming together. Maybe it's the dregs of the Elixir, but I'm listening to the intuition all the same.'

I shivered, the Elixir singing in my own veins, and feared he was right.

We hailed the first cab we found and went to Pozzi's. It was tight inside with all six of us, and we sat in a tense, awkward silence. Lily and Maske sat as far from each other as possible. Maske, squashed against Drystan's shoulder, stared out of the window. I was smooshed between Lily and Kai, but at least I was no longer exhausted. Elixir sang in my veins.

Where was Frey? And what would happen if he was upset and he couldn't control his powers?

Outside, night began to fall, and it was the Penmoon. The Penglass glowed blue, lighting the streets better than the yellow gas lights. The streets were crowded, despite the late hour. People walked through the streets in the direction of the Snakewood Palace. I saw no placards or signs that it was a late-night protest, but their stoic faces gave me chills.

We arrived on Ruby Street. All was deserted. No one wished to be this close to the Constabulary. The driver muttered we were running too close to curfew, and we paid him double. Drystan jumped down from the carriage first and asked the doorman if the Royal Physician was in, as the rest of us lingered in the gathering dusk. We were so close to the Constabulary Headquarters that it felt certain we would be arrested for breaking curfew if he didn't let us in.

'The hardest thing is standing still,' Lily said through gritted teeth. 'I want to scream, scratch, or kill whoever took Frey. Instead, I have to wait.'

Maske looked like he wanted to comfort her, but he hung back. The silence stretched.

Drystan returned. 'He's not here. Doorman says a royal carriage came to pick him up, and when I gave him a coin he told me the Royal Physician is at the palace. Maybe we can find another carriage before full nightfall?' He eyed the sky doubtfully.

As if on cue, a lone man emerged from the shadows. He wore plain clothes, but he moved like a Policier. We backed away, preparing to run.

'Wait,' he said. 'I'm here on behalf of the Steward. He requests your presence at the palace immediately. He's collecting on his favour.' He reached into his pocket, bringing out the royal crest.

We'd protest, but the palace was another potential location for Pozzi or Frey. I'd only had a brief look at our guide before he turned and led us down the winding backstreets of Imachara. He had a stocky, muscular frame, a blocky face, and short dark hair. A forgettable face, which could be useful for a policeman. I could only hope we weren't about to be arrested and unable to help Frey.

The crowds grew thicker again as we came closer to the palace. The people were no longer silent, but yelling. The wrought-iron gates of the palace were barricaded, the grounds swarming with guards and soldiers holding Vestige guns. The sight made me cold. The centre of Imachara could become a battleground at any moment.

How many people in the crowd had weapons of their own? It would take so little for the anger within the crowd to spark to violence, like it had the day we'd rescued Juliet and Tauro.

The Policier took us to the side entrance of a storefront a few streets away from the palace. The store was long closed, the paint of the door cracked and peeling, the interior filled with only broken furniture, dust, and scattered leaflets put through the letterbox.

'What you are about to see cannot be shared with anyone,' he warned. In the low light of the streetlamps, I saw he had the faint scar of a stitched harelip below his nose.

'Understood,' Maske said. It wouldn't matter much, in any case. The Steward would surely use the Lethe on us so we could not share more secrets.

The man unlocked the door and led us inside. The store had once been a pharmacy, and the wooden bar of the dispensary dominated one wall, its glass displays cracked. A few canisters still lined the shelves, neatly labelled with their contents. We went to the back, and down in the storage area was a cellar with a trapdoor. Of course. There must be a veritable maze through Imachara so people could enter and exit the palace without being seen, and there was no way we'd be able to enter the front gates with the mob above.

The man opened the drop hatch. 'I leave you here. Keep straight, and do not linger.'

The opening was pitch dark. Our guide took out a small glass globe and handed it to Drystan. Without another word, he left us there, the door of the shop clicking as he locked us in. Drystan climbed down first, then Cyan, and Kai; Lily, then Anisa, then Maske. I went last, closing the hatch behind us.

The Vestige globe did little to light our way. Down in the damp, the atmosphere was similar to Pozzi's underground lab. Kai shuddered next to me, but put one foot in front of the other.

After fifteen minutes we reached the end of the tunnel. Drystan opened the hatch and we looked up into the stern faces of no less than six guards. They stayed silent as we clambered out, none of us graceful. Anisa moved elegantly, but it was clear she was still growing used to having a body again. Her fingers moved in a ceaseless dance, skimming over the bones of her wrist, up to her elbows, to run along the moulding of the walls as we made our way down the corridor, flanked by guards.

The Steward waited for us in one of his meeting rooms. I was glad it wasn't the overlarge, over-imposing throne room. That cavernous hall had far too many nooks and crannies for curious ears to listen in.

We faced him. He sat in a chair as ornate as any throne, at the head of a wooden table made of planks of the Twelve Trees. His face was grave, his hair mussed from its usual combed-back slickness. His thin, plain coronet was slightly askew on his forehead. The circles under his eyes were so dark, he couldn't have slept in over a day and a half.

Seeing him again, knowing what Pozzi had told us, was difficult. Here was the man who had funded the Royal

Physician's experiments on who knew how many women, so they'd birth Chimaera babes. Here was the man who had created us as his army, and now he was the general calling his troops.

Cyan let out a little gasp.

The Steward's head turned towards the sound. 'You found it even through the Cricket?'

She nodded.

His shoulders slumped. 'The Princess is missing.'

It took us a beat to process his words. 'Missing, Your Highness? When?'

Lily took a step forward. 'My son has been taken today as well, Your Highness. He is Chimaera. I think it might be linked.'

The Steward's features sagged, as if he didn't even have the energy to look surprised.

'Who do you think took them?' Lily asked. She did not cry – she had spent all her tears. She was a coil of impotent rage, vibrating with the desire to move, to find her son, to kill anyone who came between her and Frey. I built up my mental walls against her, but her anger curled its way through me, too.

'The Kashura. We don't know how. They must have somehow compromised our guards, and I suppose your home would have proved no challenge. We'd heard rumours that Timur wanted a strong Chimaera, and hunted the city for one. I take it your son has powers?'

'He does. He can move objects with his mind and control weather. But if they frighten him too much, he won't be able to retain his hold on his powers. That's partly why I kept him at home. I . . . tried to keep him safe.' Her voice broke.

'I tried to do the same for the Princess. We both failed, but my hope is that you can do what I can't, and bring the Princess and your son back.' He ran a hand through his hair. 'We have an idea where they are, but I must stay here and sort out the riot outside my gates.' He did not state the real reason why he must stay. If the Princess died, the Steward would be the last remaining heir.

The crown would be his.

Pressing away the traitorous thoughts in my mind, I followed their words.

'Where are they?' Drystan asked, his voice far too sharp for speaking to our monarch. The Steward didn't seem to notice, or decided to let it pass.

'An old observatory off the coast. Remote enough for their needs. There will be about fifteen people there, as far as we can guess. They want the Princess and your son for some sort of . . . ritual, but we have no idea what its purpose would be.'

Anisa met my eyes and inclined her head, her blonde curls obscuring her new face. She whispered in my mind the words she'd said to me before the séance, just after Drystan and I left the circus: *Take heed, Child of Man and Woman yet Neither. You must look through the trees to see the play of shadow and light. Do not let the Foresters fell you. The truth of who you are and who others once were shall find you in your dreams and your nightmares.*

Anisa had seen a man with a blurred face who wished to destroy the Chimaera. At one point, I'd wondered if it was Pozzi. Yet it had been Timur from the start, preaching his hatred and twisting it towards violence. And if Frey lost control like Anisa's charge Ahti did all those centuries ago . . . all of Ellada was at stake.

'We're not fighters,' I said. 'Our abilities are limited in many ways. The Kashura will likely have Vestige weaponry. How can we hope to defeat them?'

'I can provide you with a small contingent of soldiers. I can't send an entire army, or we'd lose any chance of surprise. Weaponry I can also provide. The rest is up to you. I think you underestimate the power you hold.'

Drystan's shoulders jerked, and I took his hand. His yearning came through to me, clear as a bell. He wanted the Elixir hidden in my bag, to help us. If he asked me for it, would I be in the right to deny him?

'No time to waste. I'm sending my most trusted confidant with you, and communication devices so you can keep me updated. I'll send more troops to the shore, as many as I can spare from the riots, to follow you if you need. Bring her back.' The words should have vibrated with emotion, but they fell flat. Deep where I'd buried the traitorous thoughts in my mind, I wondered just how different Timur and the Steward were, in the end.

'We'll do our best,' I said.

The Steward left us and gave a signal as he passed the door. In came a contingent of six soldiers, dressed in their dark navy uniforms, faces grim, Vestige guns strapped to their belts.

Behind them was, of course, Doctor Samuel Pozzi, the Royal Physician of Ellada.

24

THE BLURRED MAN

I keep dreaming of the man with the blurred face. I don't know what he wanted from me. If those visions he showed me were real.

I told fortunes for the first time in over a year at the Penny Rookeries street party. I was afraid that every time I looked at the crystal ball, or spread the tarot, or held a palm, that I'd see his face and the visions of the world on fire. I didn't then. But I did when I closed my eyes.

I don't dream about anything else any more. I miss having pleasant dreams. I'd even rather dream of being Matla the owl-woman. At least she could fly.

— From Cyan Zhu's diary

What do you say, when your supposed enemies help you?

While I struggled to find the words, Lily had no such hesitation.

She flew at Pozzi, jabbing her fingers into the pressure points at his neck. She'd barely touched him before two of the soldiers held her back.

'This is your fault,' she screamed at him. 'My son, who you swore you'd help!'

'I'm helping now, as best I can.'

'What if we don't want you to come?'

'Then I won't,' he said, simply. 'But I hope you will let me.'

Lily turned to us with an aching pause.

'It's up to you, Lily and Kai. What he's done to us is terrible, but both of you have taken the brunt of his actions,' Cyan said.

Kai swallowed. 'Whatever Lily wants.' He could not look at the doctor.

Lily sighed, her body coiled with furious energy. 'Fine, but only because the Steward will likely stop us if we throw you out. One wrong move, though, and I'll kill you myself.'

'I have no doubt,' Pozzi said, bland as ever.

The guards led us back down the hidden tunnel out of the palace. Even down in the depths, we could hear the shouts of the crowd above.

'Are they fighting?' I asked Cyan in the dark.

'Not yet,' Cyan said. 'Any minute now. There are people on both sides thirsting for blood.'

A carriage, plain black and subtly armoured, waited outside the old pharmacy. We bundled inside, save for one soldier who climbed into the driver's side and started the engine. It was a tight fit for the rest of us. The soldiers wouldn't even look at us, or speak unless it was a direction. They made the rest of us uneasy. Perhaps they didn't like that we were Chimaera, or maybe it was simply the Elladan soldier way.

The ride through the crowds to the docks was tense. Sirens called through the night. Windows to apartments were boarded shut. Hands kept striking the sides of the carriage, trying to peek through the windows to make sure we weren't escaping nobles. Some of us were.

Through it all, the Penmoon glowed above us, full and watchful.

When we reached the docks, the soldier cut the engine and we clambered out. It was quieter on this side of town. Pozzi led us to a warehouse right on the water, opening the door and motioning us inside. We hesitated, but in the end, walked in after the soldiers.

Inside, the warehouse was completely empty but for a boat. It was smooth and Vestige. It'd cut through the water faster than any modern creation. Pozzi gave the soldiers a nod, and they manoeuvred the craft out to the water. Two soldiers stayed to guard us, or to stop us from running away, I wasn't sure.

Pozzi ran a hand through his hair and took off his scarf. He wore a bumblebee pin in his cravat. Cyan started at it, her mouth falling open.

'You visited me in the circus, not long before I left,' she said, her brows drawing down. 'I read your fortune. And you showed me visions of the world ending.'

'That was me.'

'I couldn't remember your face. In my mind, it was . . . blurred.'

Anisa gasped, and Drystan grabbed Lily's arm to caution her against flying at Pozzi again.

'I showed you those visions because I want to stop them. I've dreamed of them for years, and they've grown stronger. The blurred face is not unique. A simple setting on a Cricket, and it's difficult for anyone to remember a face. Cyan, with your abilities, you could probably create the same effect. And who else do we know who possesses a Cricket?'

'Timur,' she whispered.

'I know you have no cause to believe me and every cause to doubt me, but I wish no harm to Chimaera. You are my life's work. I love each and every one of you.'

'Love doesn't give you a blanket excuse to use others for your own gain,' I said.

'That was a lesson I learned far too late in life.'

The soldiers came back to tell us we were ready to head out.

'This could be a trap,' I said. 'You could be leading us right to him, to add our power to Frey's.'

'I am not. Cyan, I drop all my walls. Read me, find the truth of what I say.'

Cyan moved forward, touching his hands. She closed her eyes, and she was not gentle. Pozzi stiffened, beads of sweat appearing on his brow. At one point he staggered, only barely remaining upright.

She pulled away. 'He tells the truth, as much as he believes it. It's not a trap, unless he's very, very good at hiding it.' Her face was so haunted, I wondered what else she'd seen in Pozzi's mind.

'Let's go,' Lily said.

Out on the dock, the only sounds were the lapping of the waves and our footsteps on the wooden planks. Our group climbed into the bobbing copper craft. The ocean wind was salty and cold enough to pierce my coat. Pozzi took the helm, and the engine was almost silent.

Anisa curled at the end of the boat, looking a little green. Her blue dress was thin and she had no coat.

'Are you still immortal?' I asked her.

'As long as there are Alephs and Ampulla tanks and I have access to them, yes. You could be too, you know. It'd work on any Chimaera.'

'Pity we have no Alephs in case we die tonight.' I'd meant it to sound flippant, but the words fell heavy as rocks.

'I would have brought mine and the other empty one, had I known,' Anisa whispered.

'Too late now, Madame Damselfly,' Drystan said. 'We move forward, mortal as all the rest.'

Even one of the soldiers flinched at that.

We continued out onto the open ocean. The shore grew further away, until the city was a smear of darkness lit by Penglass blue and sodium yellow.

'I've never even heard of this observatory,' Cyan said as we cut through the cold, dark water.

'It's the old Royal Observatory,' Pozzi said. 'You'll have seen it from the beach. The tiniest speck on the horizon. It was once the hub of astronomy studies for the university, but the harsh salt wind caused it to crumble too quickly, and eventually it was abandoned for a new

Observatory erected on one of the hills in the city. It seems the Kashura have set up base there,' Pozzi continued as he steered the boat.

'Seems far. I'd have thought they'd want to have their base in the city, like the Foresters,' I said.

'Much more secretive out here,' Drystan replied. I huddled closer to him, the cold wind and the fear causing me to shiver. He put his arm around me tight. Cyan wrapped her arms around herself, and Lily considered Pozzi with narrowed eyes, her hands falling into fists. Anisa's brow was furrowed as though trying to remember something just out of reach, and Maske's sharp mind tried to fit everything together.

As we grew closer to the Observatory, Pozzi took an Eclipse from his pocket. It was a small, thin wand, with a small bulb at the end like an antenna – like the one Drystan and I had occasionally borrowed from Maske. It would temporarily turn off Vestige artefacts within a few meters in all directions.

'Cyan,' Pozzi said. 'If you would be so kind, focus your power through here. I can direct it so they won't see us as we approach. We'll have to use the oars on this boat, but we're close enough now.'

'Eclipses can do that?' she asked, amazed despite everything.

'Vestige can do so much more than we could ever begin to fathom.'

'I can help you,' Anisa said. She took Cyan's hand, lending her strength.

Cyan hesitated, still mistrustful, but then her power

flowed into the Eclipse and emerged from the tip, surrounding us in a bubble. Cyril, Drystan, and Lily probably could not see it, but to me, it had that faint rainbow sheen of Vestige metal. I could only hope that it would hide us from view as we approached, and that it wasn't a beacon advertising our arrival.

The soldiers began to row, and I was grateful for their muscle. Rain pelted us, and mist clung to the shore. The island was sparse and rocky. One side was a steep cliff face, the Observatory perched at the top like a strange growth the same dark grey as the stone. Blue light shone from a hole in the roof, meaning there was Penglass inside, yet it was strangely mixed with red and purple. The building was on the site of an Alder ruin, and other Penglass domes were scattered on the rocky island, glowing softly. To the right was a smaller cottage, barred and dark. There were no guards that I could see, and no sign that anyone was there at all, but for another, much larger boat tied up to the ruin of the old dock.

Pozzi directed the soldier to steer us to the far side of the Observatory, and we tied up at the ruins of an even older dock, which looked as though it could crumble into the sea at any moment.

'I remember this place,' Anisa said. 'From so long ago.'

'Was it an Observatory then?'

'Something like it. It's where we saw the stars. I think it's where the Alder eventually decided to leave this world.'

'What happened to them?'

'I do not know. I like to hope they survived – found another star. Another world.'

'Despite how they treated you?' I remembered the punishment she had suffered after letting one of her charges die. Had the Kashura killed that child?

'Not all of them were so harsh. Like any people, they were a mixture of the marvellous and the terrible. Look at all they created, and all they left behind.'

'All they abandoned once things became difficult, more like,' Drystan said bitterly, and no one had a response to that.

Pozzi climbed out of the boat first, assisted by two soldiers. I hated how interchangeable they all were, how they surrounded us. To help us and to watch us and send every word back to the Steward.

'Do you have a plan?' I asked Pozzi. 'I don't think we can exactly knock and walk in, can we?'

Pozzi held up the Eclipse. 'I'm hoping this will be enough to disarm the Vestige within.'

'It'll take out our weapons, too.'

'For a few minutes, yes. The Steward has provided us with non-Vestige weapons as well. Gentlemen,' he said to the soldiers, and they took off their packs. The soldiers grimly passed us each guns and knives.

Lily took a gun immediately, checking it was loaded, and looked like she'd like nothing more than to point it at Pozzi's face and press the trigger.

Drystan took another gun, as did Maske and Kai. Cyan and I hesitated. As a noble girl, I'd never been allowed to touch a gun, and in the circus, Cyan had only used little toy guns in the carnival booths.

Anisa took one and then set it down. 'I may not have

much power in this human form, but it's still more than that cold metal.'

'I've never held a gun before,' Cyan said. 'I've never liked them.'

'Take both anyway,' Pozzi said. 'Knives will only work in close contact, and guns are fairly straightforward. You point and shoot.'

'Condescending arse.' Lily's hand twitched on the gun, and Pozzi flinched.

We all took knives, even Anisa, and I checked the edge before strapping it to my belt. Sharp. The gun was cold and heavy in my hand. I could kill someone with this. And tonight, I might have to.

'We don't even know what we're walking into,' I said, helpless.

'There are around fifteen members who are in the closest rung of the Kashura,' Pozzi said. 'They are the ones Timur will likely invite for whatever he's doing tonight. Other than that, I know as much as you. How many weapons he'll have, what he's planning to do. No idea.'

'That's comforting,' Drystan said. Sarcastic to a fault, and I was grateful for it.

Pozzi still held the Eclipse, and a tiny thread of Cyan's energy still kept us surrounded in the bubble that should hide us from sight.

'Why does Timur hate us so much?' Kai asked.

Pozzi shook his head at his former assistant. 'I don't know, Kai. I wish I did. It'd be easier to take him down, to find his weaker points. Hatred, a ploy for power, a blend of both. He may even hate the Alder more than the

Chimaera, hence why he's trying so very hard to take down the monarchy. We may never know.' He stood a little straighter, pushed his shoulders back. 'Let's go.'

'Yes, let's give the Kashura a piece of our minds,' Lily said, her face hard and determined.

Though fear rattled through me, I couldn't help but react to Lily's confidence that we could do it. She gave me the slightest hope that perhaps we wouldn't all die.

She strode up the hill, holding her gun aloft, and the rest of us followed close behind, gazing up at the warm yellow lights in the Observatory.

25

THE KASHURA

Some older fragments of Alder script refer to a splinter group called the Kashura. Many scholars have spent their lives puzzling through these crumbling scrolls, yet there is much about this group we do not know. They might have been religious extremists who were against humans worshipping Chimaera. Some posit that the Kashura despised humans as well, but there's no surviving evidence to corroborate such a claim.

The scholar Professor Shawn Arbutus went one step further. A classics linguist, he spent much of his life translating Alder scrolls on all subjects, rather than concentrating on ones that referenced the Kashura. After decades, he came up with his own proposition, which many still dispute: the Kashura despised both humans and Chimaera, wanting to kill Chimaera and return humans to slavery. No one is sure what happened to the Kashura, any more than we know what happened to the Alder or the Chimaera, but in the end, it seems that only humans survived.

— 'Theories of the Alder', *A History of Ellada and its Colonies*, PROFESSOR CAED CEDAR, Royal Snakewood University

Cyan kept the barrier around us and the soldiers as we made our way up the hill.

She stumbled, and Drystan and I went to either side of her, propping her up by her elbows. 'I won't be able to do this much longer,' she warned. 'I don't have much left.'

'I am exhausted by it as well,' Anisa said. Her new body was almost corpse-pale again.

Yet within a few steps, Cyan straightened, her eyes going wide as she gazed towards the Observatory. 'That's very, very strange. I feel . . . better. There's some sort of Vestige in there. It's huge, stronger than almost anything I've felt before.'

I could feel it, too. It recharged my depleted energy. I closed my eyes, my quivering muscles stilling, my mind growing clearer.

Cyan took a shuddering breath. 'The Eclipse won't be able to turn it off, whatever it is. It's far too powerful.' She turned off the slim wand. 'There's not much point using this any more.'

'I don't like this,' Drystan muttered.

'None of us do,' I replied.

We circled the Observatory, keeping to the darkest parts. Guards were posted outside, sentries at regular points. Six to eight in total, one of the soldiers guessed. The main door dominated one curve of the Observatory, shut and barred tight.

Two soldiers peeled off from our group, sneaking up
on the sentry, another Kashura in a dark robe. I expected
them to use their weapons, but instead one made a small
scuffling noise with his shoe. The Kashura sentry's head
turned to the side, and within half a second, the second
guard was on him. One hand over the mouth to stop the
scream, another to snap his neck. The Kashura fell. We
didn't know who he had been, why he had joined. Now
he was gone.

Cyan let out a small sound, quickly stifled. She had
sensed him die. The two soldiers came back, their faces
unreadable. I suppressed a shudder.

The two soldiers went to the right to take care of the
next sentry. We waited, tense, until they came back. Cyan's
hands were over her mouth, tears falling silently from her
cheeks to the salt-stained rocks. Drystan and I put hands
on her back, rubbing softly, but we could do little to
comfort her. My own eyes were wet, as were Maske's.
Drystan, Anisa, Pozzi, and Lily were dry-eyed.

Between the two sentry points was a small structure
which held the generator. At the top was a small window
where we'd be able to see into the main atrium of the
Observatory. We moved closer. The generator buzzed,
steam escaping the vents.

One of the soldiers climbed up and reached down a
hand, hauling us up. Touching a stranger's hand was
strangely intimate. His hand was warm and dry. I was
pathetically glad he wasn't the guard who had snapped
the Kashura sentry's neck. He didn't meet my eyes, simply
turned and helped up the next member of our group. Two

guards stayed on the ground, guns at the ready in case anyone came near.

I crept towards the window and peered in, Lily following and pressing close against me. Cyan reached out and I let her in, so she looked through my eyes, and, like a ghostly echo, I felt Anisa there as well. It was strange having her inside my mind again, but not strong enough to take control of my limbs.

It took a moment to make sense of the scene before us. A group of people dressed in dark robes were clustered in the middle of the large atrium of the Observatory, the figures dwarfed by a huge Penglass globe that almost reached the hole in the ceiling. Yet where Penglass was always blue, this one was a pulsating crimson, and it did not look as though it'd grown from the ground, like others did. The globe must have been moved here, and set in the indentation where the massive telescope had once let scientists gaze up at the stars.

Smaller blue Penglass domes surrounded it, like a fairy ring I'd seen in the Emerald Bowl what seemed like a lifetime ago. The Penglass glowed, casting the entire room in a blue, red, and purple glow.

I could sense Frey's distress, his power rising and pulsing. The ground shook. Overhead, the weather grew worse, the dark storm clouds rumbling. I couldn't see him.

Dragging my eyes away from the domes, I focused again on the people clustered around one smaller blue dome in particular. Deep within its glowing heart were moving shadows.

'Do you see that?' I whispered to Lily.

'Yes.'

I squinted, and with horror, I noticed that the shadows were human-shaped, the size of children. And one of the shadows had horns. Frey and the Princess were somehow *inside* the Penglass dome.

One of the Kashura rested a palm on the Penglass, and it grew more transparent, until we could see the Princess and Frey inside. Though they'd never met each other before tonight, they clung to each other for comfort. Frey did not have his wheelchair, and his legs sprawled out, the Princess crouched protectively over him. She'd lost her Glamour, or they'd taken it, and her skin looked even bluer from behind the Penglass.

Frey's power grew stronger, until I felt like his warmth would burn me. I tried to reach out to him, but though his emotions and thoughts were clearly projected, the Penglass or something else blocked me from contacting him. His power buckled, itching across my skin, a sour taste at the back of my throat.

Timur stood before him, his back straight. His hair curled over his face, his strong jaw and heavy brow. Next to him, his followers had their hoods pushed back. Men and women, all Elladan and most brown-haired, turned their faces towards the red Penglass globe. Around twelve in total between the sentries and the Kashura inside, so we were outnumbered, yet none of them had Vestige weaponry. I guessed this was because the globe somehow interfered with other artefacts. I tried the Eclipse again, but it had no effect. All that work to steal weaponry from the Mechanical Museum, and they could not even use them tonight.

'What are they doing?' I asked.

'I don't know.' Lily's voice had gone flat and cold, as if she'd shut down all emotion so she could focus. 'But it's too far for me to shoot with any accuracy.'

'I agree,' said the main soldier. We knew none of their names. They had not offered and we had not asked. I didn't want to connect or empathize with them, in case they died before me tonight. Or I died before them. Perhaps that was cruel, but it was self-protection. My body shook with fear and Elixir, and it was a struggle to keep my mental walls strong and protect myself from the soldiers' emotions.

'Let me see,' the soldier said. I moved, and he peered in.

'There's a door at the back of the observatory,' he said, gesturing. 'If we enter we should be hidden by that red globe.'

'We don't have much time,' Lily whispered. 'Whatever they're doing, they're about to begin.'

Timur's followers put up their hoods, hiding their faces. Like in Pozzi's underground lab, there was something hushed, reverent, almost religious about how they moved through the Observatory.

We made our way down from the roof and around the perimeter of the atrium. My body felt as though it was not connected to my mind. The extra dose of Elixir I had taken before we left our apartments was in full effect, thrumming through my veins, enhanced by being so close to the strange Penglass dome. I suspected I'd need every drop of this extra power.

The small door at the back was locked, and so Drystan yet again used his lock pick. I could feel Frey's fear rise again on the other side of the steel door, and gritted my teeth. Whatever was happening in there, we didn't have much time.

We opened the door and flitted in, two guards remaining behind to cover our exit. The Lord and Lady had given us a stroke of good luck. There were several wooden crates stacked on this side of the Observatory. Not excellent cover, but better than nothing at all. We ducked behind them.

Timur was giving a grandiose speech like the ones I'd heard at his previous protests, surrounded by eleven of his closest followers. A total of twelve, like the hands on a clock. Like the Twelve Trees.

'Tonight, my friends, we fulfil our destiny. In one fell swoop, we will protect this world. From Chimaera and the Chimaera monarchy that protects them.'

I exchanged a look with Drystan. How did Timur know about the Snakewoods? Even if he didn't know they were Alder rather than Chimaera.

'By sending the Chimaera back where they belong, we will send a message that cannot be ignored. Ellada is for humans, not monsters.'

'They understand nothing of the world,' Anisa whispered.

Silently, the guards drew their weapons. 'We'll aim for Timur. If we cut off the head, this snake should die.'

It struck me as an odd yet violently poetic way to describe it, but I nodded. 'Be careful.'

'We always are,' the soldier said, and flashed me something like a smile. *No*, I wanted to say to him. *Don't make me like you. Don't make me cry if you fall.*

Tears pricked my eyes, and I sent a quick prayer to the Lord and Lady that I wasn't sure I believed in. *Please, please don't let these soldiers come to harm. Don't let Drystan die tonight, or any of these other people that I love.* For I cared so much for Cyan, Maske, Frey, and the Princess. Even Lily, who I didn't know that well, and who had spied on us. Even Kai, who I'd only met a handful of times. Even Anisa, who had so often been a mystery to me.

The soldier crouched low to the ground, moving closer to the strange dome. From this vantage point, we could see Timur motion towards the blue dome that housed the Princess and Frey. One of the hooded Kashura went to the glass and drew a glyph on its front. I recognized it from the vision dreams Anisa had sent me from the past. Though the Kashura was not Chimaera, as far as I could sense, the glyph glowed beneath his touch before the dome opened, half of it seeming to melt away. Another Kashura grabbed the Princess by her upper arm and dragged her out, and the other hefted Frey over his shoulder. Frey's fear grew stronger, his power rising to dangerous levels.

Now that he was out of the Penglass, though, I could contact him.

Frey. I sent him the tiniest tendril. He stilled, his head swivelling around as he heard me.

Micah? he wailed.

I'm here. We're going to help you. Remember all we taught you? You have to stay calm, so we can get you and the Princess out of here. Your mother is here. As is Drystan, and Cyan. We're all here to help you. Now you can help us by controlling your power. Can you do that?

I'm scared.

I know. I am too. But you can do this. You are strong.

He tried. And he managed to find a thread of calm. The power that danced along my skin lessened.

That's good, Frey.

The soldier held up his gun, pointing it at Timur. A second guard crawled low on the ground behind him. The other two stayed close to the rest of us.

'Oh, Styx,' Drystan muttered next to me, staring at the red glass globe.

It glowed brighter and it had begun to hum, the sound reverberating deep in my bones.

The Kashura had moved and we were not sure what they did. I left the cover of the boxes for a better view, ignoring Anisa's low hiss at me to stay back.

Someone had drawn a glyph on the red dome as well, and a hole gaped open like a mouth waiting to swallow the Princess and Frey. They both struggled, but the Kashura held them tightly.

'As we have read in the scrolls. Two Chimaera,' Timur intoned, blissfully ignorant of Nicolette's Alder heritage. 'Both strong in their power, and once inside this Penglass, their minds will reach out to all Chimaera within Ellada, and maybe even the rest of the Archipelago. When we trigger their powers, then all Chimaera will simply . . . disappear. We, single-handedly, will have achieved what the Kashura of old did as well. The monarchy will be gone, and we shall build from the ashes. Ellada will be the shining jewel it deserves to be.'

How much of his words did he believe? Violence was the only language this man knew. Once he'd rid the world of Chimaera, he would find someone else to hate, to blame.

He wanted to kill all of us. Frey, Cyan, Kai, me. Drystan might still have dregs of Elixir in his veins – it could hurt him too. Juliet and Tauro. All the other Chimaera out there, hiding, that I did not know. Killed for nothing more than our differences. He thought the Princess was Chimaera – would this weapon harm her, too, with her Alder blood?

The soldier aimed and fired with his non-Vestige gun. The shot rang in the round atrium. Several Kashura screamed. Timur spun, the movement saving his life. The bullet grazed the front of his chest, and he bowed forward, blood staining his shirt.

'There!' One of the Kashura to Pozzi's left spied the soldier and pointed. The soldier raised his gun to shoot again, but not quickly enough. A Kashura fired, hitting the soldier between the eyes. He fell, and before I could blink, the second soldier fell. One third of our trained fighters. The man who had given me a smile. Dead.

Lily and Maske fired, but their shots went wide. Pozzi shot and hit one of them in the leg. Kai had curled into a ball, radiating pain and fear. Behind us came more shots as the sentries fought with the two guards outside. They were outnumbered, and I feared for our soldiers out there. More bullets came our way, but Anisa managed to use her powers to shift them out of our way. She was stronger than she was in her Aleph form in some ways, but judging by the exhaustion emanating from her, she would not be able to move many more bullets.

I don't know if this will work. Cyan closed her eyes tight. *Go to sleep, go to sleep, go to sleep,* she sent to the Kashura as loudly as she could. I'd never seen her influence people in that way before. Anisa took up the call, lending her strength.

It worked on a few of them. They dropped their weapons and curled on the floor. Others shook their heads to keep themselves awake. The two remaining soldiers inside took down two sleeping Kashura, leaving two awake and Timur, who held a blood-soaked cloth to his chest.

Another Kashura fired, and Lily was hit in the shoulder. She cried out and fell.

Frey began to scream, high and echoing. He sounded almost like Anisa and her old three-toned voice.

I ran out from behind my cover, dodging the Kashura who rushed me and pushing at them with my mind so they staggered. Still gripping the knife Pozzi had given me, in my other hand I held the gun. I raised it, but my hand shook terribly.

The man who held Frey dropped him, as though burned. Frey crumbled to the floor, though he still screamed at the top of his lungs. It was a mental scream as well, and everyone in the room, Kashura and my friends, stumbled, clapping their hands to their ears. I dropped the gun and thrust the dagger into my belt. I grabbed Frey, trying desperately to contain the tide of raw power rushing through him. The Observatory grew hot and sweat dripped down my face. Up above, the sky flashed with lightning and thunder boomed deep in my chest.

Frey, I can't stop this. It has to be you. You can do this. You have to take control, or all is lost. I gasped, my lips cracking with the heat. The scales on his hands were hot enough they burned me, but I wouldn't let go of him.

'Frey,' the Princess whispered, coming closer. 'I'm here.'

'Nico,' he managed. He turned to her and she reached out her blue hand and took it in his green one. They grew stronger together. Cyan and Anisa helped, lending what strength they could. I could feel the pain of their injuries, their exhaustion.

Maske, Drystan, Kai, and the remaining soldier circled us. Humans and a Chimaera, protecting us against the Kashura who wished to destroy so many.

Though Cyan and I tried to help, it was Nico and Frey who held the true power among us. Ours paled in comparison. Their awareness spread over everyone in the atrium. Kashura and our side stopped fighting. The power drifted over the water, to Imachara.

In my mind I saw Chimaera freeze, turning as one in the direction of the Observatory. Dozens of them, far more than I would have imagined. There was Juliet, her lips pulling back from her canine teeth. Tauro, shaking his head as if chasing off a fly. A man in a dark room, his skin rough as an elephant's, his ears large, his fingers short, blinking blearily in the dim light. A woman with hair like a lion's mane, her pupils slit like a cat's, her lips dark against her tawny fur. A child with feathers sprouting from the backs of his arms, like the beginnings of wings. So many others who did not have Theri features but hid powers like mine and Cyan's. Twin boys my age. A Byssian man in his apartment, surrounded by his family. A dancer at the protests, her screams dying in her throat, surrounded by a crush of people. So many. Hidden, afraid.

Timur had wanted to destroy them all.

Nico and Frey's awareness moved beyond Imachara, to the rest of Ellada. Many other Chimaera stopped, heads turning towards us. Some were afraid, and some smiled. They sensed us, and we sensed them.

Frey and Nico pulled back. The Kashura had brought in the red Penglass globe to enhance their powers, but they hadn't needed it once they linked. The Alder and the Chimaera boy turned their attention to Timur. He lay, half-collapsed, near one of the other blue Penglass domes. His face was pale from loss of blood, but he still glared at us, and his hand rested on his gun.

Frey and Nico reached out for him and twined their way around his mind, and Cyan and I were taken with them. It was just for a moment before we pulled back, but in that instant, we knew him. The secrets that made him who he was. That his parents had been Chimaera, and he'd been angry when powers never materialized for him. He'd been raised in poverty, and had run away from home, driven enough to work his way up in the royal household. He witnessed the unfairness, the policies that kept people like his family in poverty. He tried to change it, but at every step, he was blocked. One night, he'd caught a glimpse of the Princess with her blue skin, and the hatred within bubbled up again. The Forester party had many sound politics, but Timur at the helm had twisted it. When they realized the party was primarily to serve his own agenda, they cast him out. He began studying old scrolls, piecing together information about a sect of the Alder who destroyed the Chimaera. So the Kashura were born, and the violence with it.

A gunshot startled us from Timur's mind. He held a non-Vestige gun in a shaking hand. It took me a moment to register the pain. The bullet had grazed my arm. Shallow, but bloody and painful. I hissed, but watched in horror as Timur raised the gun again and aimed it at the Princess.

Another shot echoed in the atrium like lightning, and Timur screamed, a fresh wound in his leg. Lily Verre, still lying on the floor, held a gun in a shaking hand, but dropped it, her eyes closing. Cyan assured me she wasn't dead as my panicked thoughts wondered what Frey would do if she were, but she'd lost a lot of blood and desperately needed a hospital.

Yet despite the new wound in his side, Timur fired again. Not towards Lily, but at Frey. Time froze for a moment. Anisa wailed, her powers too weak now to deflect the shot; Cyan tried to mentally push, but it was too late. I couldn't breathe. And then Pozzi threw himself forwards between Frey and Timur, taking the bullet directly in the chest. His weapon fell from his clockwork hand. Blood bloomed on his shirt. His eyes met mine as he fell to the Observatory floor.

One day, I hope you will forgive me. My walls had fallen completely, and all of his pain entered me. So much agony and so much regret.

In the roiling sky, the wind chased away the clouds. A beam of moonlight fell through the hole in the ceiling onto the Penglass dome that had held Frey and the Princess, illuminating Pozzi as he died. The angry red of the globe glowed brighter. The only way to survive was to clamp down on all my emotions. I would grieve later, if I survived.

Frey used his powers to lift Timur. Our enemy screamed at the movement, but still moved closer, his toes dragging along the ground.

What should we do with him? the Princess asked, and she cocked her head to the side. The thought of killing him did not upset her. Yet they were so young. Too young for blood on their hands. The rest of the fighting had stopped. The remaining two soldiers had subdued or killed the rest of the Kashura. Maske was tending to Lily.

I moved forward and bound Timur as he sagged against me. He'd pay for his crimes in public with a proper trial. With the powers we possessed, we couldn't afford to be judge, jury, and executioner; otherwise, we'd have turned into the very thing that Timur wanted the world to think of us. 'All this pain, all this death. For nothing,' I told Timur. 'You failed.'

Timur's face went slack. At the protests, he'd always appeared so large and powerful, but now he had collapsed upon himself. I could lift him with ease, but Anisa came and helped me.

I understand your sentiments, little Kedi, Anisa said. *But, while we will not kill him, he must not be permitted to go out into the world again. He is too much of a threat. Place him in the red globe.*

I wondered why Anisa would ask that of me. Timur thrashed weakly as we dragged him closer to the globe. He had lost a lot of blood. We pushed him through the small opening, and it closed immediately, swallowing him. He smashed his fists against the glass pitifully, and I stumbled back.

Close your eyes and turn away, Anisa commanded us. Drystan threw his arms around me, and I buried my face in his neck, closing my eyes tight. Even behind my eyelids, the bright red light was almost too much. Our screams tore from our throats, our ears ringing. The floor shook so violently I feared the roof of the old Observatory would cave in on us.

Eventually the light dimmed, the shaking stopped. Drystan's breathing was ragged in my ear. We broke apart, peering at the wreckage.

The red dome had sunk into the stone of the atrium, only the very top peeking out of the grey. It no longer glowed, and the dark red surface was pocked and bubbled, as if partly melted. Around us, the blue Penglass domes had shattered, small pieces of dark blue glass scattered across the floor of the atrium. I picked one up in wonder, and it did not glow beneath my touch despite the faint moonlight.

'He's dead, isn't he?' I asked. 'Anisa . . .'

'I lied, yes. You may not have wanted to kill him, but I had no such hesitations. That is on me. I take responsibility, I take that death.' Her gaze was as distant and ancient as I remembered. Turning from her, I threw up the contents of my stomach. She may have claimed responsibility, but I had still put him within that globe. I was the one that trusted her.

When I'd finished, my mouth sour, I checked the others. Focusing on actions was the only way to keep myself together. Drystan was all right, with only a few scratches and bruises. The same for Cyan, though she'd re-injured her ankle. Anisa had been knifed in the arm, and it bled worryingly. Lily was fully unconscious, her heartbeat erratic. Kai's jacket was splattered in blood that was not his own. At some point, he had either attacked or defended himself.

Only one of the soldiers survived. I made sure to ask his name: Noel. The ones outside had taken out the rest of the sentries, at the cost of their own lives. The Kashura had perished, their hoods pulled back to show faces frozen in fear and pain. I looked away. Though they had wanted to destroy me and those I held dear, it was hard to relish the death of others.

Pozzi was cold. I reached down and unpinned the bumblebee from his cravat, putting it in my pocket.

'I don't forgive you,' I whispered to him. 'But I

understand why you did it, even if your methods were horrifically wrong.'

Our diminished number limped from the broken atrium of the Royal Observatory, bundling ourselves into the small craft. Kai carried Frey, and Maske carried Lily. Drystan and Noel worked the oars until we were far enough from the strange red Penglass to call for help on Noel's Vestige communicator. The engine hummed back to life and Drystan and Noel set aside their oars. Hopefully the Steward had actually sent backup to the docks, as he'd promised.

'What was that red globe?' I asked Anisa.

'The Alder lived in red Penglass, or Venglass as we called it back then. The Chimaera lived in blue. Most of the Penglass disappeared along with the Chimaera, all those years ago, but a few of the smaller domes remain. The secret of Penglass is only that they were our homes. Smooth castles of glass that glowed under the moon. Some were mausoleums, housing the bodies and Alephs of our ancestors. Still others were grand meeting places, filled with gardens and light. The old world was a beautiful place.' She gazed out towards Imachara. Her voice was faint and her skin was too pale. The bleeding on her arm had slowed, but she needed stitches and rest.

'Where did the red Penglass go?' Drystan asked.

'They took it with them.' She tilted her head back, gazing up. 'To the stars.'

All of us lay back in the boat. Drystan put his arm around my shoulders, and Cyan lay nestled against my other side. Maske had Lily's head in his lap, and her eyes

were closed. He stroked her hair. Frey lay propped against
Maske's other side, his hand still linked with Princess
Nicolette's. Of all of us, they were the least tired. Noel
kept to himself, mourning for his fallen friends. Kai was
hunched underneath his jacket, his hands shaking. Anisa
sat in the centre of the boat, her head still tilted towards
the sky, and the rest of us watched the stars with her as
we moved back to land.

26
The Aftermath

We have no fairy stories starring the Alder. Though they were the inspiration for many, they still remain too far away from our understanding to feature in our tales. They created us, perhaps, they watched us for aeons, yet they never let us know their secrets. And then they left – they were too powerful to ever be destroyed. They've been gone long enough for history's wheel to turn again.

Any clear night, I look up at the stars. And I always think:

The Alder left. I think they will return one day, too curious about what they created.

And sometimes, I swear, one of the stars brightens in response to my thought, or my wish. Whichever it is.

— From the unpublished notes of Professor Shawn Arbutus, Royal Snakewood University

My mother called my name.

I tried to respond to her, and though my voice echoed in the mist, I couldn't find her.

She called again. I saw her figure, a dim shadow in the grey. I could tell she would be dressed as perfectly as always. Tightly corseted, pert bustle, black crinoline and silk. The perfect coiffure, the jet-black beads. I never knew what she was perpetually mourning, but she always wore black except for the white of her gloves.

'Mother!'

She turned. 'Iphigenia.'

'That's not my name any longer.'

'Is it not?' Her brow drew down in confusion.

She drifted away.

I called out after her. There was no answer.

I woke up in the hospital.

We'd gone there late in the night, after we'd returned. Soldiers had been waiting on the shoreline, as promised, and escorted us to the Royal Snakewood Hospital. The hospital had been busy with injuries from the riots, but no large-scale violence had broken out, though it had been a very near thing.

One of the nurses told us what had happened. Lorna Elderberry, the new leader of the Foresters, had stood up and pleaded for patience and peaceful protest. She reminded them of the Chimaera, who had asked for nothing more than the same desire to be heard. That they must stand for what was right without resorting to the same base violence as the Kashura. Her speech had worked, and people had stood silent in front of the palace, and the Steward himself had come out towards the gates. Lorna Elderberry reached the entrance, and they let her in. As soon as she'd passed through, the rest of the crowd stayed in a silent vigil while the sun rose before dispersing. Oh, plenty were still angry and others thirsted for a fight, but most were tired and wanted actual change.

The ward I was in was empty but for my friends. Lily lay in the bed across from me, her head turned to the side towards Frey's bed. He did not wear a Glamour. He was awake and raised a scaled hand in greeting. I returned it. Noel, the guard, was gone. The Princess was also not there. I gathered she was back at the palace, yet she would not be looked over by the Royal Physician. *Don't think of Pozzi*, I told myself. *Not yet.*

Drystan, Cyan, Anisa, Kai, and Maske weren't there, but they had not been as badly injured, so they must have returned home. I wanted Drystan with a physical ache. The last time I'd woken up like this, he had been the first person I'd seen.

Every part of me hurt, and a headache lurked just within reach. I tried to sit up but my muscles did not obey. A nurse passing by in the hallway spied my laboured movements. She came in and forced me to drink two large glasses of water, taking my temperature, looking at the whites of my eyes.

'Where are the others?' I asked her, but the clicking of her retreating footsteps was my only answer.

She had put something in the water. I drifted in and out of consciousness.

When I woke up the next time, a warm hand held my own.

My eyelids fluttered open, and I turned to see Drystan. I let out a strangled sob. He did not look healthy. His skin was pale, dark circles under his eyes.

'Are you all right?' I managed to ask.

'I fared better than you.' He smiled at me, and I could sense the relief washing over him. But it was . . . dampened from how it'd felt while I was on Elixir. I reached for his mind, but sensed nothing. It was more like my powers had been before this all began – weak, unreliable. The drug must have worked its way through my system faster than usual.

'How long was I out?'

'Just a night. It's early afternoon, now.'

'What happened after we came here?'

The Steward's guards had taken Noel and the Princess, wearing her Glamour, back to the palace. Drystan, Maske, and the other uninjured went with them. The Kashura were all gone, or at least all that had been present at the Observatory. Snakewood intelligence suggested the fringe group was not large, so hopefully any other members would scatter rather than regroup.

'We don't seem to be under arrest,' I said, holding up my unshackled hands.

'No. Rescuing the Princess means we're in the Steward's good books.' He gave me his first smile. 'She could not stop singing our praises, and demanded we all have medals.'

'No public ceremonies.'

'I requested that, so we'll see if she listens. She's also demanded Frey comes to live with her at the palace, along with his mother. The Steward agreed to that, too, surprisingly.'

'They should.' They fitted together. I'd seen the friendship between them. If there was one thing the two extraordinary, lonely children needed, it was each other.

'On the way out, I ran into my father,' he continued.

'Oh,' I said.

'Yes. Oh.' He gave me a rueful look. 'I was covered in soot and dust and not a little blood, but he recognized me right away.'

'Did you two . . . talk?'

'Yes. It went all right, amazingly. There were no tearful hugs and falling to our knees, overcome with emotion. But he asked me to come home for a visit, and I accepted. It'll be awkward as all Styx, but I'll go.'

'What if they ask you to return to the Hornbeam family?' I asked. I imagined him taking up his place as first-born son, and it struck fear into me. If he went back to that world, would I have a place with him there?

He shook his head. 'I have no interest in that life. But they all know I'm all right now. And if we stay in Imachara, I probably won't be able to avoid my mother and sisters forever.'

'And you wanted to?'

'I thought I did.'

I took his hand and squeezed. 'I'm glad. Really. That was a wound that had never healed. Maybe now it can start to.'

Drystan shrugged. 'Perhaps.'

My head fell back against the pillow. 'When can I leave here?'

'Tomorrow, the doctors say. I'll be here to take you back to the Kymri Theatre. It's all fixed now. We can go home.'

'That'll be nice. Though I've grown a bit fond of the creaky old apartment in the Penny Rookeries.'

'The hot water broke yet again. Fancy an ice-cold shower?'

'Not a bit. Goodbye, mould-stained walls and sagging beds.' I sighed. 'We still have plenty of other messes to sort through, though, don't we?'

His lips brushed my forehead with a kiss. 'Aye, but we'll get through it.'

When I woke up the morning I was meant to leave, Drystan wasn't there. But Cyril was.

It took me a moment to come to myself. I thought I must have dreamed of my mother again, but I couldn't remember the details.

'Hello,' I said softly, jolting him from his reverie.

'Micah,' he said, smiling. 'I'm so glad you're all right.'

'Just battered and bruised,' I said with a smile, though in truth, those had already healed. 'I take it they told you everything that happened?'

He looked down at his hands. 'Yes, they did. And, well, something else occurred. That's why I'm here instead of Drystan. I don't think you should go home right away.'

I frowned. 'What? Why? Is someone hurt?'

'Because . . . Mother woke up. And she's here. Just a few floors above us.'

I stared at him, my tongue stuck to the roof of my mouth. Then I gazed upwards, as if I could stare through the ceiling and see her.

'I . . .' My words trailed off. 'When did she wake up?'

'The night of the Penmoon. But she only started speaking this morning.'

I said nothing.

'You need to see her, Micah. You owe it to her, and to yourself. Despite everything.'

'You mean despite what she almost did to me. Her and Father deciding my life, with me having no say in the matter.' I breathed out loudly, staring at his open features. 'Are you forcing me to see her?'

'That's tempting. I could probably pick you up and drag you up there, you scrawny thing. But I won't. It's up to you in the end, whether or not you want to talk to her.'

'Styx.'

'I know.' He stood up and held out his hand to me. 'I'll come with you, if you want.'

'No. No. I'll do this on my own.' I swung my legs over the side of the hospital bed and stood. The world wobbled. 'Though maybe you can help me to the door?'

Cyril waited for me while I changed out of the hospital gown into the spare clothes he had brought. Changing made me nervous. No one had bathed me, except to sponge off the worst of the blood and dust. My Lindean binder was undisturbed and my medical chart had no mention of anything except my injuries.

'They don't seem to know,' Cyril said, noting my unease.

I leaned against him as we made our way out of the ward, and halfway up the stairs I had to rest. By the time I reached the door I was stronger, at least physically.

I didn't want to open the door. I didn't want to have to face her. Would I feel like Gene again in front of her? An unhappy girl, stuck in a life she didn't want?

Cyril squeezed my shoulder. 'Thank you. This will be good for both of you.'

Cyril left me, walking back down the corridor.

Over his shoulder, he called, 'I'll be back by your bed. Come see me when you're done and I'll take you back to the theatre. Take as long as you need.'

Then he was gone.

Staring at the door, I debated leaving, going down to the canteen for a drink, then finding Cyril and pretending I had gone to visit my mother. That was useless. He would know in an instant that I lied.

Drystan had taken the step to heal his past. The least I could do was try for the same.

I pushed open the door.

My mother was in one of the beds by the window, awake, propped up against pillows, looking out over the buildings to the thin, blue strip of sea. She was much changed from that woman who was never seen without pristine white gloves, like in my dream. The woman before me now wore no cosmetics, and the light through the window illuminated every line on her face, every grey hair showing at the roots, the dark smudges beneath her eyes.

Her skin was slightly jaundiced, and her form diminished. She didn't look like the mother I'd once feared.

At the sound of my footsteps, she turned. Her eyes almost slid over me, and then they fixed on me like a magnet to a pole. She jerked back in her bed. I slowed my steps. I didn't say anything. What could I say?

What she must see before her – a boy in trousers, a buttoned shirt, a waistcoat and jacket. Brogues. Auburn hair grown long for a boy's, curling about his ears. Hands that fluttered nervously before settling in the trouser pockets. A boy in every respect, except that he had the face of her lost daughter.

'No,' she said. 'It can't be. I'm still dreaming, and you're the phantom to haunt me.'

I slipped still closer. I sat beside her. Her eyes quivered as they drank in every detail of my face.

'Hello, Mother,' I managed.

'Iphigenia.' She breathed the name I'd hated so much, and that no one had called me in over a year. The exact same intonation as in the dream.

I shifted in my seat, uncomfortable with her close stare.

'You look so different,' she said after a moment.

'I expect so.'

'I dreamed of you, I think.'

Though I had dreamed of her, too, I said nothing. Guilt pecked at me. I'd only tried to reach her once. If I'd tried harder, perhaps she could have awoken weeks ago.

'Iphigenia . . .' Her words trailed away. 'I expect you do not call yourself that any longer.'

'No, I don't. I'm Micah Grey, now.'

'Micah Grey,' she repeated, and my name sounded so strange in her voice.

Her eyes were slightly unfocused; she was still on a mixture of medication. The skin on her arms was slack from lost muscle.

'I don't know where we go from here,' she said. Gone were the imperial tones she'd so often used with me. Gone the affront she'd exhibit at my wayward behaviour. It was almost as if I didn't know her at all. And I never had, not really. She'd hidden behind her facade as Lady Laurus, so desperate to seem like she belonged in the nobility, to hide her merchant-class background. I had no idea what she'd been like when she was younger, or even how she'd met my father. No stories, no memories. She'd encased herself in a stiff masquerade, and only my running away had broken through it.

'I'm still angry at you,' I said. 'I don't know how to forgive you for what you were going to do. And never tell me. Never give me a choice. That was horrific.'

She looked away, unable to meet my eyes. 'How did you find out?'

'I listened at the door. The night I ran away.'

'I thought . . . it would be for the best.'

'For who? For you? For your precious reputation?'

'I didn't want you to have to grow up alone and without prospects.'

'I don't give a fig for prospects. You were going to castrate me. You can't pretend it was more than that.'

Her fingers worked at the cloth of the blanket covering her. 'It was wrong,' she said. 'I was wrong. I'm sorry.'

I blinked. I'd had so many adults apologize to me lately. Anisa. Pozzi. Now my mother. I could never recall my mother apologizing to me, unless it was to say 'I'm sorry to say, but . . .' and then berate me for another one of my many infractions.

'Thank you,' I said. 'It means much that you would say that. I'm afraid I cannot apologize for running away, because, despite all the awful things that happened, becoming Micah was the best choice I could ever have made.'

Her mouth opened, but no words came.

'So, like you I don't know where we go from here, either. You know I'm alive, and I'm well enough.' I swallowed, trying not to think of the sound of the scream in the atrium, everything drenched in blue and red light. Of the bodies that remained when we opened our eyes. Of that anger and hatred in Timur's eyes before we'd buried him alive in ancient Alder Penglass.

'I'm glad to see you well. I am.'

'But you're not going to reclaim me as your daughter, now son, are you?' I asked. 'You'd have to field the questions, risk your reputation, all of it.'

Her gaze flicked away again, which was my answer. It hurt, and I couldn't pretend otherwise. Not that I even wished to go back to life as a member of the Laurus family. Manoeuvring through the nobility as a boy held no more allure than when I'd had to do it as a girl. I'd rather stay in my working-class existence, performing magic shows for the masses in my true home.

'I wish I didn't care,' she whispered. 'That I could throw it all to the wind, and damn the nobility to Styx.'

'You worked your way up from a merchant girl, and you want to stay there,' I said, and I couldn't keep the bitterness from my voice. But I wasn't as bitter as I might have been, even this time last year. 'You can't change who you are any more than I can change who I am.'

I made to stand.

'Wait,' she said. Her mouth worked as she tried to find the words. 'I want you to know that I do love you. I wanted you so badly, and when I first held you in my arms, it was one of the happiest moments of my life.'

'Until you unwrapped the diaper.'

She shook her head. 'That frightened me, yes, but I never loved you any less, even if I know now I was terrible at showing it. I wanted . . . wanted to make sure you had everything in life I had to work so hard for. A good marriage. Security. A place in society. I wanted that for both you and Cyril, and I thought I had to be strict to get you there.'

The onslaught of pure, unfettered emotion from her shocked me. 'I never knew you. You closed yourself to me. And no matter what, I was never good enough for you. For a time, I worked harder, wondering whether if I could be a better girl, you'd loosen. But you never did, and so I rebelled from my corsets and my crinoline. Why bother trying to be perfect, when I thought you saw me as forever broken?'

A tear ran down her cheek. 'I'm sorry. I know it doesn't undo all those years, but I am sorry.'

When I was small, I'd thought my parents were perfect beings. Almost gods. And now, I'd discovered that they were just as flawed as everyone else. My father, too distant and detached, too afraid to stand up to his wife. My mother, hiding behind the power and prestige she'd clawed her way to, pushing away the real things that mattered. Dosing herself with drink and laudanum to numb her pain and loneliness. Me, the daughter who ran away. Cyril, the son caught in the middle of it all. A broken family, and I didn't think we'd ever be puzzle pieces that fitted together.

I held my hand out to her. I held my hand out to the woman who had terrified me, who had also tried to change me entirely for her own, misguided beliefs. She clasped my palm so hard it hurt, and I squeezed, once, and took my hand back.

'Goodbye, Mother.'

'Will I see you again?'

I paused. 'Maybe.'

She sniffed. 'I'll take maybe.'

I managed something resembling a smile, and then I left. I did look back. She stared at me, from her hospital bed and her white sheets. Tears fell down her face freely. I'd never seen her cry before.

I raised the hand she'd held in an almost-salute, and then I turned away.

27

HOMECOMING

*Home. A nebulous concept, far more than the stones we
build around us and the slates we put over our head. It's
where we feel safe. Where those who love us dwell. Sometimes that's not a physical place, but a state of mind.*
— From the earlier work of philosopher ALVIS TYNDALL

It was a strange homecoming.

I hadn't been to the Kymri Theatre in a month and a
half, or perhaps closer to two months. It was not quite
noon when we pulled up in front of it. The roof had been
restored. The columns repaired and repainted. The broken
glass replaced. It looked just like it did when I returned
from Pozzi's after my fever and first dose of Elixir. I
remembered the first time I had walked up these steps
and stared at these oaken doors and their swirling brass
tendrils. Soon, the Kymri Theatre would be open for
business again.

I walked past the empty box office in the entryway and
through to the kitchen. There they all were, waiting for

me. Cyril went to sit next to Cyan, loosening his bow tie, and something about their body language made me raise an eyebrow at them, and they blushed. Well. Maske had been reading a book, but he glanced up as we entered, his eyes ringed with dark circles. Anisa was drawing with a piece of charcoal, and I recognized ancient Linde and a portrait of her old friend, Matla. Kai was studying a medical textbook. He was going to finish his studies despite losing Pozzi as his mentor. Even Lily and Frey were there, though I noticed Lily and Maske were not sitting next to each other. They still had much to work through.

My eyes rested on Drystan.

Tufts of his blonde hair stuck up from his scalp. I'd only seen him a few hours ago, but I'd missed him. He rose and came to me, and I folded into his embrace, resting my cheek against his shoulder.

I'd not seen most of them since the Observatory. It was almost as if that memory was a presence in the room with us, the blue and red light so bright we couldn't look at each other. I hunched my shoulders, sliding into an empty seat.

'Coffee?' Drystan asked.

I nodded.

No one spoke. Yet the unspoken words we wanted to say floated all around us.

Drystan passed me the coffee, heavily sugared and milky. I took a sip, and the taste grounded me more.

'What do we do now?' I asked. So much had changed, and we'd all nearly died. It was unreal to be sitting in a warm kitchen, clutching the cup of coffee in my hands. How could I find my balance after my world had shifted from underneath my feet?

'Now . . . we take back our lives.' Cyan said. 'We heal from our wounds. We perform magic. We watch it all change in front of us.'

'I don't know about you, but I think the first thing I want is a nap,' I said, and they laughed. Drystan stood and offered his hand. I took it, and kept it clasped in mine as we climbed the stairs to the loft.

It was strange to be back in the loft instead of our cramped bedroom in the Penny Rookeries. Drystan had unpacked and the place was already back to its usual level of disarray. Clothes piled on top of chests instead of neatly folded within. The bed unmade, Ricket slept curled up on the crumpled sheets, his tail covering his eyes. A few plates that should be carried down to the kitchen at some point. My heart lifted to see it, so familiar. The early afternoon light shone through the recreated stained-glass window of the dragonfly on the far wall, dotting the floorboards with green, blue, and red.

It reminded me of Anisa. 'She never found Relean, the Chimaera she'd loved for lifetimes.'

'She still has most of a lifetime left. Knowing her, she'll find him if she wants to. If he's out there. Or she'll find someone else, or she'll surround herself with a new family. That's the joy of life. Endless possibilities, endless ways to love. Right?' His mouth twisted sardonically.

It was good to be home. I crawled into the bed,

pulling the covers around myself. Ricket mewled in protest and jumped off the bed, trotting away in search of food. 'That is true. You big softie.'

He laughed, lying in the bed next to me, tucking his arms behind his head. His shirt rode up, showing a sliver of white skin dusted with blonde hair.

I emerged from the cocoon of blankets I had just made and fitted myself next to him, slipping my palm under his shirt to rest on the warm skin. His hair tickled me as I pressed my cheek against his chest. His heartbeat soothed me, as it always did.

'How are you, through all of this?' I asked.

'I'm . . . all right. I haven't taken any more Elixir, since I don't know where you hid the rest of it. If you hadn't, I probably couldn't say the same.'

'Wonder what we should do with it,' I said. 'Burn it, bury it.'

'Keep it,' he said. 'Don't tell me where, but keep it. It might prove useful one day. But at least Pozzi was lying about you and Frey needing it to survive.'

'True. My body doesn't seem to be attacking itself.'

'It's healing faster still, though, isn't it?' He touched the fading scratch on my face. 'That needed stitches when you were unconscious, and it's almost gone. I doubt you'll even have a scar.'

'Well, I'm never going to go back to normal, for I've never been that, anyway.'

'Me neither.' He sighed. 'I do think taking Elixir that once changed me, though.'

I propped myself up on one elbow, looking down into his blue eyes. 'How?'

'Nothing concrete. I can't fly or make anything levitate. But . . . I don't know. I feel like the world isn't as mysterious any more. And my dreams are more vivid, like I'm peeking into peoples' lives.'

'Maybe you are.'

'Perhaps. I don't mind the dreams, anyway. Not so far.'

'What do you dream of?' I asked.

'Of a girl and a boy, playing with toys in their home as a fire burns in the hearth. A man walking through a park, stopping to gaze up at the clouds. A far-away island, palm fronds shifting in the breeze, a woman wearing an Elladan dress looking out to sea, her son at her side. He carries a little mechanical Minotaur with him, like a doll. Most are silent, and short. Maybe they're only dreams.'

I shifted a little on the bed. Drystan's hands moved, stroking the hair back from my face, his fingertips dancing down my neck. My body had felt numb after all the events of the past few days, but now it came alive. Every inch of my body tingled, my stomach clenching with desire. I reached up and drew his lips to mine, kissing him fiercely. His mouth opened and I met my tongue with his.

He sat up, pulling me up with him. My fingers fumbled at his belt as he unbuttoned my shirt. He pulled the shirt open, and I wriggled from it, throwing it to the floor. I pushed his shirt up over his shoulders, and it joined mine. His fingers made quick work of the Lindean corset, and I pressed him to the bed, my skin against his.

We shed the rest of our clothes, and it felt like it had

been so long since we had last been this close. Drystan gasped as my hands moved lower, and he gripped me close. My kisses trailed down his neck and chest, until, too impatient, we moved together.

I didn't close my eyes, and he didn't close his. We drank in every detail of the other, finding ourselves.

At the end, when we lay back in the bed, spent and sleepy, our limbs heavy, I was finally at home.

EPILOGUE: THE MASQUE

Masque: a court entertainment with music, singing, dancing, and acting. Sometimes members of the court will take part in the festivities, and sometimes they are content simply to watch the display. Most characters dress up as Chimaera from older myths, and occasionally the Alder. Often the masque will feature an allegory tying into the political actions of the time. There may be a silent procession as part of it, to better showcase costumes. Afterwards, there is often a masquerade ball, with all guests disguised for the evening's entertainment.

— 'Court Entertainment', *A History of Ellada and its Colonies*, PROFESSOR CAED CEDAR, Royal Snakewood University

Six months later

All dressed up in our new costumes, we waited in the lobby of the Kymri Theatre. I shifted from foot to foot. Drystan took my hand to calm me, and I stilled. Cyan wore a Temnian robe. Cyril, Maske, and Kai looked dapper in their suits. Lily was there, wearing that red dress I'd seen in a long-ago vision. The former Shadow and the magician had decided to begin again, without the lies, though Maske's trust was slow to heal. Frey was in his wheelchair, wearing no Glamour. After that night of the full moon, he'd decided against the facade. 'They can accept me or they won't,' he'd said. 'But I'm not going to hide.' It had taken people aback, but no one had said anything rude to him.

Drystan and I had done the same, retiring the Glamour and the lives of Sam Harper and Amon Fletcher. It was a relief to no longer wear faces that were not ours. Pretending to be Elladans raised in Temne had never sat well with me. Cyan had told us she hadn't minded, but I knew she was glad to see the last of our alter egos as well. We performed with our true faces for Maske's Marionettes, never offering a definitive reason for the change. Rumours flew thick and fast. That Amon and Sam had died, or gone on the run from the law. Now we were Drystan and Micah. No more lies. No more hiding. Somewhat surprisingly, no one matched us with the runaways from R. H. Ragona's Circus of Magic. Or if they did, they didn't bother going to the Constabulary.

The carriage that pulled up in front of the theatre was the grandest I had ever seen, large enough for twelve people rather than our eight. The edges were gilt, bright plumage rising from the top of the roof, nodding in the gentle breeze. The driver tilted his hat to us before climbing down to open the door. Autumn was turning into winter, and I shivered beneath my coat.

I took a deep breath as we climbed in, and settled by the window. As the carriage twined its now familiar route towards the palace, I wished I didn't have to go. Large crowds of nobility still made me more than a little nervous, especially those who had once known me as Lady Iphigenia Laurus. I'd seen my mother and father once or twice over the past half year. They had not offered to accept me back into the family and present me as a Laurus. I had not asked. Drystan's family did ask, but he turned them down gently. He saw his family more often than I saw mine.

We went through security. I did not spy Noel among them. He'd been promoted to one of the Princess's main guards, last I'd heard.

Time to put on our masks.

Maske wore the mask I had given to him as a gift last Lady's Long Night, of black velvet with embroidered moons and stars. Lily wore a simple one of dark red velvet, and Frey one the same shade of green as his true skin. Cyan wore a mask of peacock feathers and Cyril wore a lion's mask. Kai's was bat wings, naturally, and Drystan wore a mask patterned in a jester's motley. As for me: I wore a dragonfly mask.

When we entered the large ballroom, no heads turned towards us.

I'd never been to the ballroom before. It was enormous, about three times the size of the Beach Ballroom in Sicion, where I'd had my debut. Glass globe chandeliers glimmered above us, the ceiling painted with the Twelve Trees of Nobility, the family shields between them. The floor was smooth marble, shiny but not too slippery for dancing. The far wall had a raised proscenium stage, where the masque would be held.

Tables were clustered about the edges, should people tire, and there was an upper storey, so people could watch the dancing from above. The Steward was there, watching the festivities but not yet joining in. He too wore a mask, though the crown gave away his identity. Again, he met my eyes, but this time he did not look away. He nodded, and I nervously returned the gesture.

A few people gave us lingering looks, wondering who we were underneath our disguises. I was so glad that the Steward had decided to let us keep our anonymity. Had he not, then we would have been announced with the greatest fanfare, and no one would have left us alone.

Cyril broke away from us, spying some of his friends. One of them was Rojer Cyprus, a boy I used to know. He looked at me curiously, so I reached towards him with my thoughts, for the first time since the Observatory. But the Elixir was out of my system and I couldn't sense anything from him now.

Cyan recognized my fumblings. 'That boy Rojer thinks he recognizes you. He's not sure, though, because of the mask.'

The thought of him recognizing me didn't frighten me as much as it would have, once.

Cyan rested her hand on my arm, offering wordless comfort. I gave her a smile and sat down at one of the tables at the side. Drystan came with me, while the others were content to mingle.

Drystan was not in a speaking mood either. He went to fetch us drinks and a plate of food neither of us touched. He held my hand under the table, and we watched the people twirl about in their dresses and suits, masks sparkling with jewels or metal scales. Drystan's eyes lingered on his father, and then his mother and his siblings, but he made no move to go to them.

'Have people outside of your family recognized you?' I asked him.

'I'm sure they have, but they've all been far too polite to mention it, since we're so favoured by the Crown just now.' His sarcasm was biting.

I sipped the wine Drystan had brought me before making a face and setting it aside. I still didn't care for the taste. But it reminded me of seeing Cyan and Maske connect and learn how they were related at the party after the magicians' duel. My smile faded as I remembered the wine I'd tasted that night had been poisoned by Pozzi, so he could trick me into receiving his treatments.

I went back to the food table and found a glass of sparkling strawberry juice, which tasted much better.

Frey sat in his wheelchair, speaking to the Princess. The Princess still wore her Glamour, but I wondered when she would throw it off. She did not strike me as a person who would willingly stay hidden for long.

It was not only nobility here tonight. Over the last six months, Ellada had changed significantly. A parliament was being finalized, and after the first election, Lorna Elderberry was the first Prime Minister of Ellada, working with the Steward to make sure the will of the people was heard. Taxes had been reformed, with nobility giving higher yields and those funds being used directly to help the poor. It was slow, and there was still much to be done, but the people, on the whole, were much happier with the new arrangement. I wasn't sure if the Steward was as keen to give any of his power to Elderberry and the new Parliament, but he recognized that, long-term, it was the best way to retain his crown. At least until the Princess was of age.

Elderberry wore a dress of green linen, simple and understated compared to the silken finery of much of the nobility. The members of Parliament likewise wore simple dresses and suits, their only ornaments flowers in their hair or buttonholes. For along with the Twelve Trees of nobility was the Garden of the People, each member wearing a different flower. A member wearing a rose in his lapel leaned over and spoke to Lord Hawthorne, and they both burst into good-natured laughter.

The lights overhead dimmed. The promised court masque was about to begin. I sat there on my own, waiting for the spectacle. The glass globes over the tables dimmed, while the ones up on the stage brightened. Horns blared. Most of the inner court participated in the affair, and the poor palace seamstresses must have been run ragged, preparing all of the costumes.

Once I realized the story they told, I couldn't help but laugh aloud, to the mystified looks of those around me. They had chosen none other than the romance of *Leander and Iona*, by the playwright Godric Ash-Oak. We'd performed a version of it at R. H. Ragona's Circus of

Magic, which felt like a lifetime ago. Yet it was a strange tale to pick. Leander and Iona fell in love. Iona's overbearing father, King Zimri, forbade it, locking her away in a Penglass prison, far too much like the true Princess had been locked up. I overheard a noblewoman whisper to her friend that the Princess had asked for this tale. That I understood: it was a way for her to tell the story of what had happened to her, even if it was warped by the fairy tale. She had escaped the prison. We had all defeated the monsters. She had found a happy ending.

And so I sat there, holding my glass of sparkling strawberry juice, surrounded by strangers, yet with the people I loved most in the world not far from me. I watched the masque of Leander and Iona, clad in their fantastic costumes, the stage set with glowing glass globes. After the tale was told, I would find my strange, wonderful family, and we would return home to the Kymri Theatre.

I smiled.

ACKNOWLEDGEMENTS

I first dreamt up *Pantomime* while filing at my first job back in December 2009. I'd already started another manuscript that took a different direction with an older Micah as a detective solving crimes, but I thought I'd try writing from the point of view of Micah as a teenager joining the circus. I thought it'd be a short story. Seven-ish years later and there are 300,000 words of the trilogy and around 80,000 words of the tie-in Vestigial Tales (available on e-readers!). There are so, so many people to thank who helped me along this sometimes bumpy road.

The first person I told about the book was Craig, my husband. He's read almost every draft, listened to me talk through plot problems, held me as I laugh-cried through the good times and sobbed through the bad bits. Thank you and sorry for salt-staining your shirts. Thank you to my mom, (the ever-stalwart cheerleader) Sally Baxter, and to Erica Bretall, Shawn DeMille, Wesley Chu, Lorna McKay, and Mike Kalar, who have consistently been early readers on all three books. Cheers to Joseph Morton,

J. B. Rockwell, Corinne Duyvis, and Josh Vogt for their time and excellent comments. Thanks to Katharine Stubbs and Kale Levin, readers of *Pantomime* who ended up being beta readers for *Masquerade* and giving very insightful notes. More appreciation to Laya for all your awesome fan art – it never fails to brighten my day when a new one pops up. I really hope I haven't forgotten anyone!

On the publishing side, huge, huge gratitude to my agent, Juliet the Leopard Lady, for selling this series twice and being consistently amazing. Thank you to Julie Crisp, Bella Pagan, Phoebe Taylor, and everyone at Tor UK. They've been such a delight to work with the past few years and I'm very grateful. Merci to Amanda Rutter for seeing the early promise in *Pantomime*, way back when. It might have just stayed on a hard drive otherwise, my confidence was so low.

Last and not least, endless thanks (I feel like I say thanks a million time in all the acknowledgements, but there aren't that many synonyms!) to everyone who has taken the time to read and review these books. Thank you especially to Gay YA and Bisexual Books for consistently signal boosting on social media. The series continued because of my readers' love for these books – you helped me keep writing when times were tough. That's why this book is for you. Thanks for meeting Micah Grey and his friends and finishing his tale. His story is over for now, but I hope he stays with you.

extracts reading groups
books competitions books new
discounts extracts extracts
competitions extracts events
books new discounts reading groups
events books extracts discounts events
extracts new titles reading groups
interviews reading groups
events extracts extracts books
discounts events new
new books events interviews new books extracts
events new books

www.panmacmillan.com

discounts extracts discounts books
extracts events reading groups
competitions books extracts new